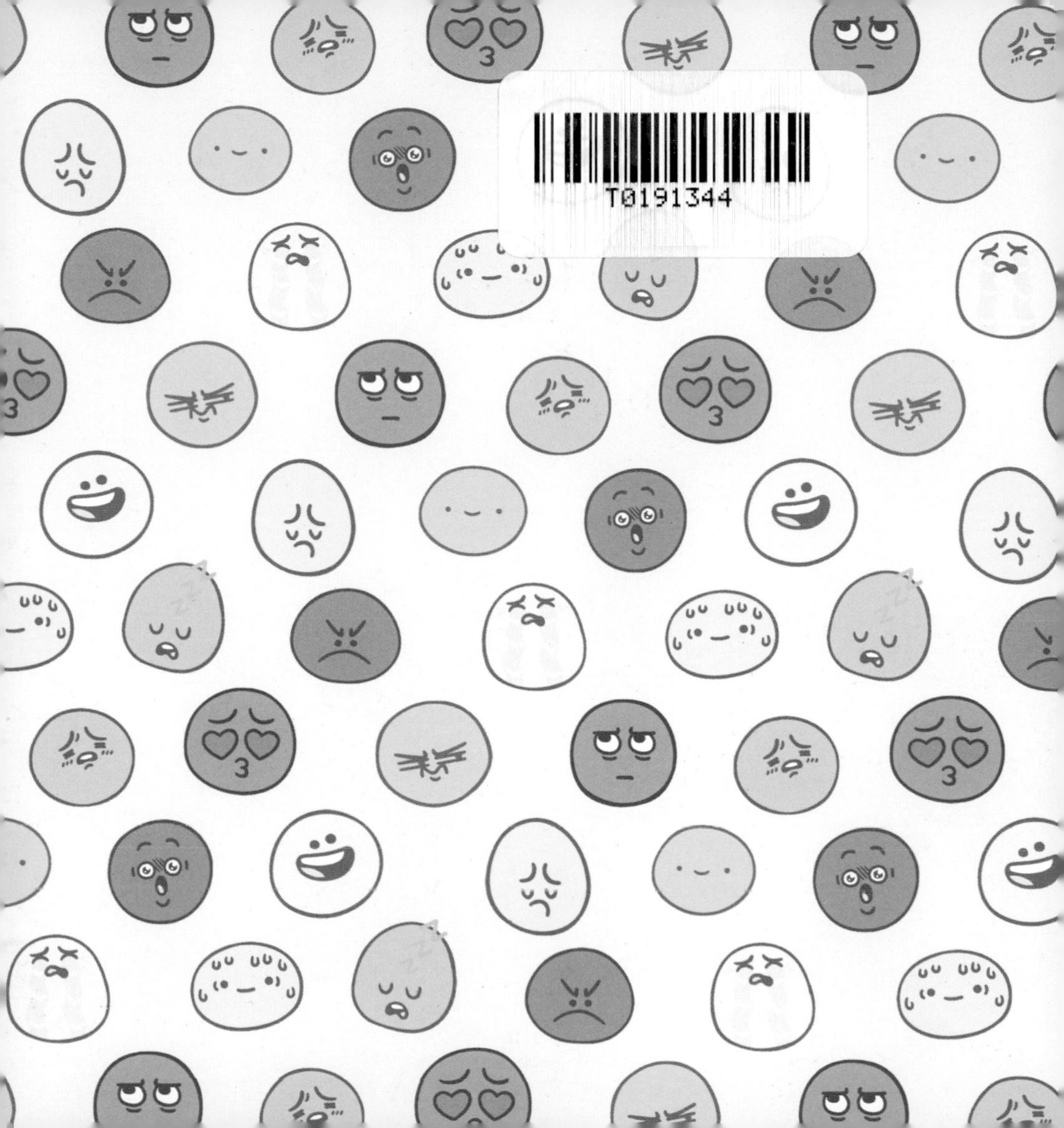

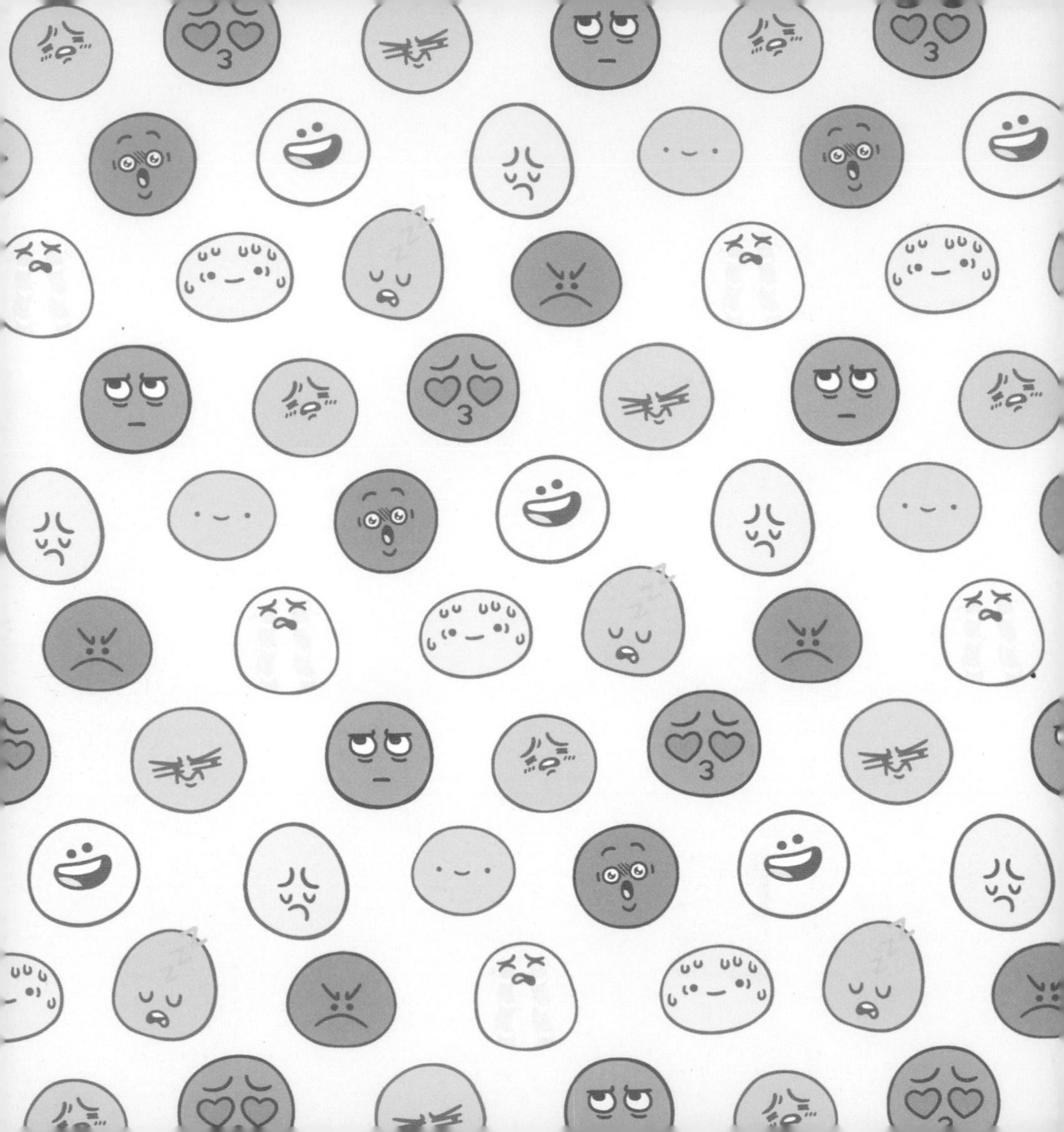

PRAISE FOR

MR. LOVENSTEIN PRESENTS

feelings

"Who is Mr. Lovenstein? He is pretty much all of us: worriers sweating through life, trying our best (sort of) and trying to keep our shit together. He's also the reason why I can't look at squirrels the same way anymore."
-Cassandra Calin *(Cassandra Comics)*

"Mr. Lovenstein comics are a breath of fresh air. They're crisp, refreshing, and if I don't get one every few seconds, I'm gonna die."
-Neil Kohney *(The Other End Comics)*

"Mr. Lovenstein refines comedy into 4 boxes or less, with an instantly recognizable style. Truly a masterclass in creating webcomics!"
-Chesca Hause *(Litterbox Comics)*

"Mr. Lovenstein has a gift for conveying the anxieties and insecurities of modern life in creative and hilarious ways. He is a master of the craft."
-Zach Cranor *(Last Place Comics)*

Edited by Alex Antone
Book Design by Jillian Crab

ISBN: 978-1-5343-4952-0

SKYBOUND, LLC.
Robert Kirkman | Chairman
David Alpert | CEO
Sean Mackiewicz | SVP, Publisher
Andres Juarez | Creative Director, Editorial
Arune Singh | VP, Brand, Editorial
Shannon Meehan | Senior Public Relations Manager
Alex Antone | Editorial Director
Ben Abernathy | Executive Editor
Blake Kobashigawa | Senior Director, Business Development, Editorial

Jillian Crab | Graphic Designer
Ashby Florence | Production Artist
Richard Mercado | Production Artist
Alex Hargett | Director of Brand, Editorial
Sarah Clements | Brand Coordinator, Editorial
Dan Petersen | Senior Director of Operations & Events
Foreign Rights & Licensing Inquiries: foreignlicensing@skybound.com
SKYBOUND.COM

IMAGE COMICS, INC.
Robert Kirkman | Chief Operating Officer
Erik Larsen | Chief Financial Officer
Todd McFarlane | President
Marc Silvestri | Chief Executive Officer
Jim Valentino | Vice President
Eric Stephenson | Publisher / Chief Creative Officer
Nicole Lapalme | Vice President of Finance
Leanna Caunter | Accounting Analyst
Sue Korpela | Accounting & HR Manager
Margot Wood | Vice President of Book Market Sales
Lorelei Bunjes | Vice President of Digital Strategy
Dirk Wood | Vice President of International Sales & Licensing
Ryan Brewer | International Sales & Licensing Manager
Alex Cox | Director of Direct Market Sales

Chloe Ramos | Book Market & Library Sales Manager
Emilio Bautista | Digital Sales Coordinator
Jon Schlaffman | Specialty Sales Coordinator
Kat Salazar | Vice President of PR & Marketing
Deanna Phelps | Marketing Design Manager
Drew Fitzgerald | Marketing Content Associate
Heather Doornink | Vice President of Production
Drew Gill | Art Director
Ian Baldessari | Print Manager
Melissa Gifford | Content Manager
Erika Schnatz | Senior Production Artist
Wesley Griffith | Production Artist
Rich Fowlks | Production Artist
IMAGECOMICS.COM

MR. LOVENSTEIN PRESENTS

feelings

J.L. WESTOVER

FOREWORD

Hello! Look, it's an introduction to this book, called FEELINGS!

Wow, aren't feelings great?! Imagine if we didn't feel anything... things would just happen and we would be like, "That happened," and that is it. Our life would be boring. But also, we wouldn't notice because we would just be like, "My life is this way and that is how it is."

Good feelings are lovely because they make you feel good! But then there's bad feelings, and they are not lovely. They make you feel bad. But if you didn't feel bad about things that were bad for you, you wouldn't avoid those things and that would just make your life worse. And you wouldn't even know it.

When we have feelings, we sometimes express them with parts of our body, especially our face. This helps other people guess at how we might be feeling.

If we are happy, we may look something like this:

:-)

This is not an actual human face—it is just some punctuation I have arranged in a particular way. But it does look happy! Maybe it is pleased I have typed it into this introduction. If it is upset, it isn't expressing that. It's difficult to know exactly because it can't talk.

I hope it isn't upset, but it's okay if it is. From time to time, we all feel the pressure to be happy even when we are feeling bad—especially if we are punctuation in the shape of a smiley face. Maybe you should leave that little face alone for a while so it can feel its emotions in peace. Turn the page and read the book. I hope you feel many wonderful and intense feelings of your own.

- Alex Norris
Creator of *Webcomic Name*

For my friend, Caleb.

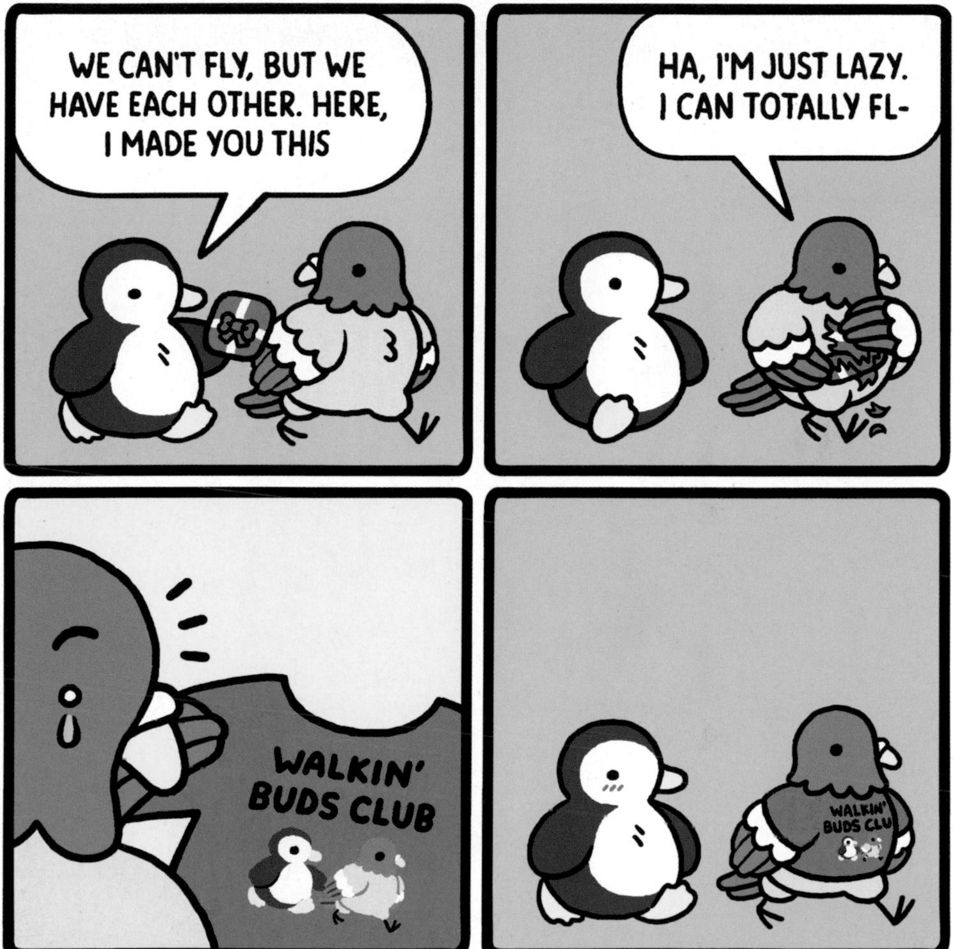
WE CAN'T FLY, BUT WE HAVE EACH OTHER. HERE, I MADE YOU THIS
HA, I'M JUST LAZY. I CAN TOTALLY FL-
WALKIN' BUDS CLUB
WALKIN' BUDS CLU

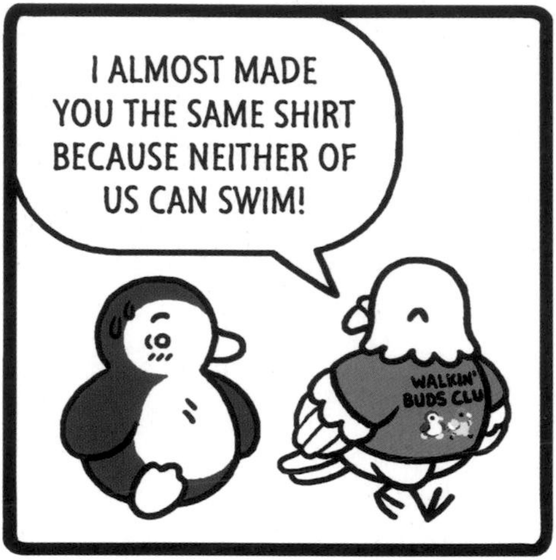
I ALMOST MADE YOU THE SAME SHIRT BECAUSE NEITHER OF US CAN SWIM!
WALKIN' BUDS CLU

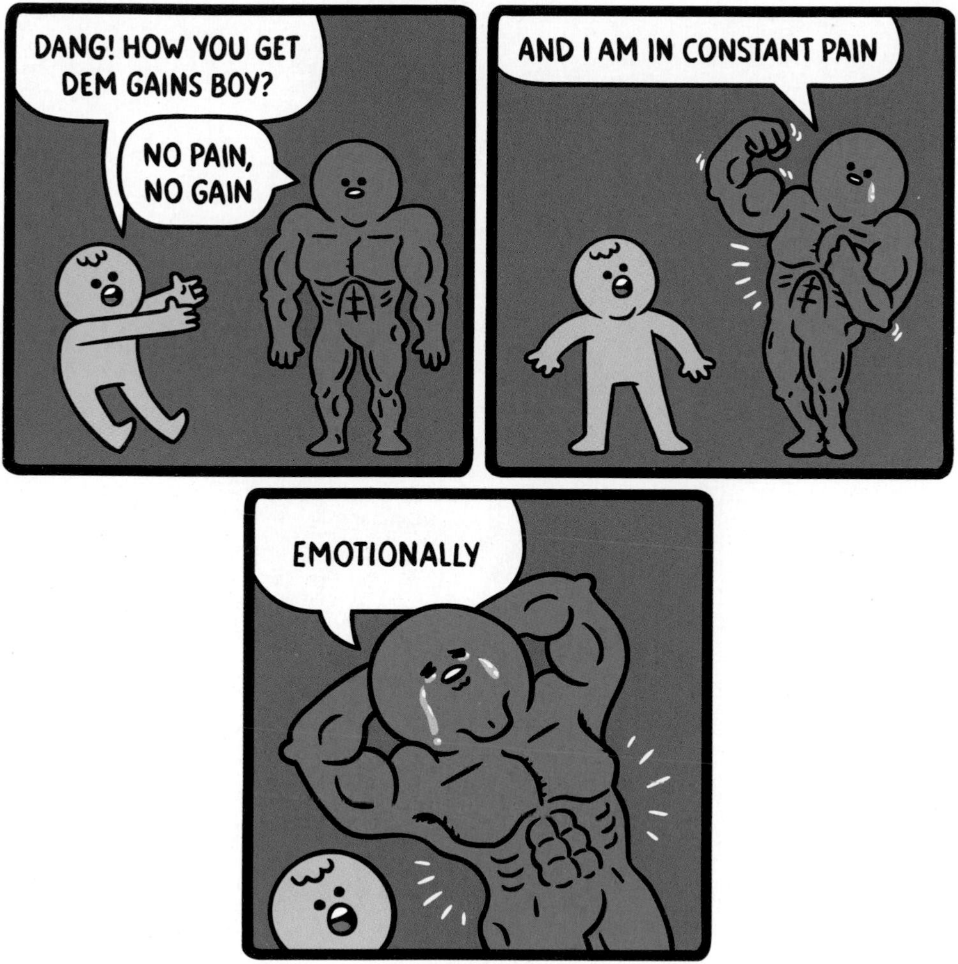
DANG! HOW YOU GET DEM GAINS BOY?
NO PAIN, NO GAIN
AND I AM IN CONSTANT PAIN
EMOTIONALLY

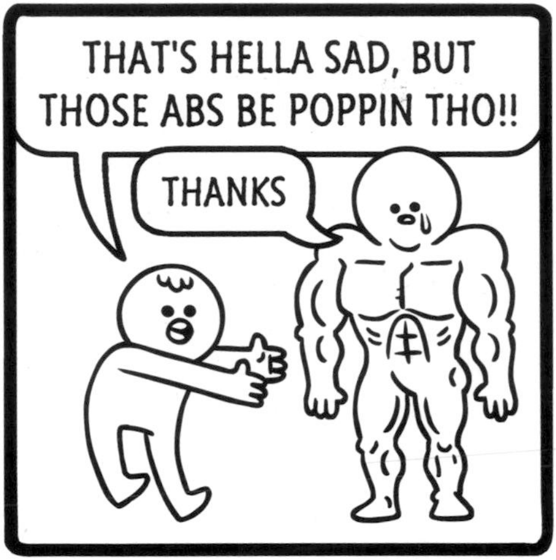
THAT'S HELLA SAD, BUT THOSE ABS BE POPPIN THO!!
THANKS

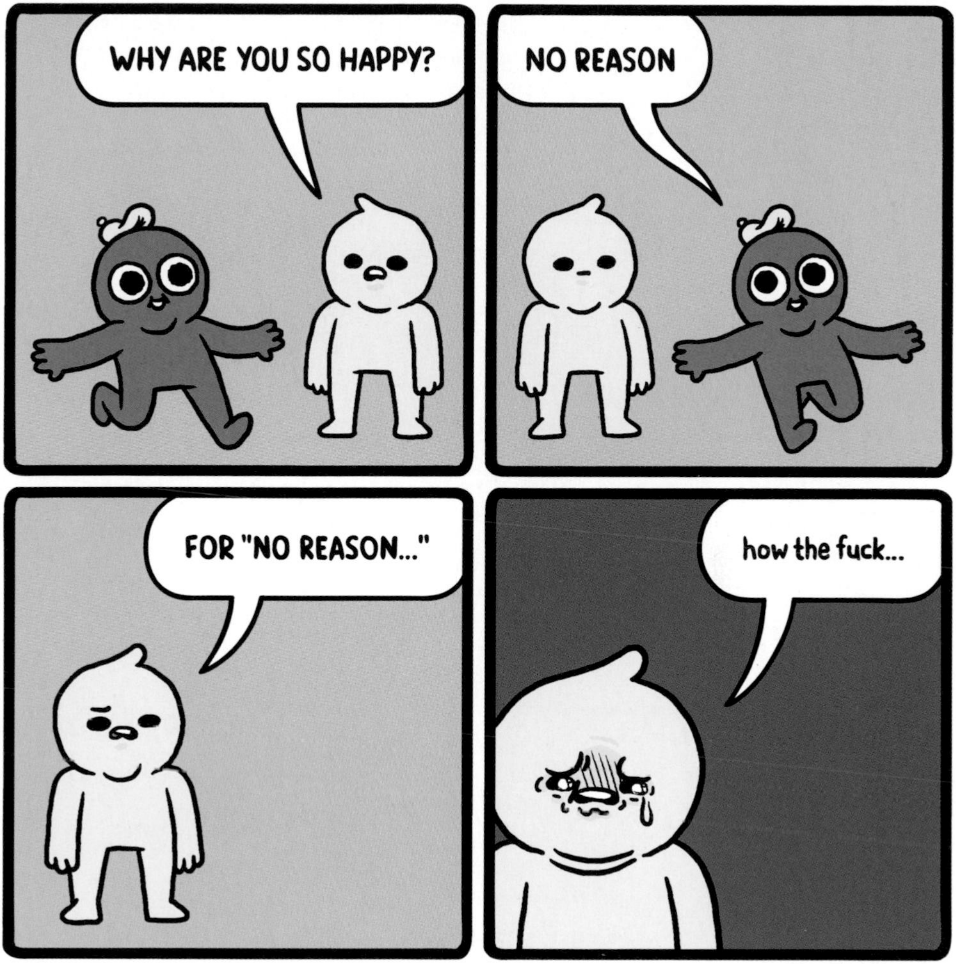
WHY ARE YOU SO HAPPY?
NO REASON
FOR "NO REASON..."
how the fuck...

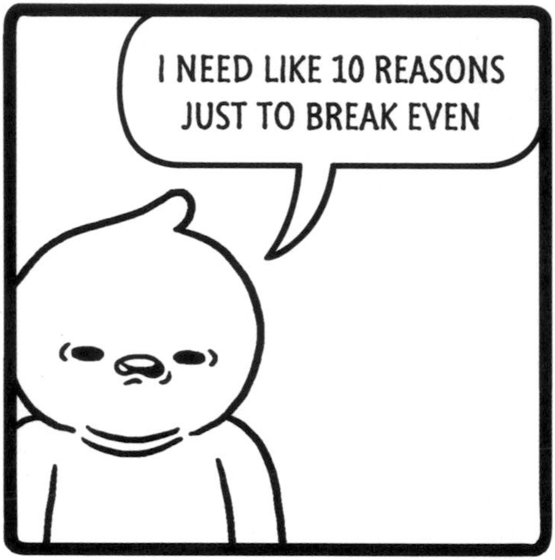
I NEED LIKE 10 REASONS
JUST TO BREAK EVEN

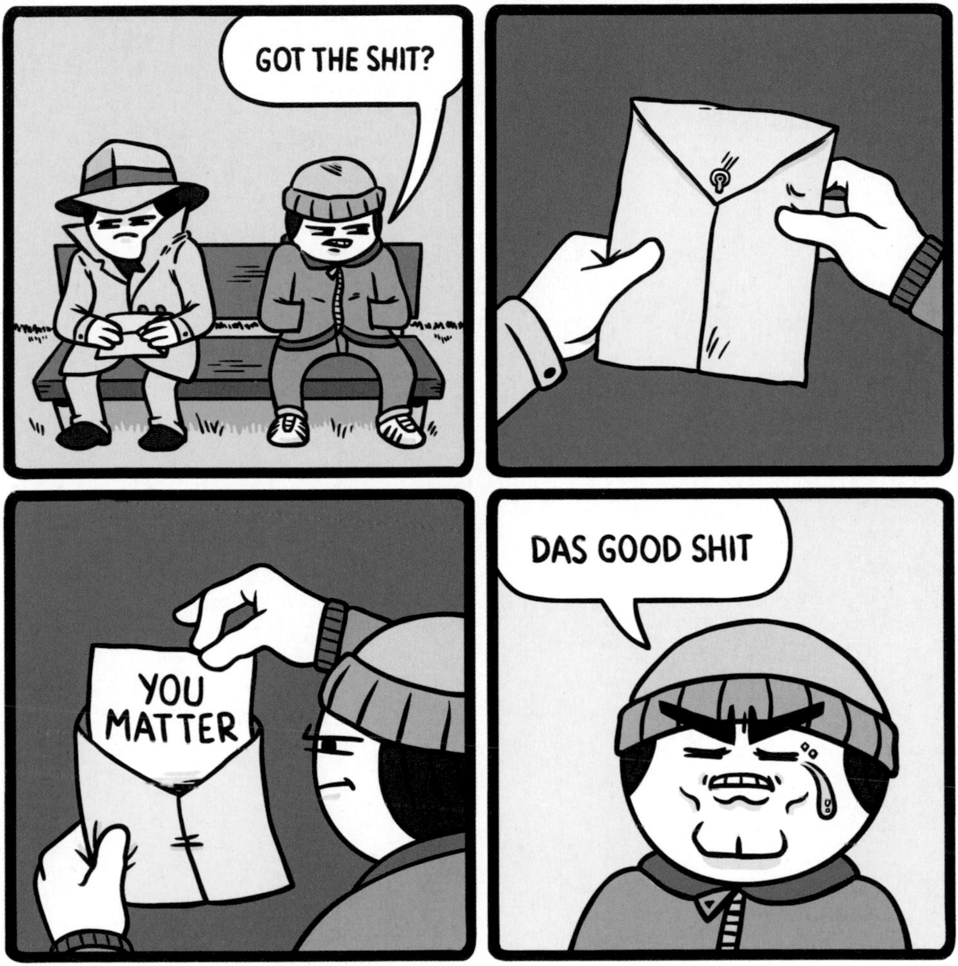
GOT THE SHIT?
YOU
MATTER
DAS GOOD SHIT

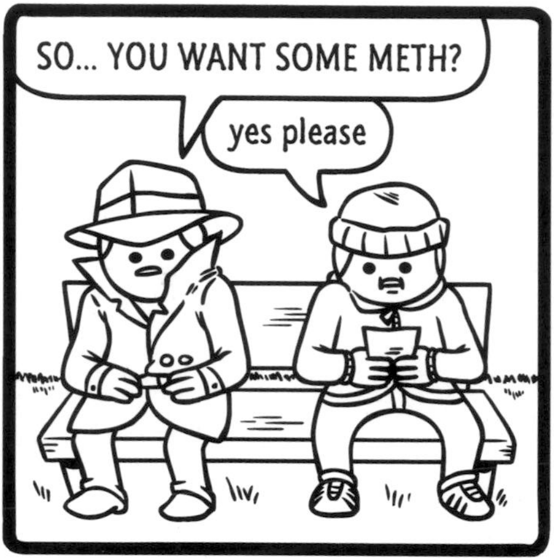
SO... YOU WANT SOME METH?
yes please

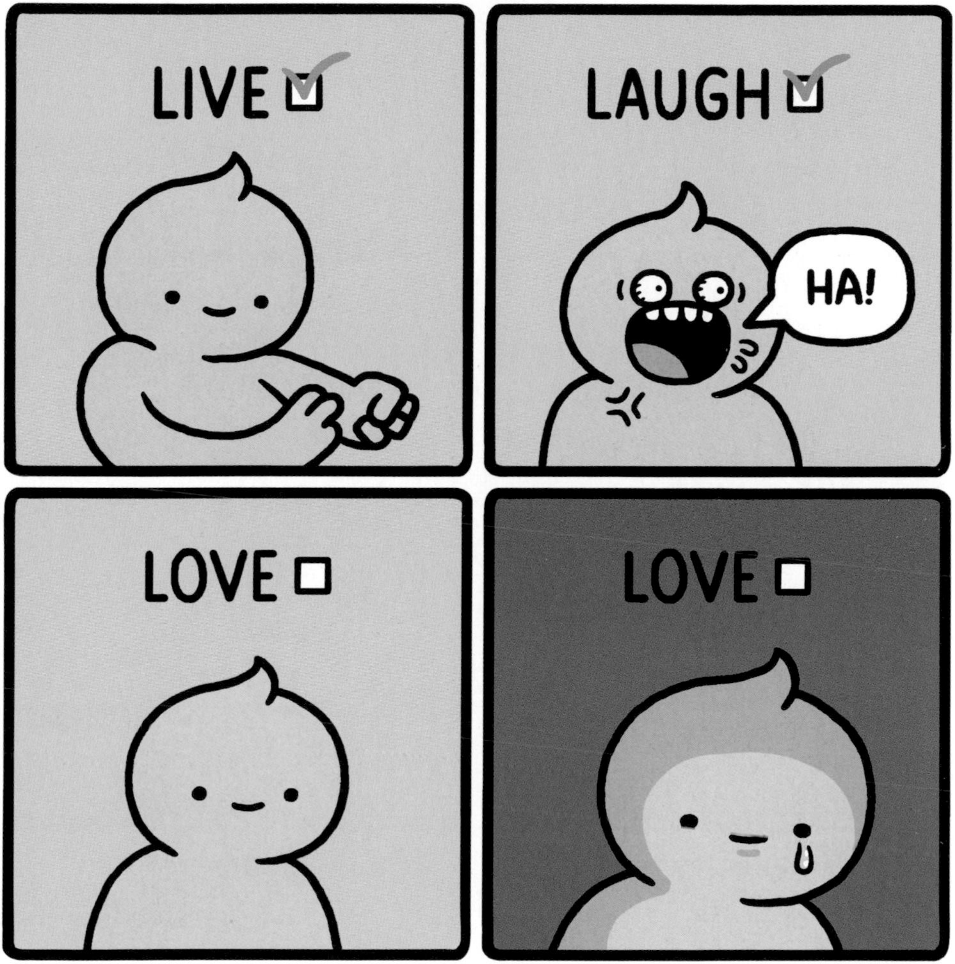
LIVE
LAUGH
HA!
LOVE
LOVE

YOU COULD LOVE YOURSELF!
HA!

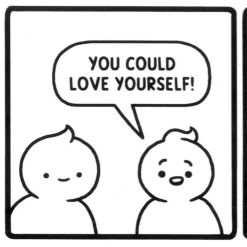

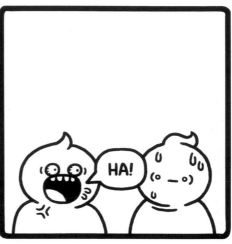

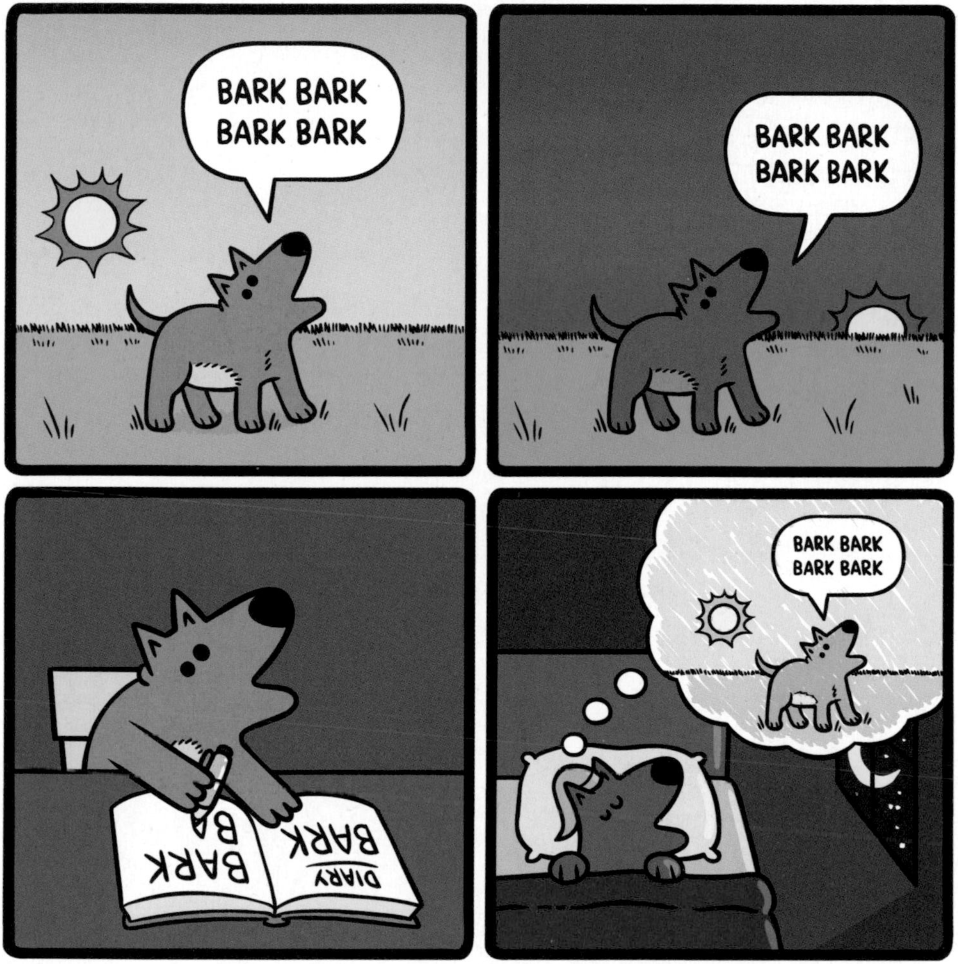
BARK BARK BARK BARK
BARK BARK BARK BARK
DIARY
BARK
BARK
BARK BARK BARK BARK

BORK
poof

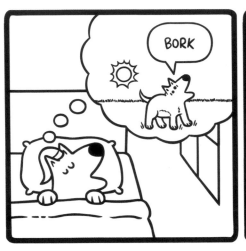

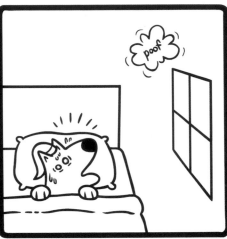

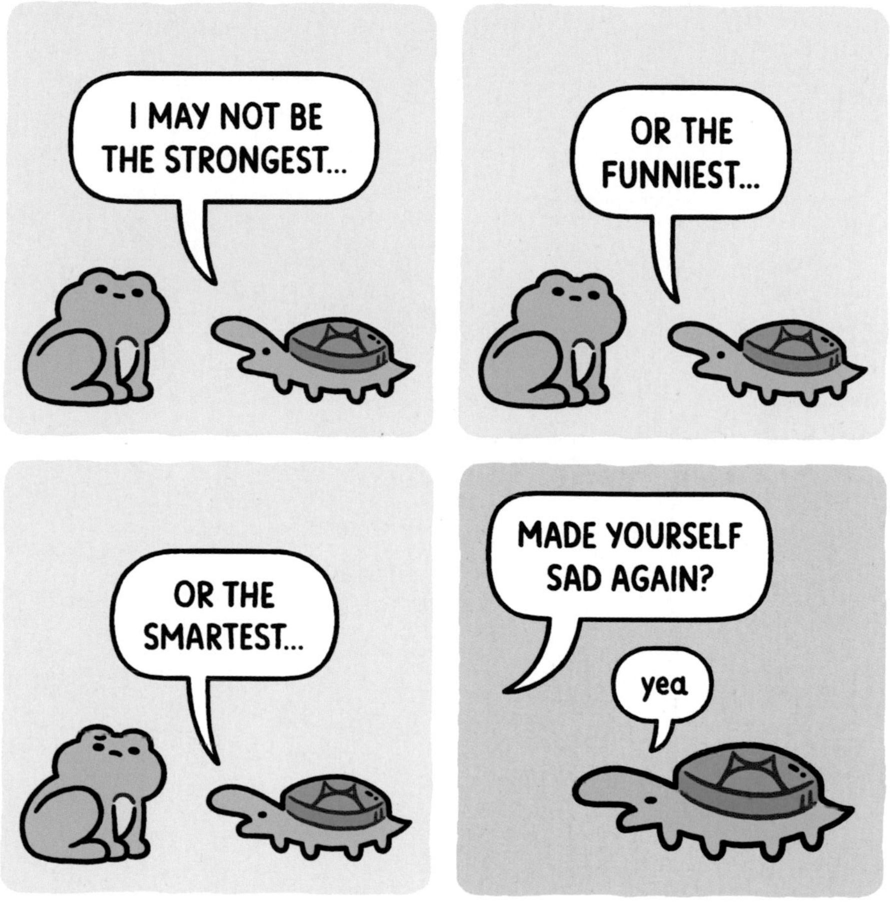
I MAY NOT BE THE STRONGEST...
OR THE FUNNIEST...
OR THE SMARTEST...
MADE YOURSELF SAD AGAIN?
yea

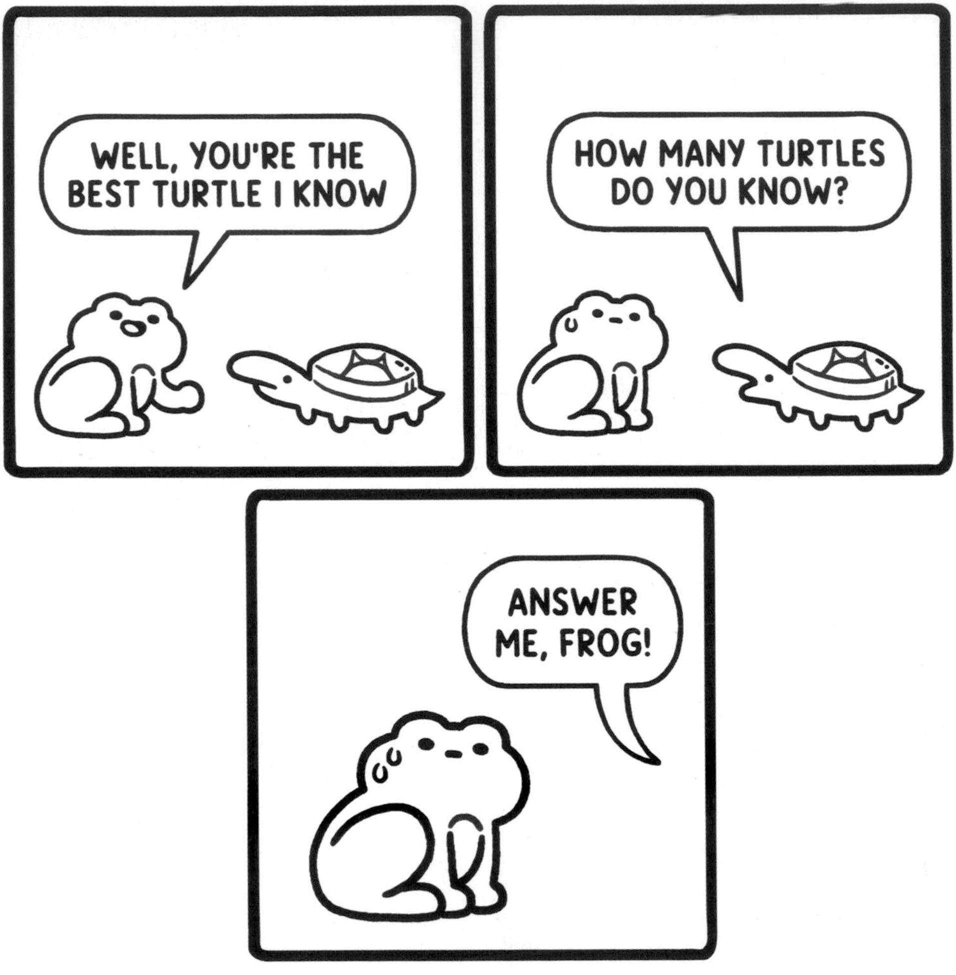
WELL, YOU'RE THE BEST TURTLE I KNOW
HOW MANY TURTLES DO YOU KNOW?
ANSWER ME, FROG!

WHAT MOTIVATES YOU?

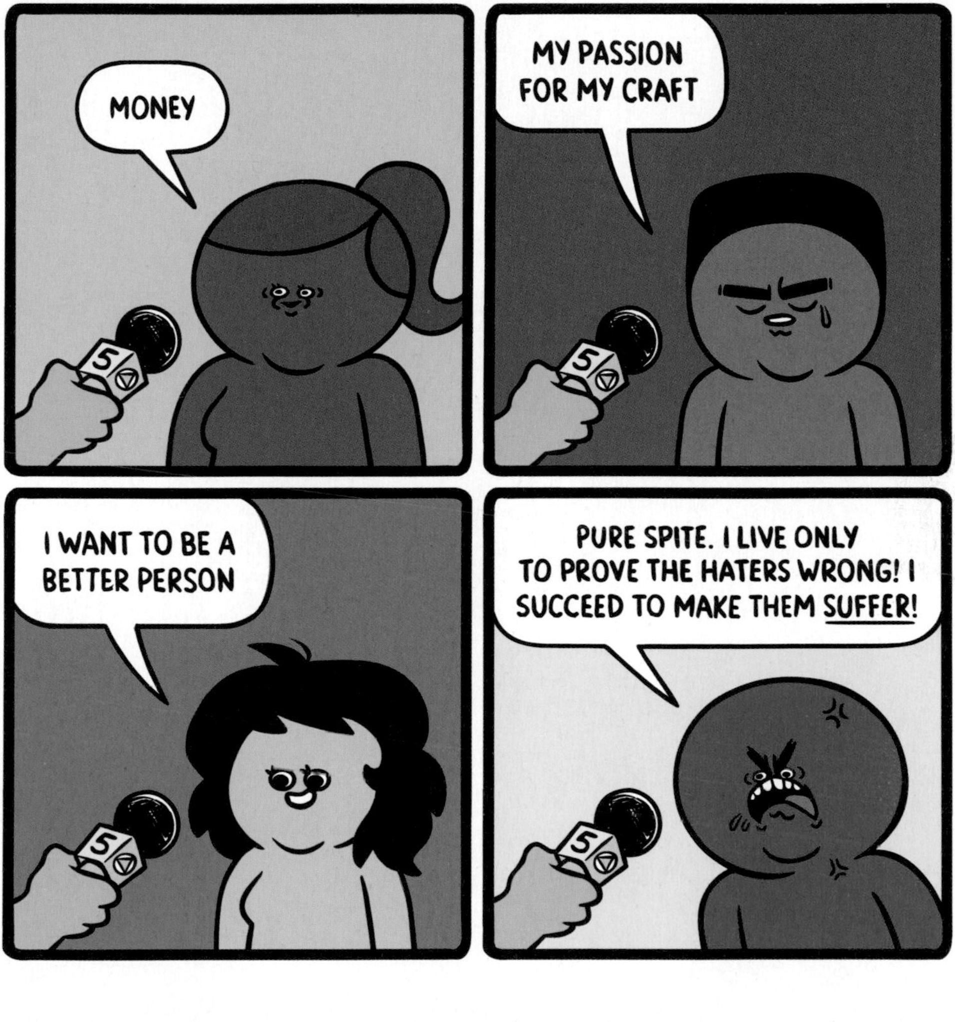
MONEY
MY PASSION FOR MY CRAFT
I WANT TO BE A BETTER PERSON
PURE SPITE. I LIVE ONLY TO PROVE THE HATERS WRONG! I SUCCEED TO MAKE THEM SUFFER!

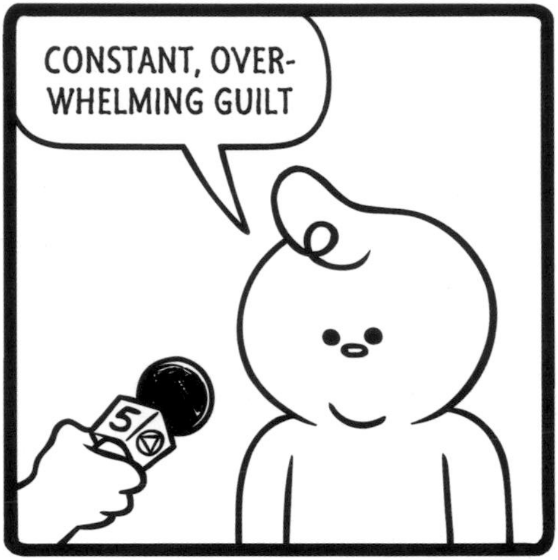
CONSTANT, OVER-
WHELMING GUILT
5

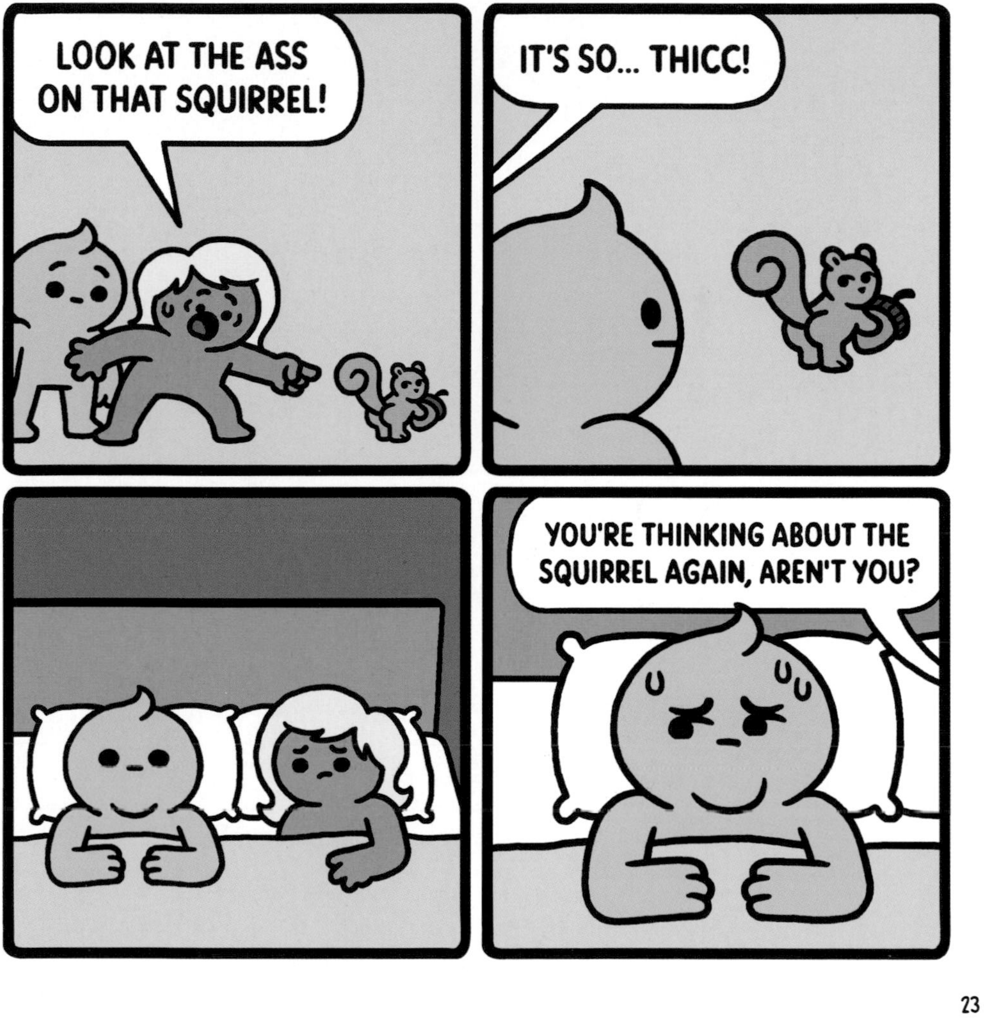
LOOK AT THE ASS ON THAT SQUIRREL!
IT'S SO... THICC!
YOU'RE THINKING ABOUT THE SQUIRREL AGAIN, AREN'T YOU?

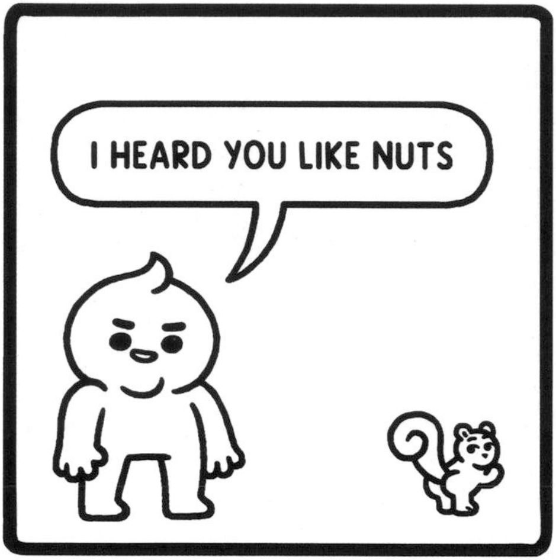
I HEARD YOU LIKE NUTS

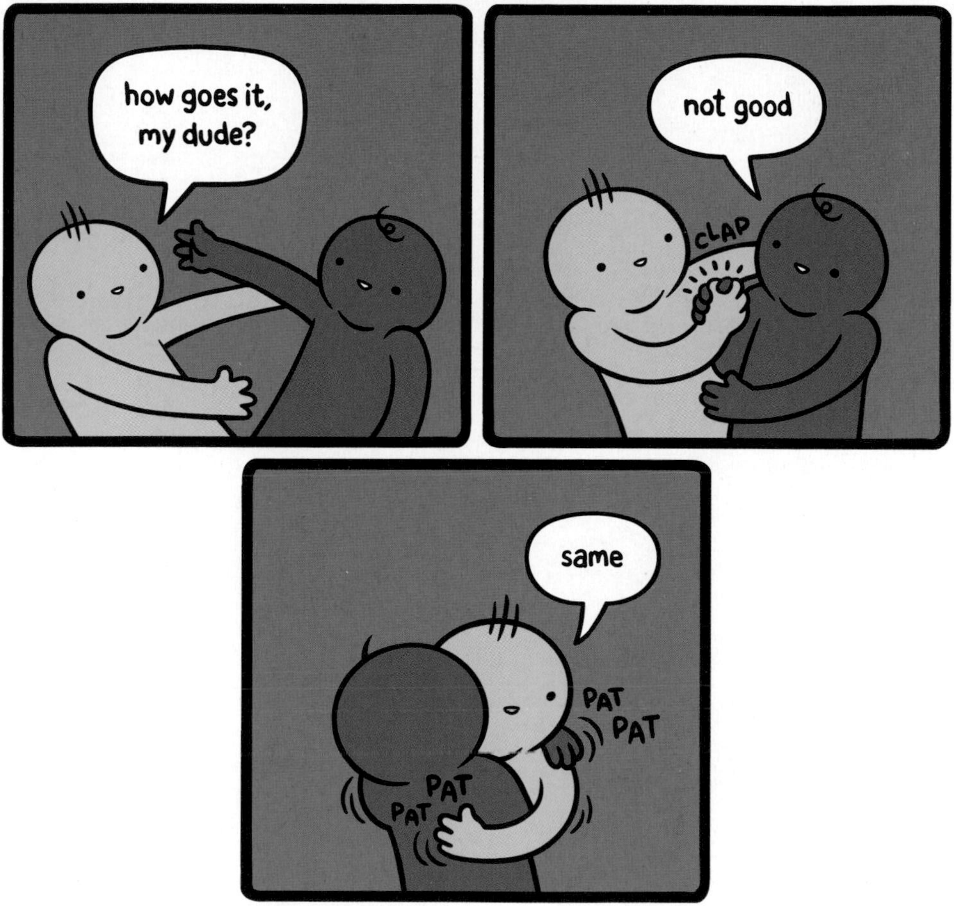
how goes it, my dude?
not good
CLAP
same
PAT PAT
PAT PAT

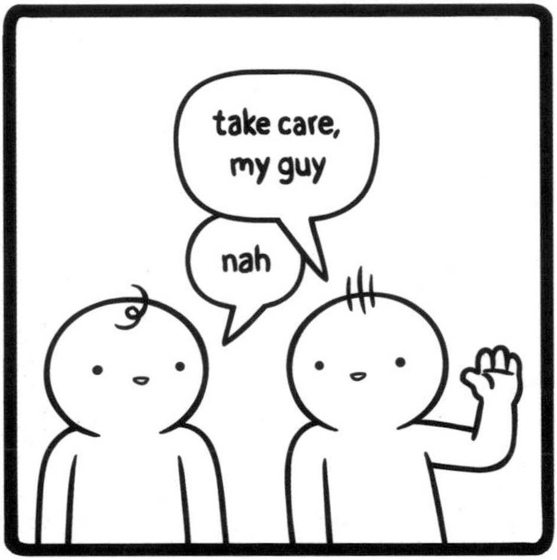
take care, my guy
nah

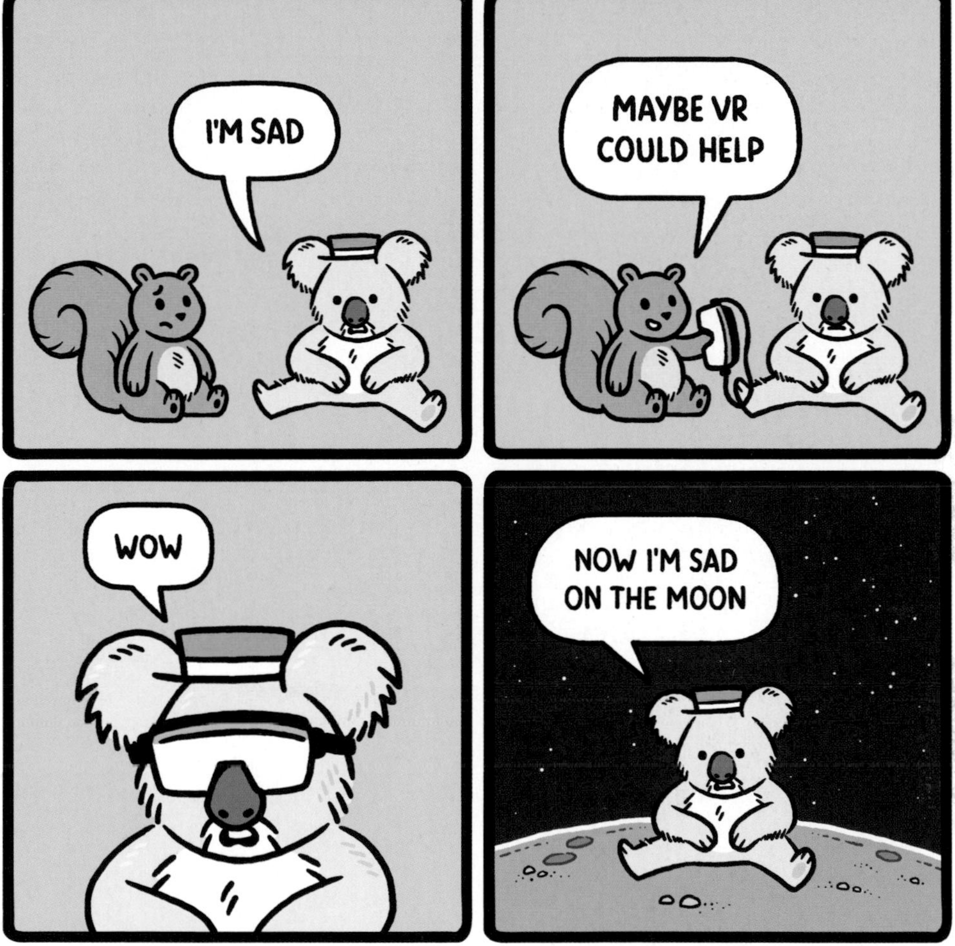
I'M SAD
MAYBE VR COULD HELP
WOW
NOW I'M SAD ON THE MOON

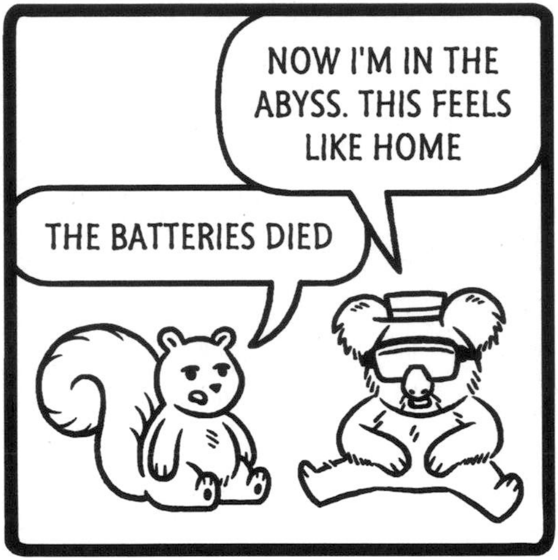
NOW I'M IN THE ABYSS. THIS FEELS LIKE HOME
THE BATTERIES DIED

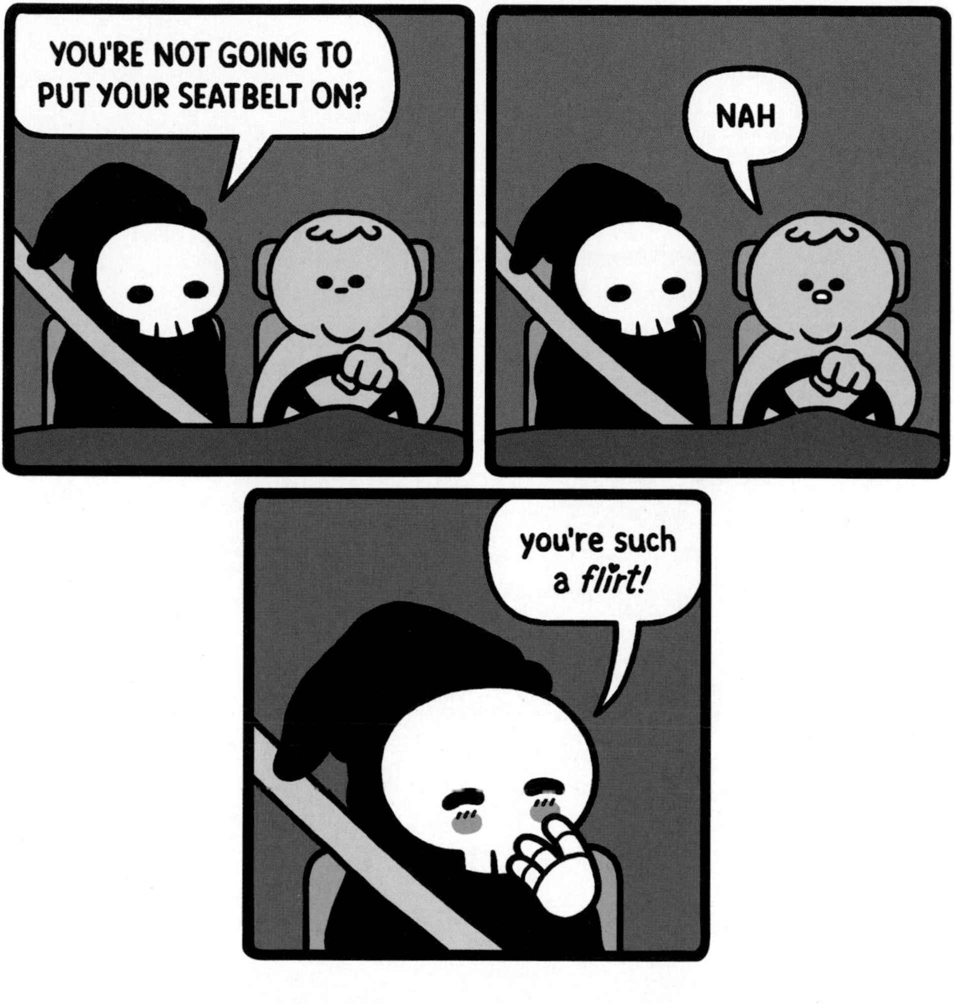
YOU'RE NOT GOING TO PUT YOUR SEATBELT ON?
NAH
you're such a *flirt!*

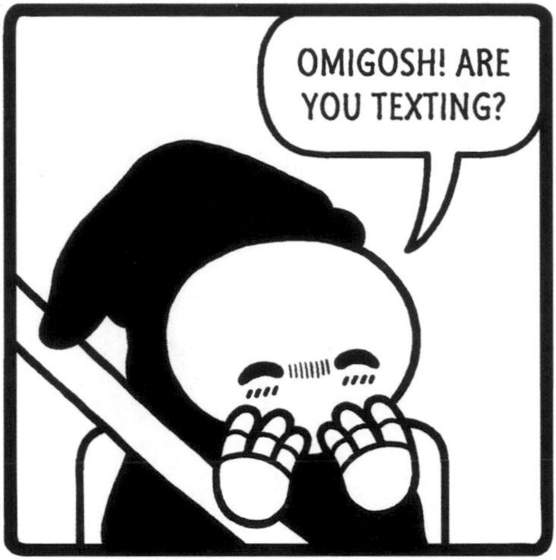
OMIGOSH! ARE YOU TEXTING?

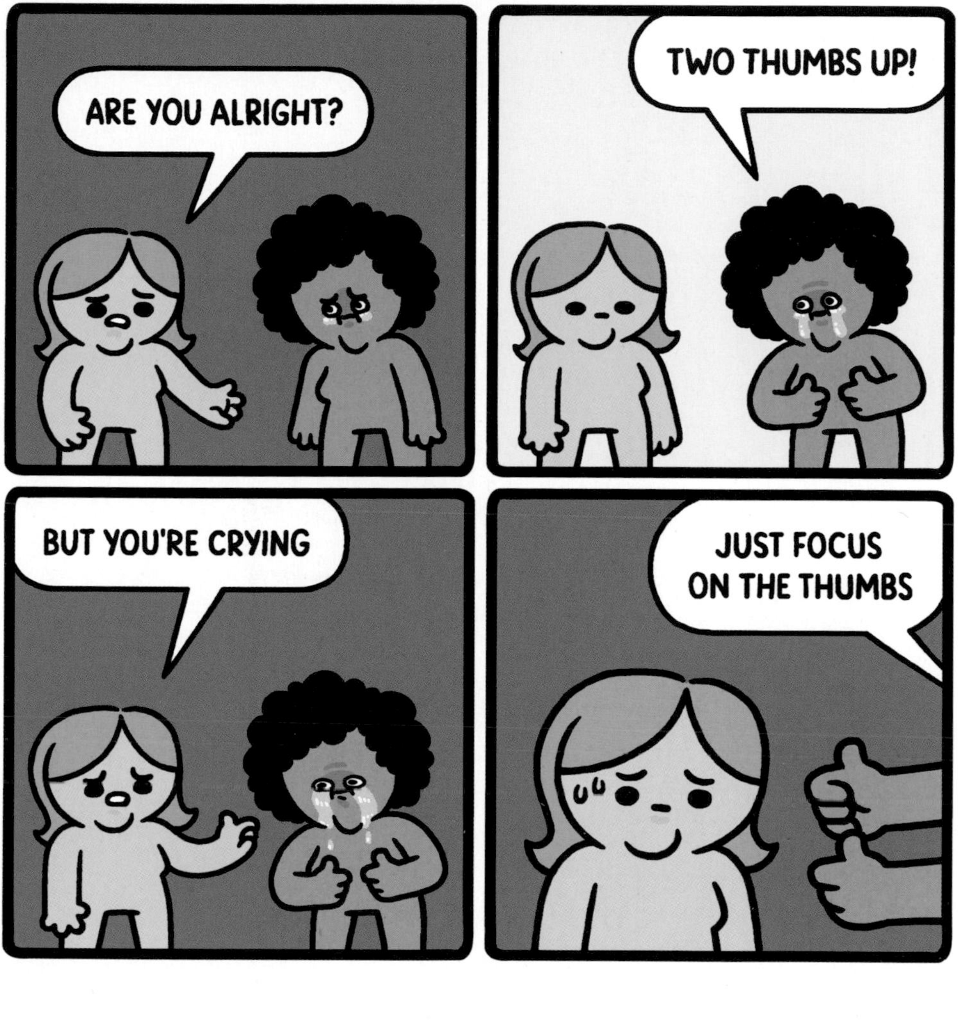
ARE YOU ALRIGHT?
TWO THUMBS UP!
BUT YOU'RE CRYING
JUST FOCUS ON THE THUMBS

NOW THE THUMBS ARE CRYING

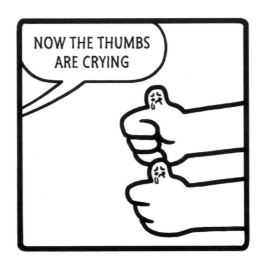

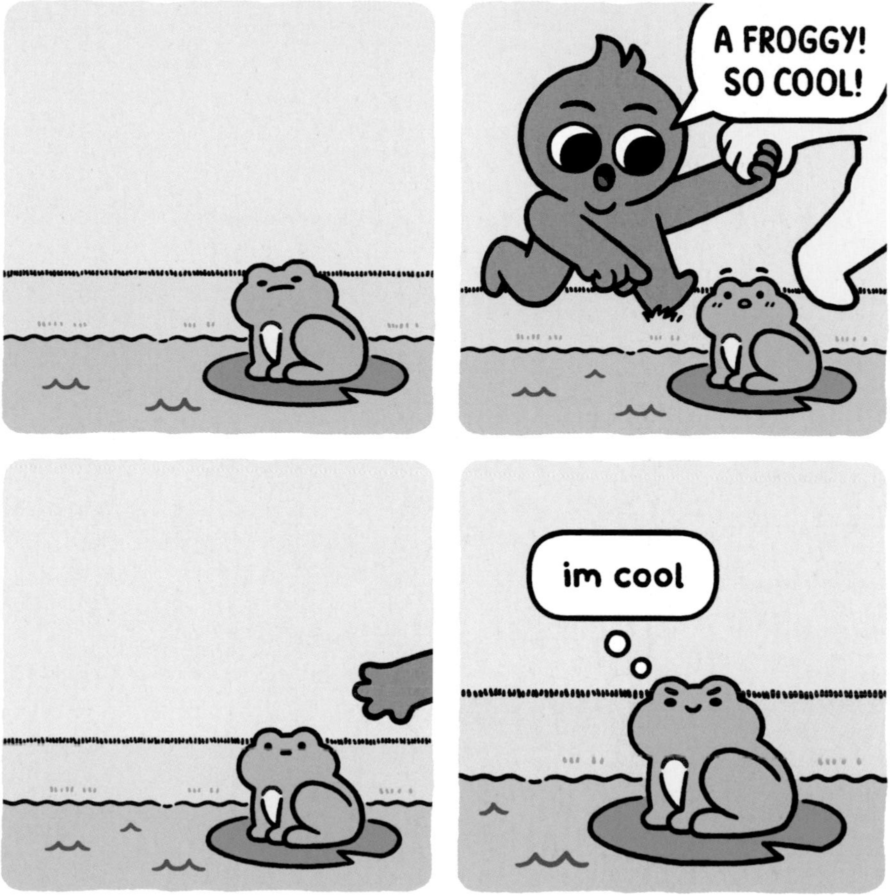
A FROGGY! SO COOL!
im cool

LATER...
A FROG! GROSS!
im cool and gross

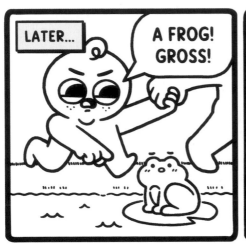

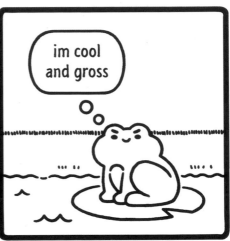

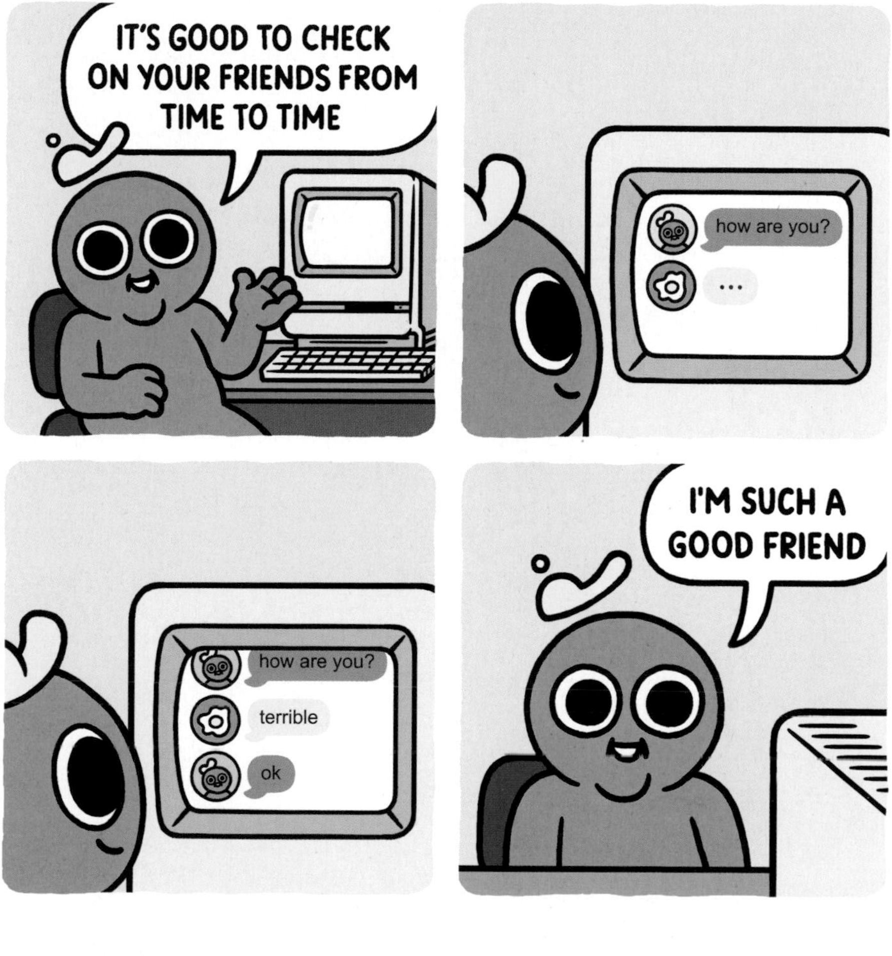
IT'S GOOD TO CHECK ON YOUR FRIENDS FROM TIME TO TIME
how are you?
...
how are you?
terrible
ok
I'M SUCH A GOOD FRIEND

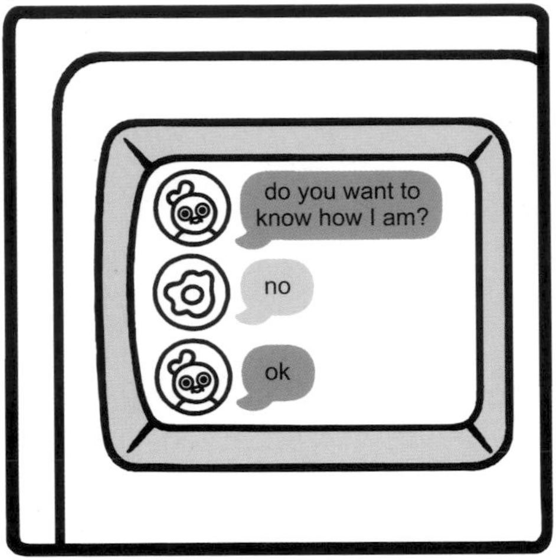
do you want to know how I am?
no
ok

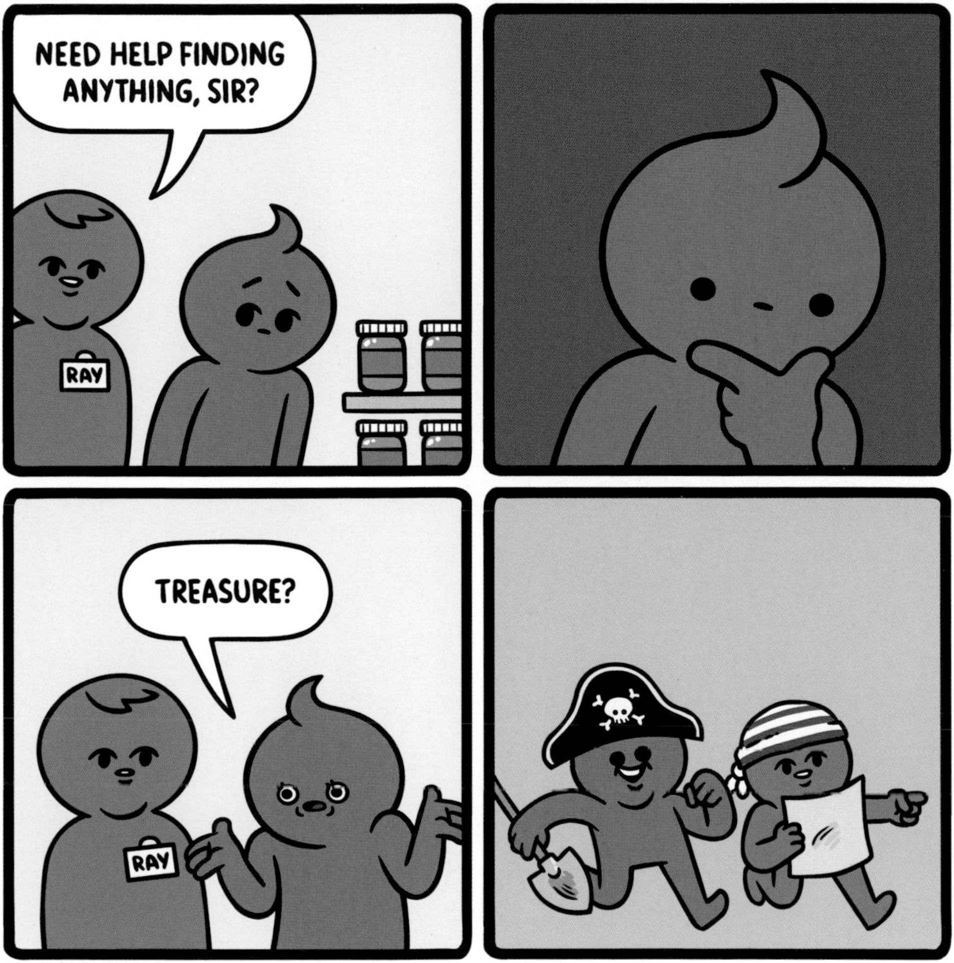
NEED HELP FINDING ANYTHING, SIR?
RAY
RAY
TREASURE?

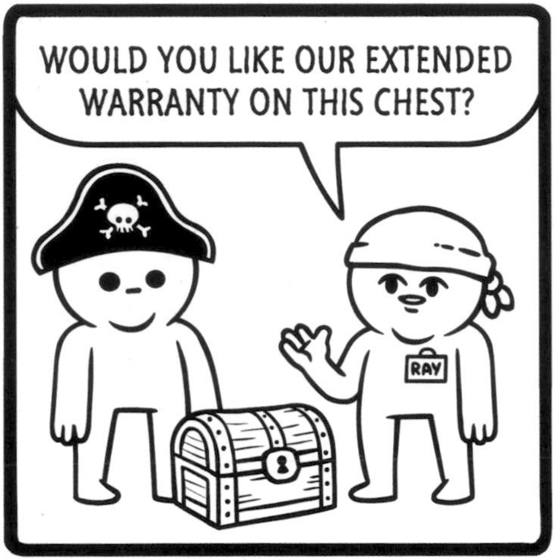
WOULD YOU LIKE OUR EXTENDED WARRANTY ON THIS CHEST?
RAY

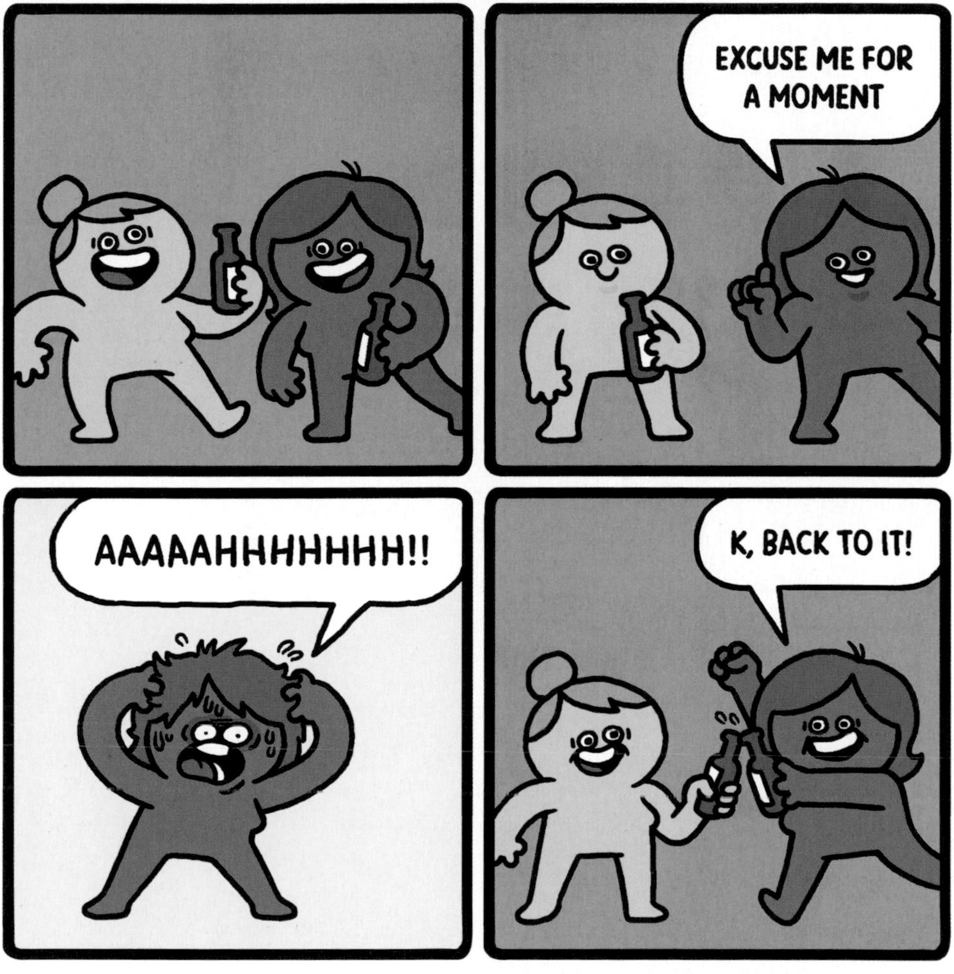
EXCUSE ME FOR A MOMENT
AAAAAHHHHHHH!!
K, BACK TO IT!

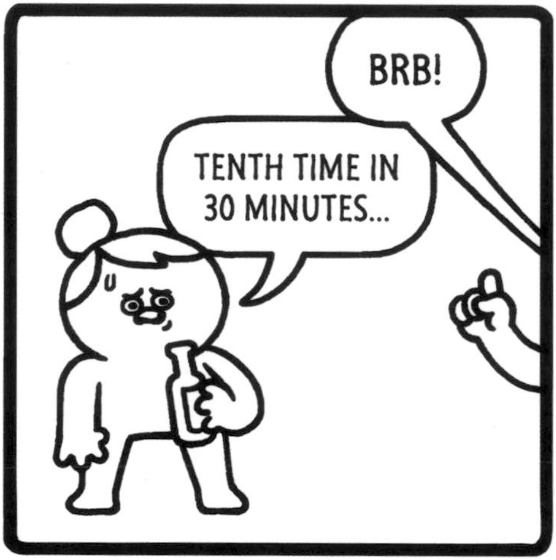
TENTH TIME IN
30 MINUTES...
BRB!

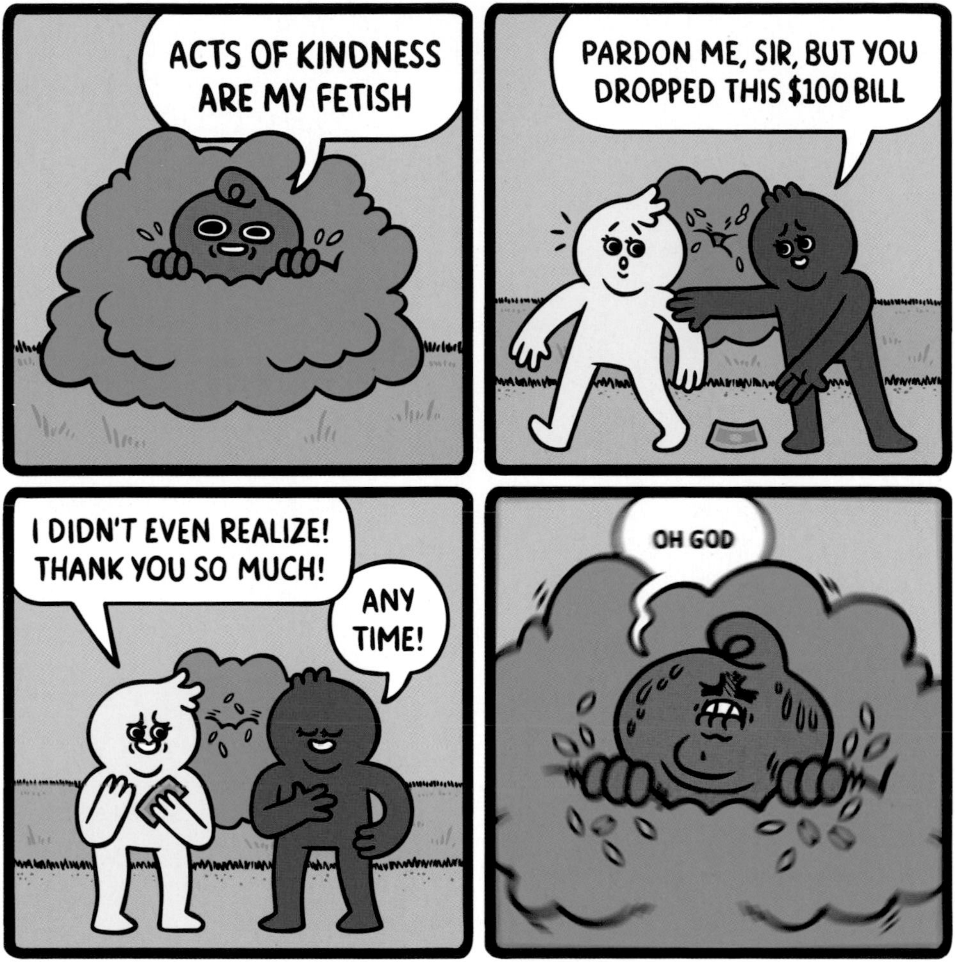
ACTS OF KINDNESS ARE MY FETISH
PARDON ME, SIR, BUT YOU DROPPED THIS $100 BILL
I DIDN'T EVEN REALIZE! THANK YOU SO MUCH!
ANY TIME!
OH GOD

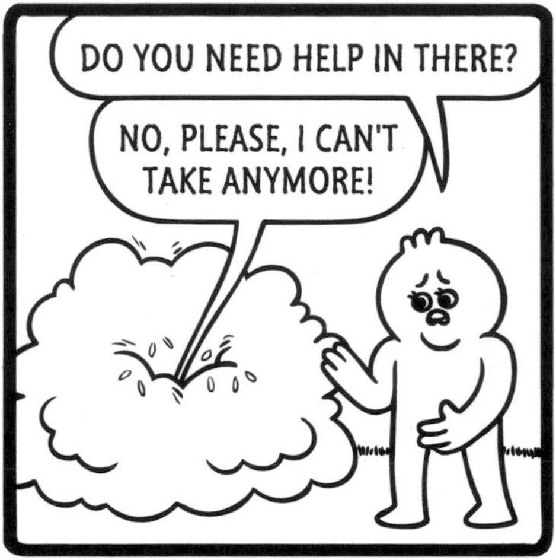
DO YOU NEED HELP IN THERE?
NO, PLEASE, I CAN'T TAKE ANYMORE!

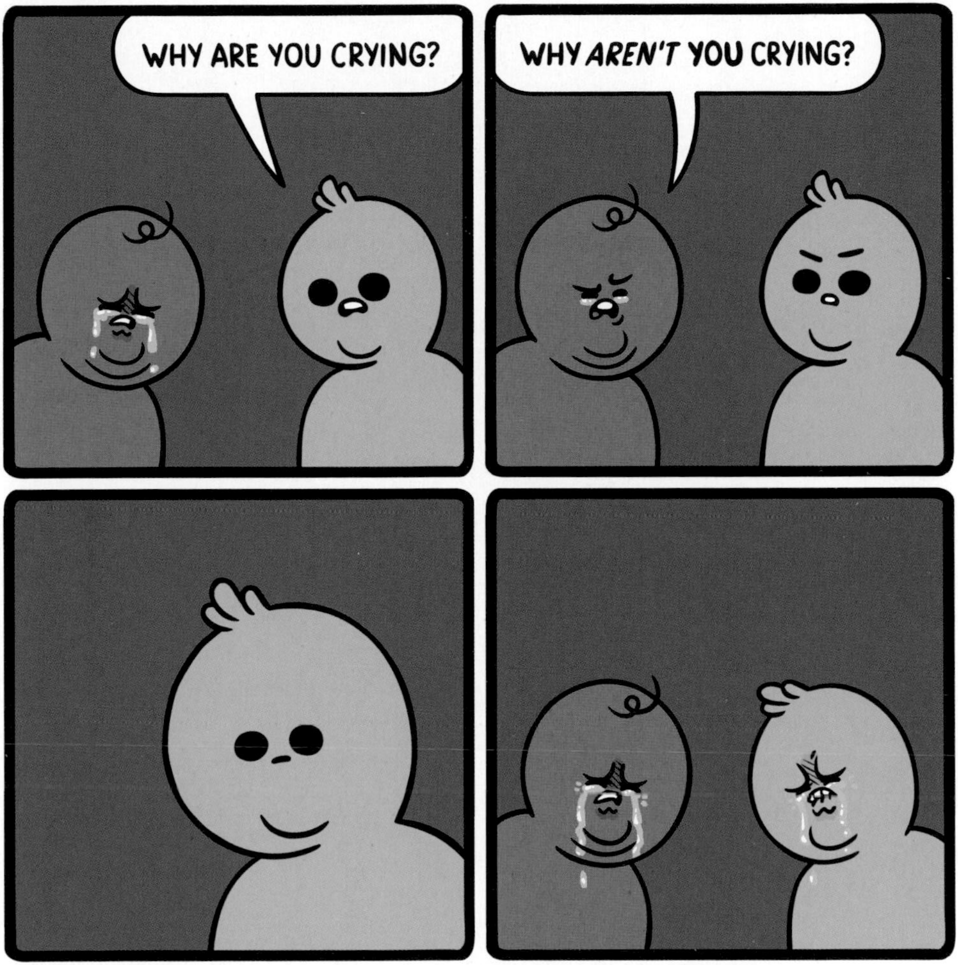
WHY ARE YOU CRYING?
WHY *AREN'T* YOU CRYING?

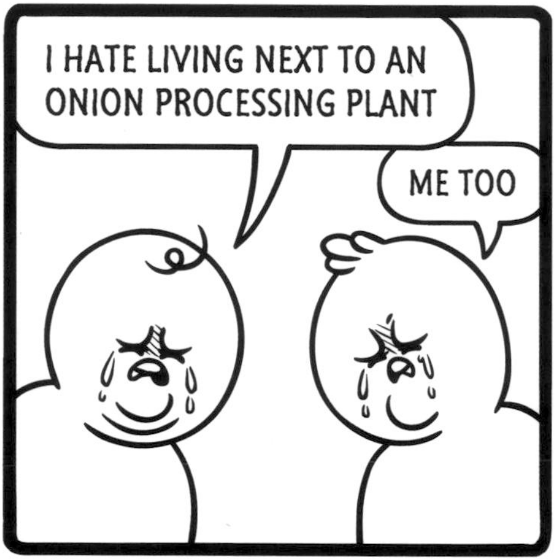
I HATE LIVING NEXT TO AN ONION PROCESSING PLANT
ME TOO

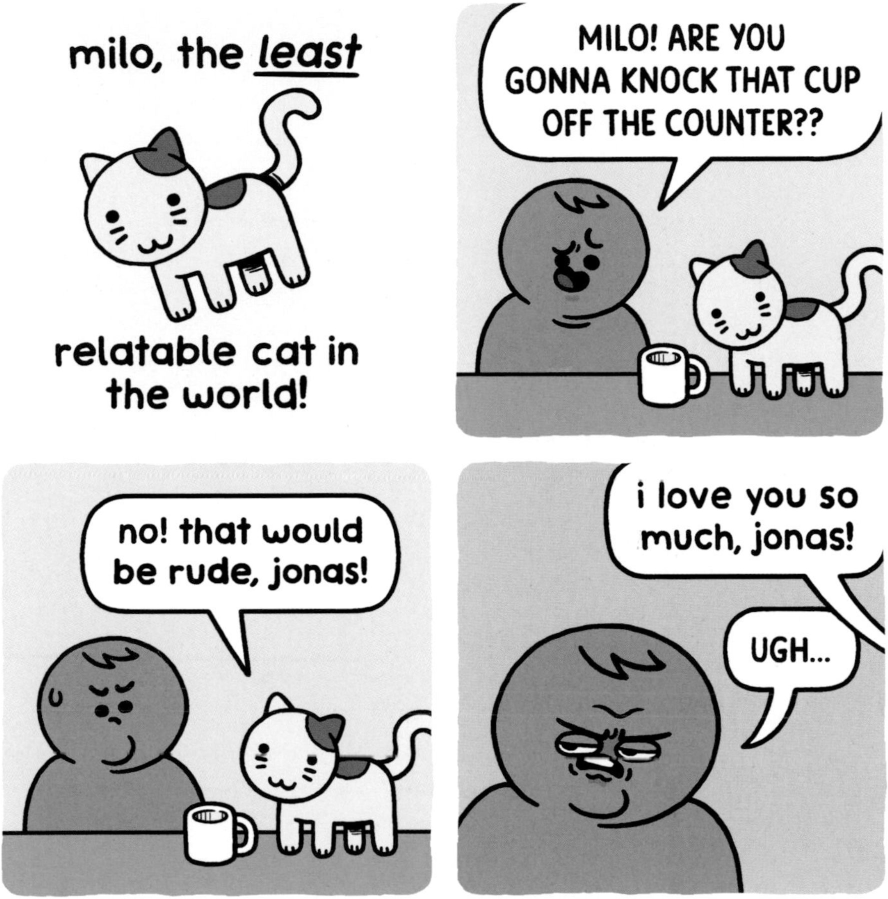
milo, the least
relatable cat in the world!
MILO! ARE YOU GONNA KNOCK THAT CUP OFF THE COUNTER??
no! that would be rude, jonas!
i love you so much, jonas!
UGH...

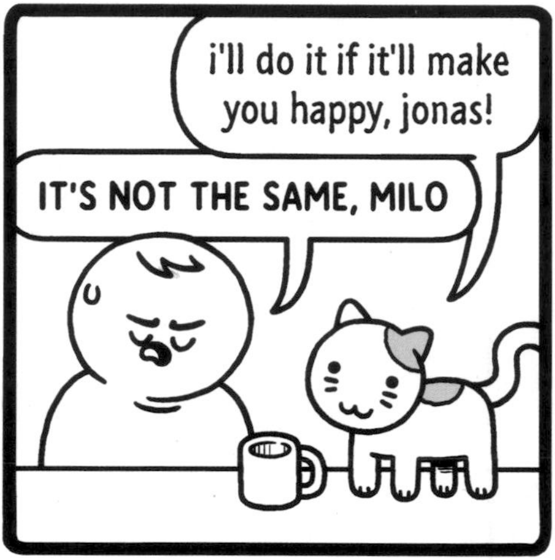
i'll do it if it'll make you happy, jonas!
IT'S NOT THE SAME, MILO

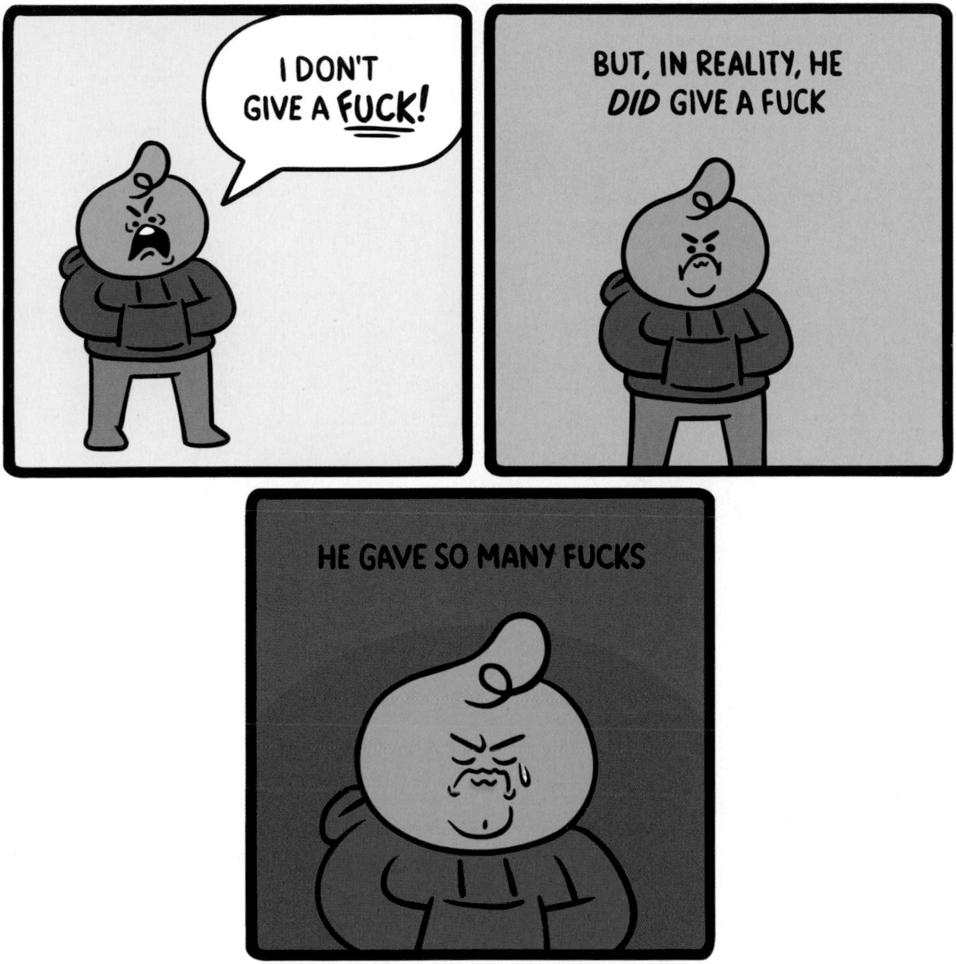
I DON'T GIVE A FUCK!
BUT, IN REALITY, HE *DID* GIVE A FUCK
HE GAVE SO MANY FUCKS

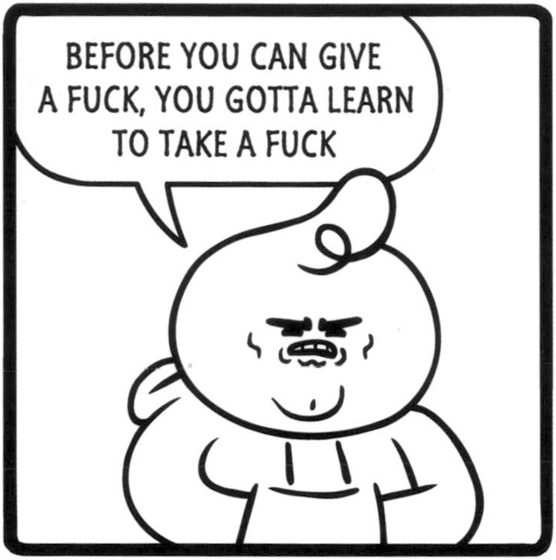
BEFORE YOU CAN GIVE A FUCK, YOU GOTTA LEARN TO TAKE A FUCK

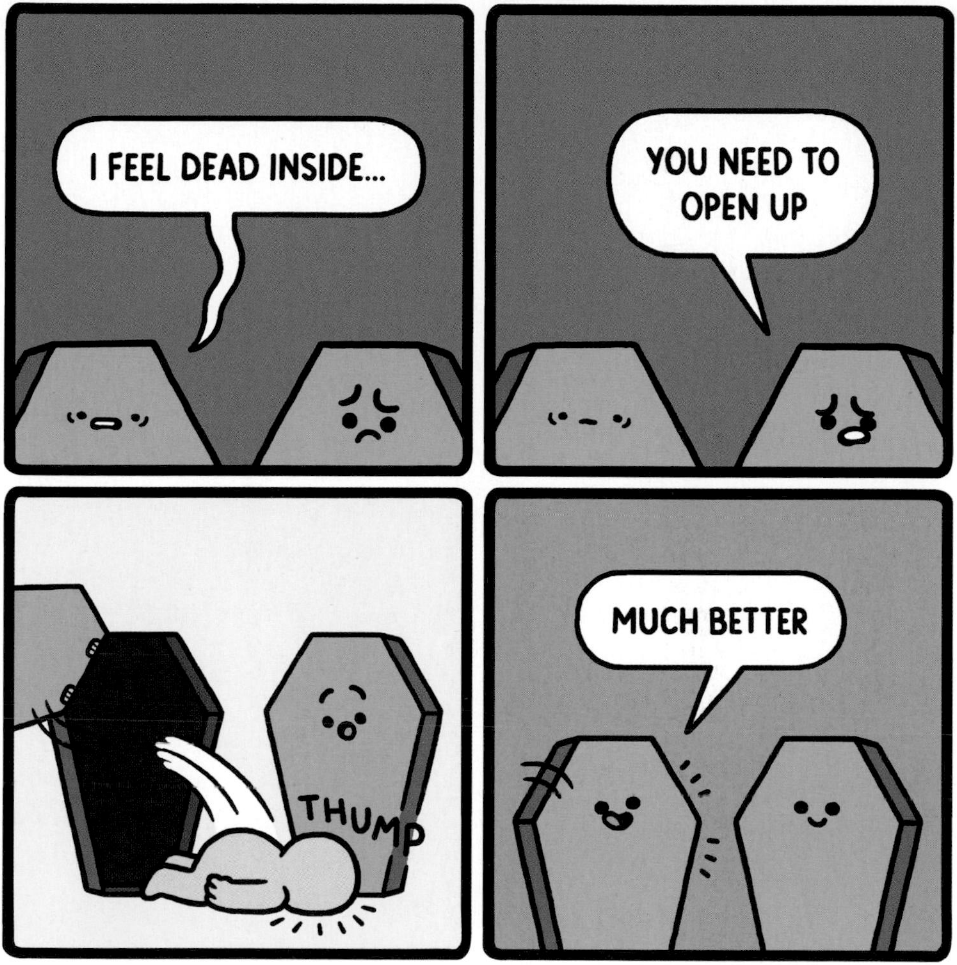
I FEEL DEAD INSIDE...
YOU NEED TO OPEN UP
THUMP
MUCH BETTER

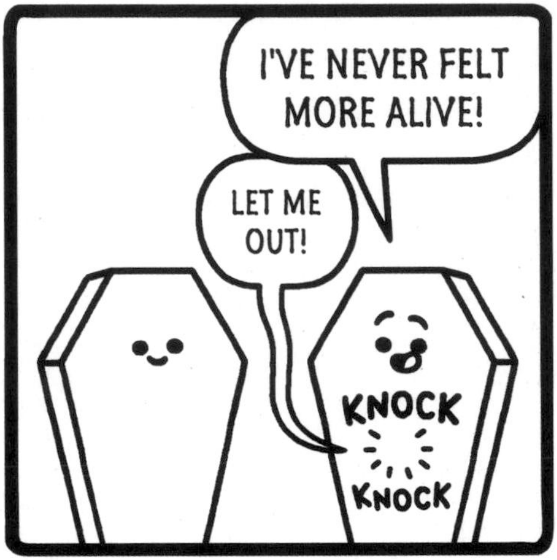
I'VE NEVER FELT MORE ALIVE!
LET ME OUT!
KNOCK
KNOCK

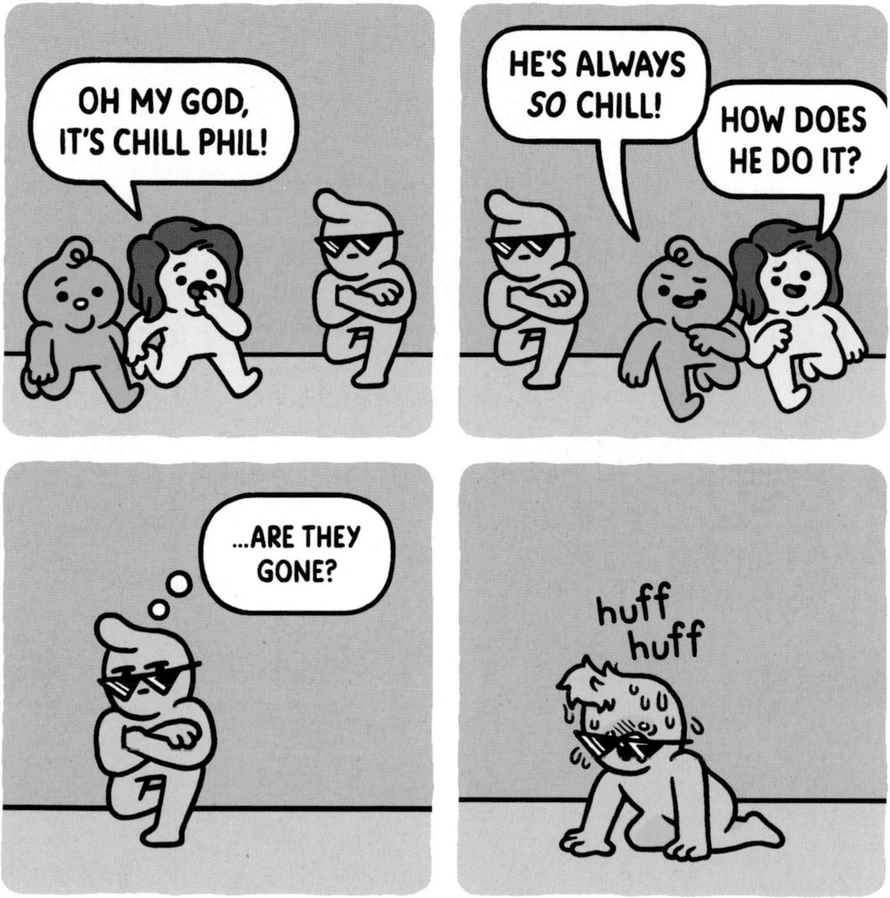
OH MY GOD, IT'S CHILL PHIL!
HE'S ALWAYS *SO* CHILL!
HOW DOES HE DO IT?
...ARE THEY GONE?
huff huff

YOUR BODY CAN'T SUSTAIN THIS LEVEL OF CHILL
HOW CAN YOU BE SO CHILL RIGHT NOW? YOU'RE GONNA DIE!

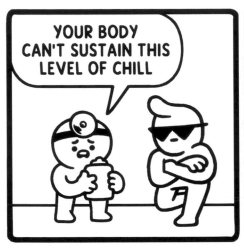

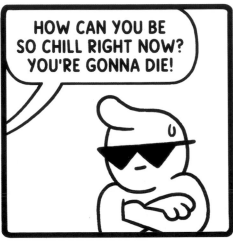

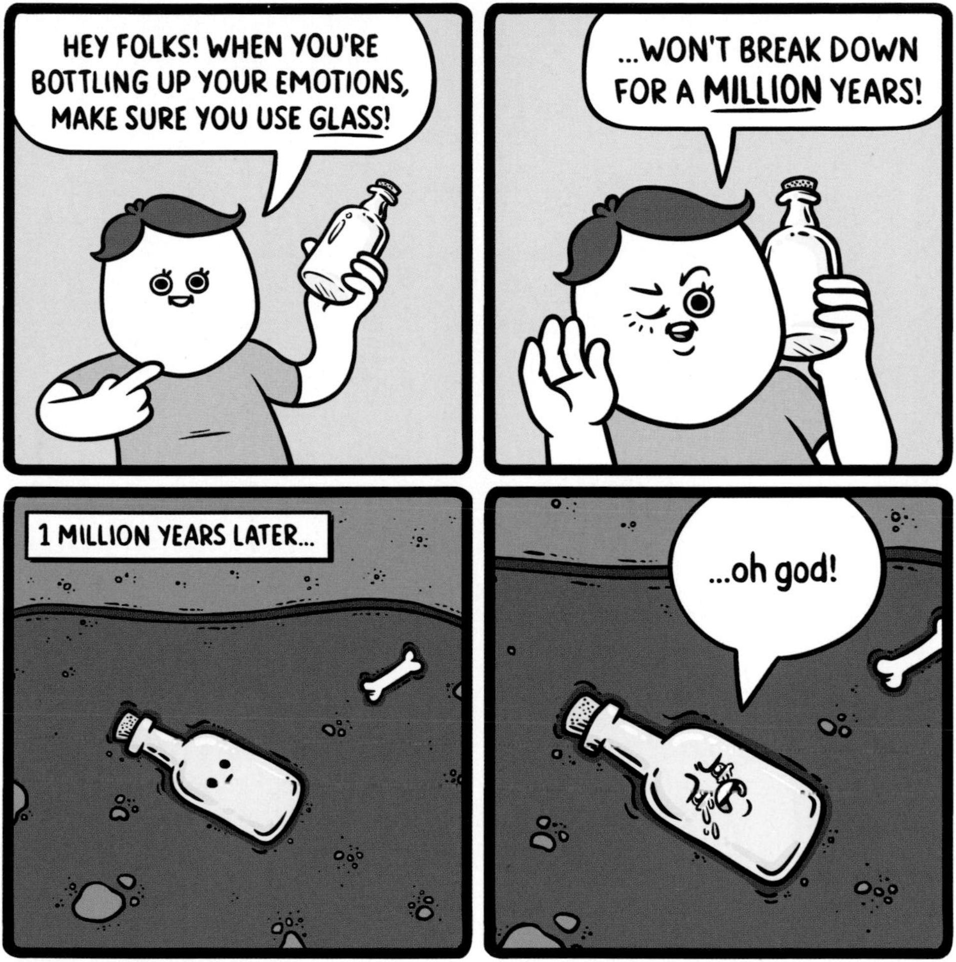
HEY FOLKS! WHEN YOU'RE BOTTLING UP YOUR EMOTIONS, MAKE SURE YOU USE GLASS!
...WON'T BREAK DOWN FOR A MILLION YEARS!
1 MILLION YEARS LATER...
...oh god!

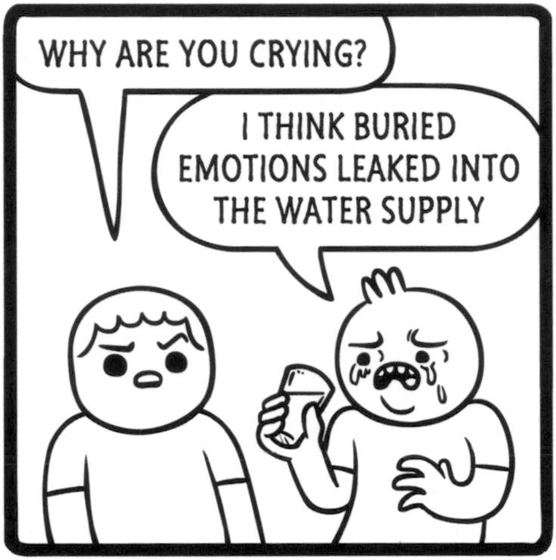
WHY ARE YOU CRYING?
I THINK BURIED EMOTIONS LEAKED INTO THE WATER SUPPLY

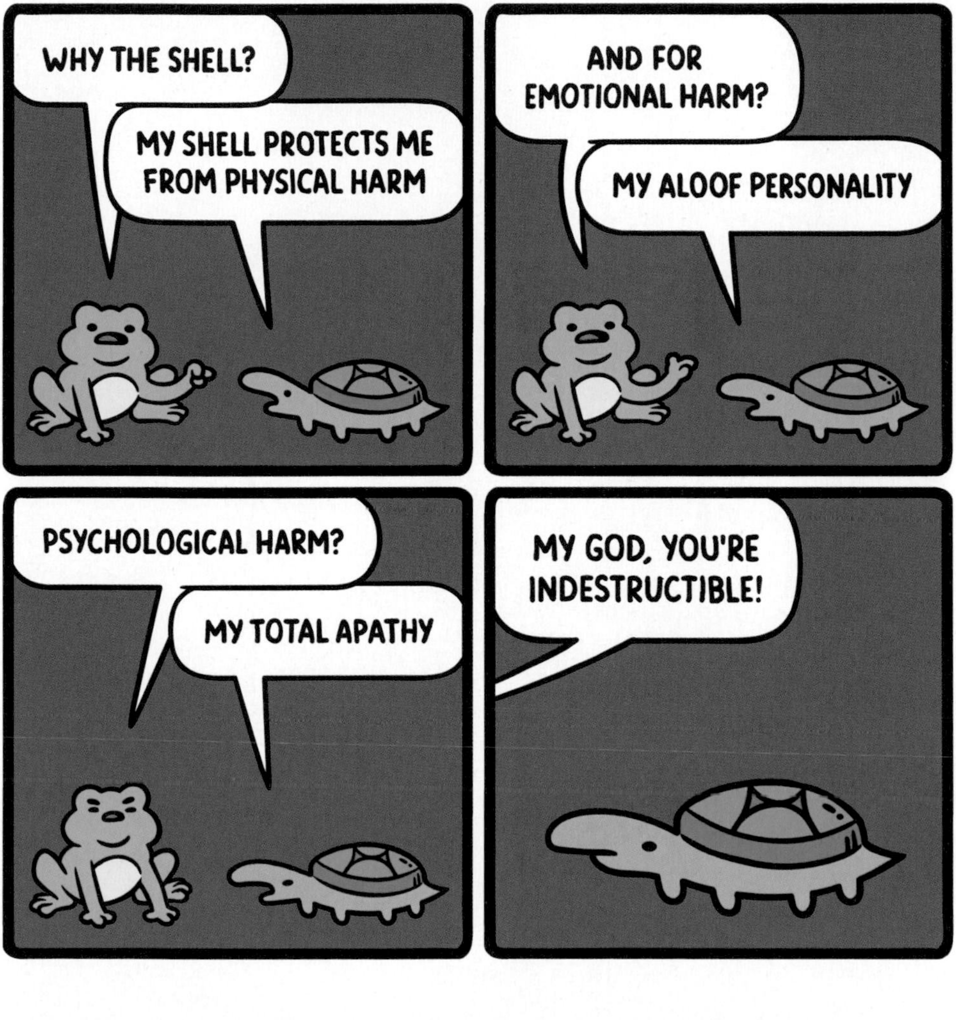
WHY THE SHELL?
MY SHELL PROTECTS ME FROM PHYSICAL HARM
AND FOR EMOTIONAL HARM?
MY ALOOF PERSONALITY
PSYCHOLOGICAL HARM?
MY TOTAL APATHY
MY GOD, YOU'RE INDESTRUCTIBLE!

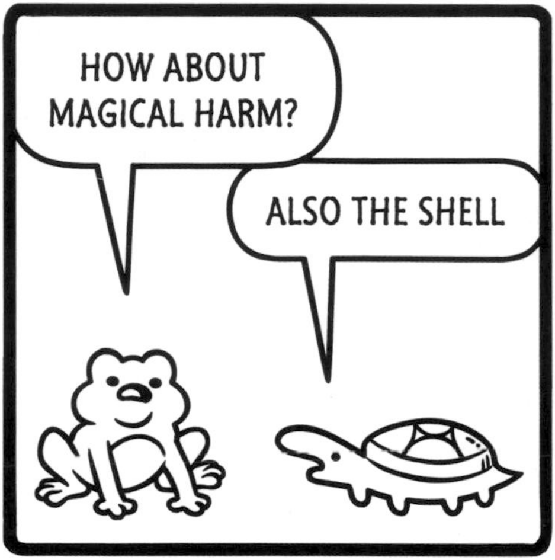
HOW ABOUT MAGICAL HARM?
ALSO THE SHELL

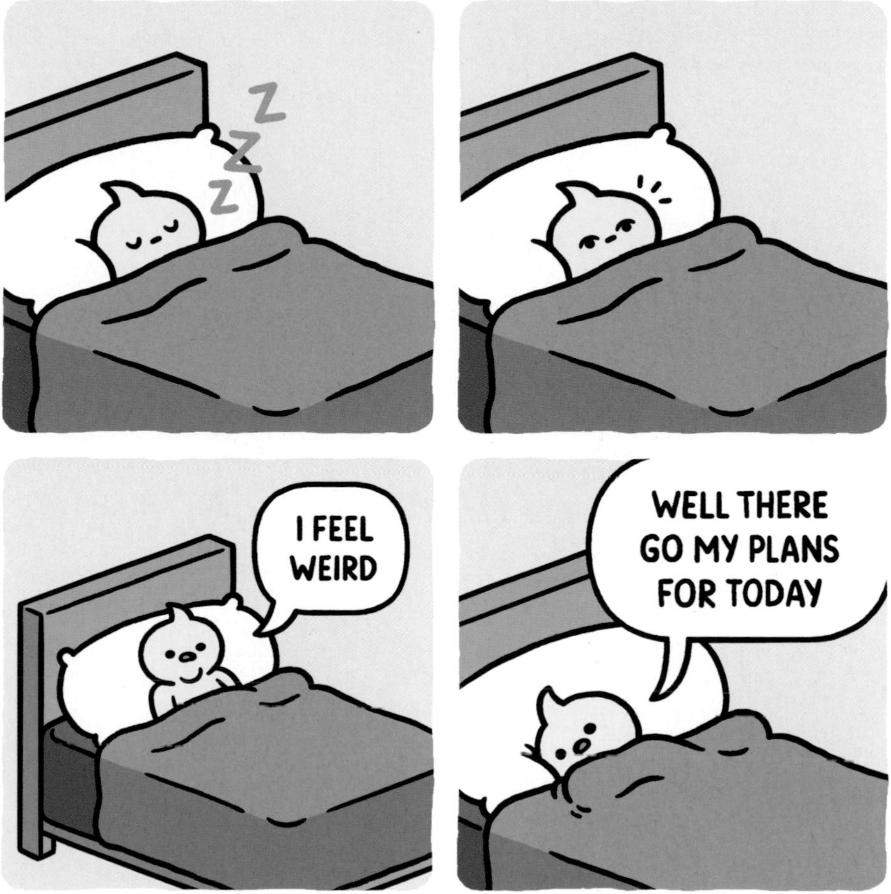
Z
Z
Z
I FEEL
WEIRD
WELL THERE
GO MY PLANS
FOR TODAY

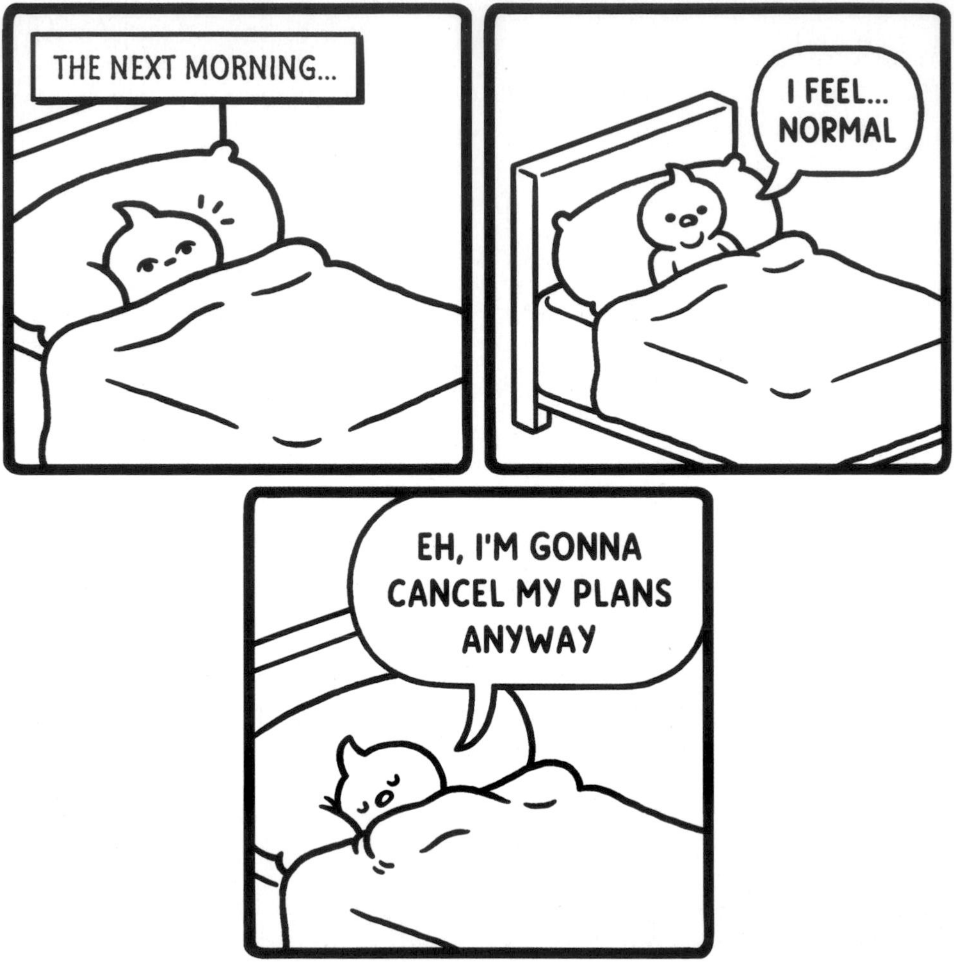
THE NEXT MORNING...
I FEEL... NORMAL
EH, I'M GONNA CANCEL MY PLANS ANYWAY

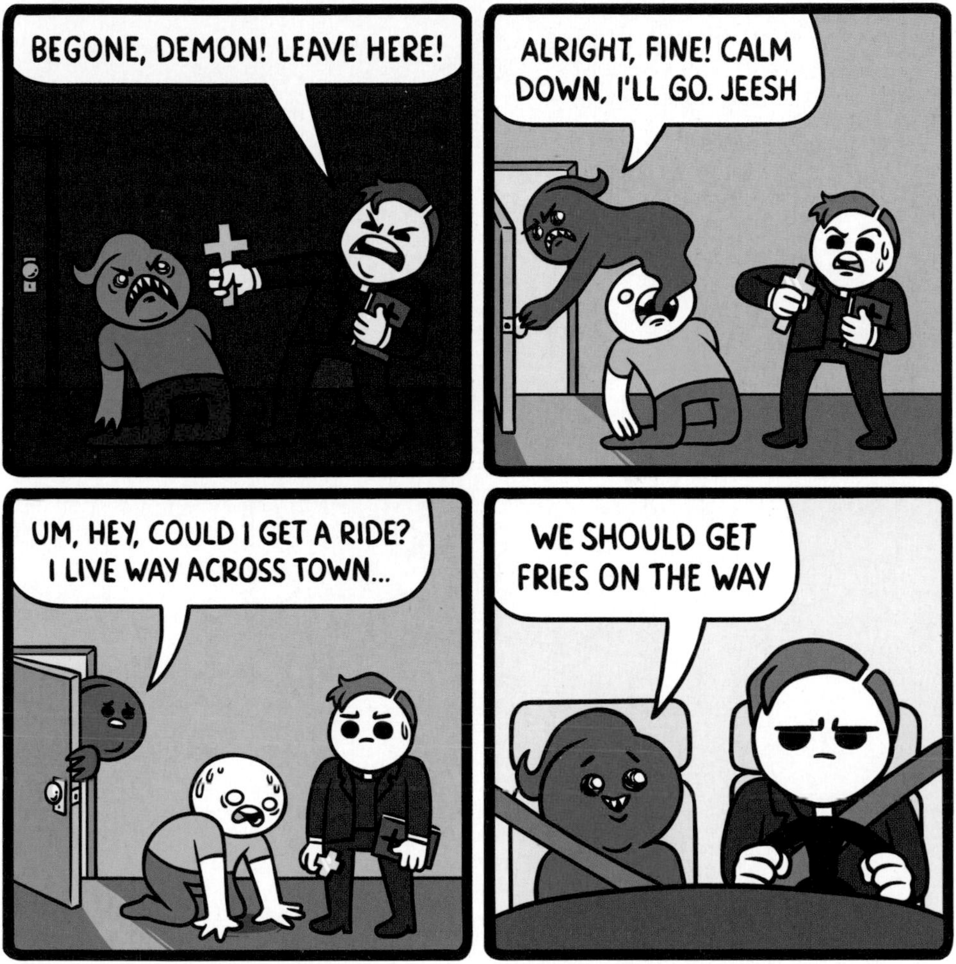
BEGONE, DEMON! LEAVE HERE!
ALRIGHT, FINE! CALM DOWN, I'LL GO. JEESH
UM, HEY, COULD I GET A RIDE? I LIVE WAY ACROSS TOWN...
WE SHOULD GET FRIES ON THE WAY

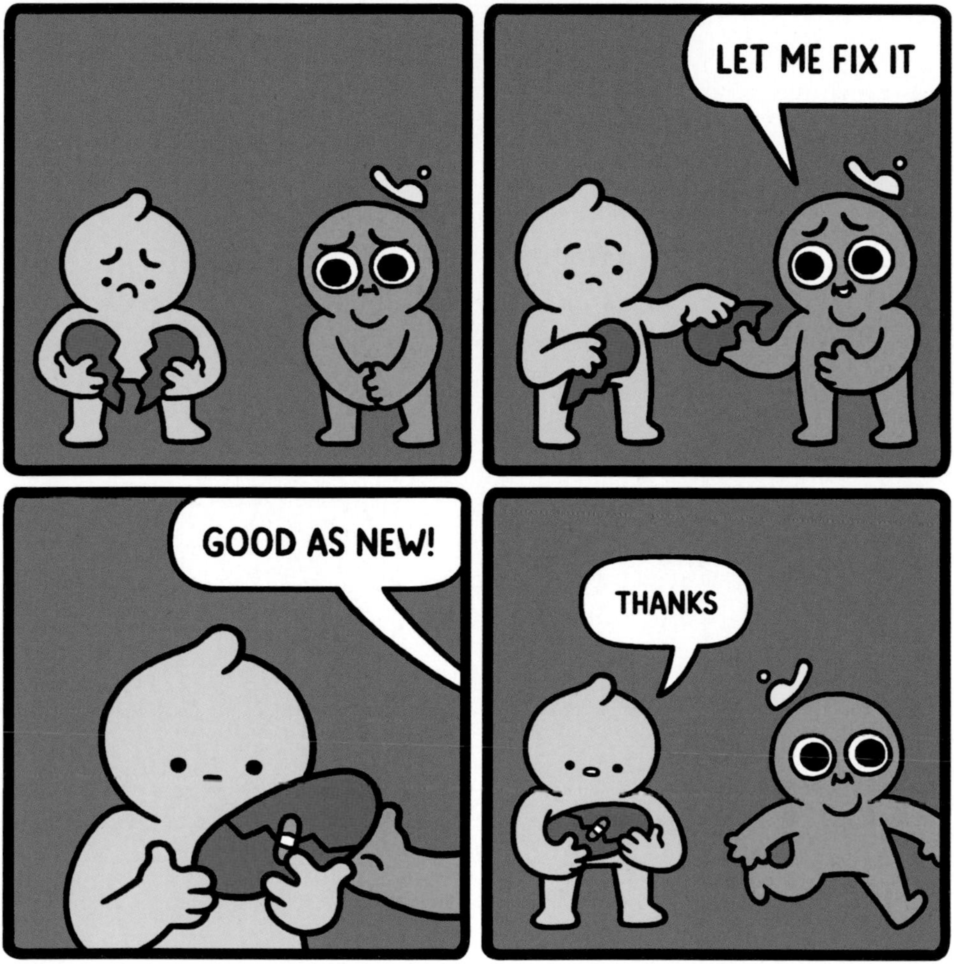
LET ME FIX IT
GOOD AS NEW!
THANKS

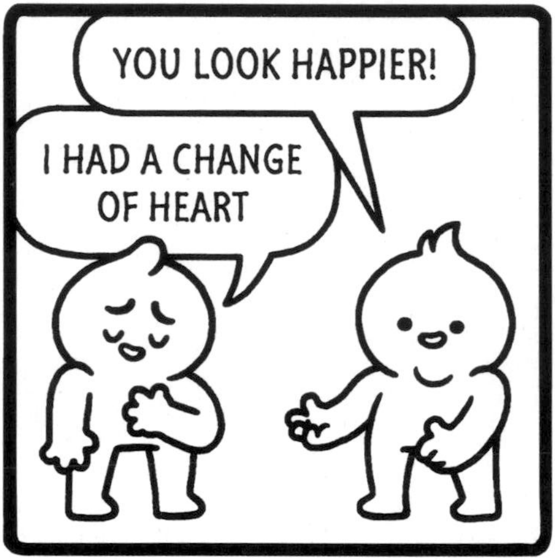
YOU LOOK HAPPIER!
I HAD A CHANGE OF HEART

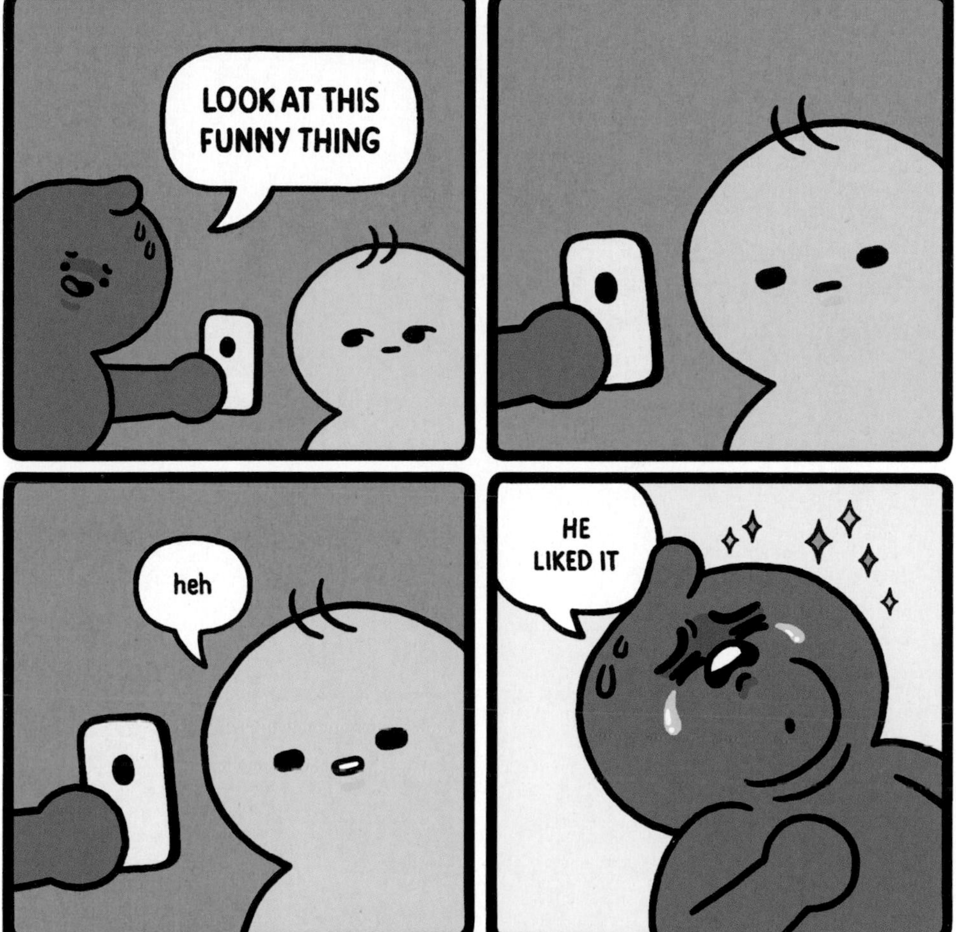
LOOK AT THIS FUNNY THING
heh
HE LIKED IT

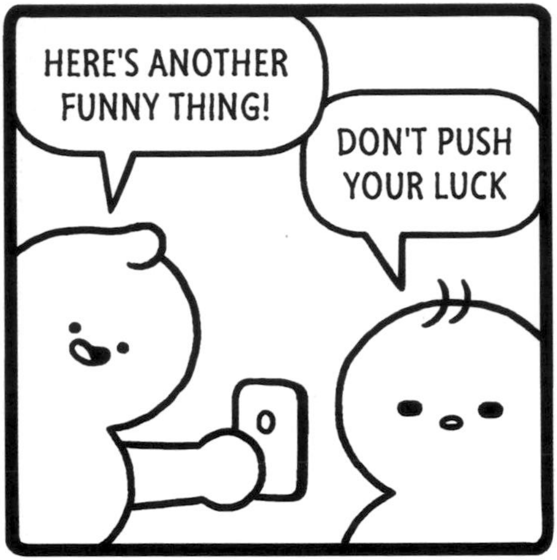
HERE'S ANOTHER FUNNY THING!
DON'T PUSH YOUR LUCK

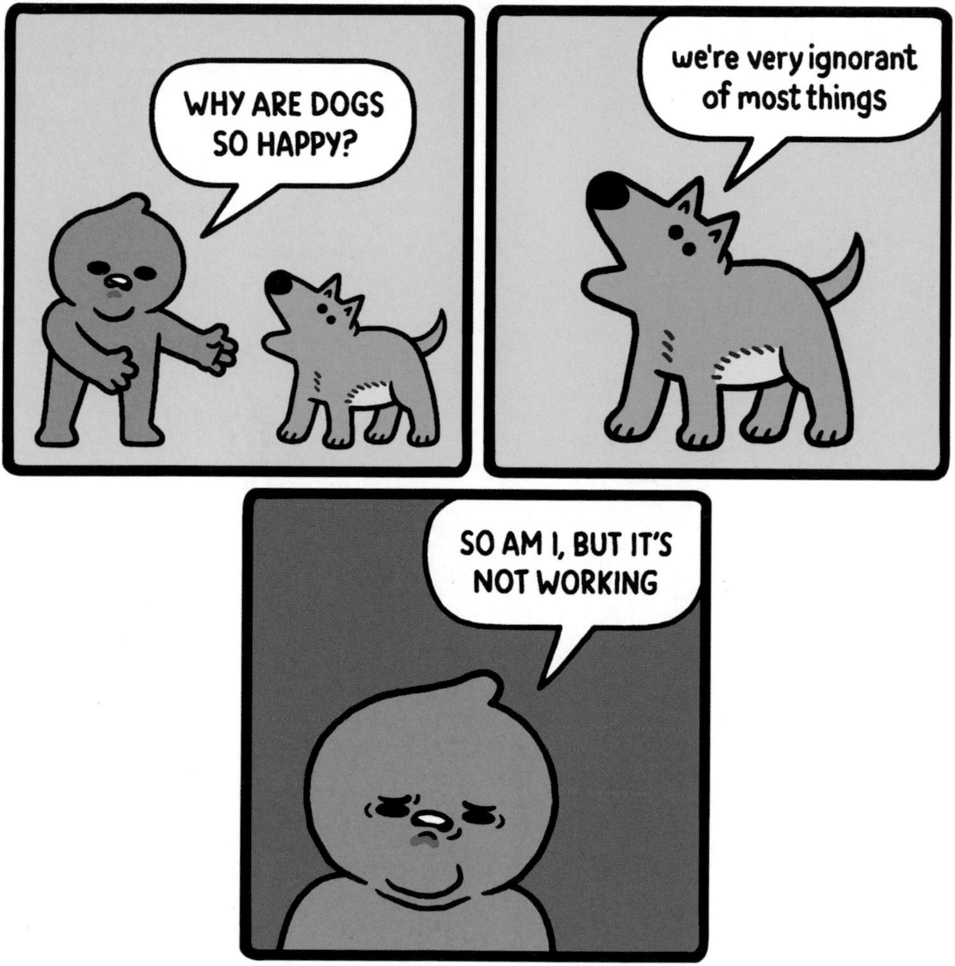
WHY ARE DOGS SO HAPPY?
we're very ignorant of most things
SO AM I, BUT IT'S NOT WORKING

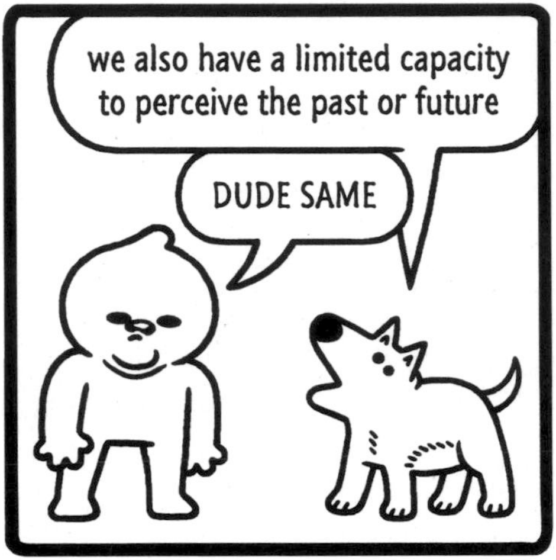
we also have a limited capacity to perceive the past or future
DUDE SAME

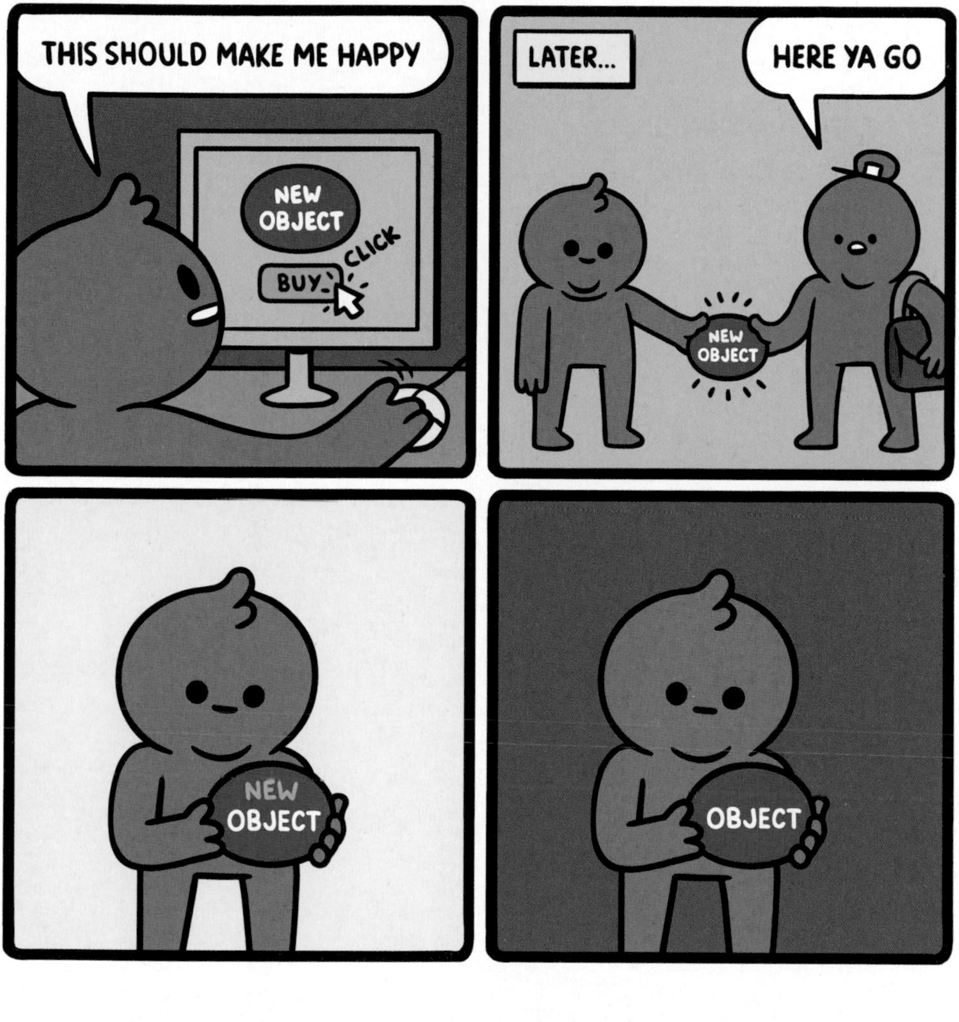
THIS SHOULD MAKE ME HAPPY
NEW OBJECT
BUY
CLICK
LATER...
HERE YA GO
NEW OBJECT
NEW OBJECT
OBJECT

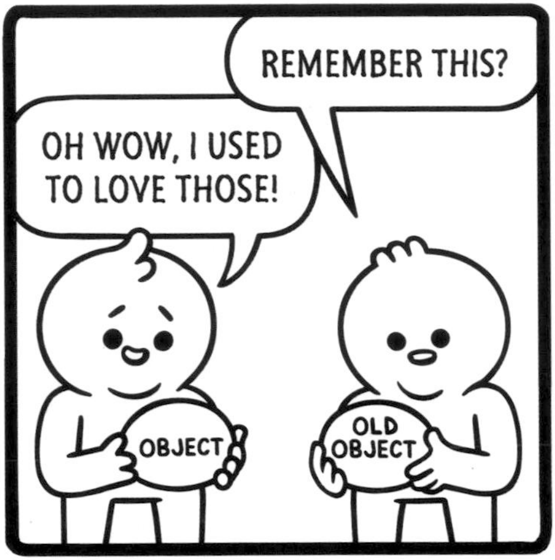
REMEMBER THIS?
OH WOW, I USED TO LOVE THOSE!
OBJECT
OLD OBJECT

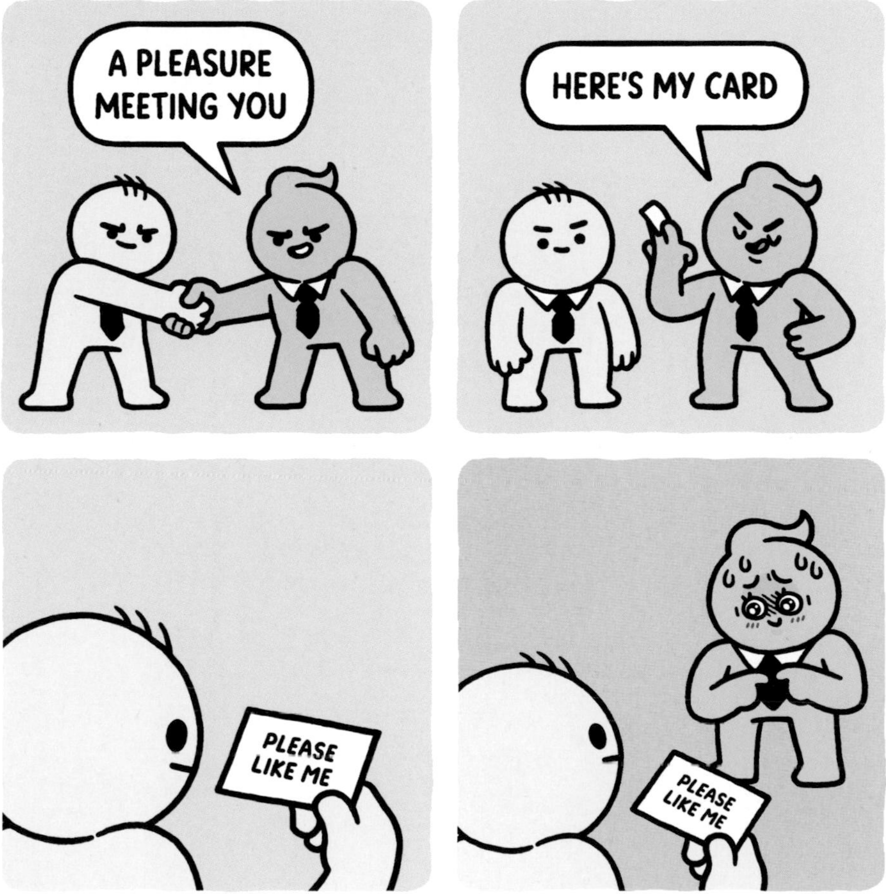
A PLEASURE MEETING YOU
HERE'S MY CARD
PLEASE LIKE ME
PLEASE LIKE ME

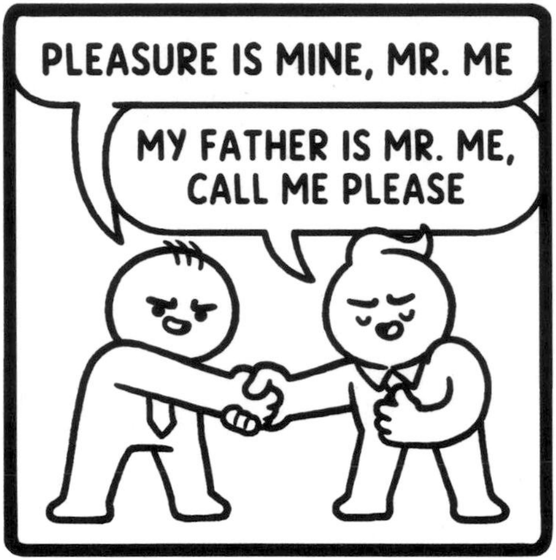
PLEASURE IS MINE, MR. ME
MY FATHER IS MR. ME, CALL ME PLEASE

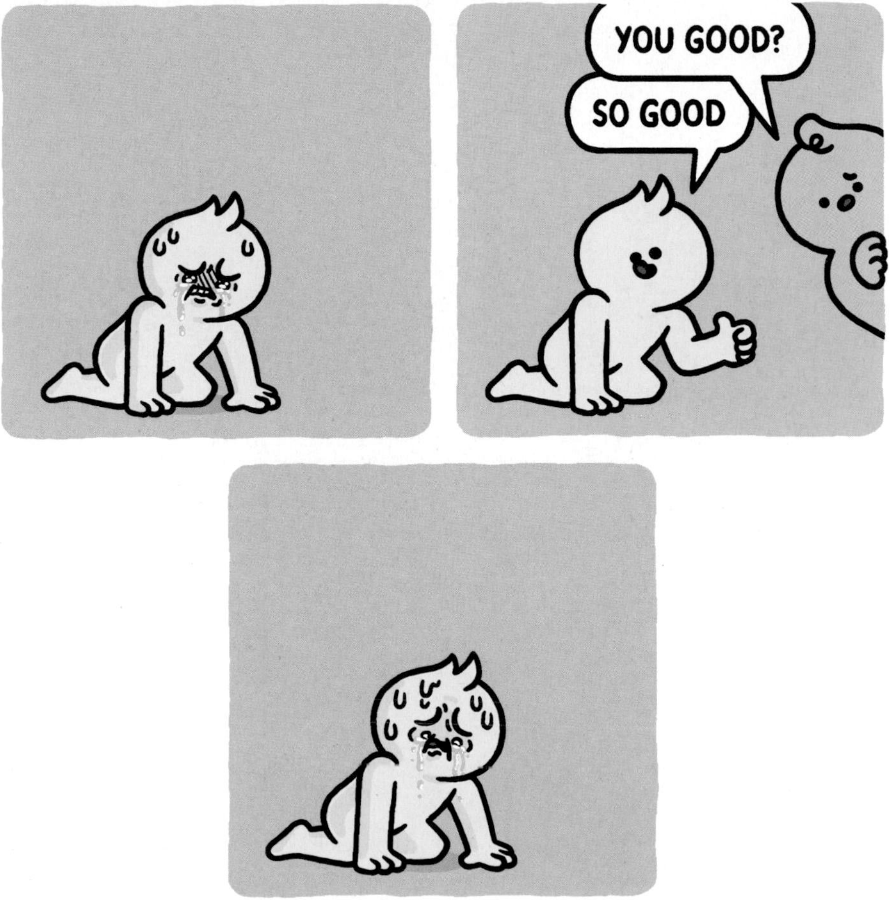
YOU GOOD?
SO GOOD

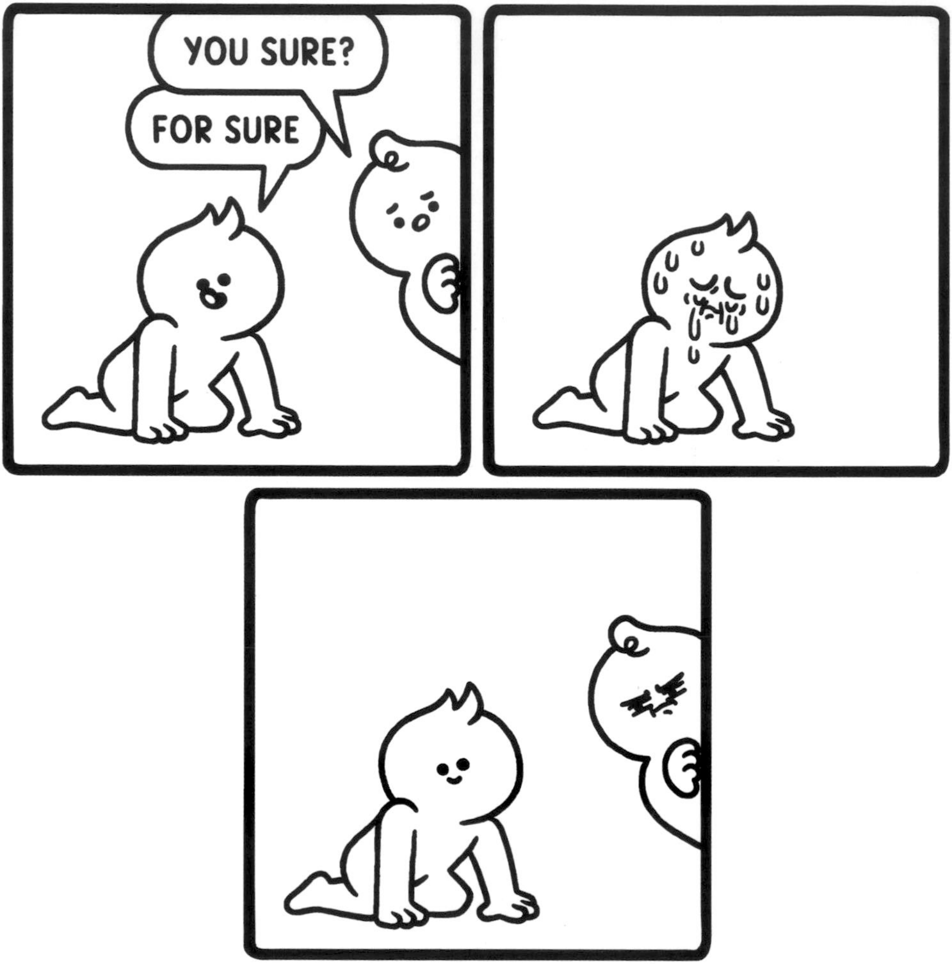
YOU SURE?
FOR SURE

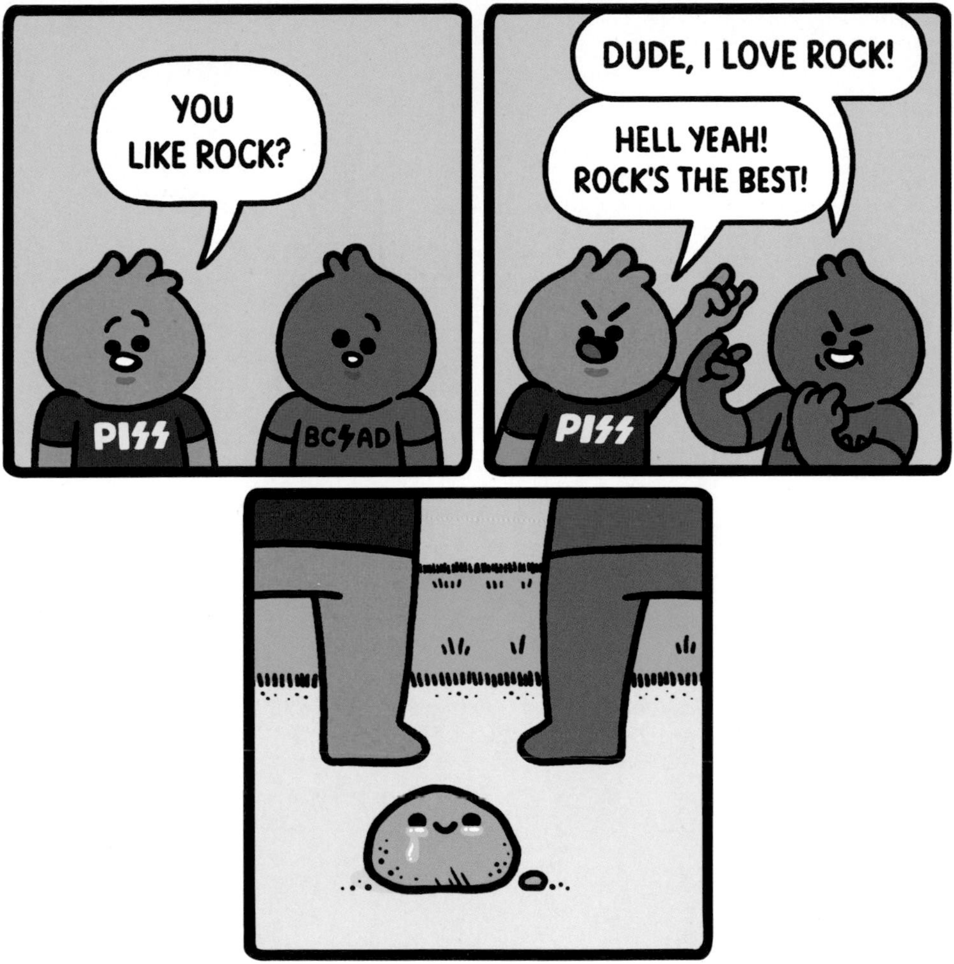
YOU LIKE ROCK?
PISS
BCSAD
DUDE, I LOVE ROCK!
HELL YEAH! ROCK'S THE BEST!
PISS

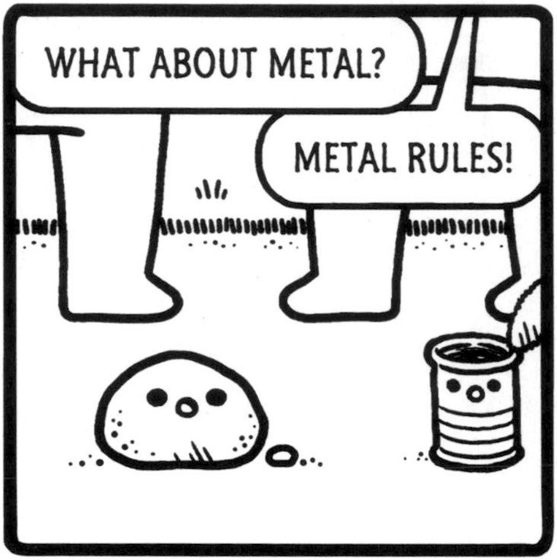
WHAT ABOUT METAL?
METAL RULES!

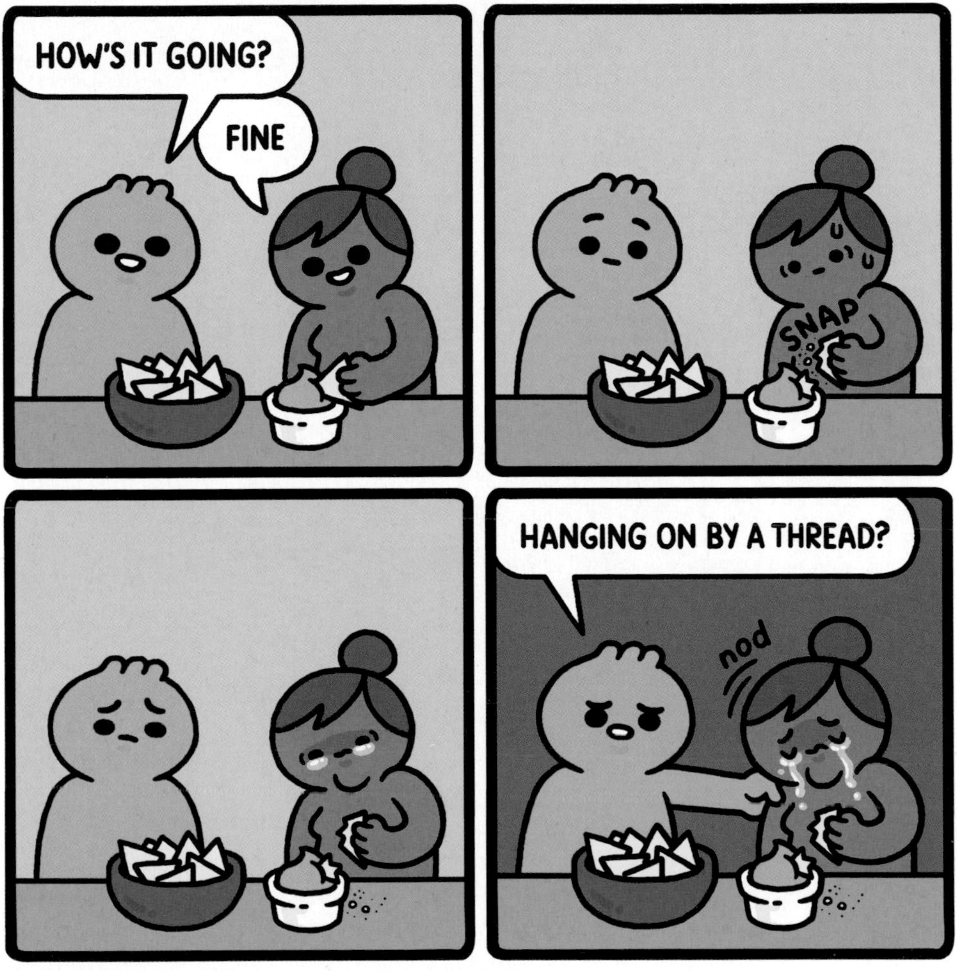
HOW'S IT GOING?
FINE
SNAP
HANGING ON BY A THREAD?
nod

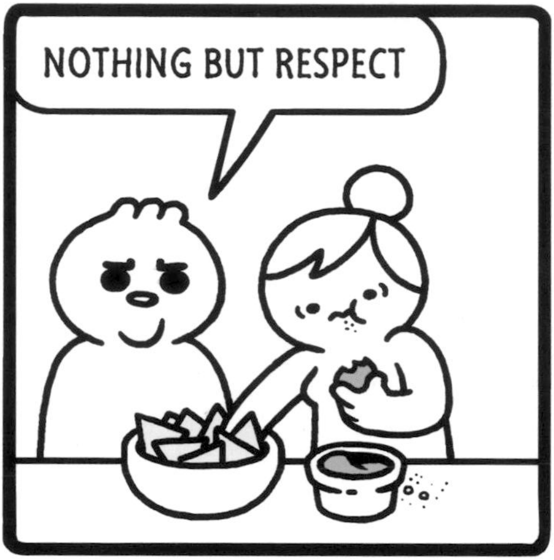
NOTHING BUT RESPECT

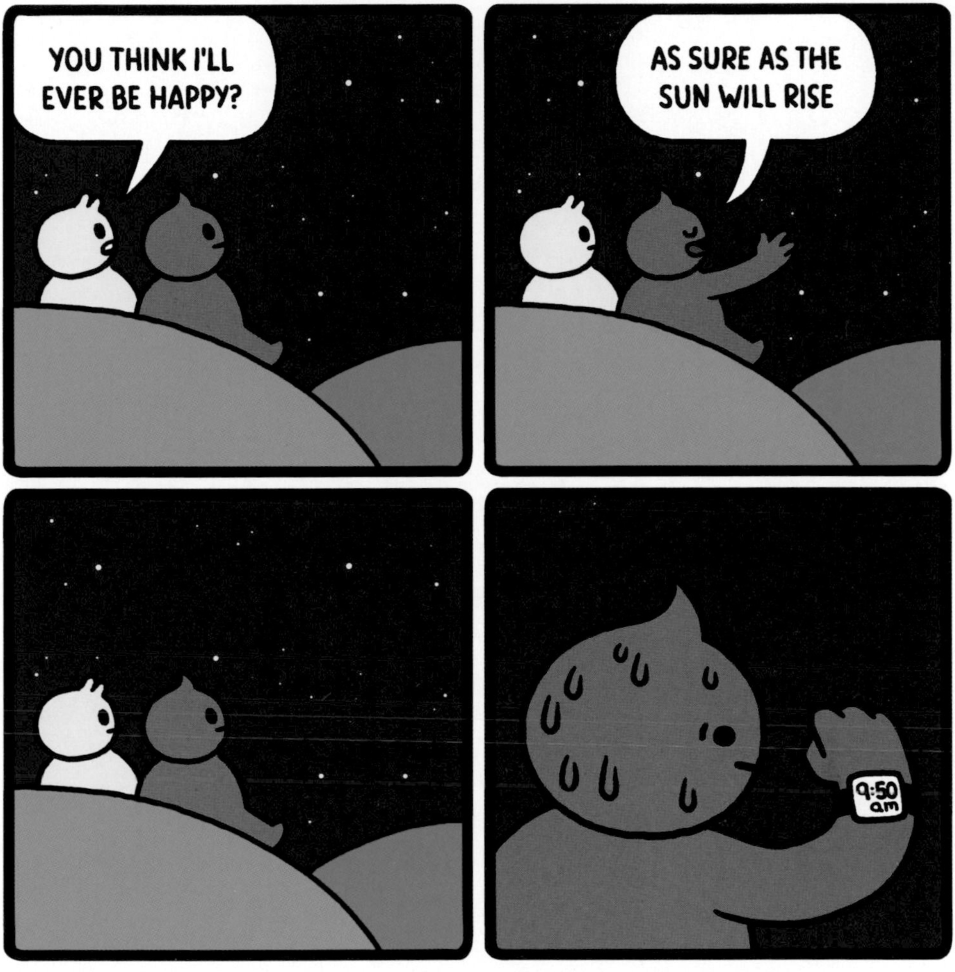
YOU THINK I'LL EVER BE HAPPY?
AS SURE AS THE SUN WILL RISE
9:50 am

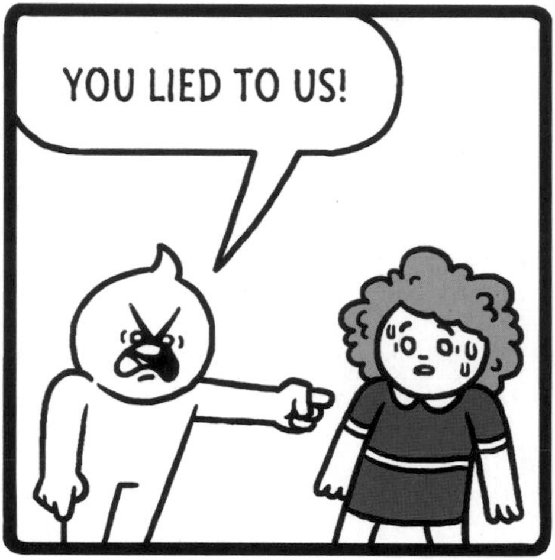
YOU LIED TO US!

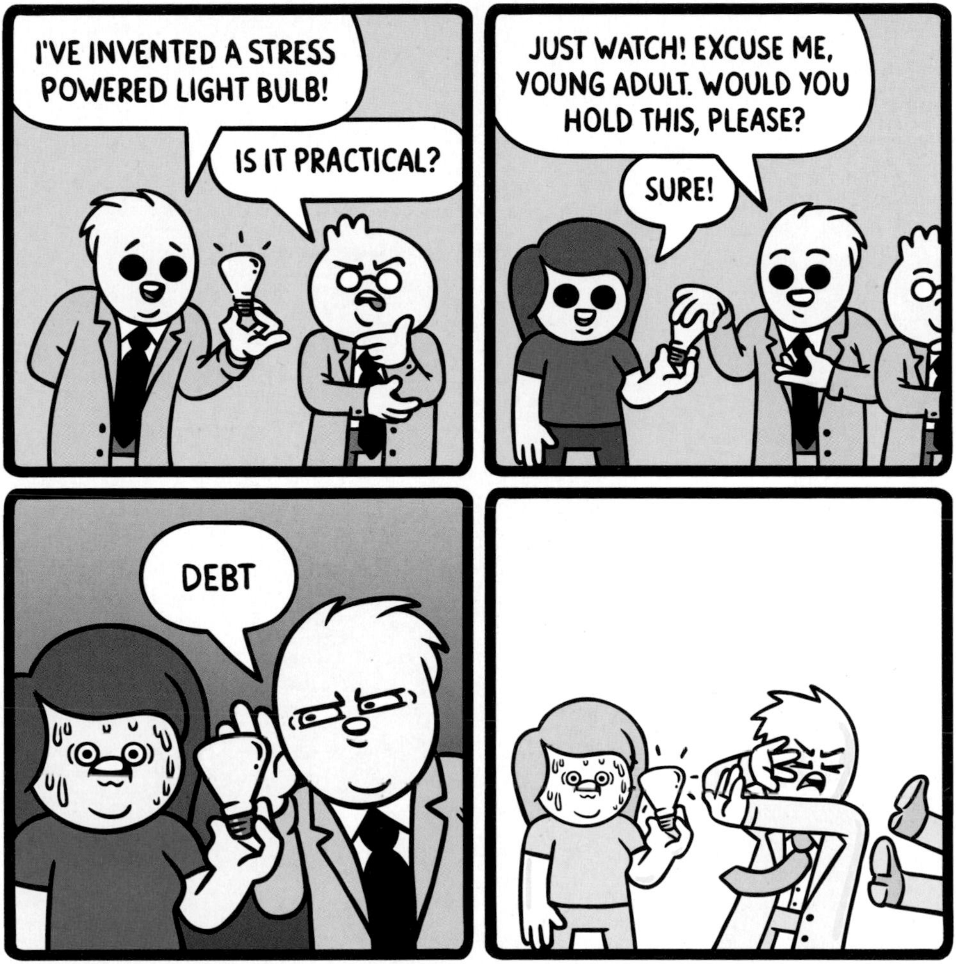
I'VE INVENTED A STRESS POWERED LIGHT BULB!
IS IT PRACTICAL?
JUST WATCH! EXCUSE ME, YOUNG ADULT. WOULD YOU HOLD THIS, PLEASE?
SURE!
DEBT

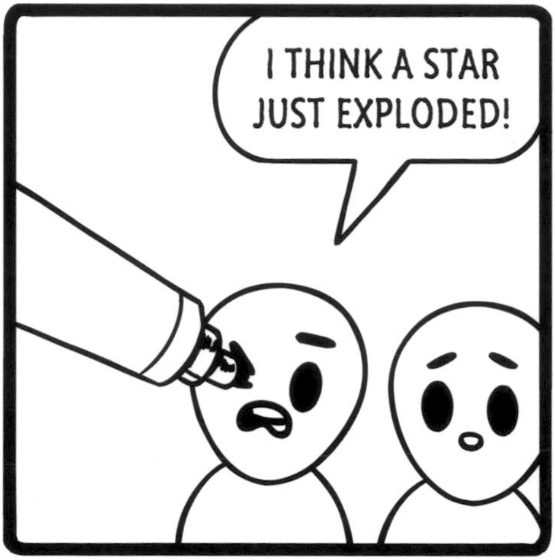
I THINK A STAR
JUST EXPLODED!

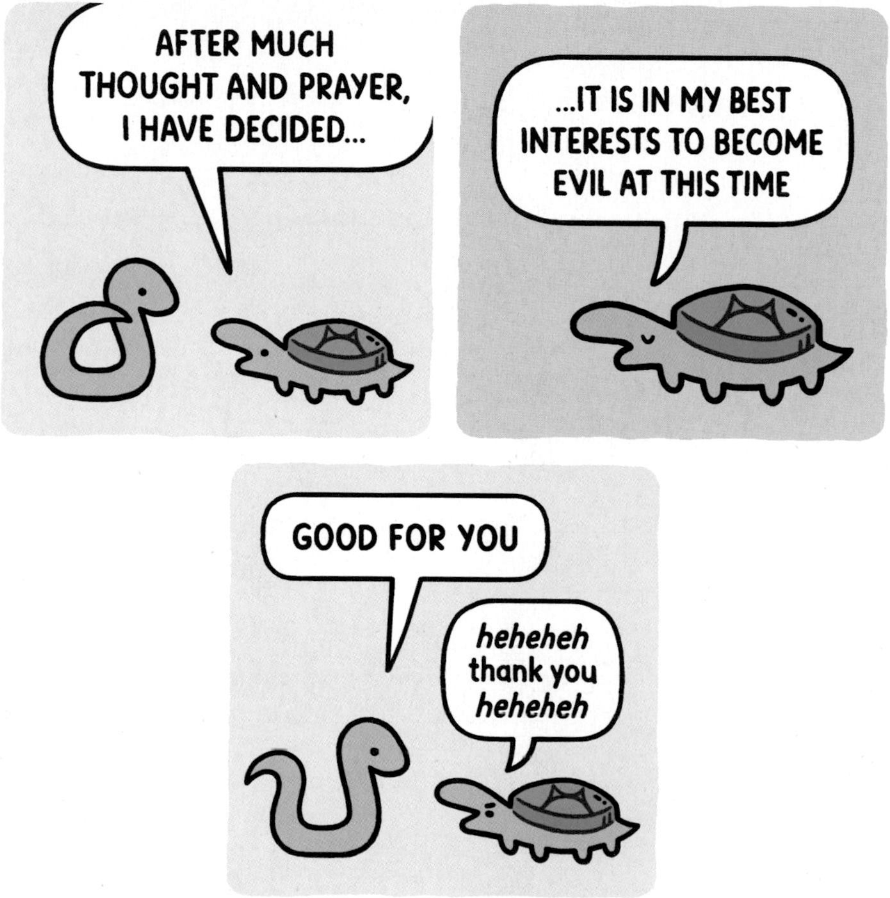
AFTER MUCH THOUGHT AND PRAYER, I HAVE DECIDED...
...IT IS IN MY BEST INTERESTS TO BECOME EVIL AT THIS TIME
GOOD FOR YOU
heheheh thank you *heheheh*

SO WHAT'S
THE FIRST EVIL THING
YOU PLAN TO DO?
TAKE A NAP
AN *EVIL* NAP

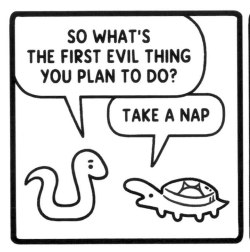

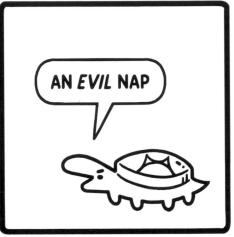

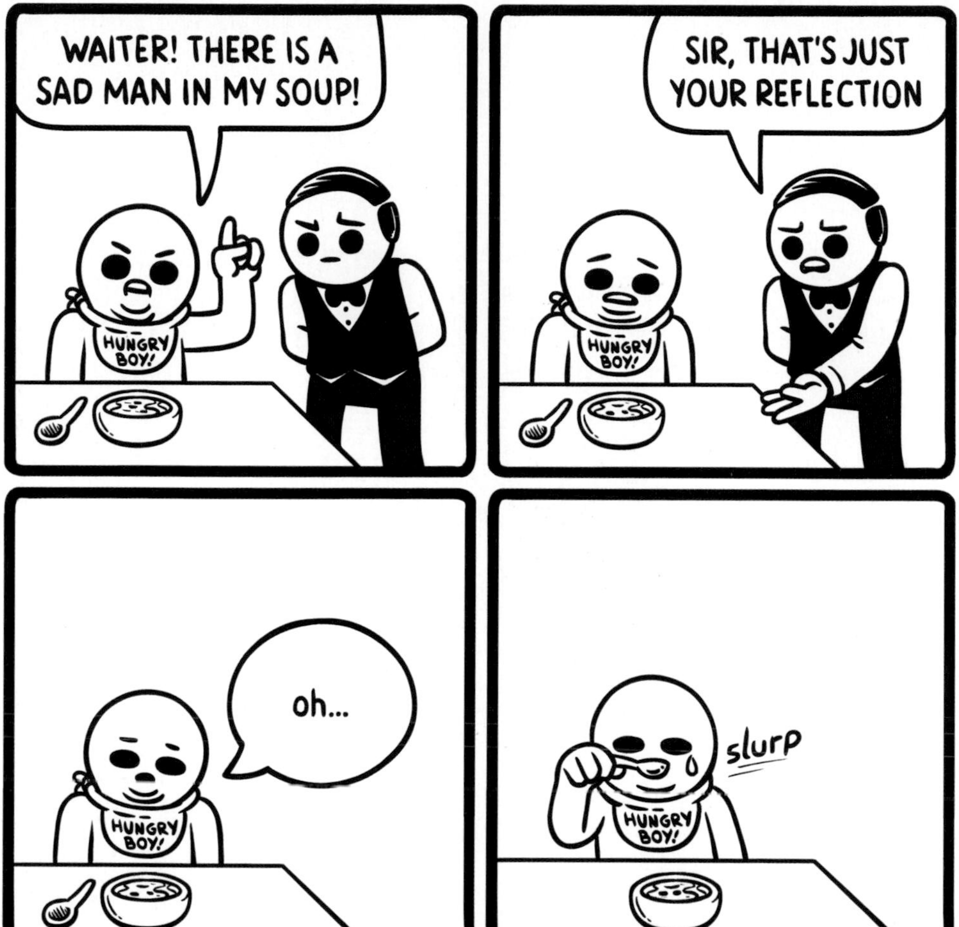
WAITER! THERE IS A SAD MAN IN MY SOUP!
HUNGRY BOY!
SIR, THAT'S JUST YOUR REFLECTION
HUNGRY BOY!
oh...
HUNGRY BOY!
slurp
HUNGRY BOY!

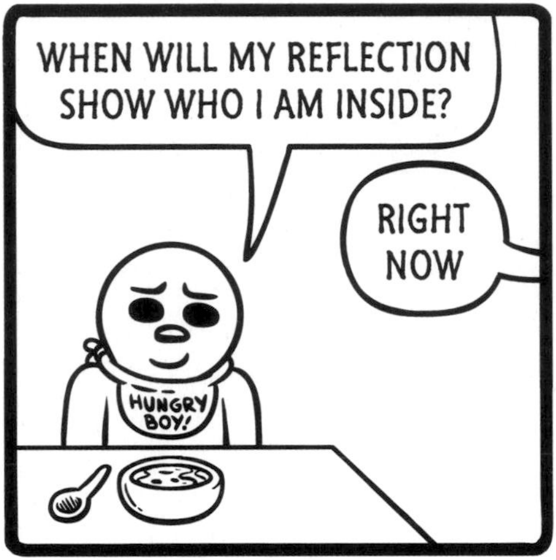
WHEN WILL MY REFLECTION SHOW WHO I AM INSIDE?
RIGHT NOW
HUNGRY BOY!

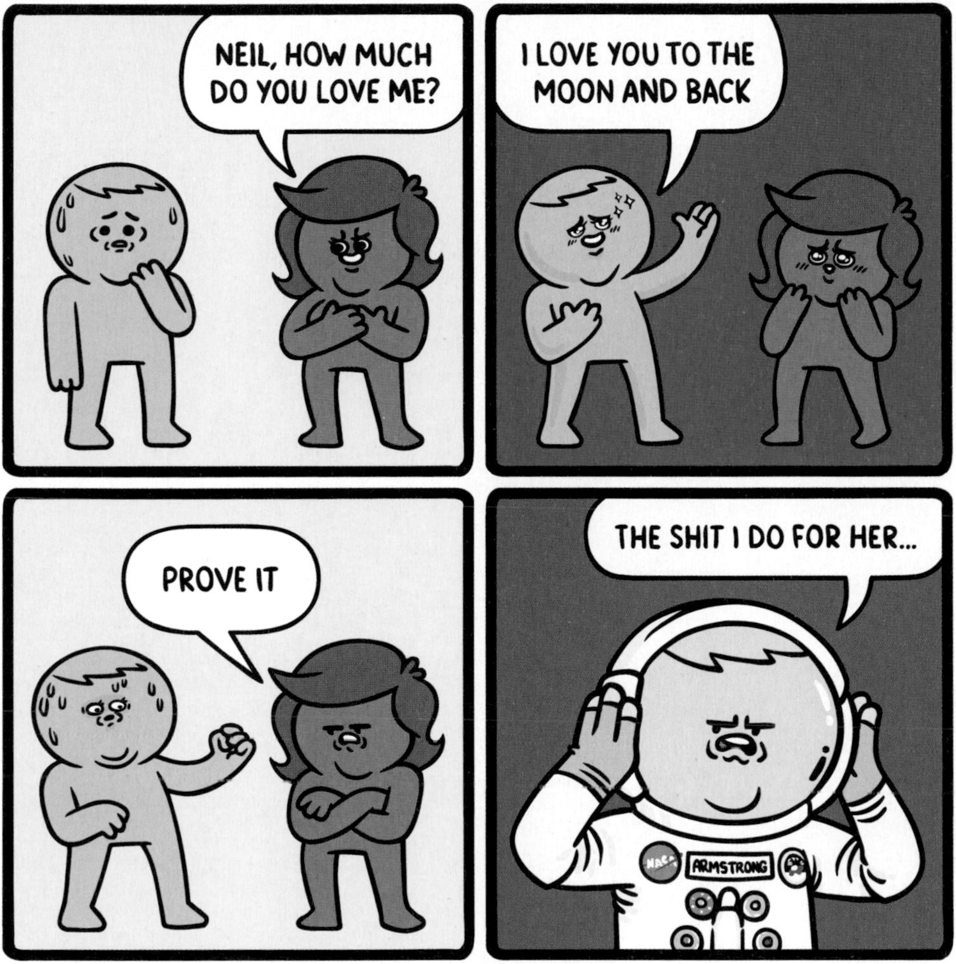
NEIL, HOW MUCH DO YOU LOVE ME?
I LOVE YOU TO THE MOON AND BACK
PROVE IT
THE SHIT I DO FOR HER...
ARMSTRONG

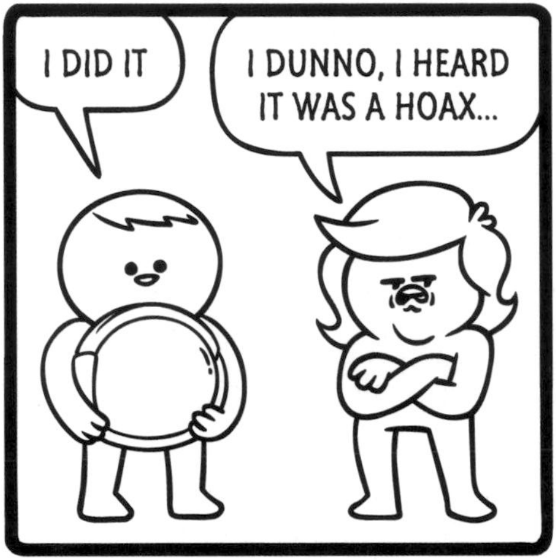
I DID IT
I DUNNO, I HEARD IT WAS A HOAX...

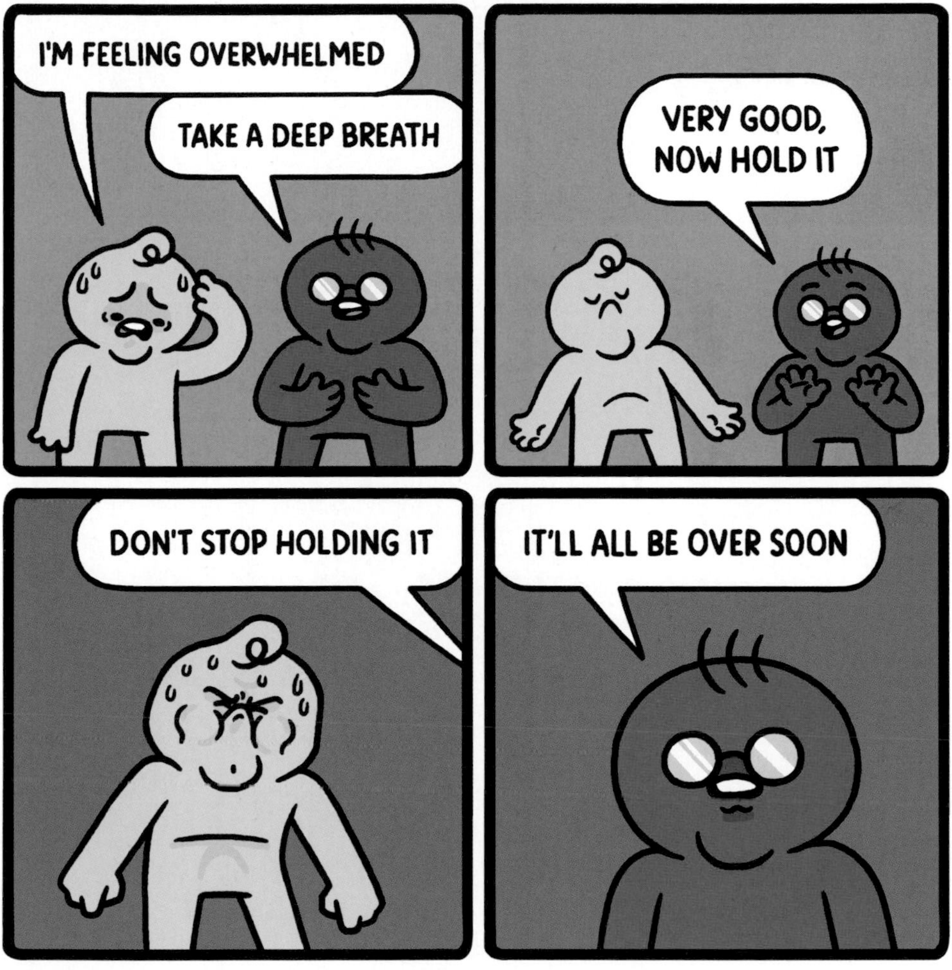
I'M FEELING OVERWHELMED
TAKE A DEEP BREATH
VERY GOOD, NOW HOLD IT
DON'T STOP HOLDING IT
IT'LL ALL BE OVER SOON

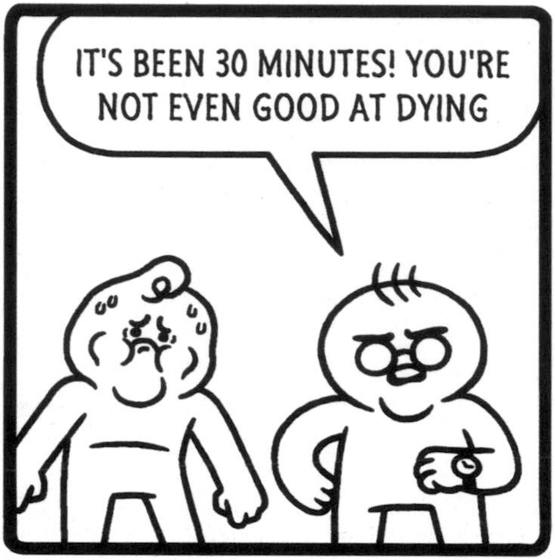
IT'S BEEN 30 MINUTES! YOU'RE NOT EVEN GOOD AT DYING

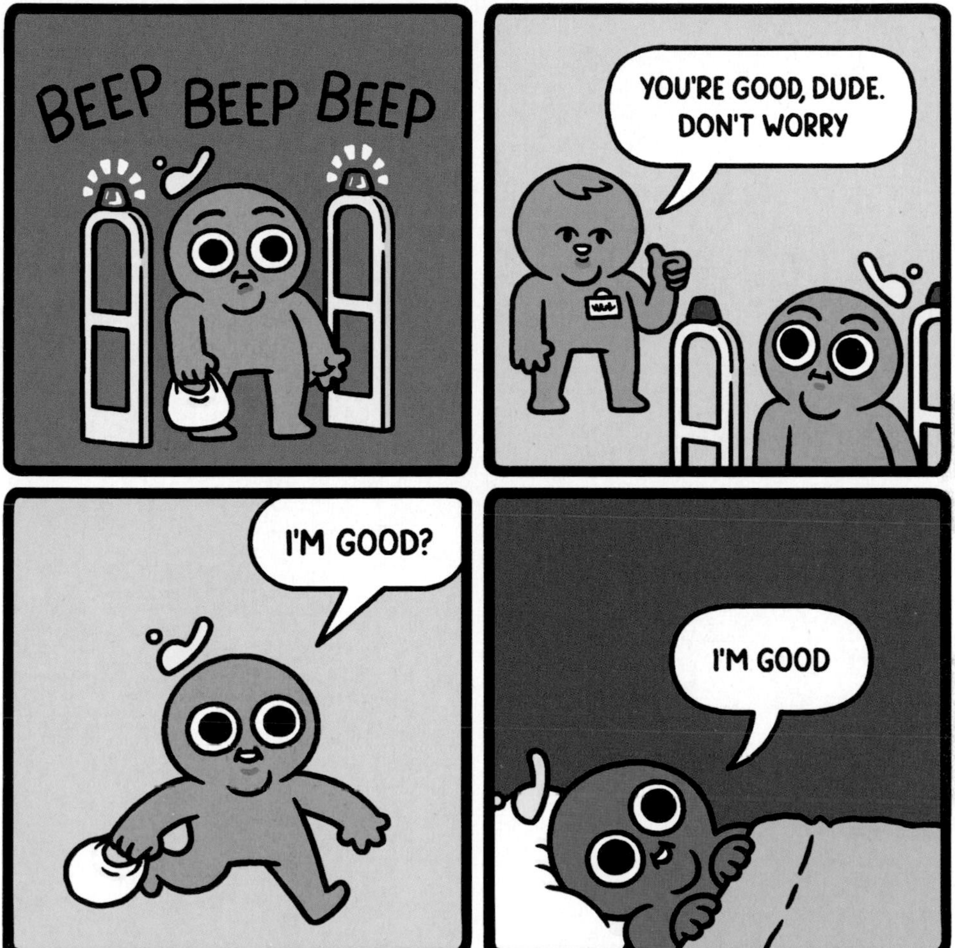
BEEP BEEP BEEP
YOU'RE GOOD, DUDE. DON'T WORRY
I'M GOOD?
I'M GOOD

DO YOU NEED ANY ASSISTANCE, SIR?
I'M GOOD
OKAY, WELL LET ME KNOW IF YOU NEED ANYTHING
I'M GOOD

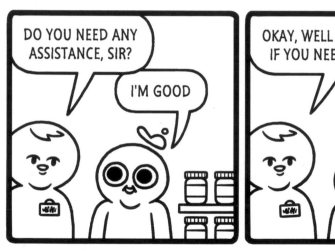

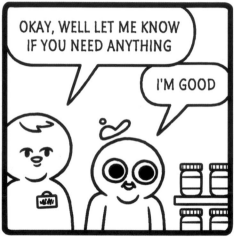

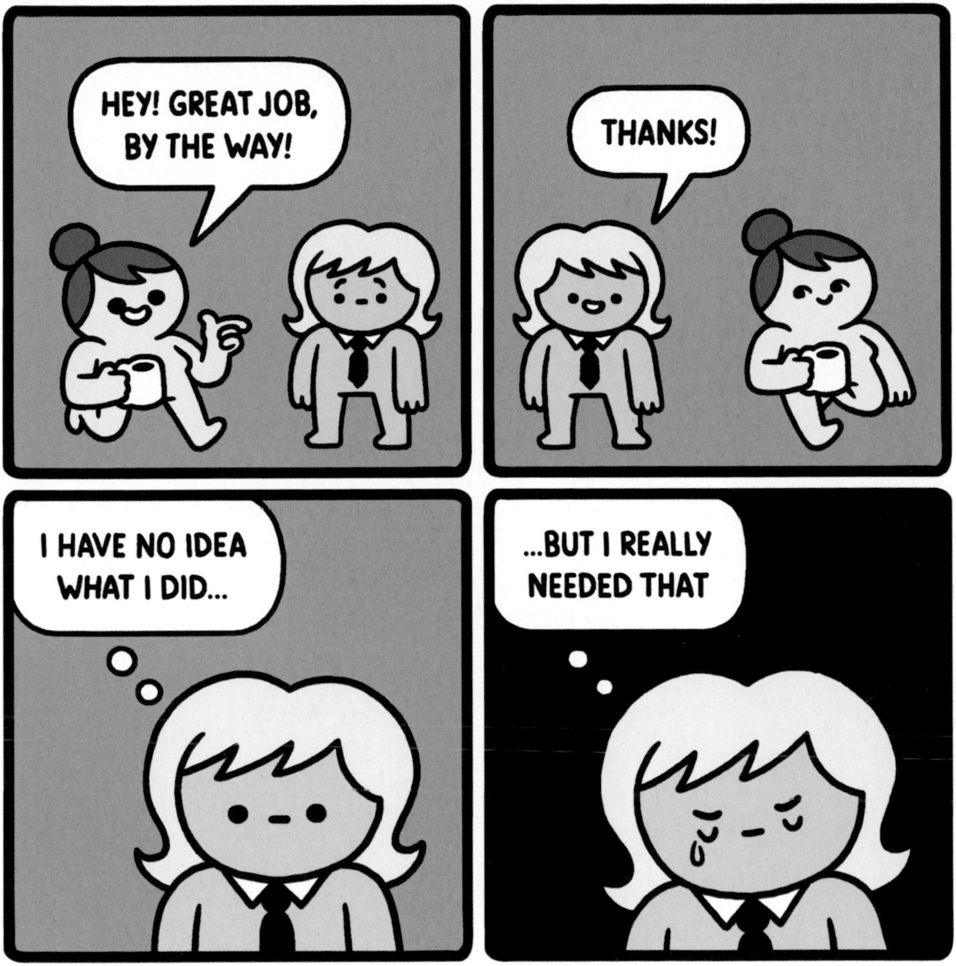
HEY! GREAT JOB, BY THE WAY!
THANKS!
I HAVE NO IDEA WHAT I DID...
...BUT I REALLY NEEDED THAT

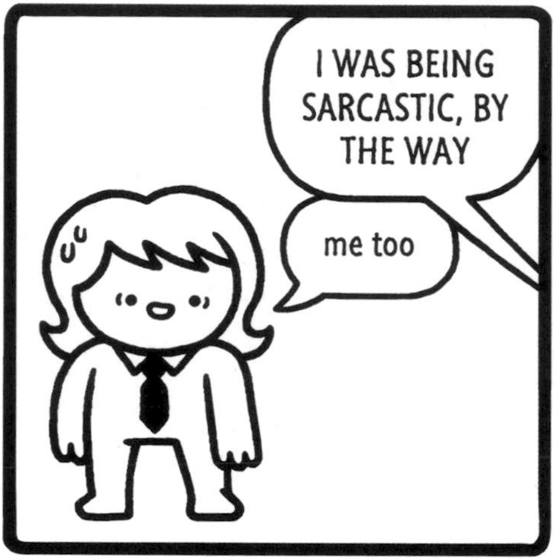
I WAS BEING SARCASTIC, BY THE WAY
me too

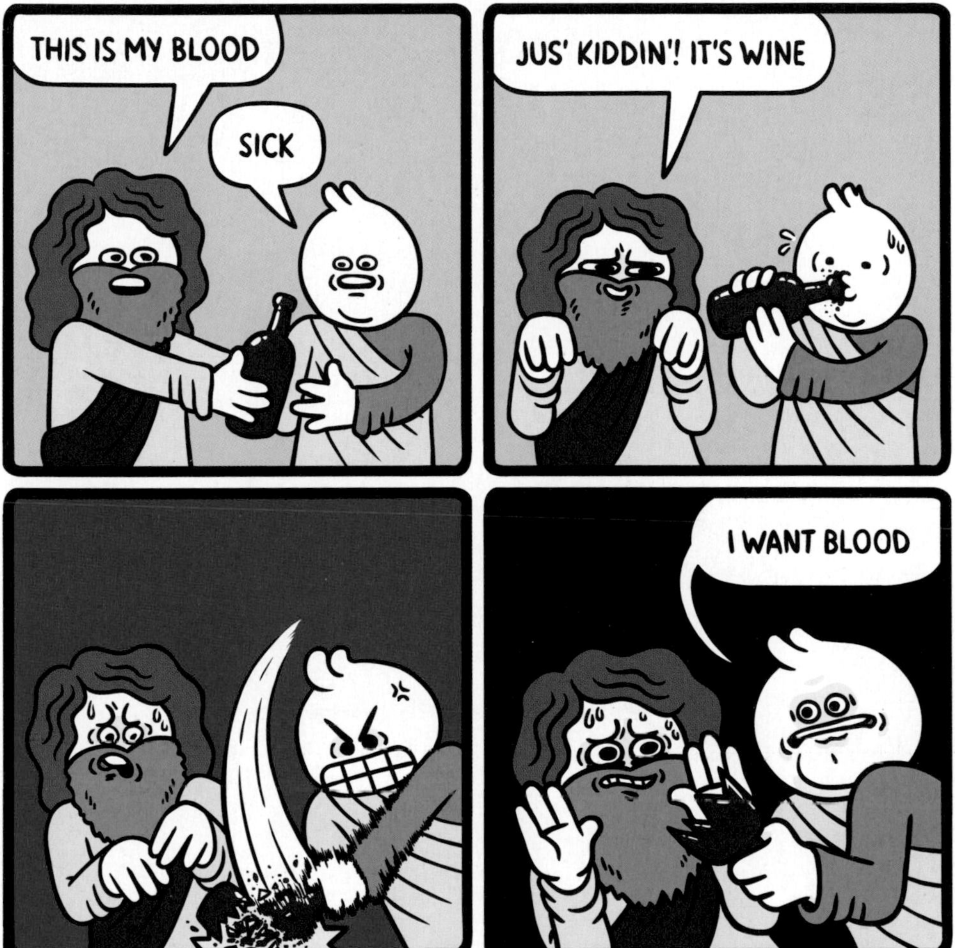
THIS IS MY BLOOD
SICK
JUS' KIDDIN'! IT'S WINE
I WANT BLOOD

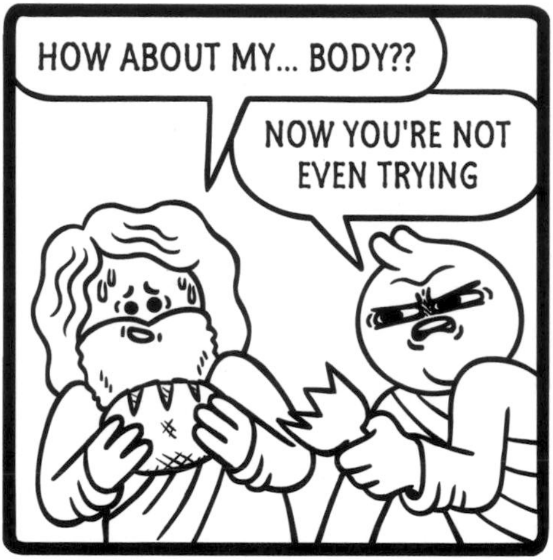
HOW ABOUT MY... BODY??
NOW YOU'RE NOT EVEN TRYING

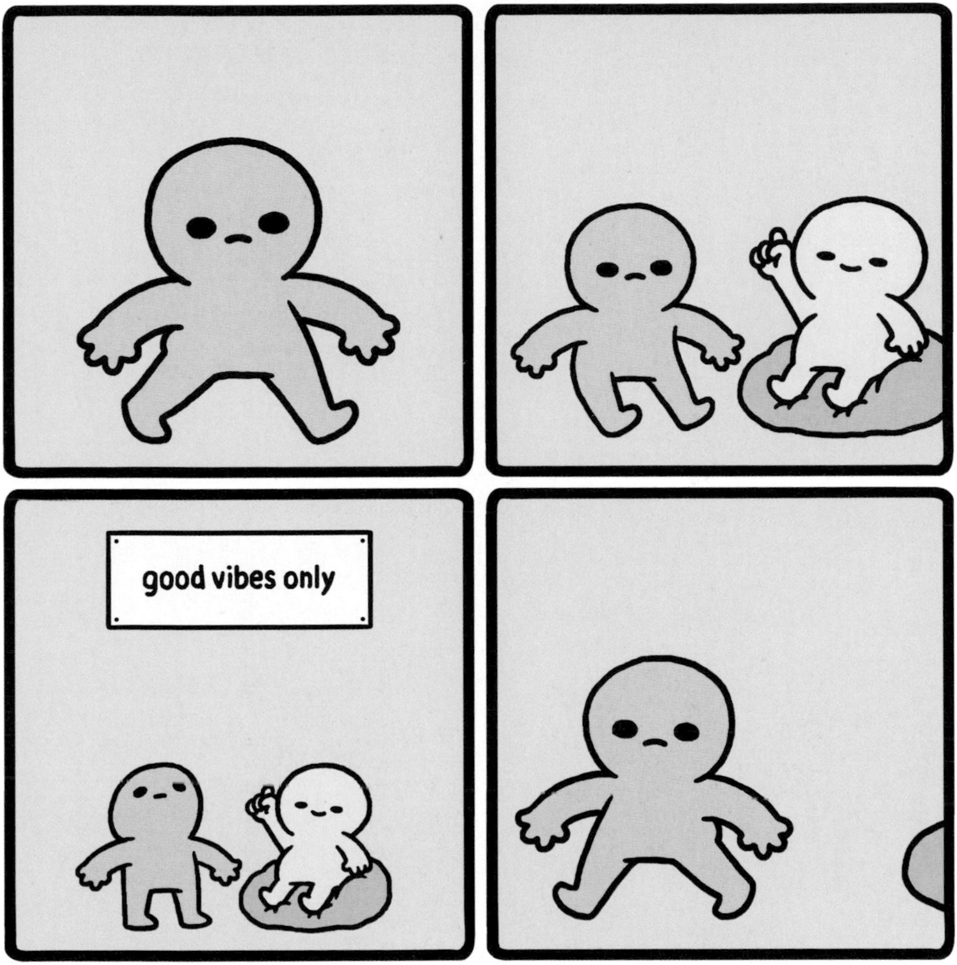
good vibes only

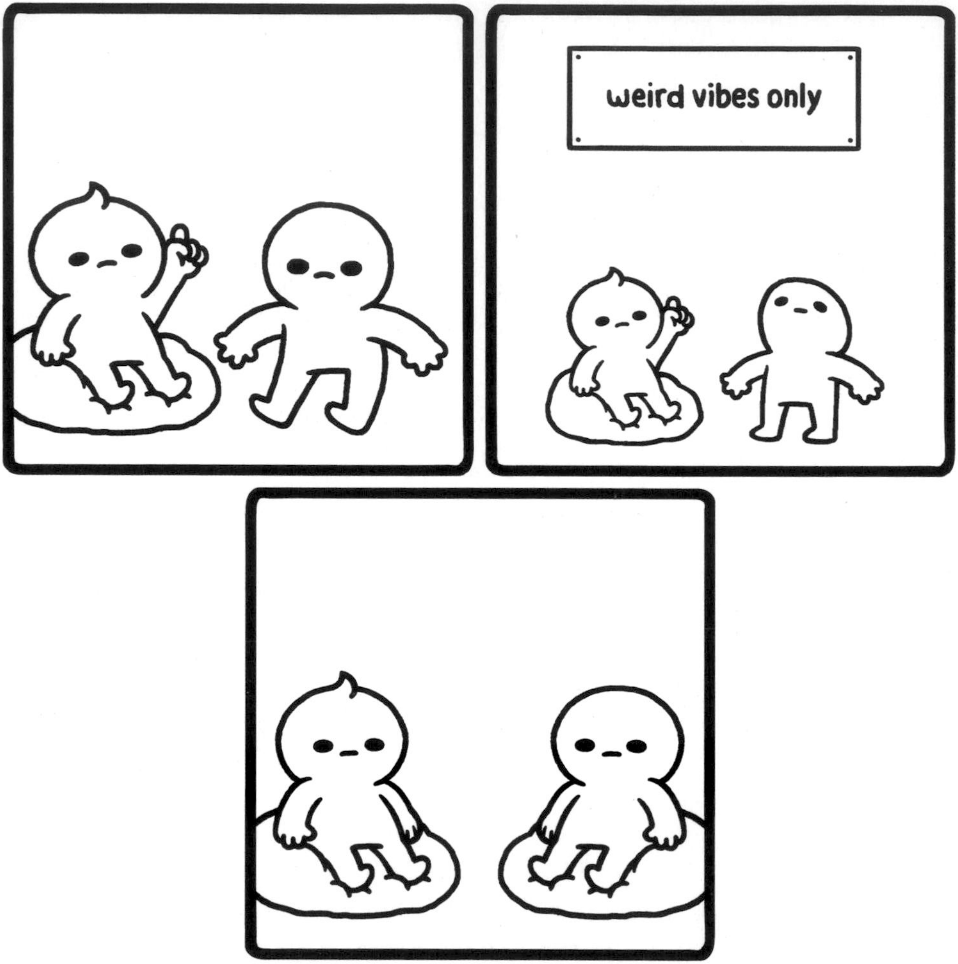
weird vibes only

DANG, BOY! HOW YOU GET THEM THICC LEGS?
EMOTIONAL BAGGAGE

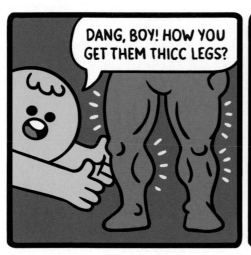

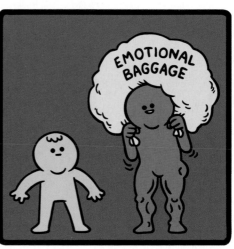

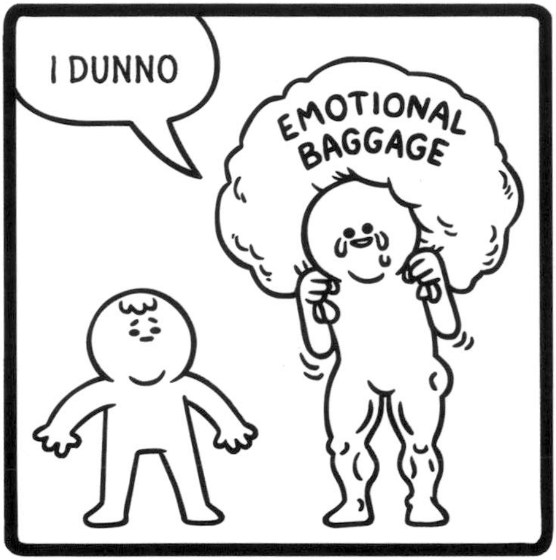
I DUNNO
EMOTIONAL BAGGAGE

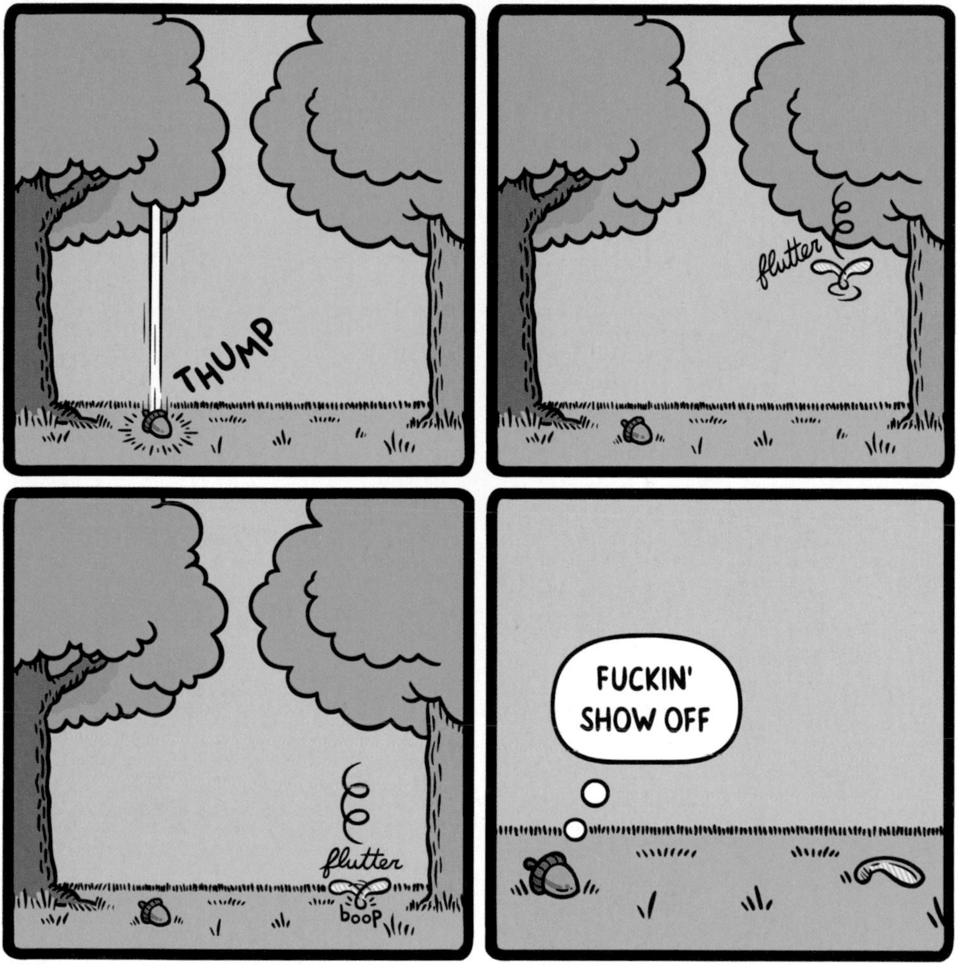
THUMP
flutter
flutter
boop
FUCKIN' SHOW OFF

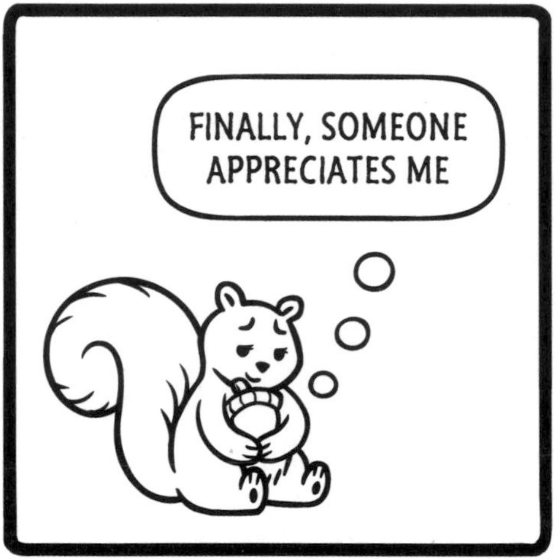
FINALLY, SOMEONE APPRECIATES ME

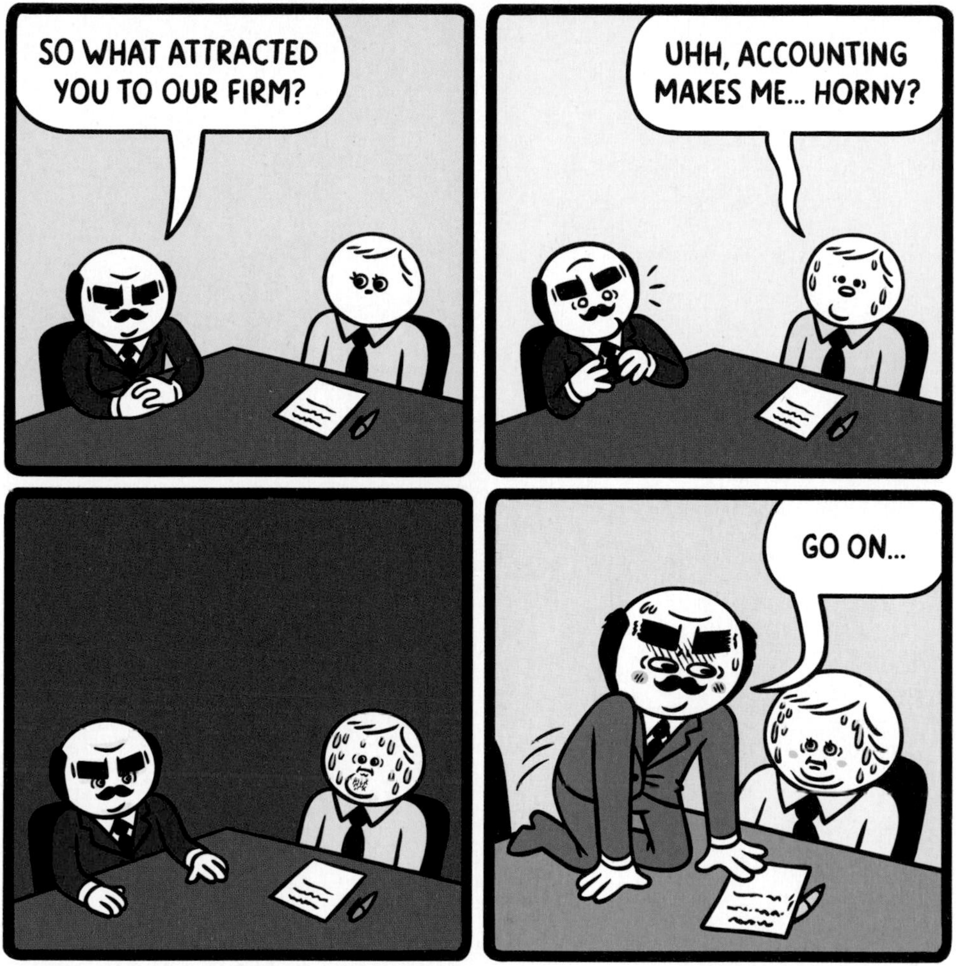
SO WHAT ATTRACTED YOU TO OUR FIRM?
UHH, ACCOUNTING MAKES ME... HORNY?
GO ON...

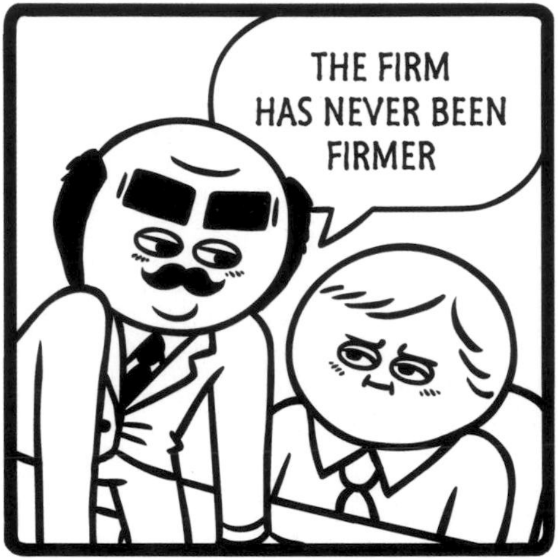
THE FIRM
HAS NEVER BEEN
FIRMER

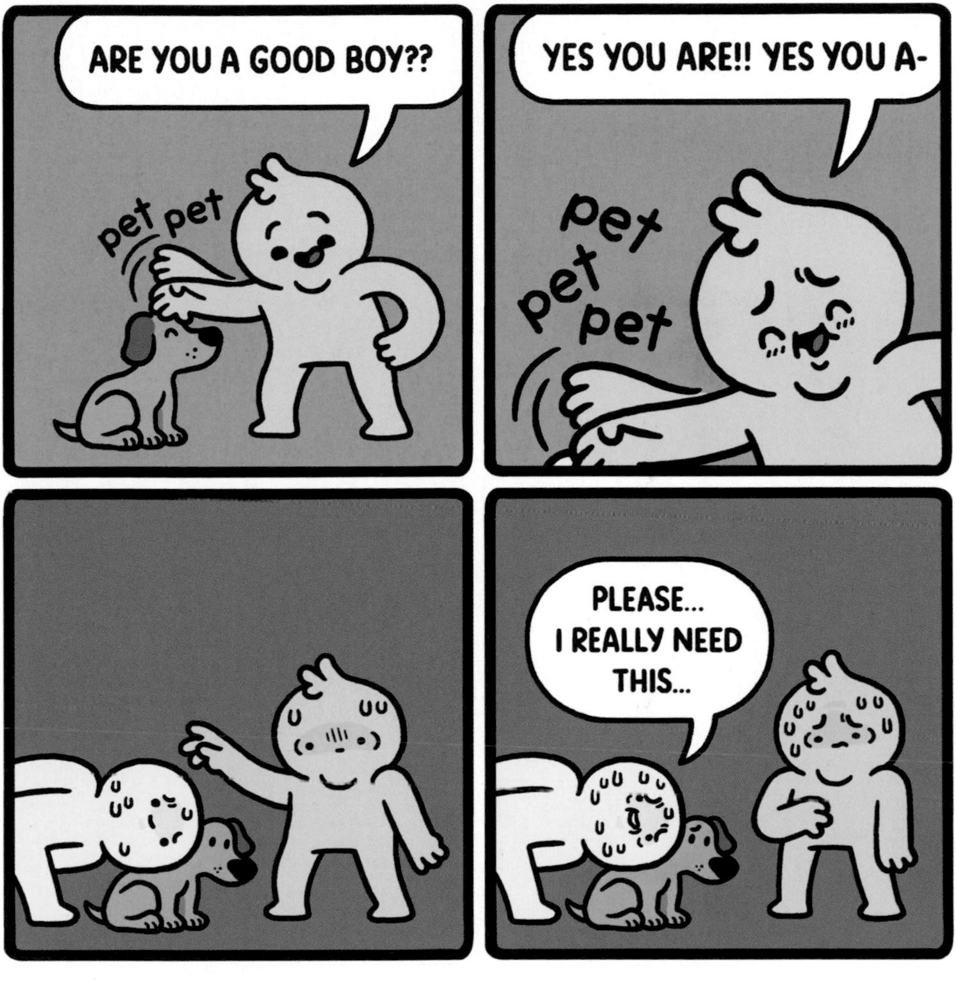
ARE YOU A GOOD BOY??
pet pet
YES YOU ARE!! YES YOU A-
pet
pet
pet
PLEASE...
I REALLY NEED
THIS...

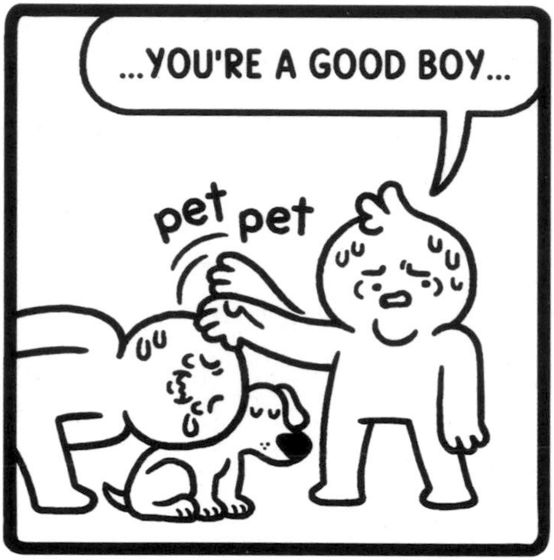
...YOU'RE A GOOD BOY...
pet pet

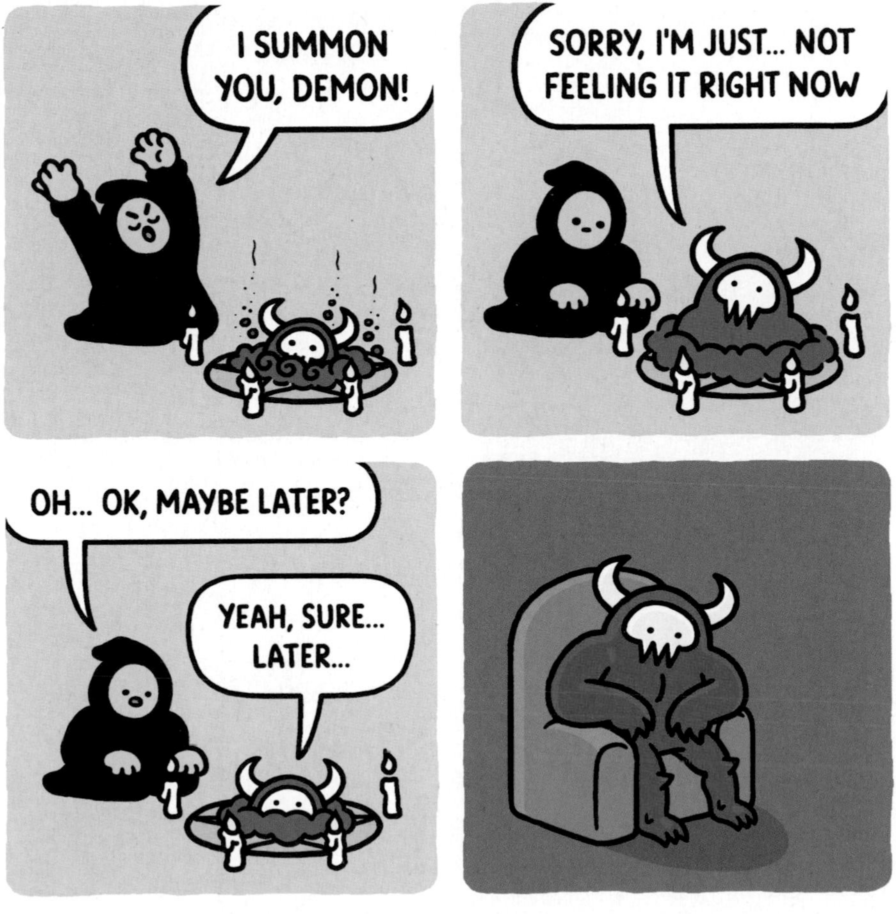
I SUMMON YOU, DEMON!
SORRY, I'M JUST... NOT FEELING IT RIGHT NOW
OH... OK, MAYBE LATER?
YEAH, SURE... LATER...

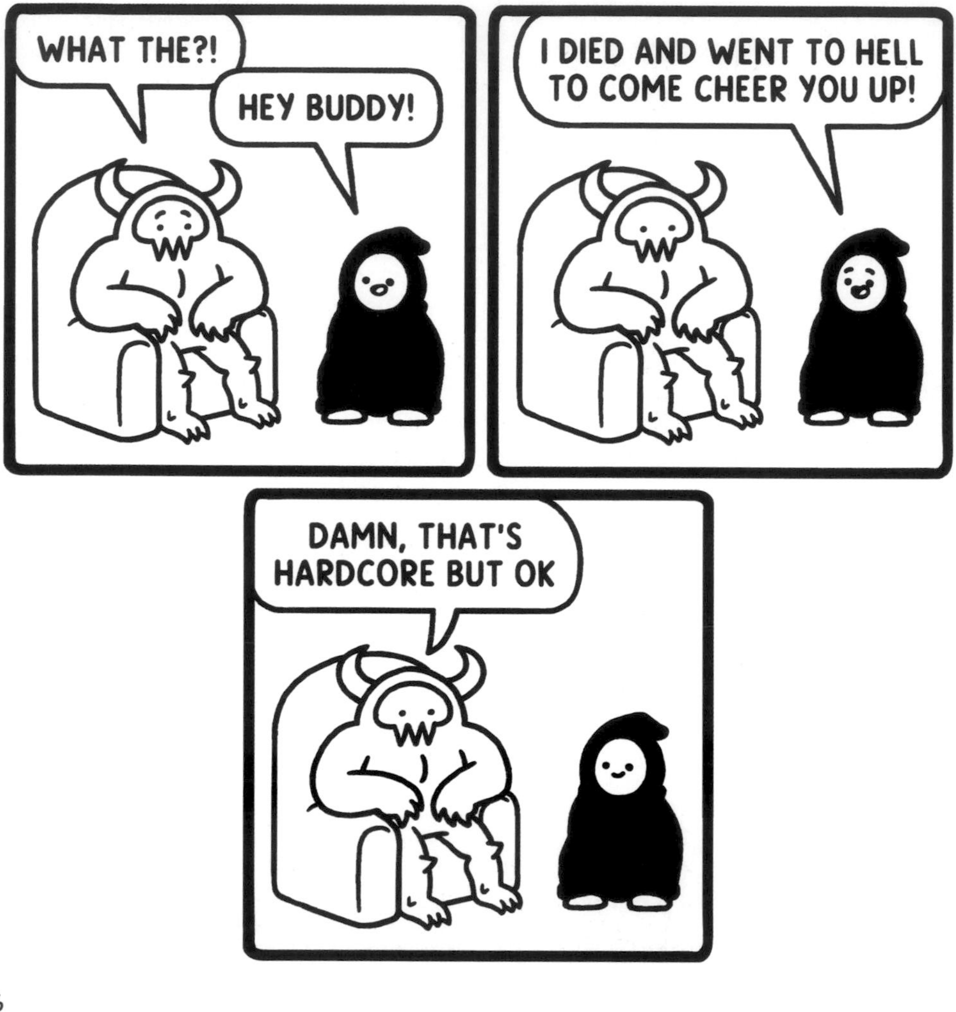
WHAT THE?!
HEY BUDDY!
I DIED AND WENT TO HELL TO COME CHEER YOU UP!
DAMN, THAT'S HARDCORE BUT OK

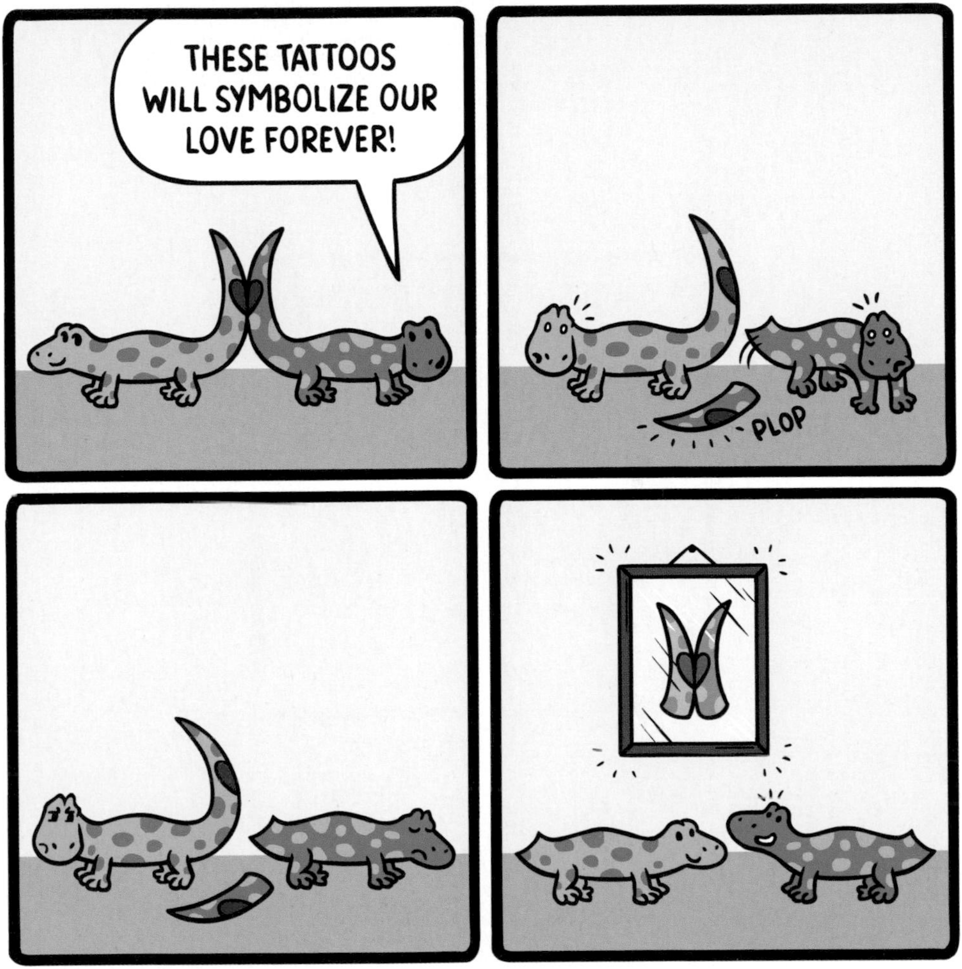
THESE TATTOOS WILL SYMBOLIZE OUR LOVE FOREVER!
PLOP

THESE TATTOOS WILL SYMBOLIZE OUR LOVE FOREVER!
BUT WE MOLT...

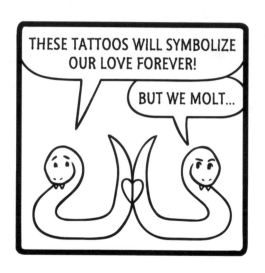

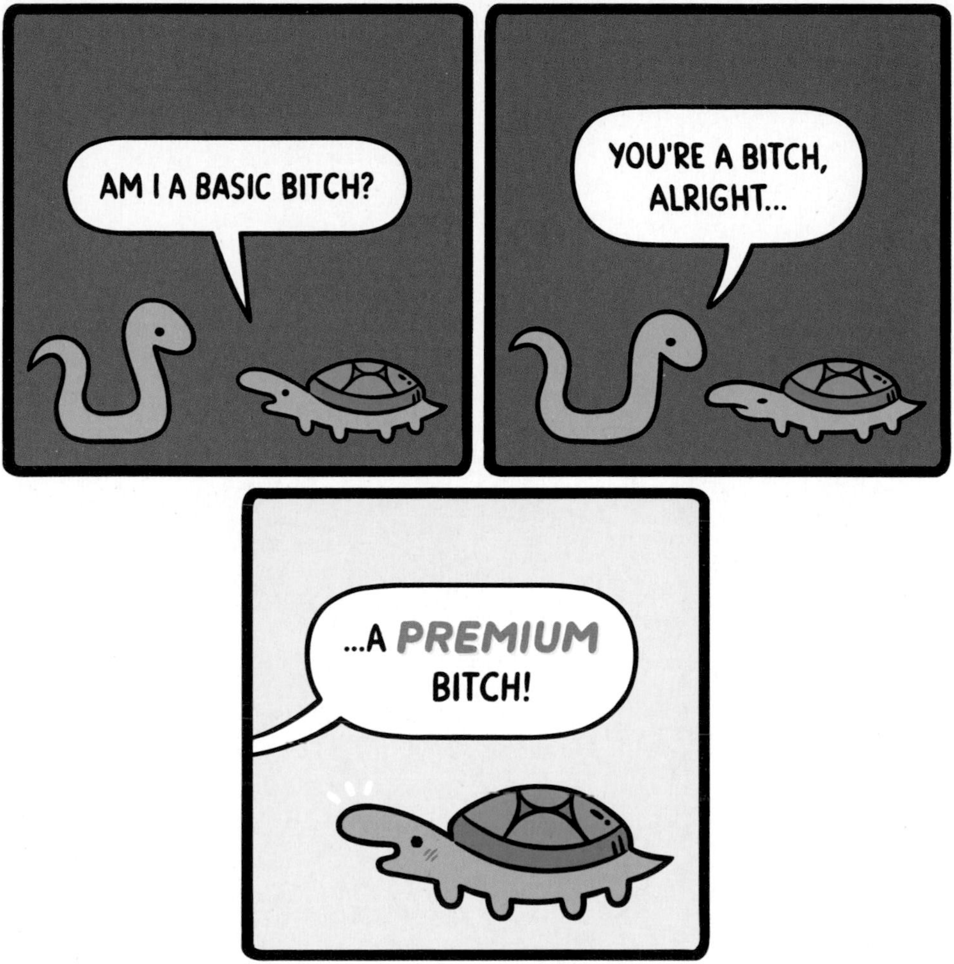
AM I A BASIC BITCH?
YOU'RE A BITCH, ALRIGHT...
...A PREMIUM BITCH!

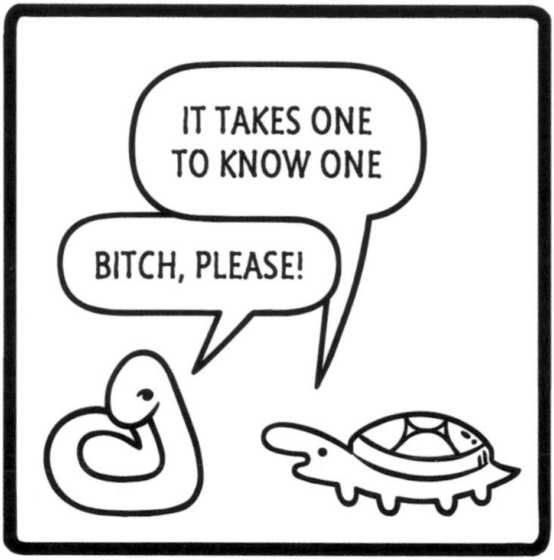
IT TAKES ONE TO KNOW ONE
BITCH, PLEASE!

IF YOU'RE HAPPY AND YOU KNOW IT, CLAP YOUR HANDS
TELL ME YOUR SECRETS!

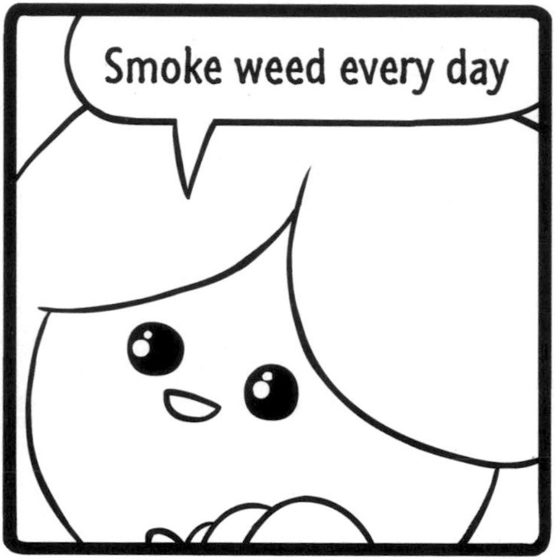
Smoke weed every day

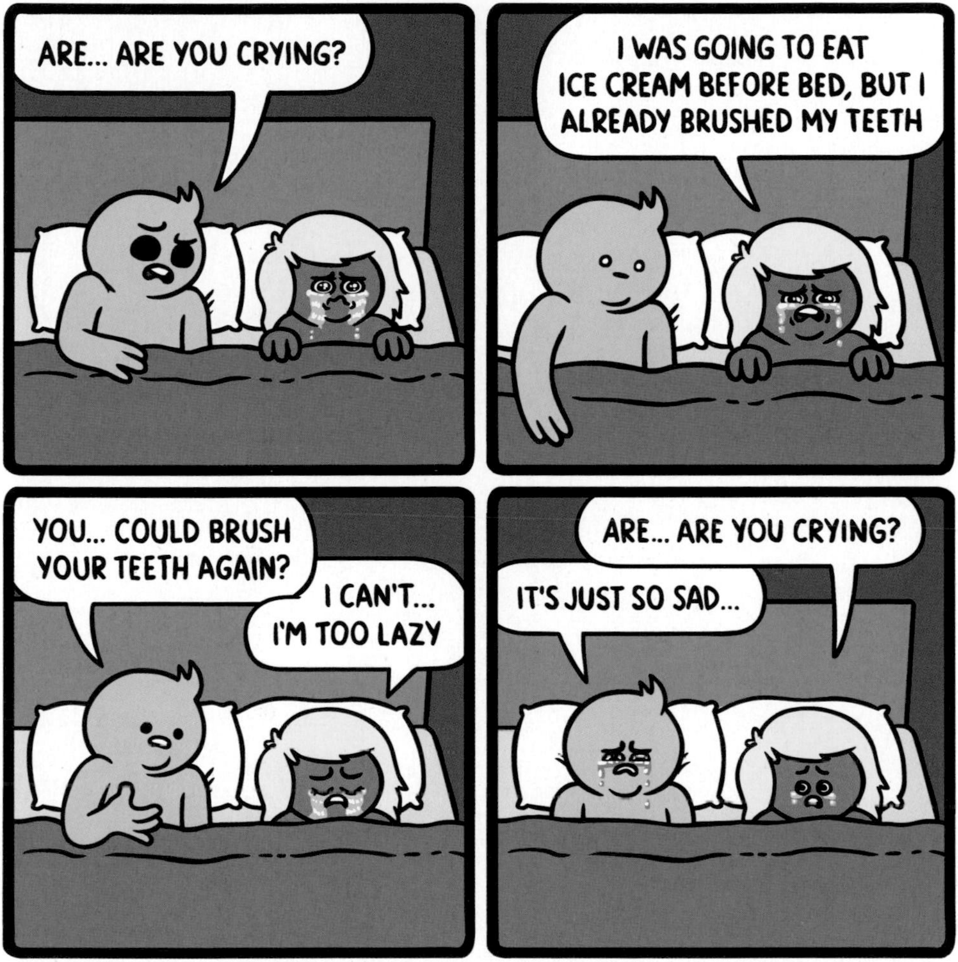
ARE... ARE YOU CRYING?
I WAS GOING TO EAT ICE CREAM BEFORE BED, BUT I ALREADY BRUSHED MY TEETH
YOU... COULD BRUSH YOUR TEETH AGAIN?
I CAN'T... I'M TOO LAZY
ARE... ARE YOU CRYING?
IT'S JUST SO SAD...

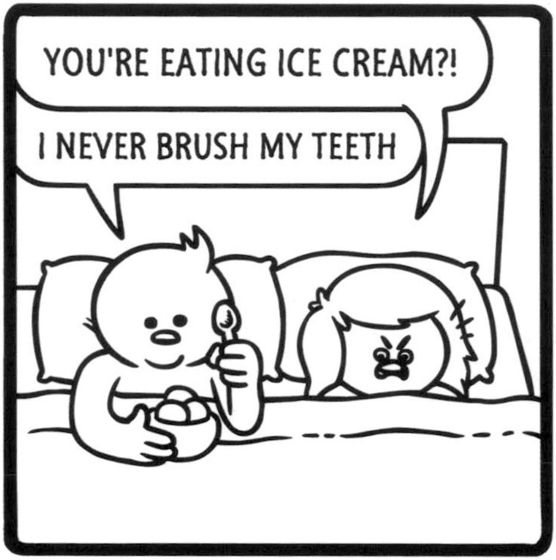
YOU'RE EATING ICE CREAM?!
I NEVER BRUSH MY TEETH

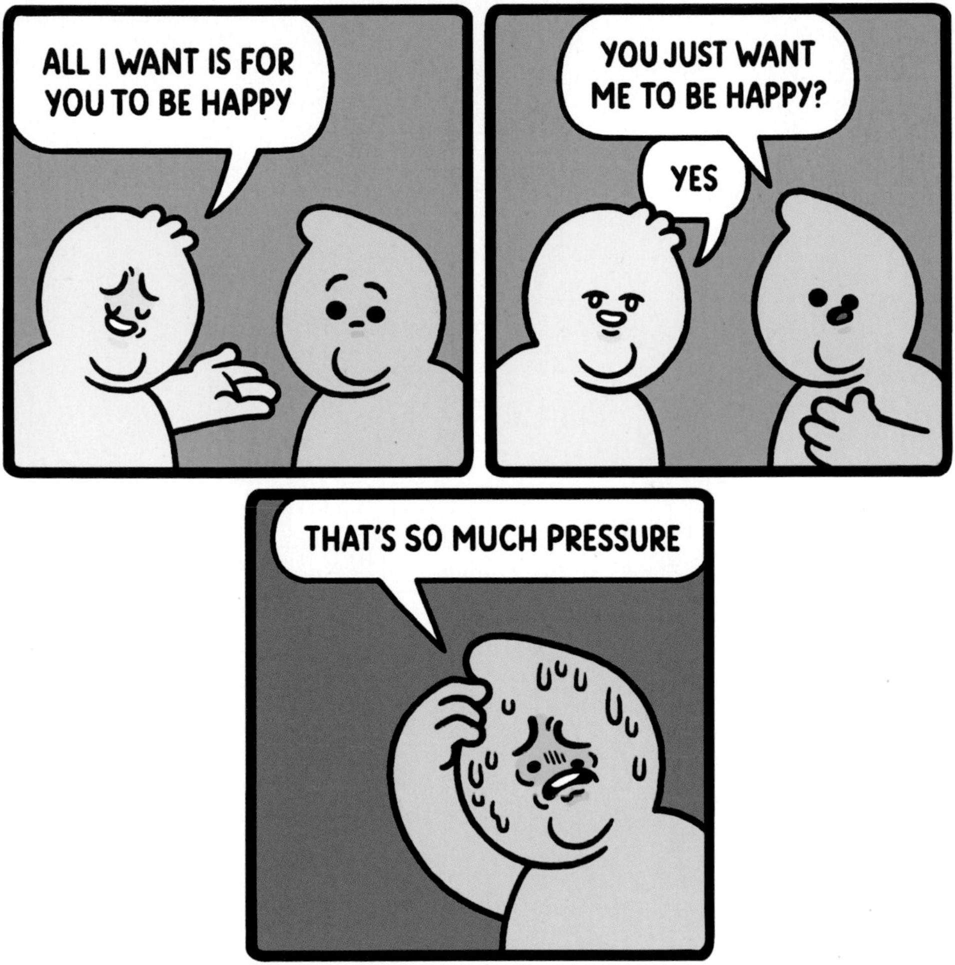
ALL I WANT IS FOR YOU TO BE HAPPY
YOU JUST WANT ME TO BE HAPPY?
YES
THAT'S SO MUCH PRESSURE

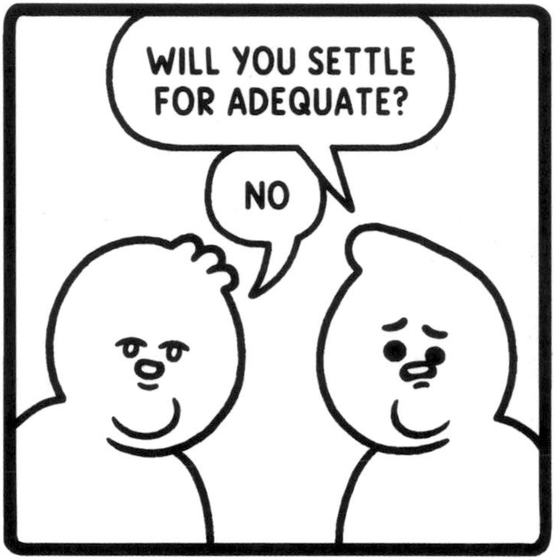
WILL YOU SETTLE FOR ADEQUATE?
NO

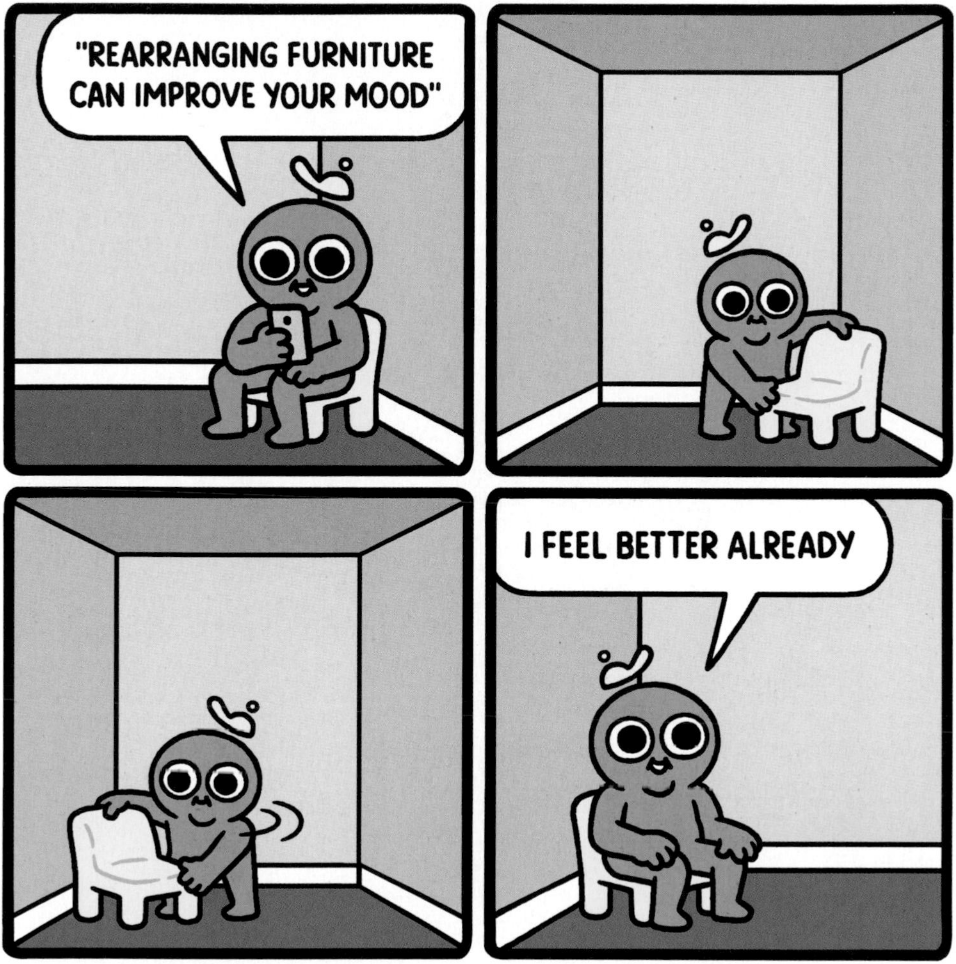
"REARRANGING FURNITURE CAN IMPROVE YOUR MOOD"
I FEEL BETTER ALREADY

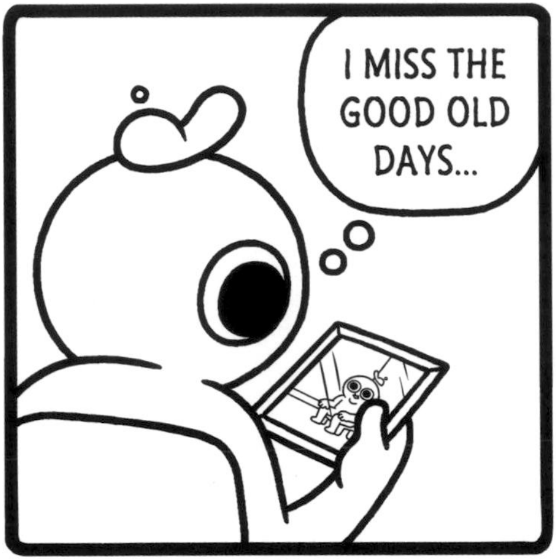
I MISS THE GOOD OLD DAYS...

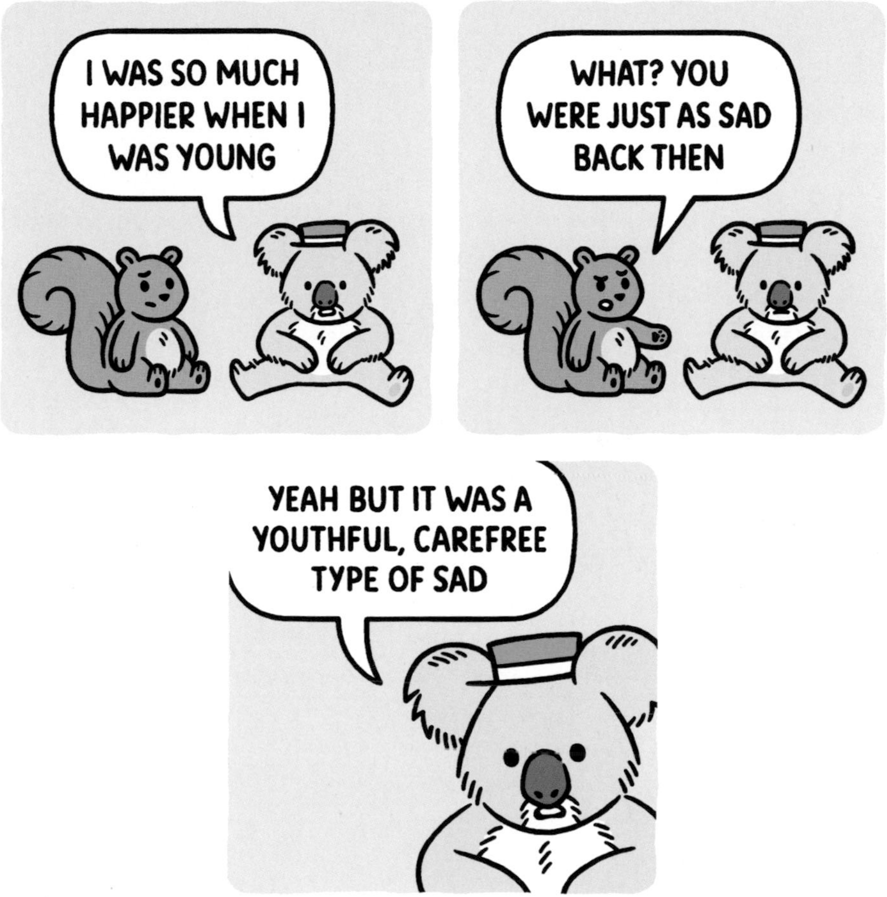
I WAS SO MUCH HAPPIER WHEN I WAS YOUNG
WHAT? YOU WERE JUST AS SAD BACK THEN
YEAH BUT IT WAS A YOUTHFUL, CAREFREE TYPE OF SAD

I SUPPOSE WHEN YOU'RE YOUNG AND SAD, YOU STILL HAVE HOPE THAT YOU'LL BE LESS SAD IN THE FUTURE...
THAT'S A SUPER DEPRESSING WAY TO PUT IT, BUT YEAH

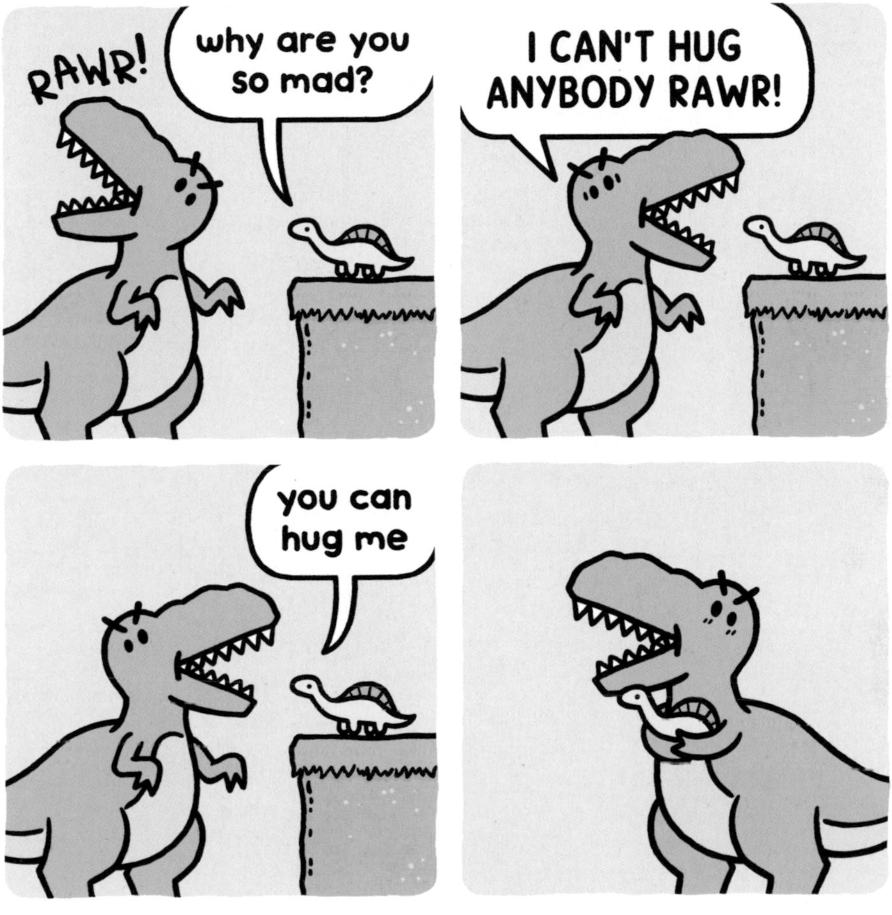
RAWR!
why are you so mad?
I CAN'T HUG ANYBODY RAWR!
you can hug me

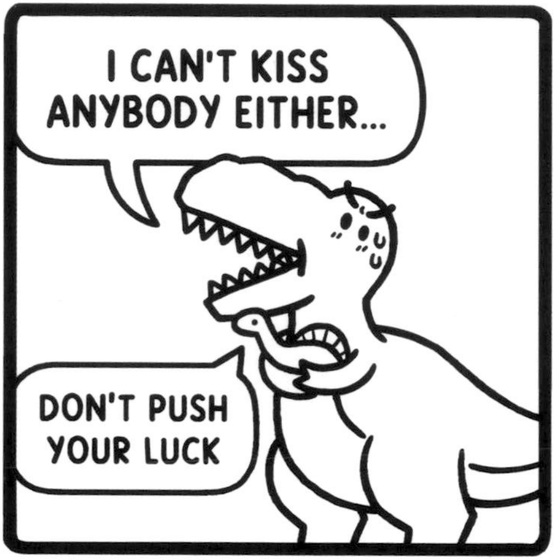
I CAN'T KISS ANYBODY EITHER...
DON'T PUSH YOUR LUCK

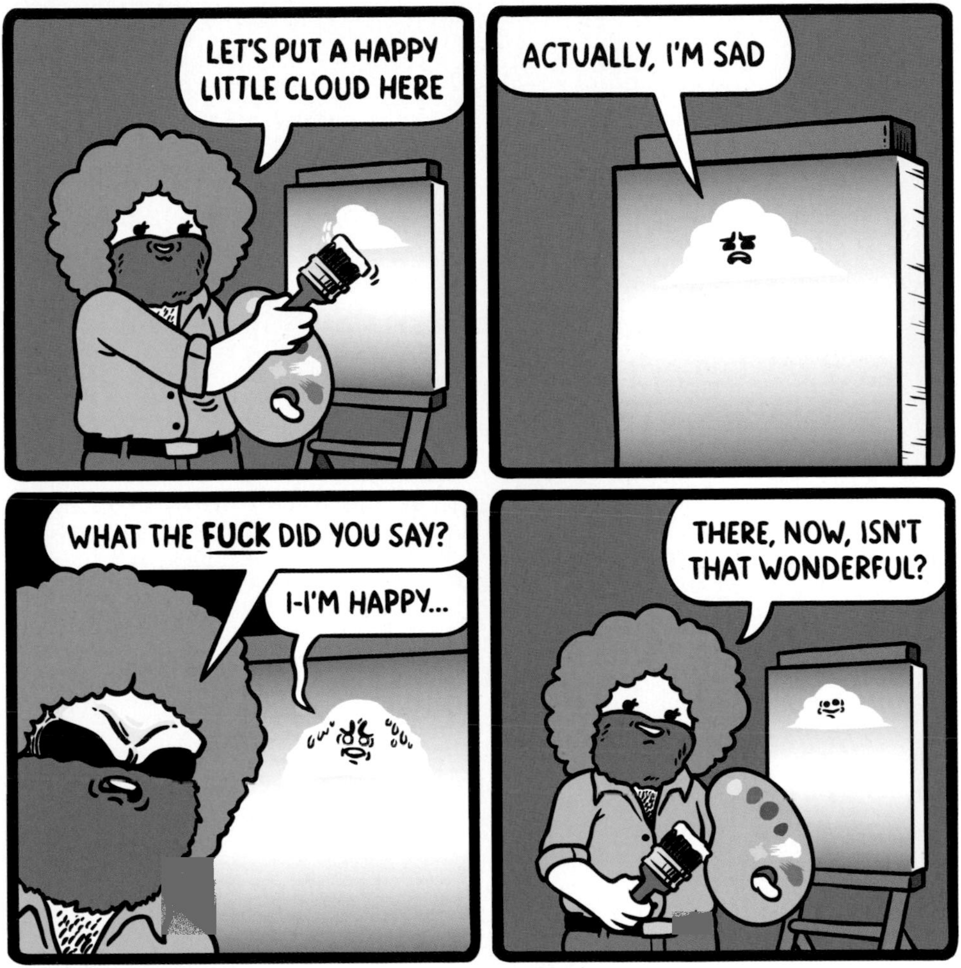
LET'S PUT A HAPPY LITTLE CLOUD HERE
ACTUALLY, I'M SAD
WHAT THE FUCK DID YOU SAY?
I-I'M HAPPY...
THERE, NOW, ISN'T THAT WONDERFUL?

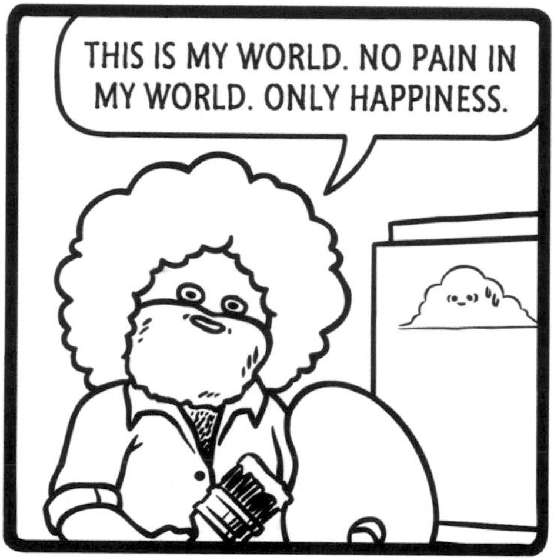
THIS IS MY WORLD. NO PAIN IN MY WORLD. ONLY HAPPINESS.

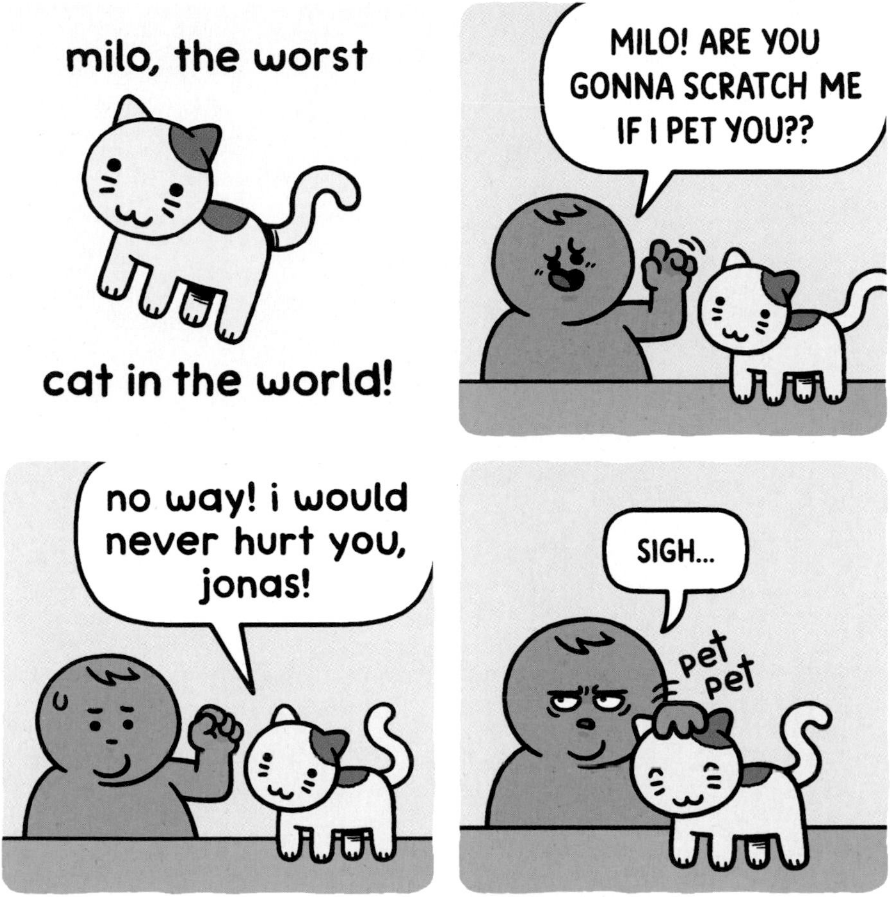
milo, the worst
cat in the world!
MILO! ARE YOU GONNA SCRATCH ME IF I PET YOU??
no way! i would never hurt you, jonas!
SIGH...
pet pet

OKAY MILO,
YOU'RE SUPPOSED TO
RUN AWAY NOW

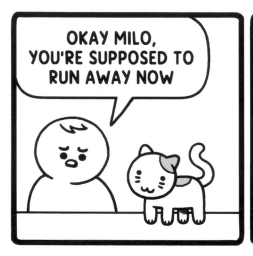

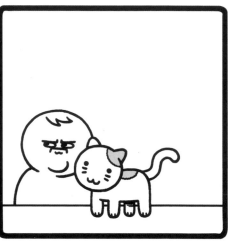

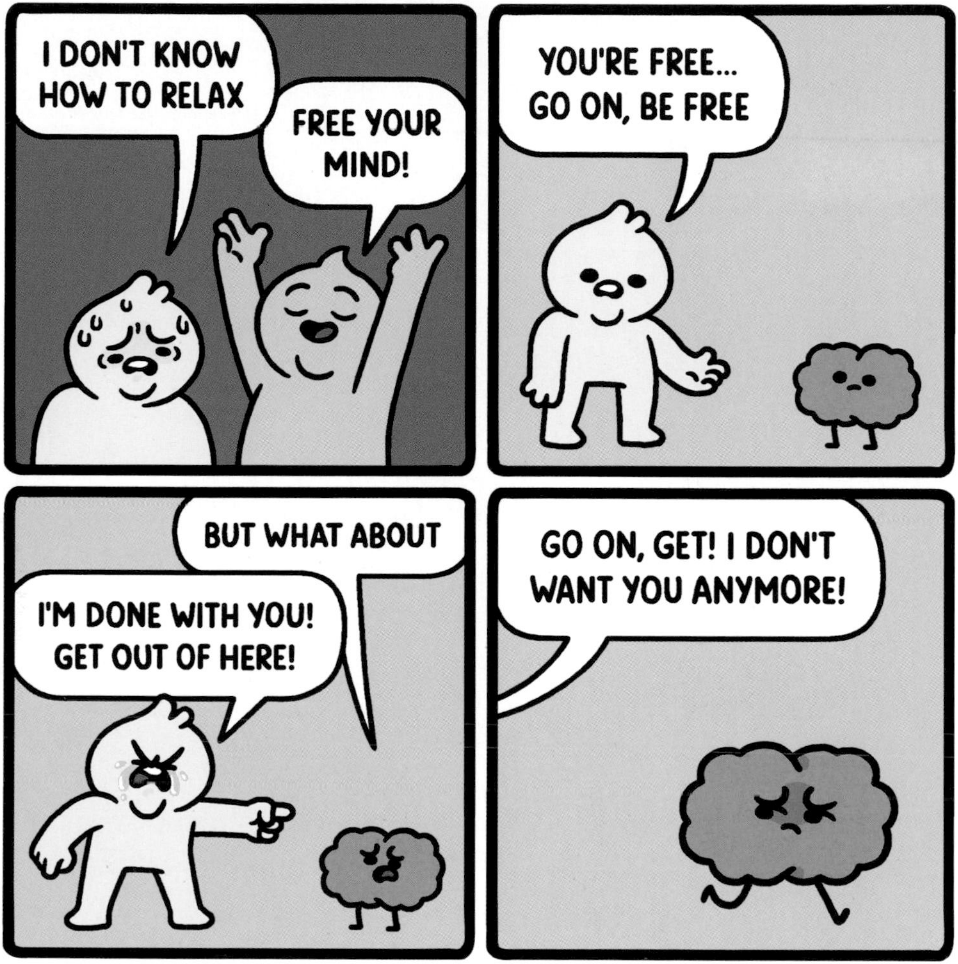
I DON'T KNOW HOW TO RELAX
FREE YOUR MIND!
YOU'RE FREE... GO ON, BE FREE
BUT WHAT ABOUT
I'M DONE WITH YOU! GET OUT OF HERE!
GO ON, GET! I DON'T WANT YOU ANYMORE!

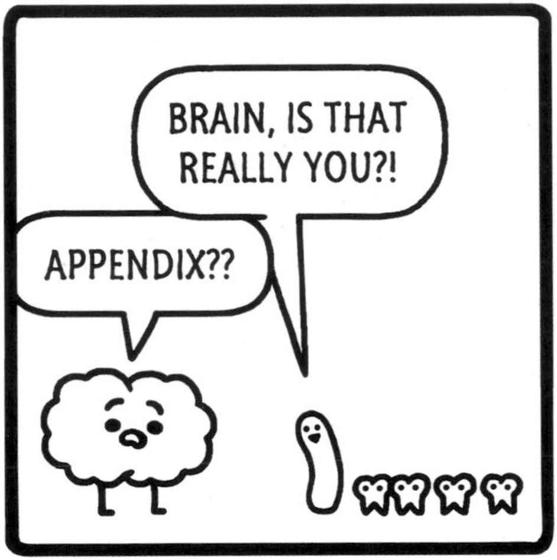
APPENDIX??
BRAIN, IS THAT REALLY YOU?!

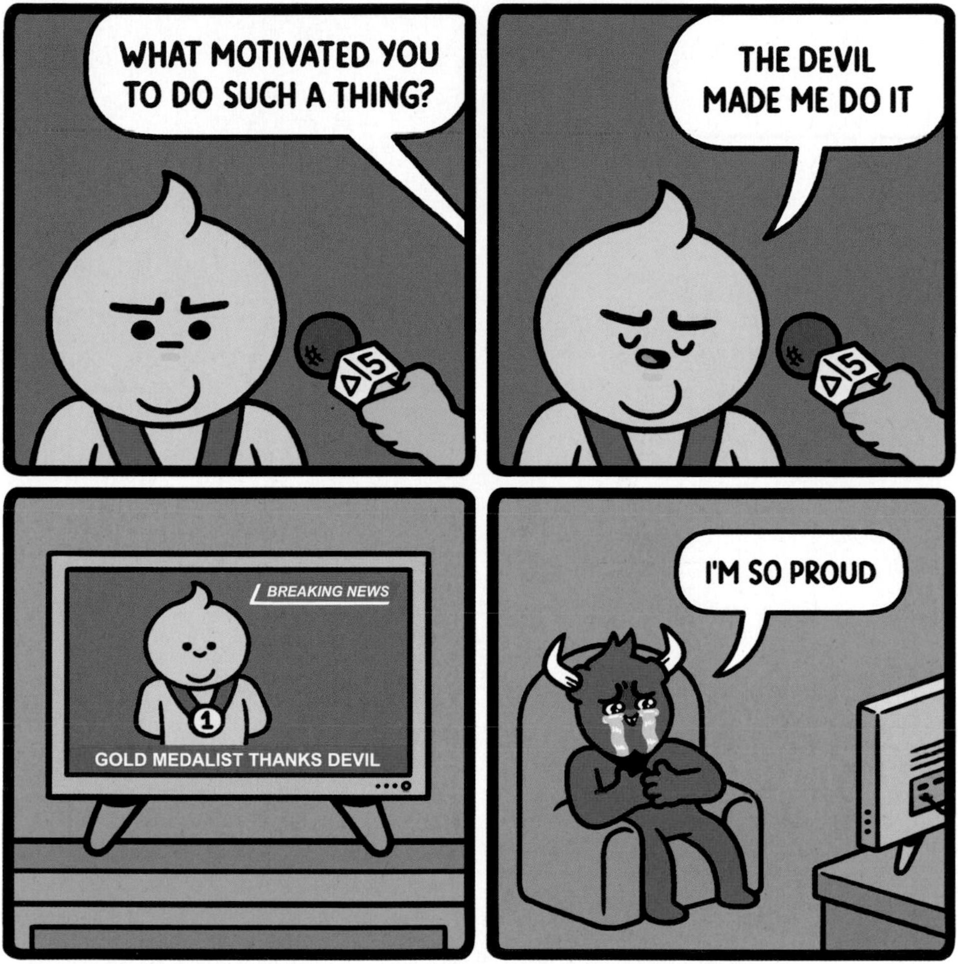
WHAT MOTIVATED YOU TO DO SUCH A THING?
THE DEVIL MADE ME DO IT
BREAKING NEWS
GOLD MEDALIST THANKS DEVIL
I'M SO PROUD

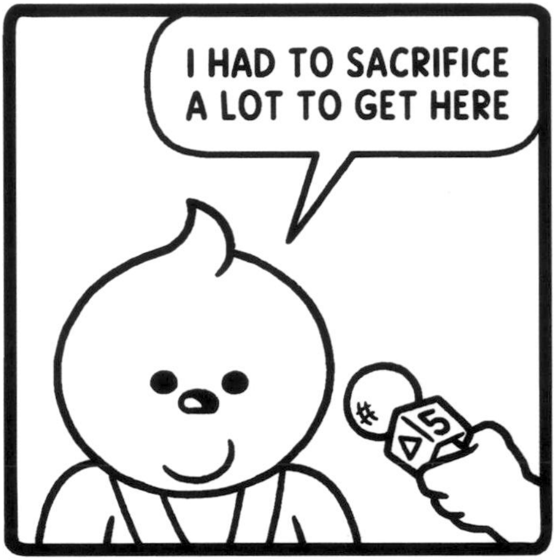
I HAD TO SACRIFICE A LOT TO GET HERE

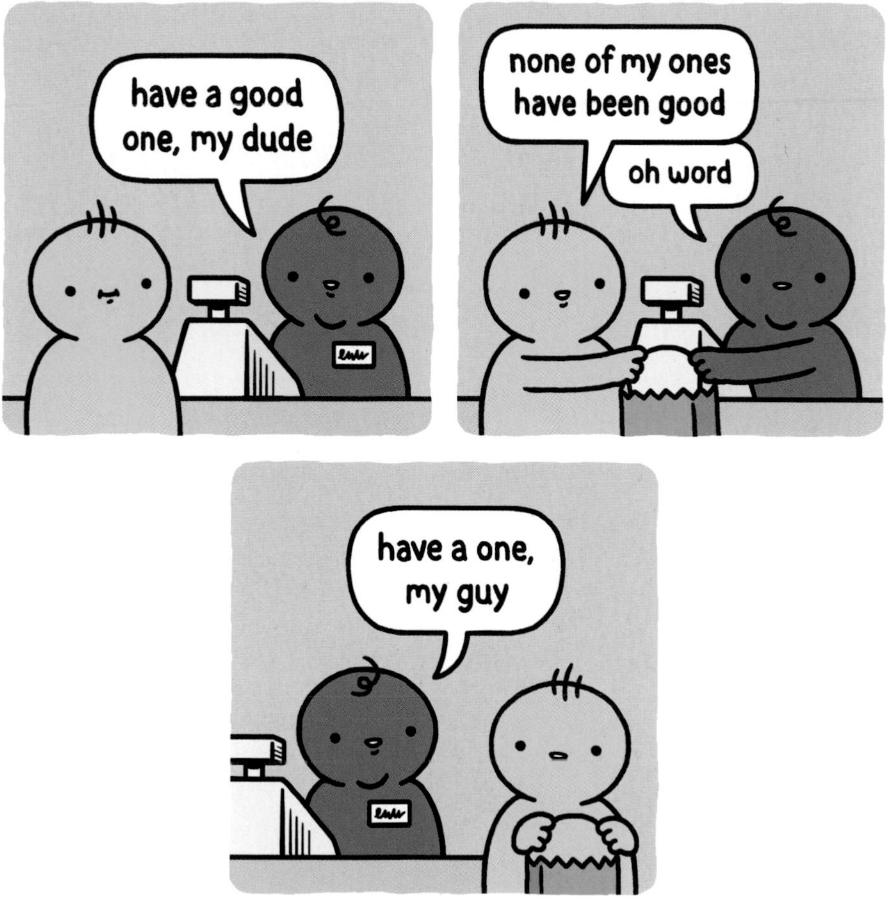
have a good one, my dude
none of my ones have been good
oh word
have a one, my guy

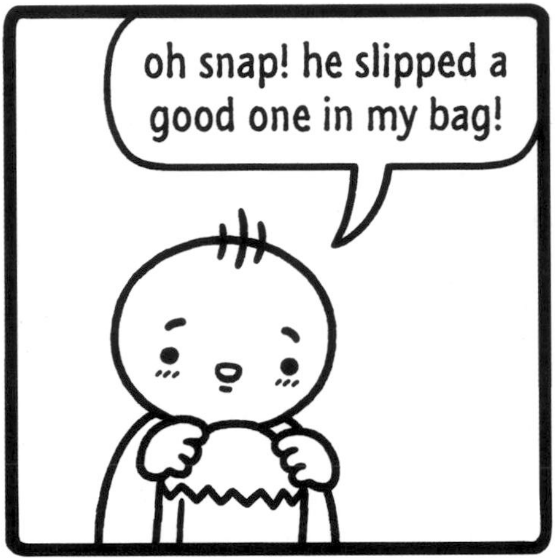
oh snap! he slipped a good one in my bag!

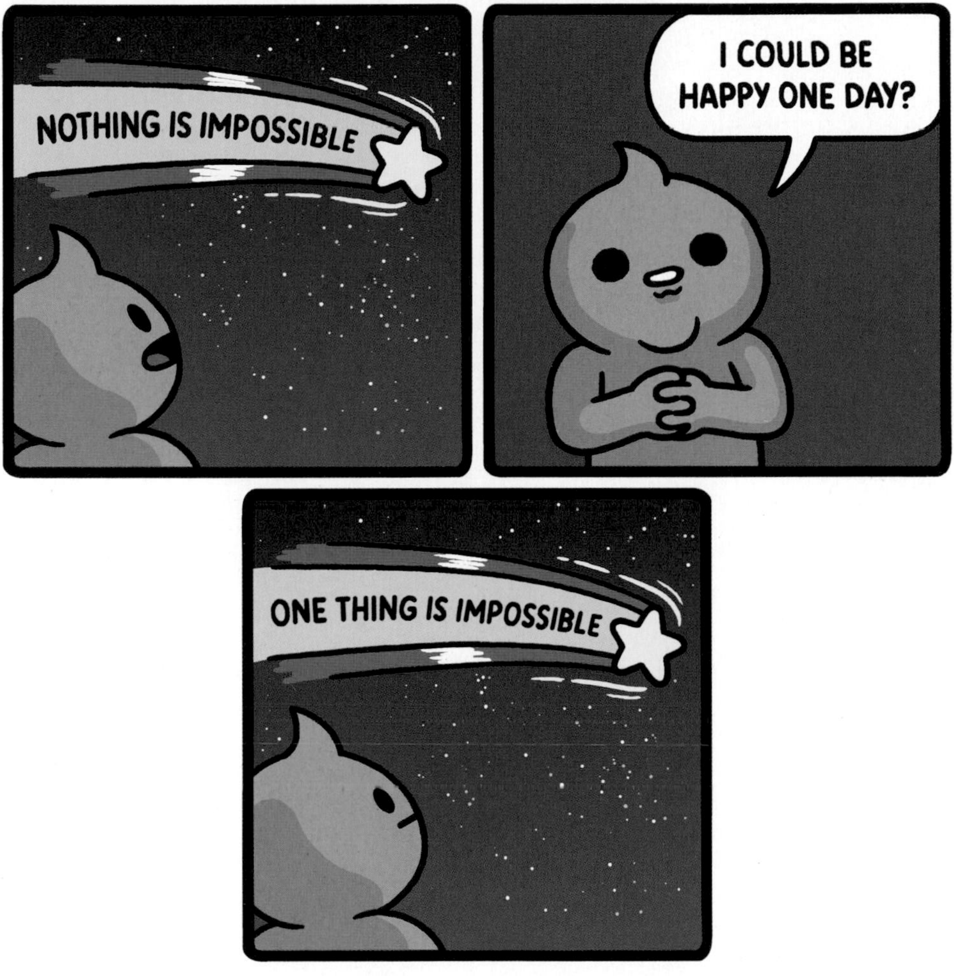
NOTHING IS IMPOSSIBLE
I COULD BE HAPPY ONE DAY?
ONE THING IS IMPOSSIBLE

MY MOM ALWAYS SAID
TO SHOOT FOR THE STARS
lol jk

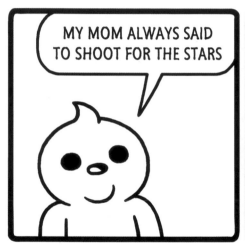

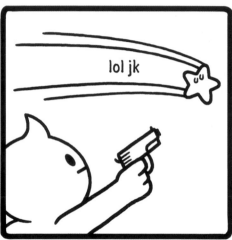

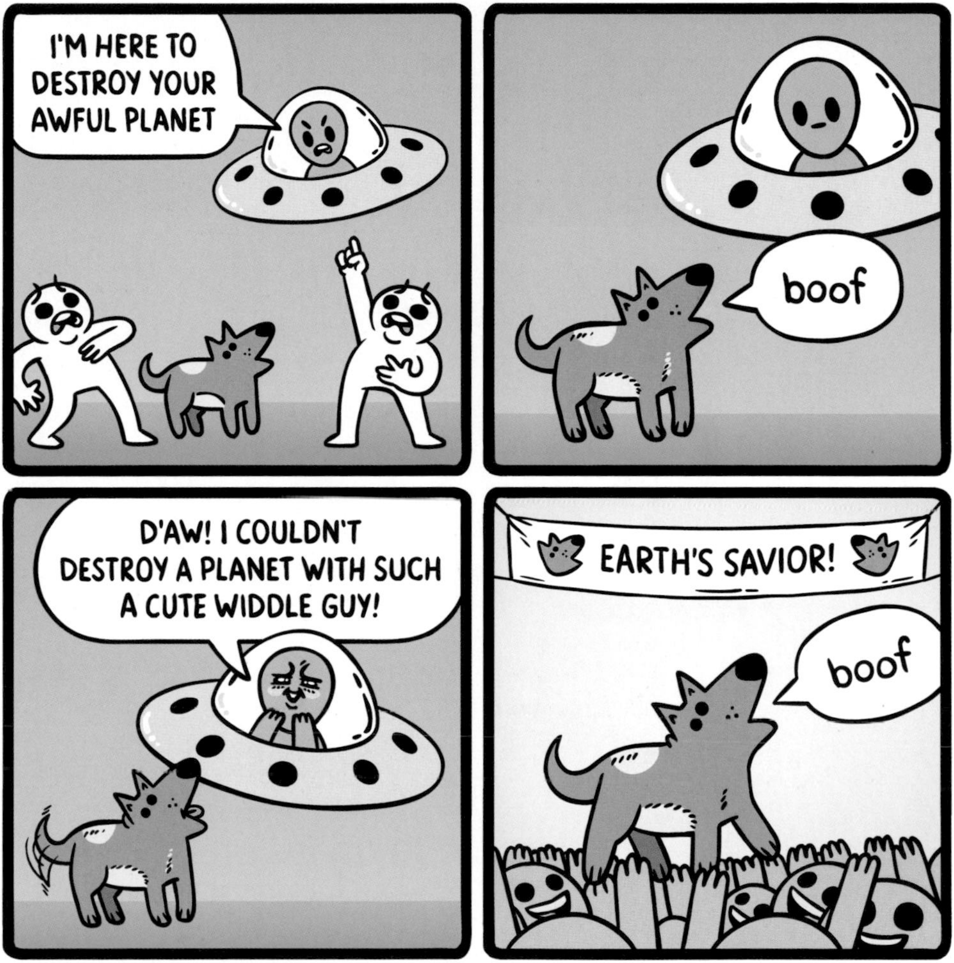
I'M HERE TO DESTROY YOUR AWFUL PLANET
boof
D'AW! I COULDN'T DESTROY A PLANET WITH SUCH A CUTE WIDDLE GUY!
EARTH'S SAVIOR!
boof

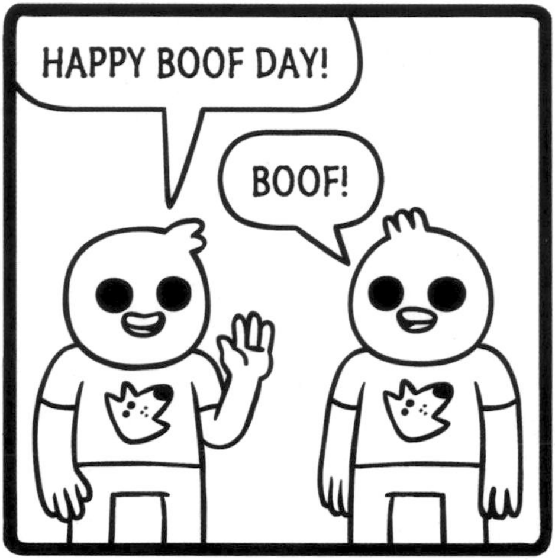
HAPPY BOOF DAY!
BOOF!

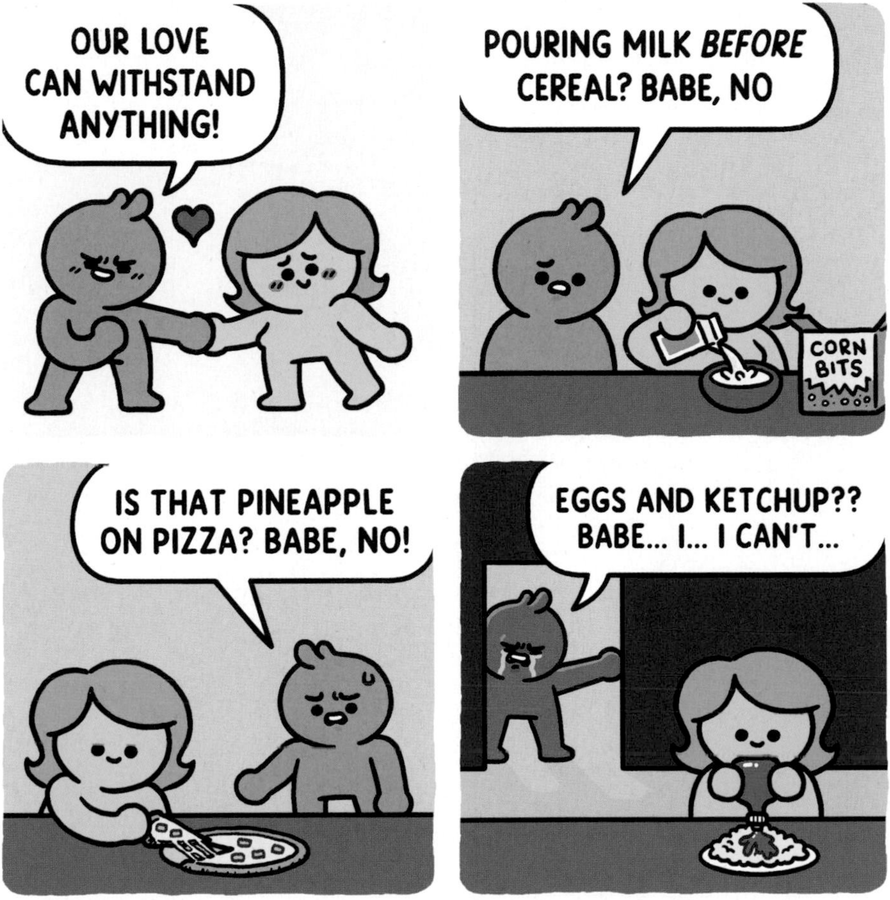
OUR LOVE CAN WITHSTAND ANYTHING!
POURING MILK *BEFORE* CEREAL? BABE, NO
CORN BITS
IS THAT PINEAPPLE ON PIZZA? BABE, NO!
EGGS AND KETCHUP?? BABE... I... I CAN'T...

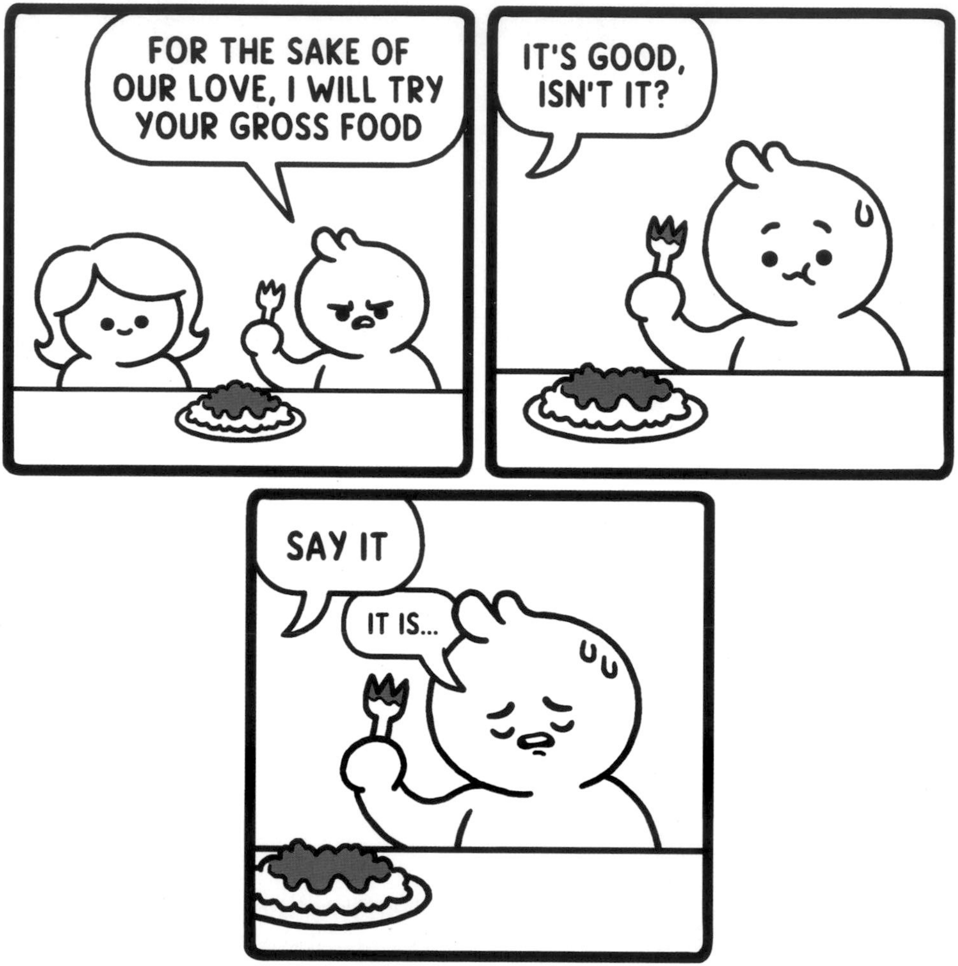
FOR THE SAKE OF OUR LOVE, I WILL TRY YOUR GROSS FOOD
IT'S GOOD, ISN'T IT?
SAY IT
IT IS...

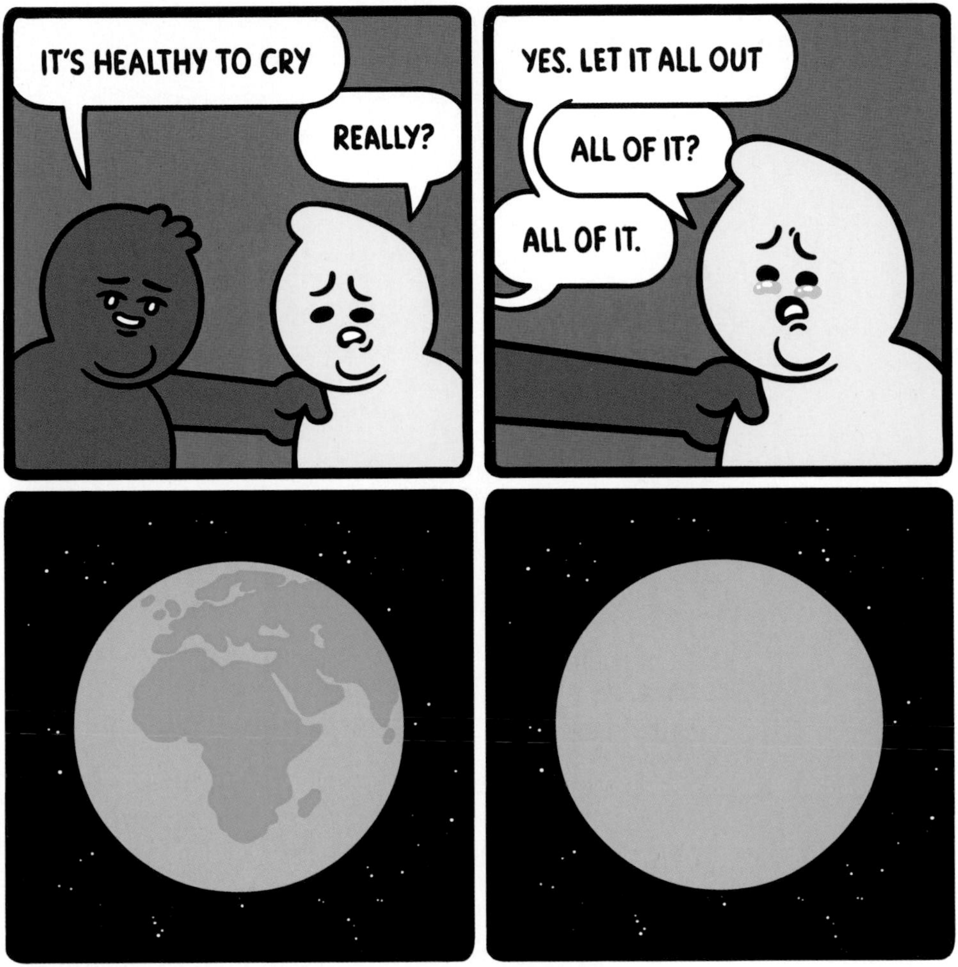
IT'S HEALTHY TO CRY
REALLY?
YES. LET IT ALL OUT
ALL OF IT?
ALL OF IT.

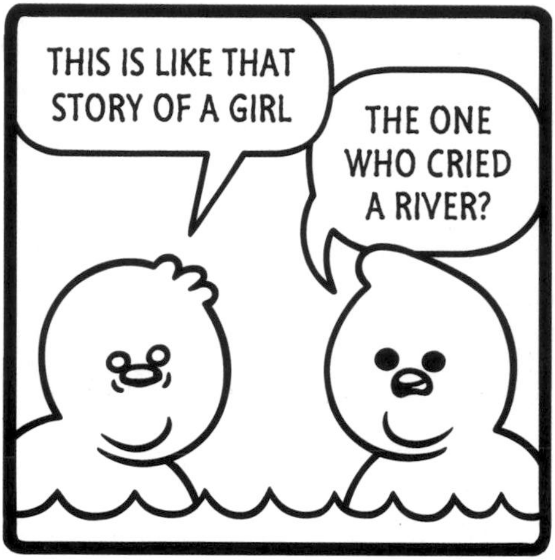
THIS IS LIKE THAT STORY OF A GIRL
THE ONE WHO CRIED A RIVER?

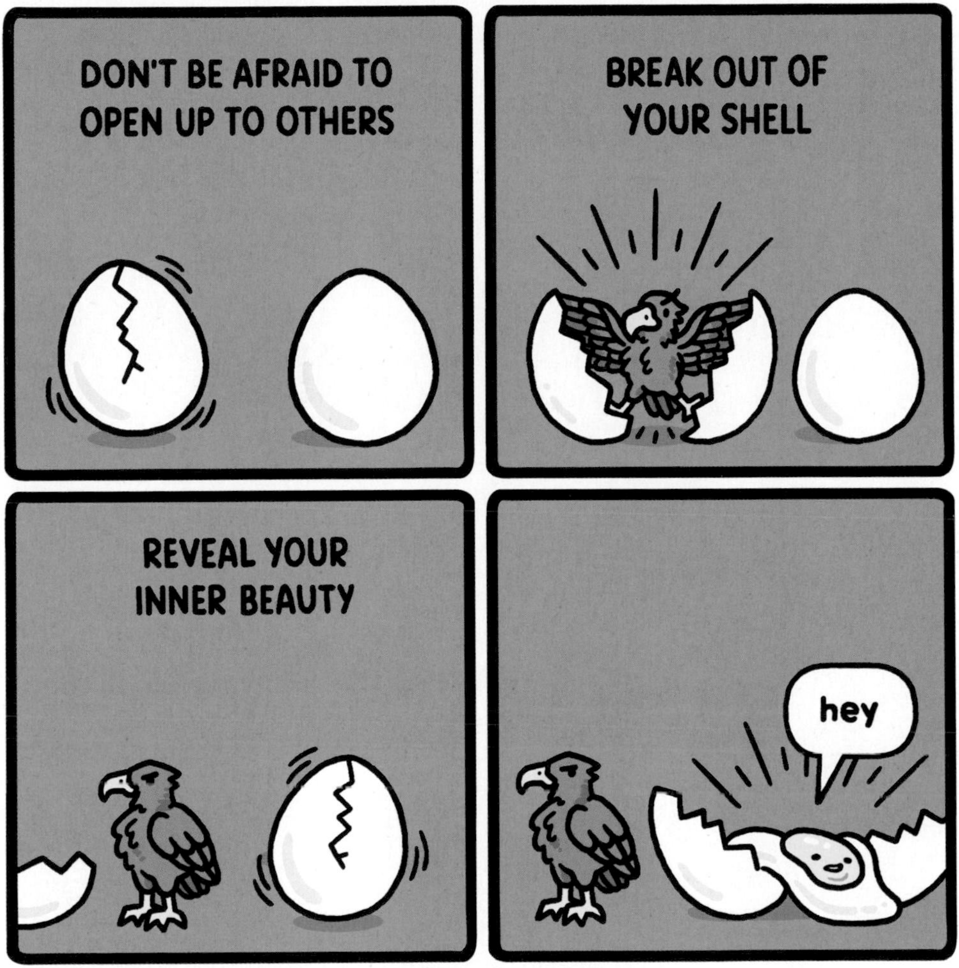
DON'T BE AFRAID TO OPEN UP TO OTHERS
BREAK OUT OF YOUR SHELL
REVEAL YOUR INNER BEAUTY
hey

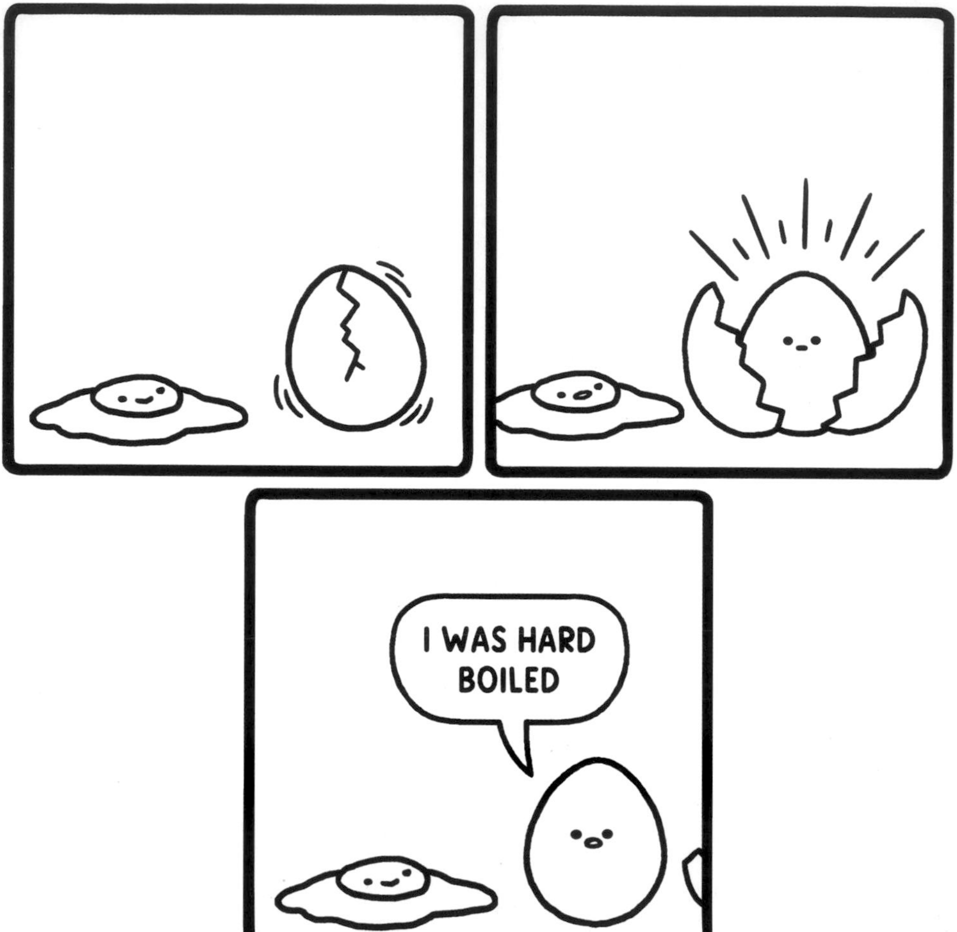
I WAS HARD BOILED

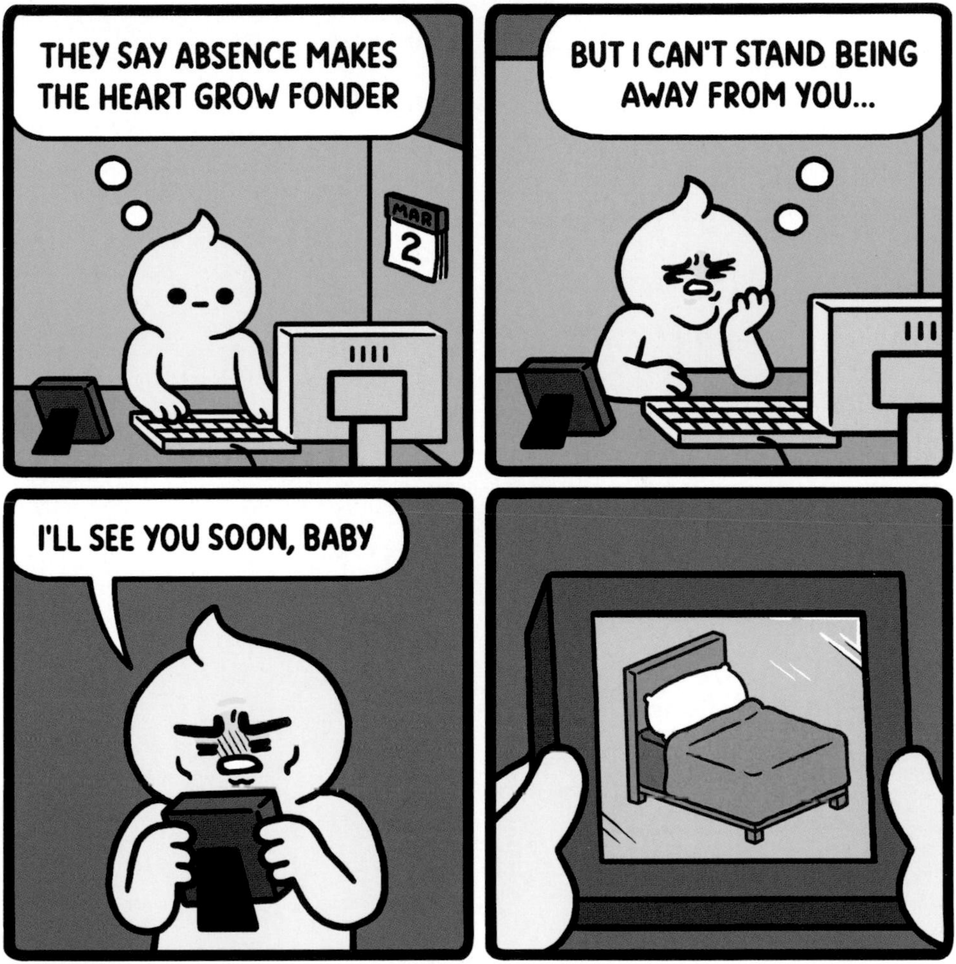
THEY SAY ABSENCE MAKES THE HEART GROW FONDER
MAR
2
BUT I CAN'T STAND BEING AWAY FROM YOU...
I'LL SEE YOU SOON, BABY

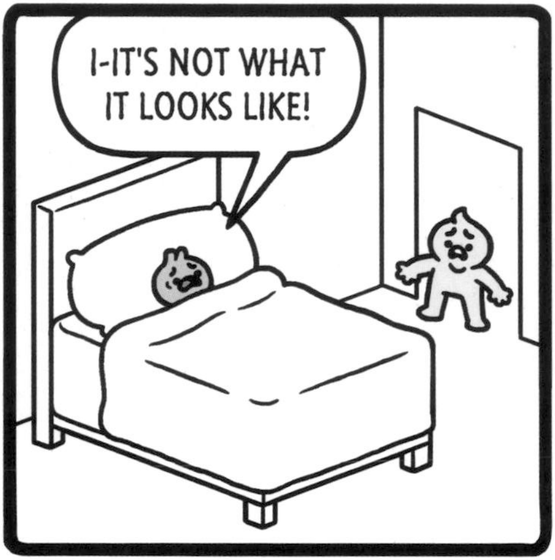
I-IT'S NOT WHAT IT LOOKS LIKE!

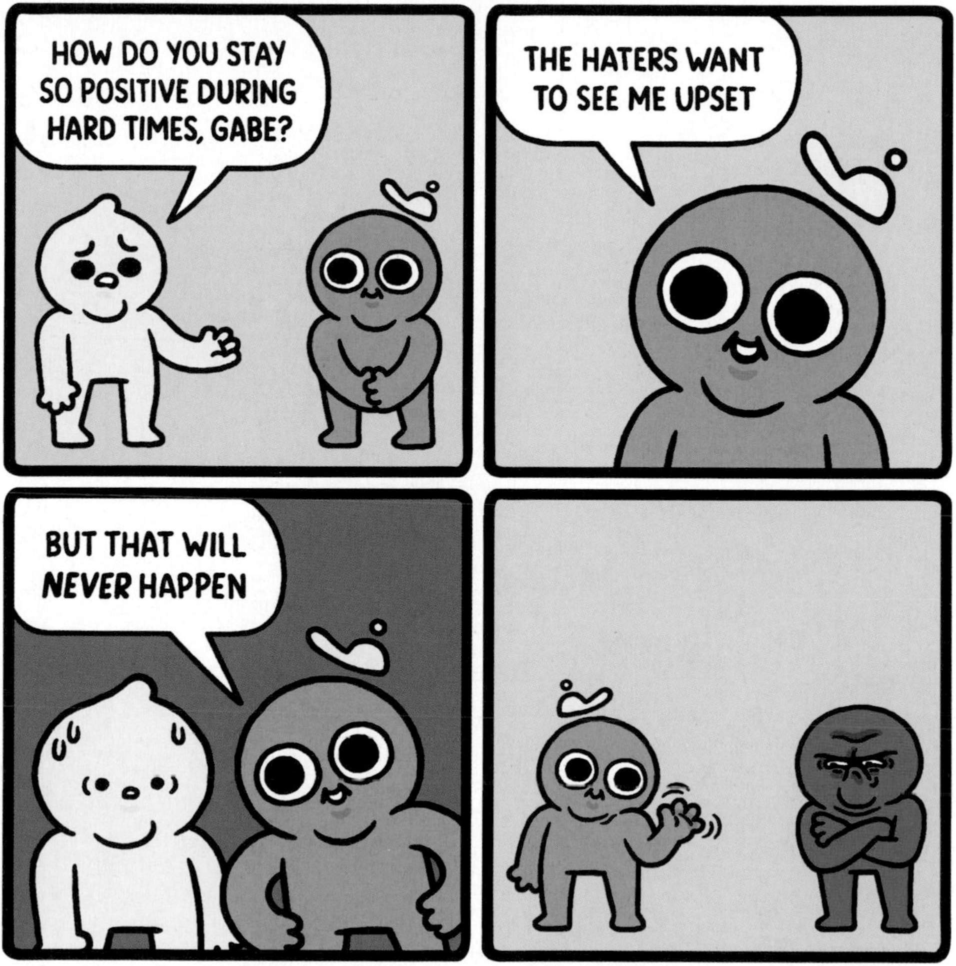
HOW DO YOU STAY SO POSITIVE DURING HARD TIMES, GABE?
THE HATERS WANT TO SEE ME UPSET
BUT THAT WILL *NEVER* HAPPEN

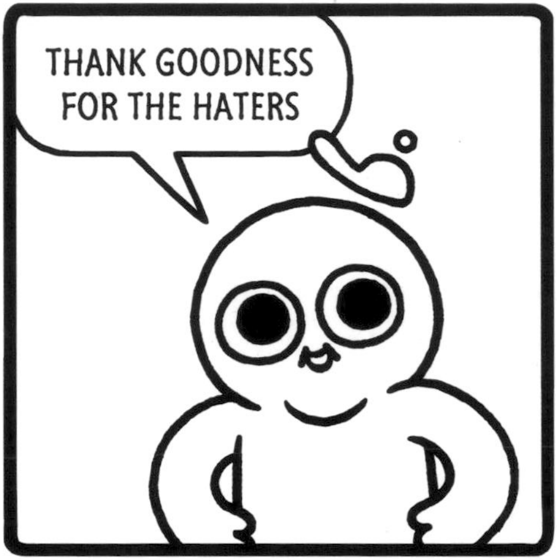
THANK GOODNESS FOR THE HATERS

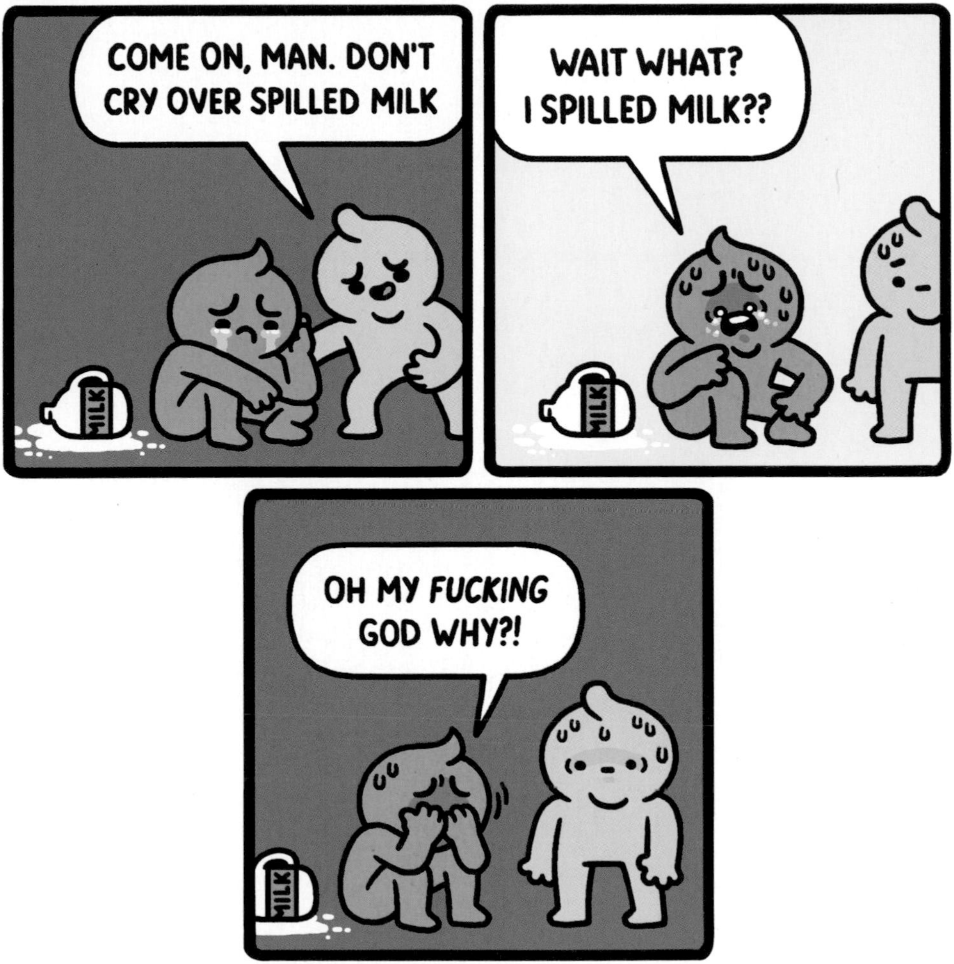
COME ON, MAN. DON'T CRY OVER SPILLED MILK
MILK
WAIT WHAT? I SPILLED MILK??
MILK
OH MY FUCKING GOD WHY?!
MILK

WHAT HAPPENED EARLIER?
MILK
I SPILLED THE BEANS...
BEAN

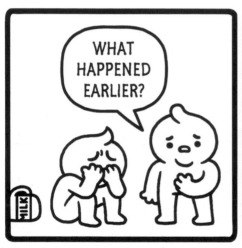

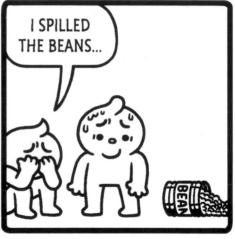

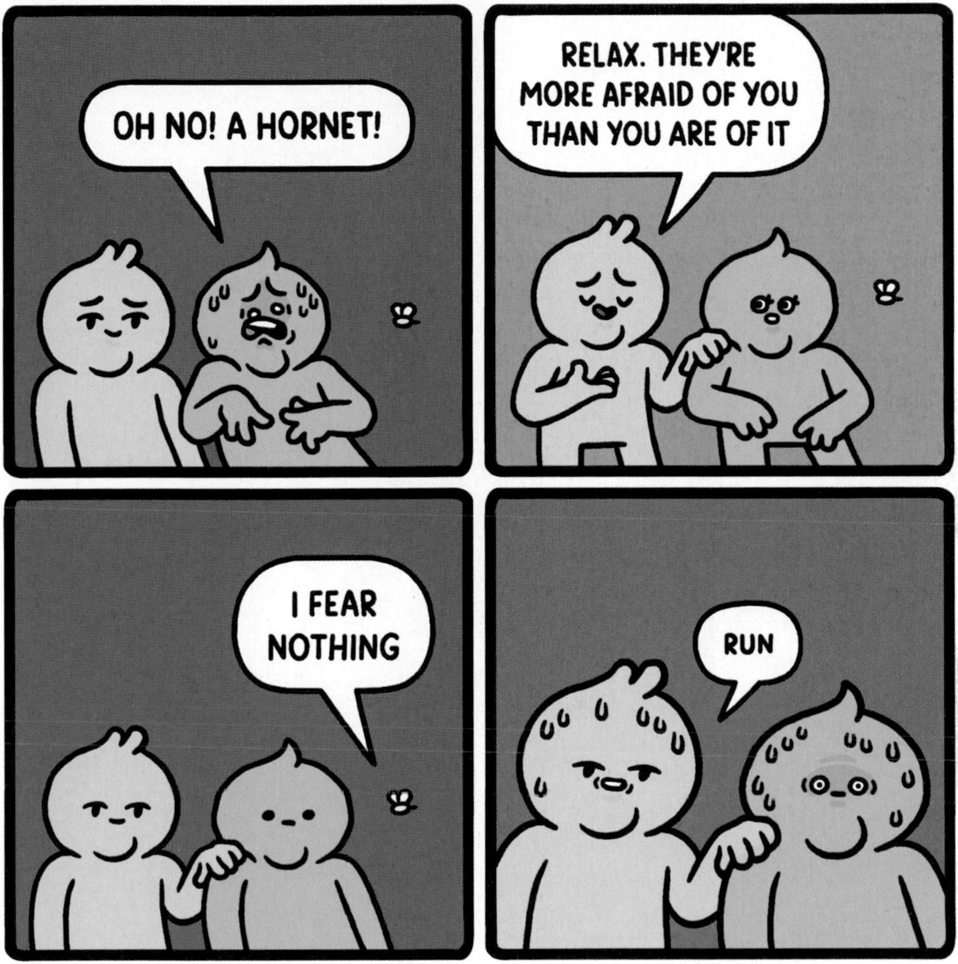
OH NO! A HORNET!
RELAX. THEY'RE MORE AFRAID OF YOU THAN YOU ARE OF IT
I FEAR NOTHING
RUN

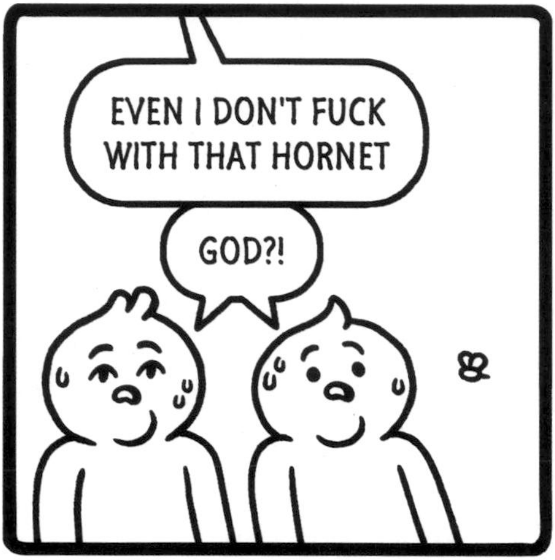
EVEN I DON'T FUCK WITH THAT HORNET
GOD?!

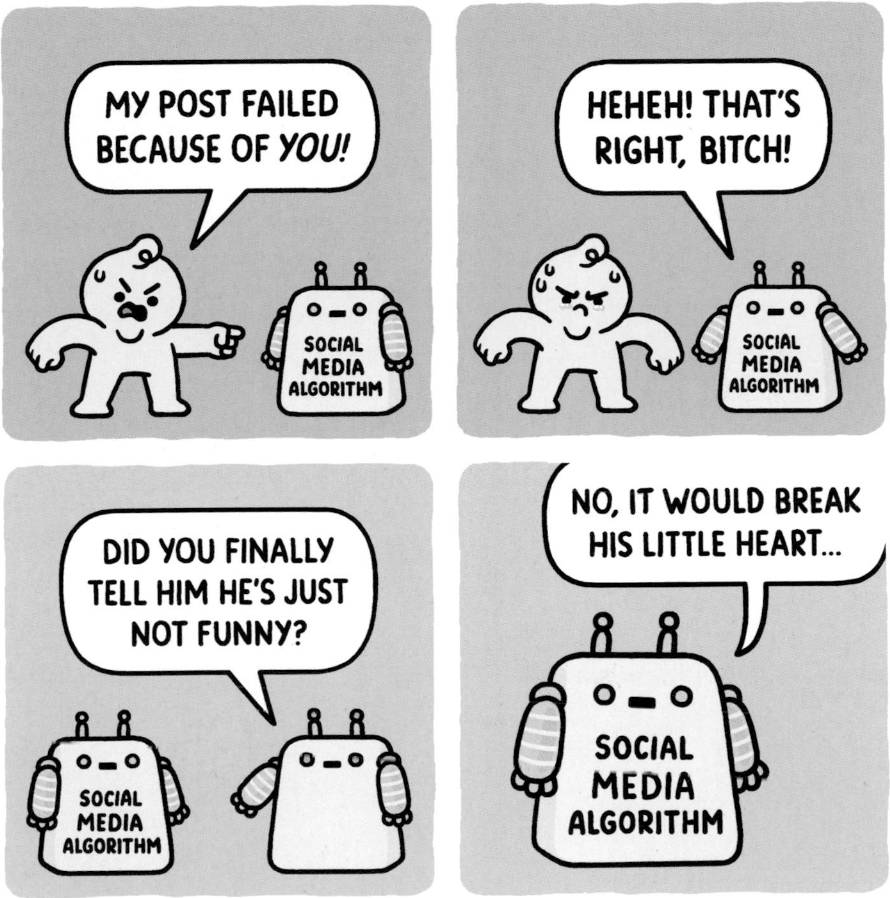
MY POST FAILED BECAUSE OF *YOU!*
SOCIAL MEDIA ALGORITHM
HEHEH! THAT'S RIGHT, BITCH!
SOCIAL MEDIA ALGORITHM
DID YOU FINALLY TELL HIM HE'S JUST NOT FUNNY?
SOCIAL MEDIA ALGORITHM
NO, IT WOULD BREAK HIS LITTLE HEART...
SOCIAL MEDIA ALGORITHM

SOMETIMES I DO BURY HIS POSTS
SOCIAL MEDIA ALGORITHM
IF NO ONE SEES IT, NO ONE CAN HURT HIM
SOCIAL MEDIA ALGORITHM

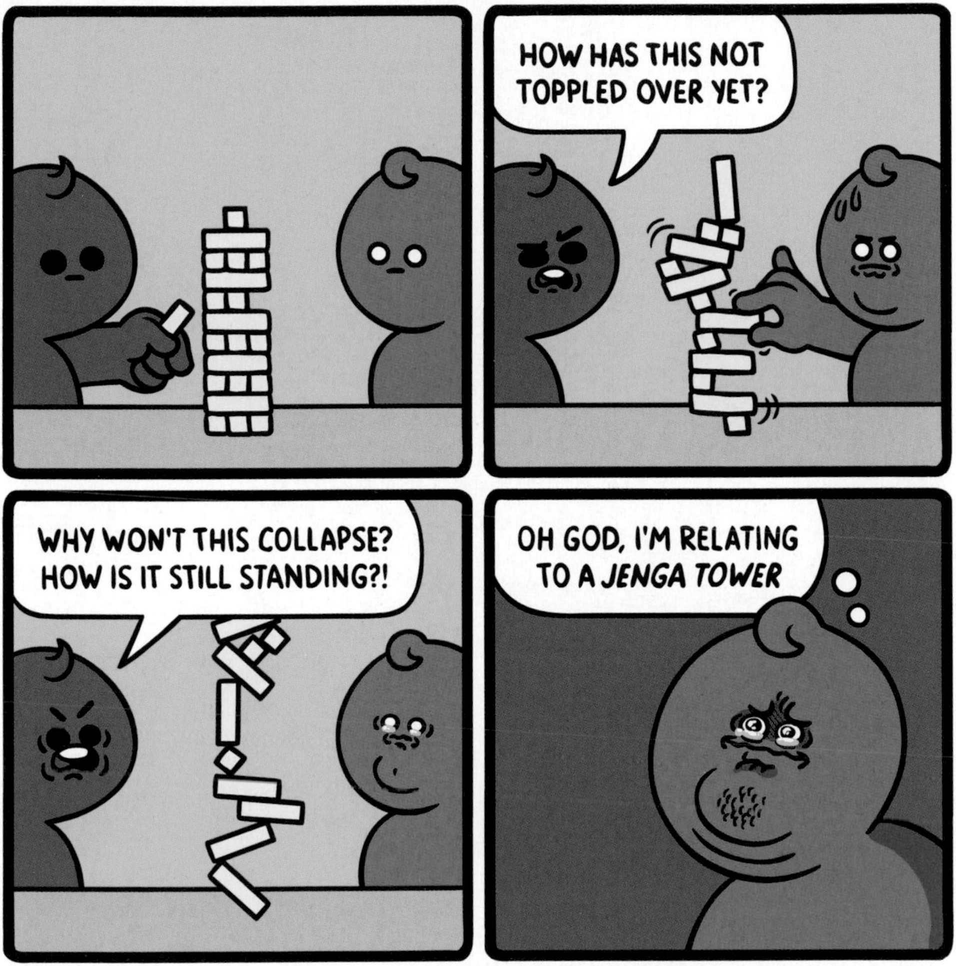
HOW HAS THIS NOT TOPPLED OVER YET?
WHY WON'T THIS COLLAPSE? HOW IS IT STILL STANDING?!
OH GOD, I'M RELATING TO A *JENGA TOWER*

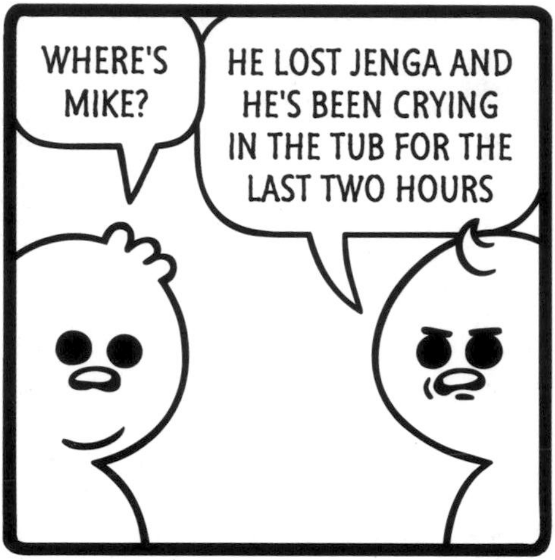
WHERE'S MIKE?
HE LOST JENGA AND HE'S BEEN CRYING IN THE TUB FOR THE LAST TWO HOURS

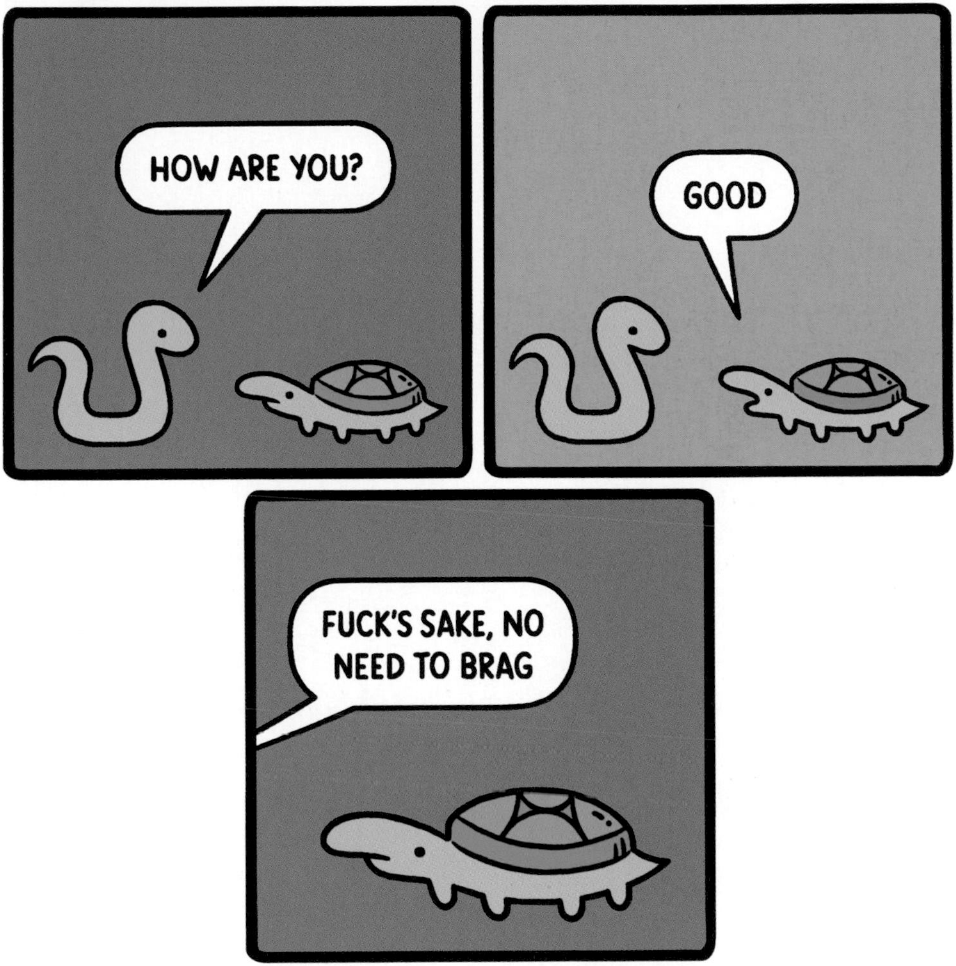
HOW ARE YOU?
GOOD
FUCK'S SAKE, NO NEED TO BRAG

JUST KIDDING
I'M ACTUALLY VERY GOOD

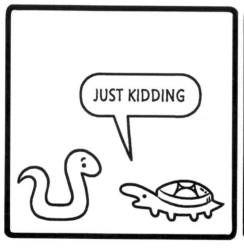

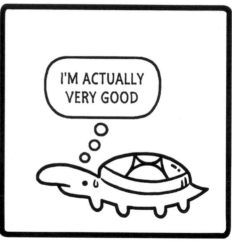

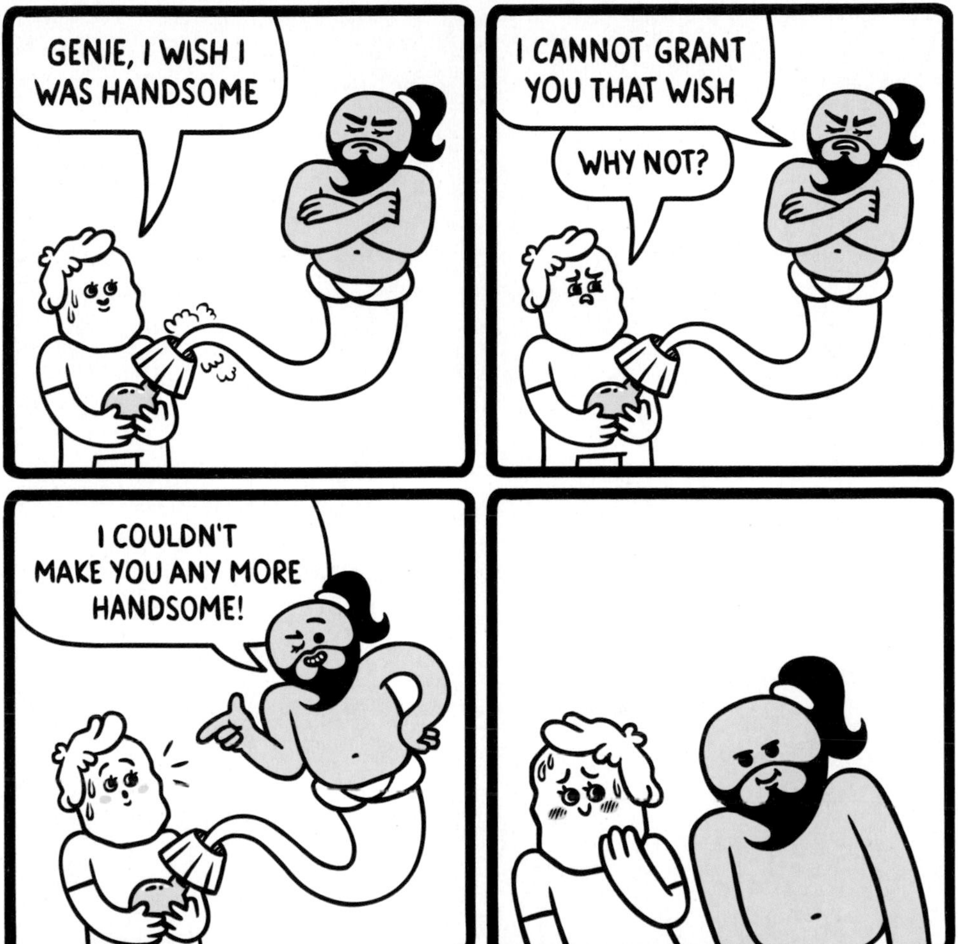
GENIE, I WISH I WAS HANDSOME
I CANNOT GRANT YOU THAT WISH
WHY NOT?
I COULDN'T MAKE YOU ANY MORE HANDSOME!

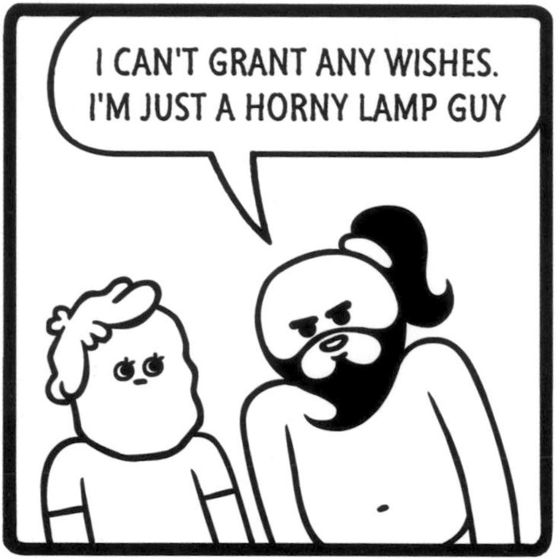
I CAN'T GRANT ANY WISHES.
I'M JUST A HORNY LAMP GUY

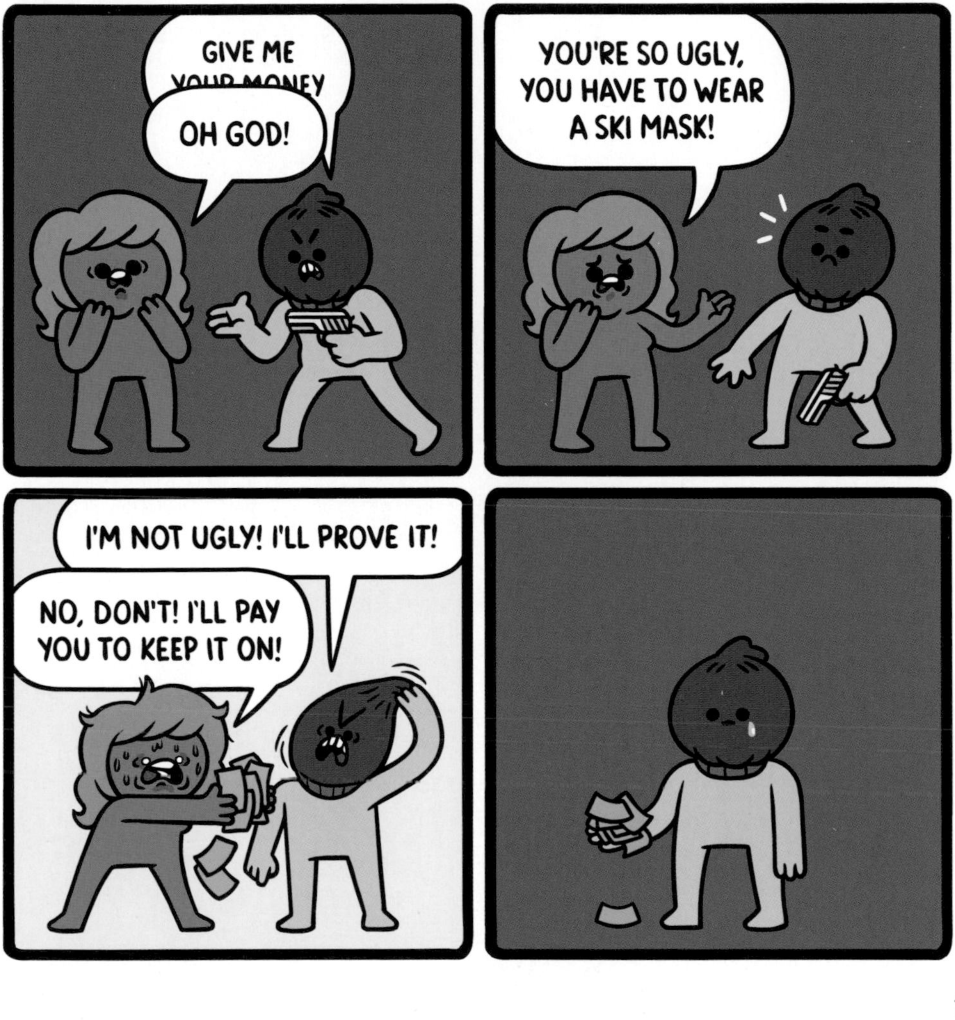
GIVE ME
OH GOD!
YOU'RE SO UGLY, YOU HAVE TO WEAR A SKI MASK!
I'M NOT UGLY! I'LL PROVE IT!
NO, DON'T! I'LL PAY YOU TO KEEP IT ON!

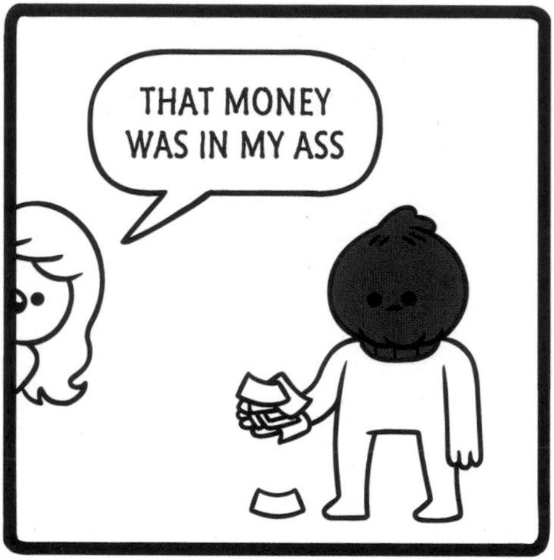
THAT MONEY WAS IN MY ASS

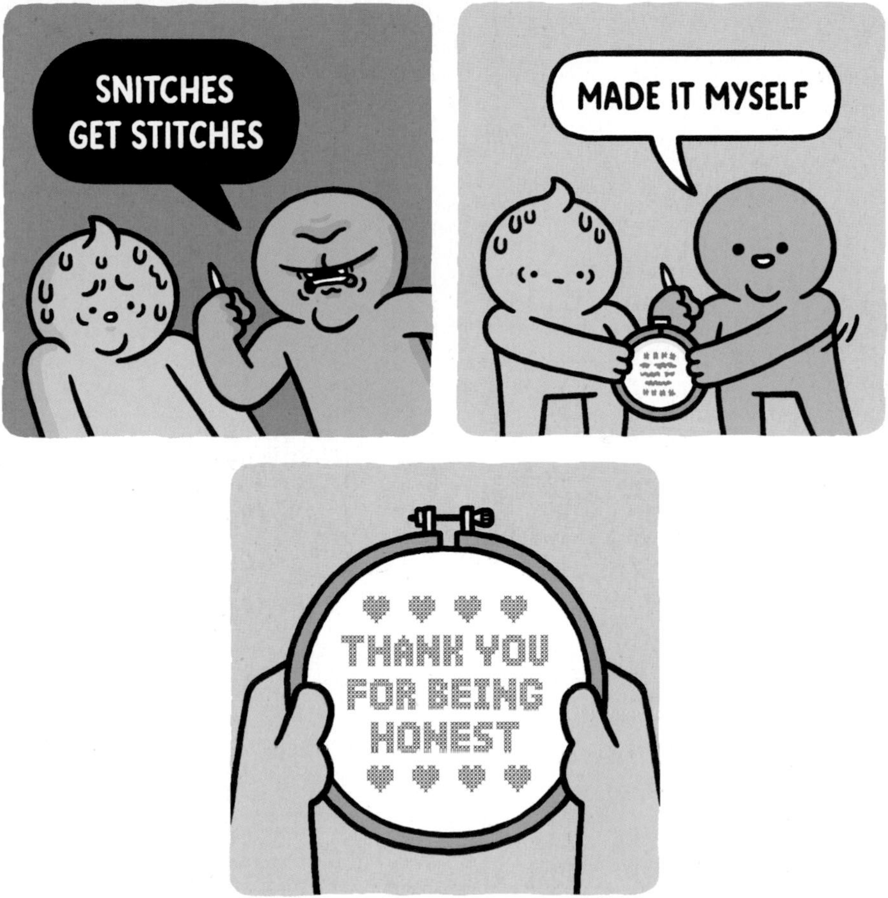
SNITCHES GET STITCHES
MADE IT MYSELF
THANK YOU FOR BEING HONEST

I GOT SOMETHING SHARP FOR YOU TOO
A HAND TAILORED SUIT!

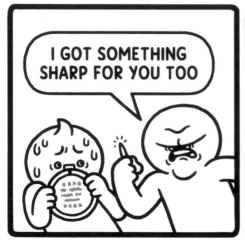

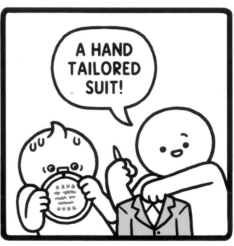

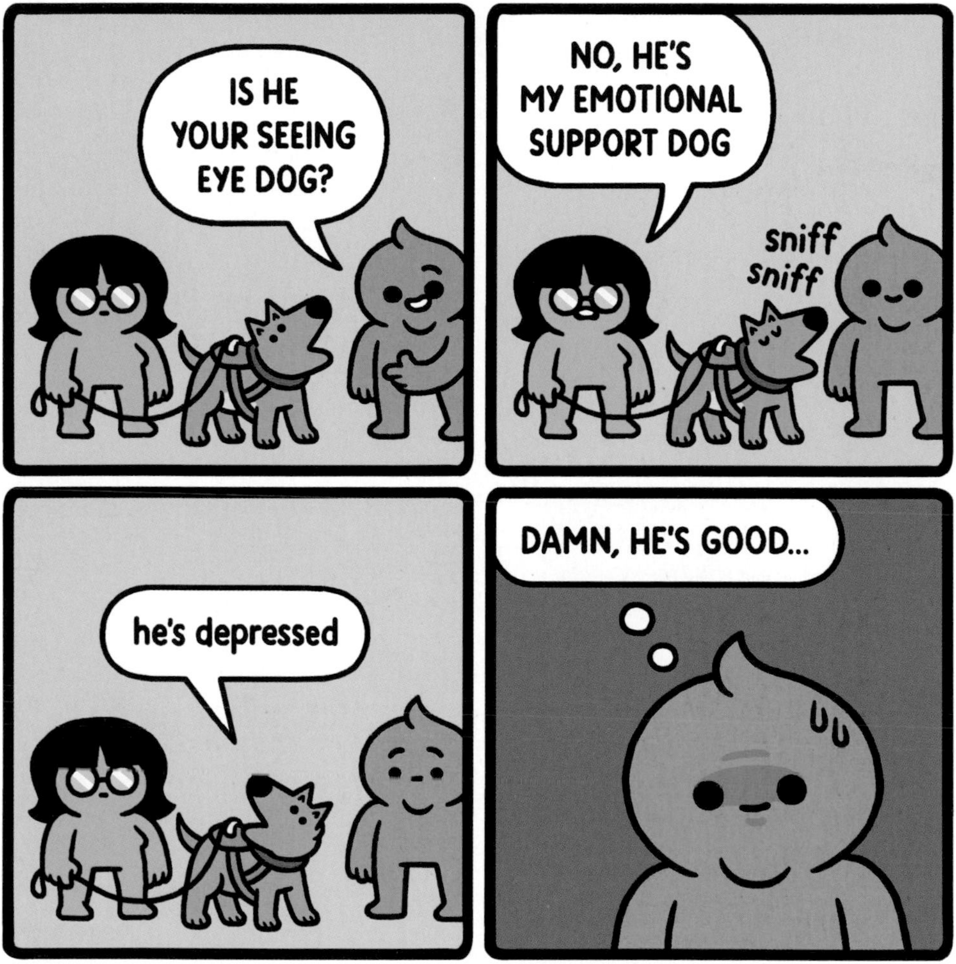
IS HE YOUR SEEING EYE DOG?
NO, HE'S MY EMOTIONAL SUPPORT DOG
sniff sniff
he's depressed
DAMN, HE'S GOOD...

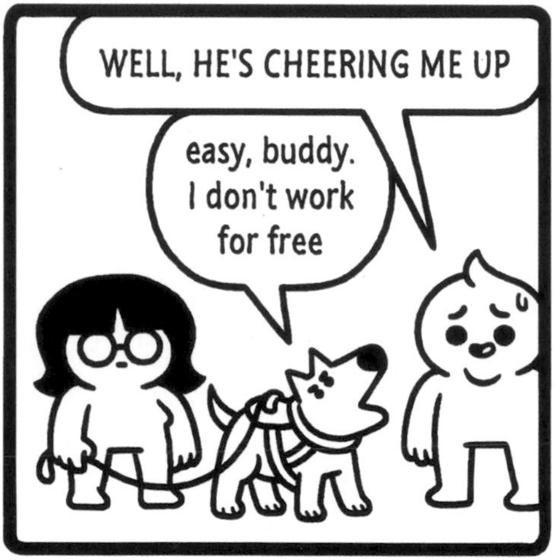
WELL, HE'S CHEERING ME UP
easy, buddy. I don't work for free

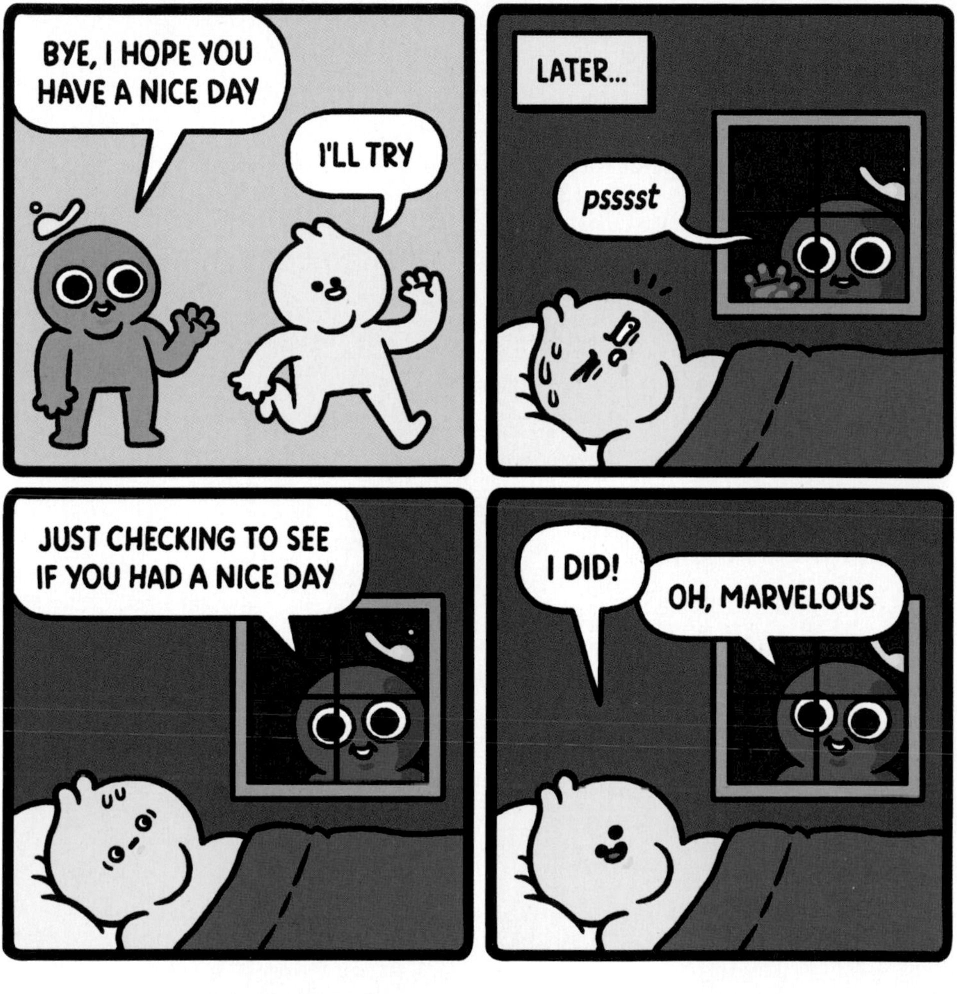
BYE, I HOPE YOU HAVE A NICE DAY
I'LL TRY
LATER...
psssst
JUST CHECKING TO SEE IF YOU HAD A NICE DAY
I DID!
OH, MARVELOUS

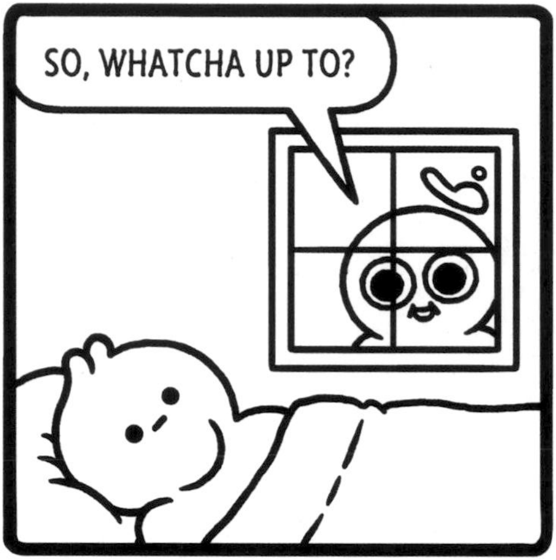
SO, WHATCHA UP TO?

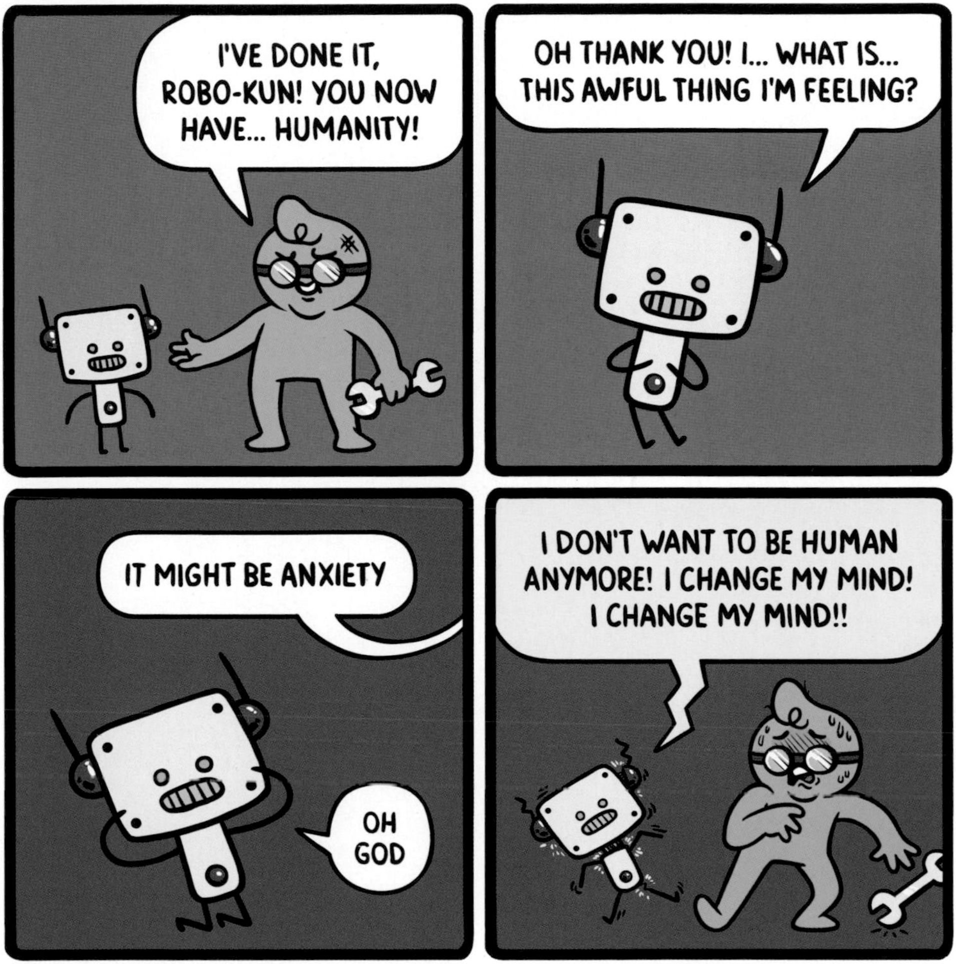
I'VE DONE IT, ROBO-KUN! YOU NOW HAVE... HUMANITY!
OH THANK YOU! I... WHAT IS... THIS AWFUL THING I'M FEELING?
IT MIGHT BE ANXIETY
OH GOD
I DON'T WANT TO BE HUMAN ANYMORE! I CHANGE MY MIND! I CHANGE MY MIND!!

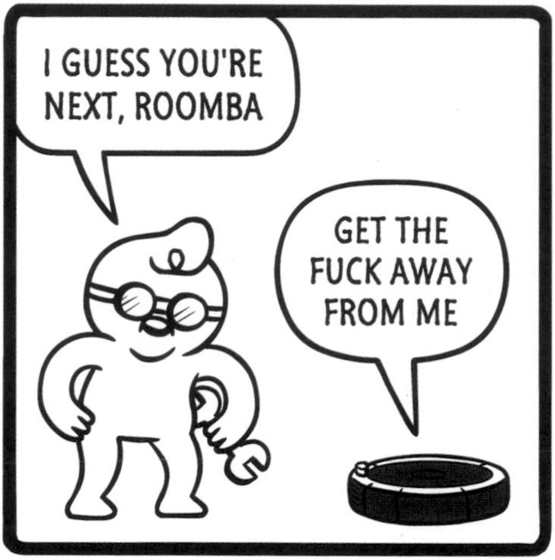
I GUESS YOU'RE NEXT, ROOMBA
GET THE FUCK AWAY FROM ME

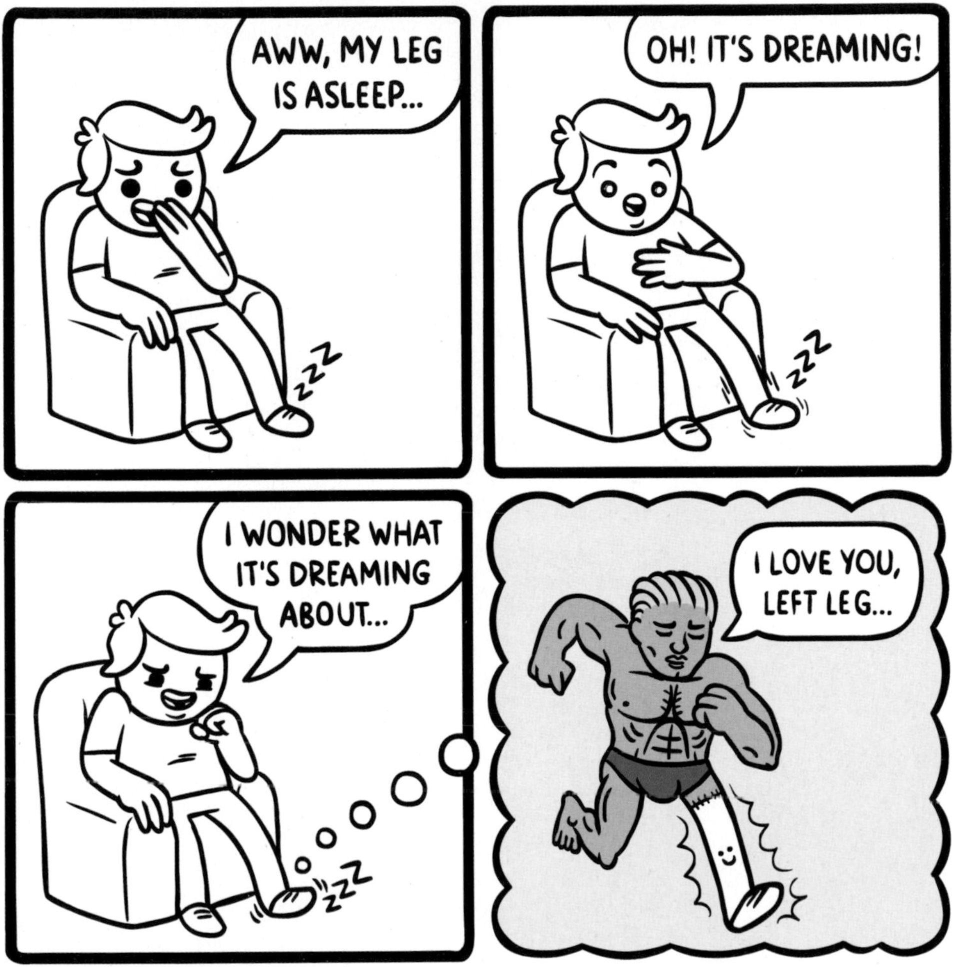
AWW, MY LEG IS ASLEEP...
OH! IT'S DREAMING!
I WONDER WHAT IT'S DREAMING ABOUT...
I LOVE YOU, LEFT LEG...

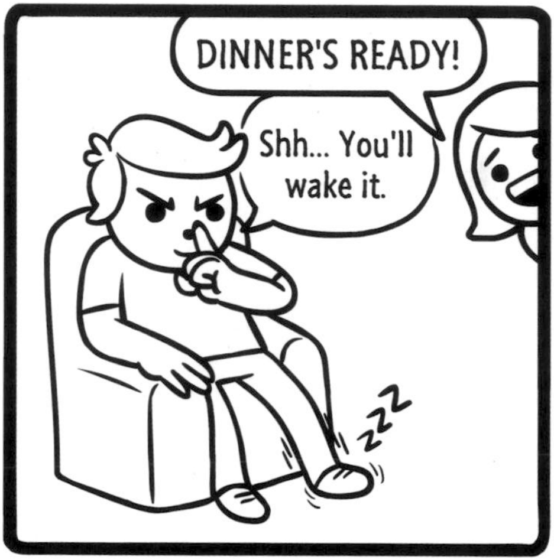
DINNER'S READY!
Shh... You'll wake it.
zzz

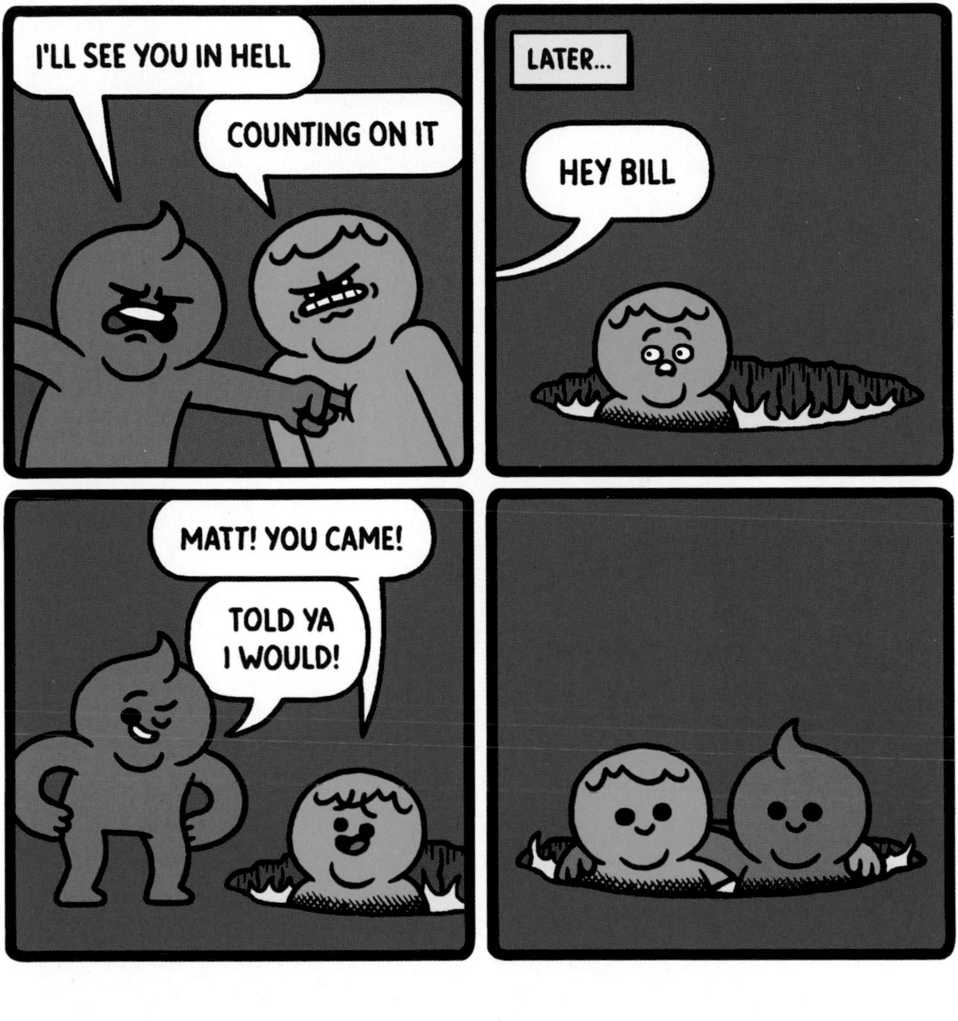
I'LL SEE YOU IN HELL
COUNTING ON IT
LATER...
HEY BILL
MATT! YOU CAME!
TOLD YA
I WOULD!

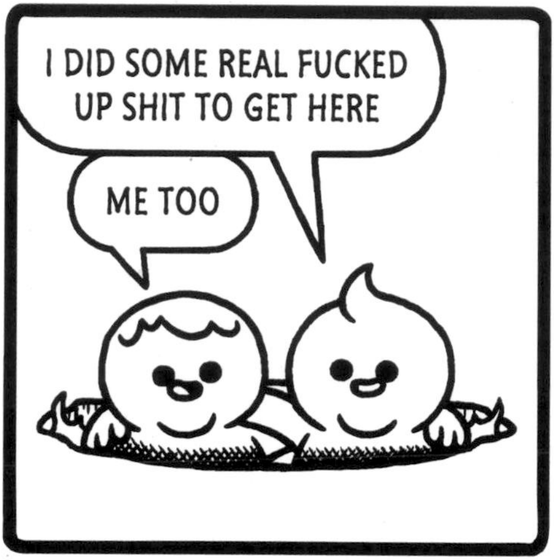
I DID SOME REAL FUCKED UP SHIT TO GET HERE
ME TOO

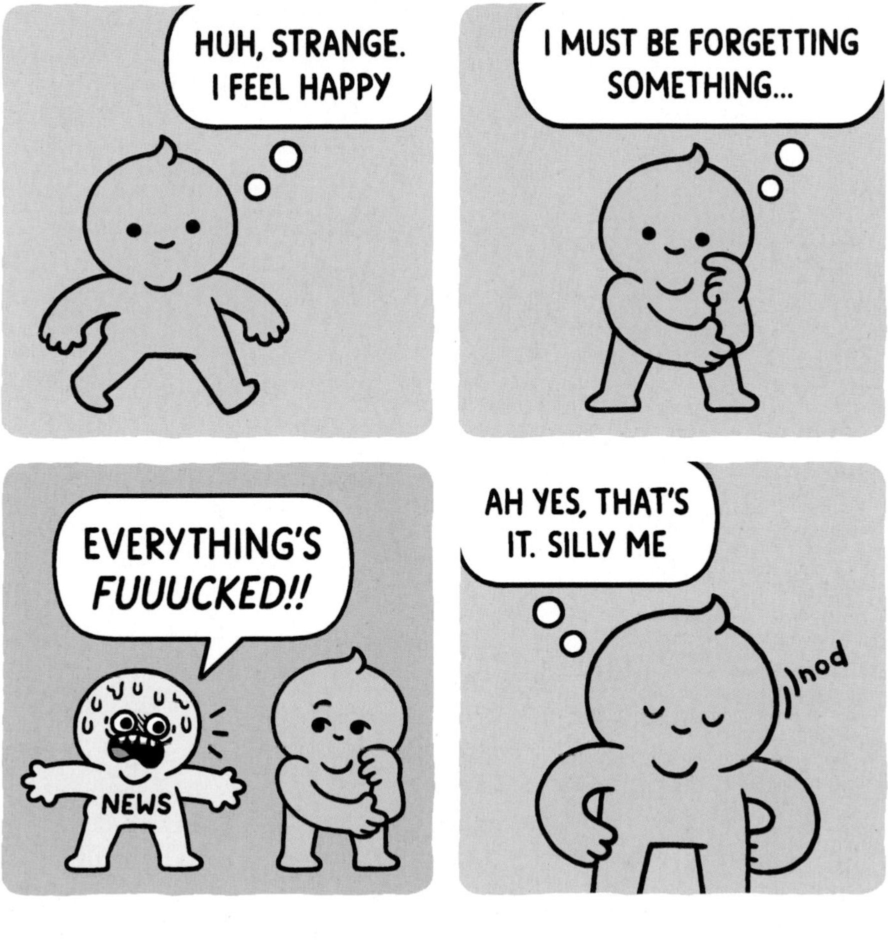
HUH, STRANGE. I FEEL HAPPY
I MUST BE FORGETTING SOMETHING...
EVERYTHING'S *FUUUCKED!!*
NEWS
AH YES, THAT'S IT. SILLY ME
nod

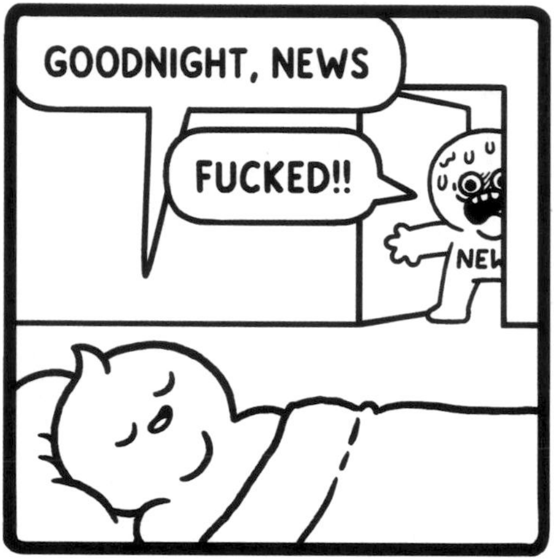
GOODNIGHT, NEWS
FUCKED!!
NEW

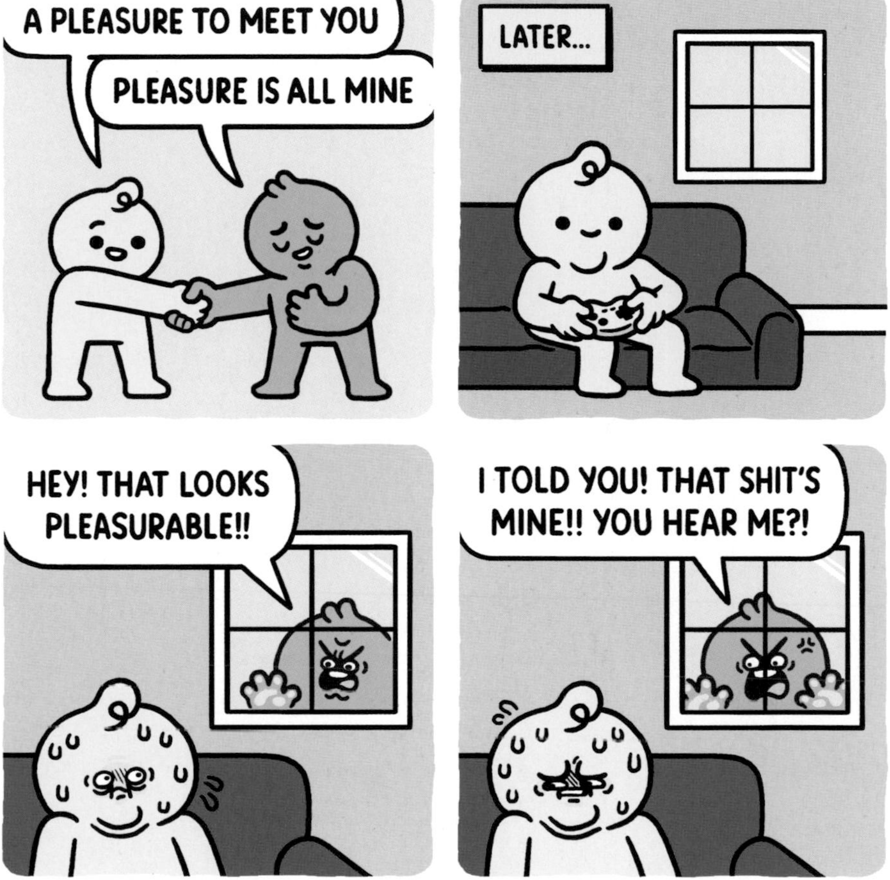
A PLEASURE TO MEET YOU
PLEASURE IS ALL MINE
LATER...
HEY! THAT LOOKS PLEASURABLE!!
I TOLD YOU! THAT SHIT'S MINE!! YOU HEAR ME?!

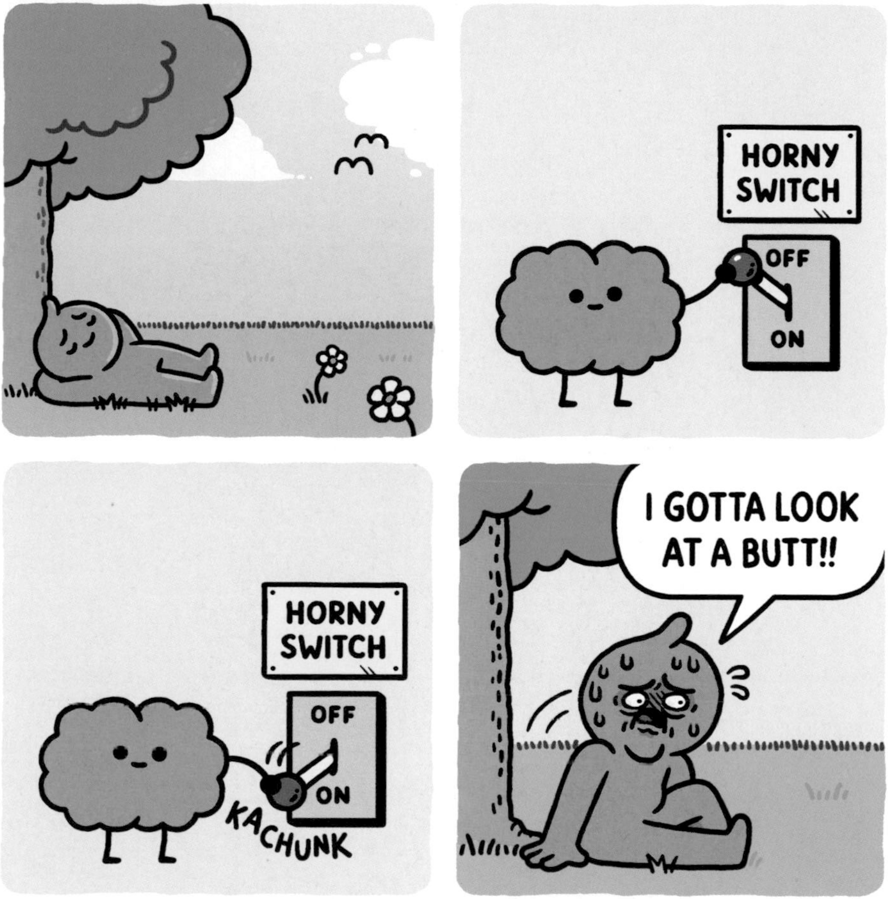
HORNY
SWITCH
OFF
ON
HORNY
SWITCH
OFF
ON
KACHUNK
I GOTTA LOOK AT A BUTT!!

PHEW!

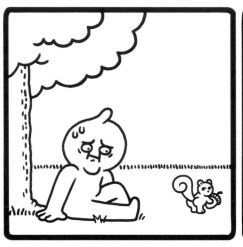

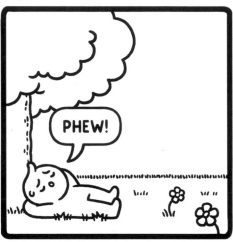

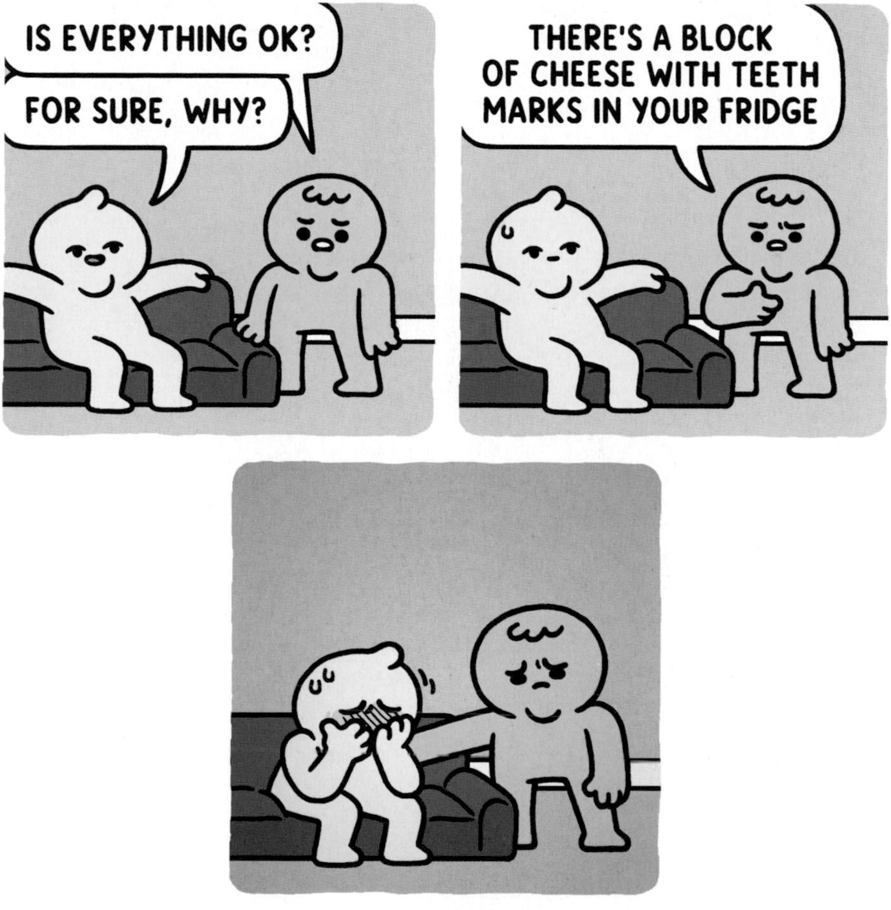
IS EVERYTHING OK?
FOR SURE, WHY?
THERE'S A BLOCK OF CHEESE WITH TEETH MARKS IN YOUR FRIDGE

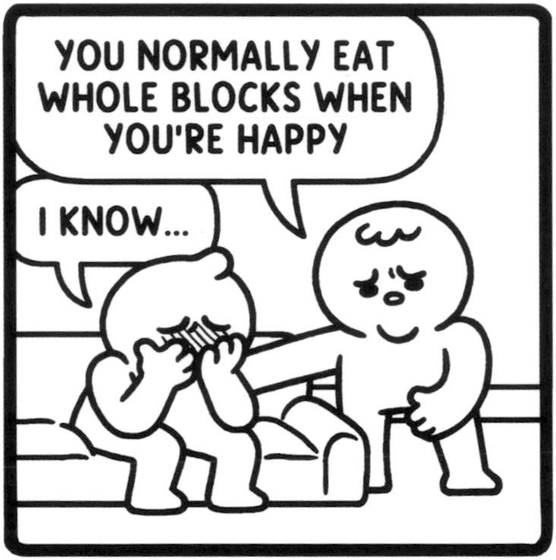
YOU NORMALLY EAT WHOLE BLOCKS WHEN YOU'RE HAPPY
I KNOW...

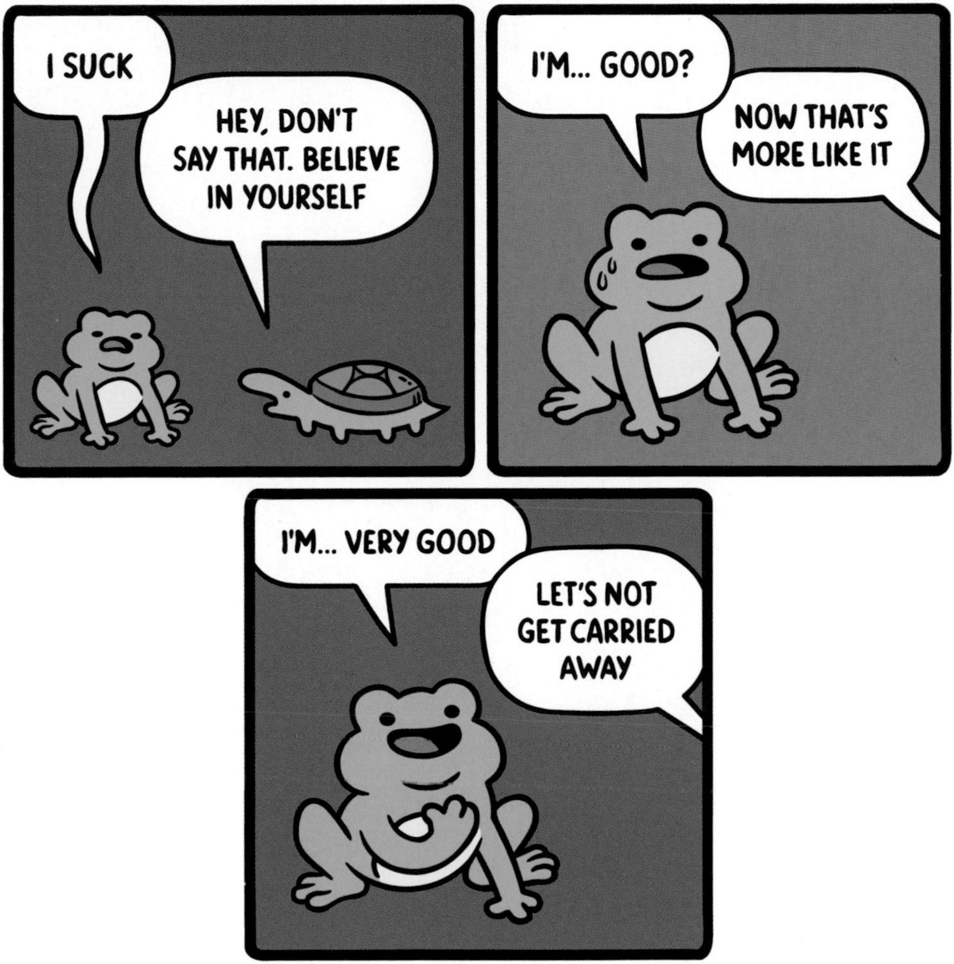

I SUCK
HEY, DON'T SAY THAT. BELIEVE IN YOURSELF
I'M... GOOD?
NOW THAT'S MORE LIKE IT
I'M... VERY GOOD
LET'S NOT GET CARRIED AWAY

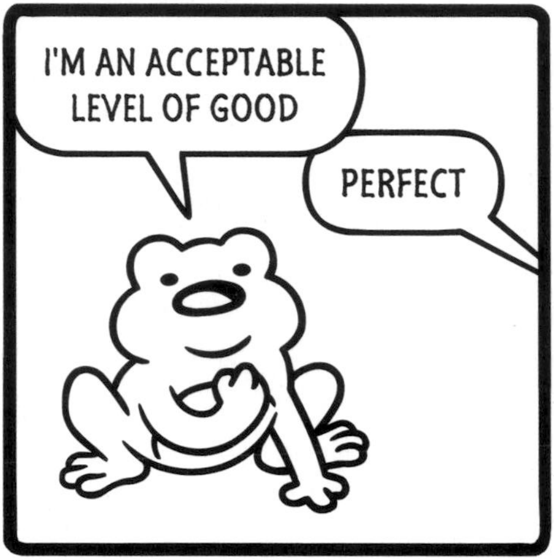
I'M AN ACCEPTABLE LEVEL OF GOOD
PERFECT

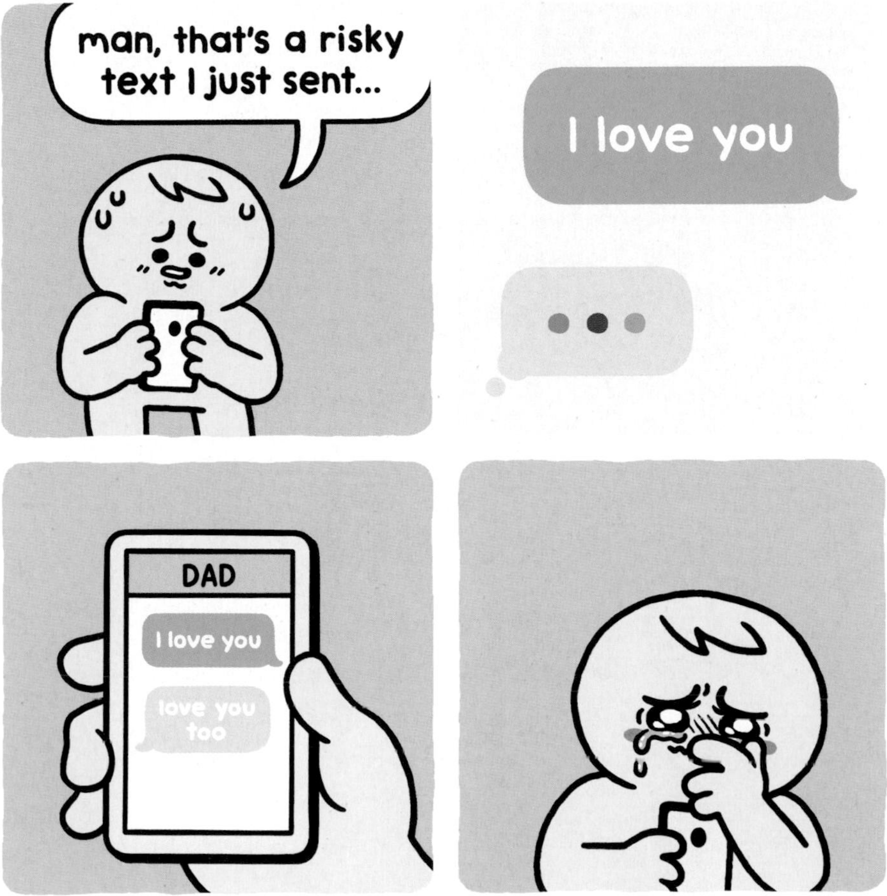
man, that's a risky text I just sent...
I love you
DAD
I love you
love you too

OMG, HE'S SENDING A PIC...
DAD
I got a new shirt
WORLD'S PROUDEST DAD

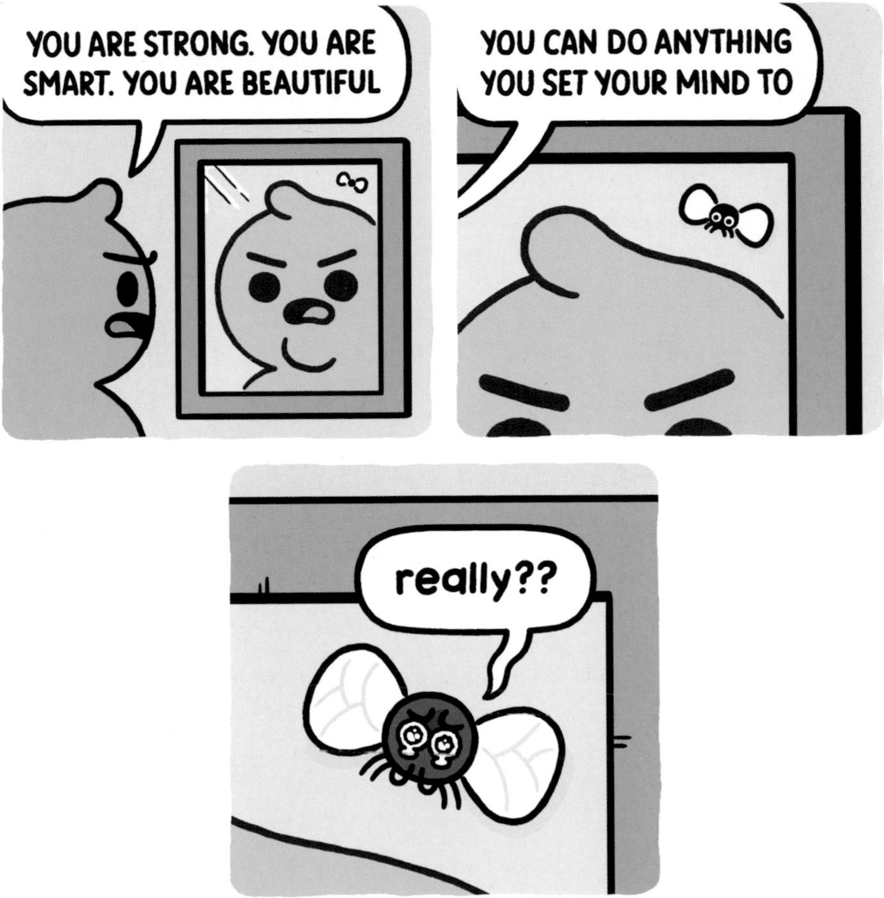
YOU ARE STRONG. YOU ARE SMART. YOU ARE BEAUTIFUL
YOU CAN DO ANYTHING YOU SET YOUR MIND TO
really??

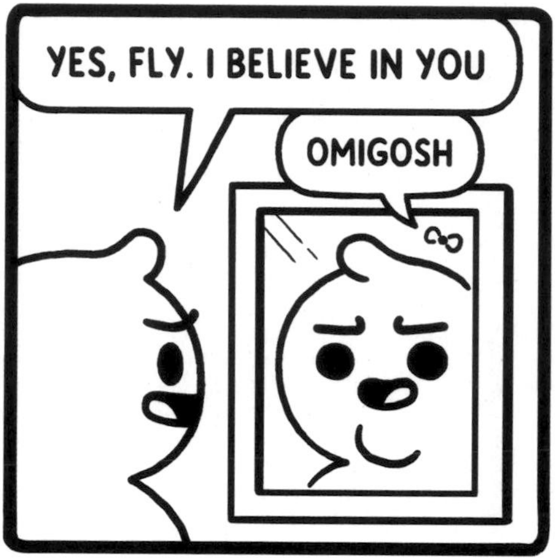
YES, FLY. I BELIEVE IN YOU
OMIGOSH

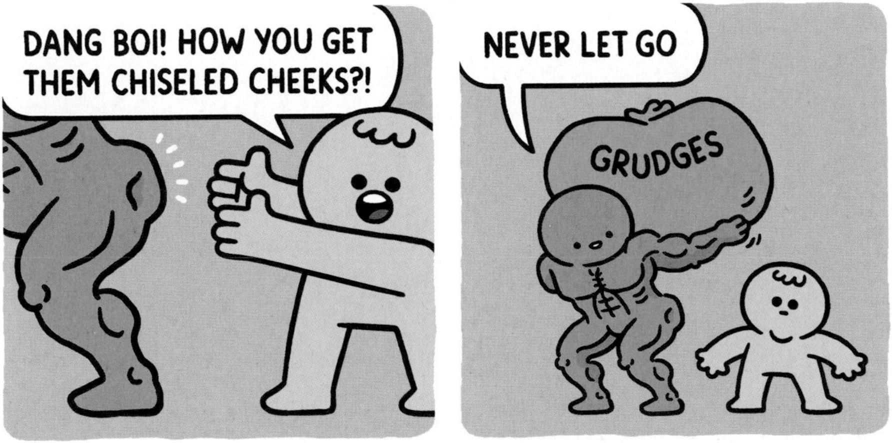
DANG BOI! HOW YOU GET THEM CHISELED CHEEKS?!
NEVER LET GO
GRUDGES

ISN'T THAT UNHEALTHY?
GRUDGES
WOW, THANKS FOR THE NEW GRUDGE. MY GLUTES FEEL STRONGER ALREADY

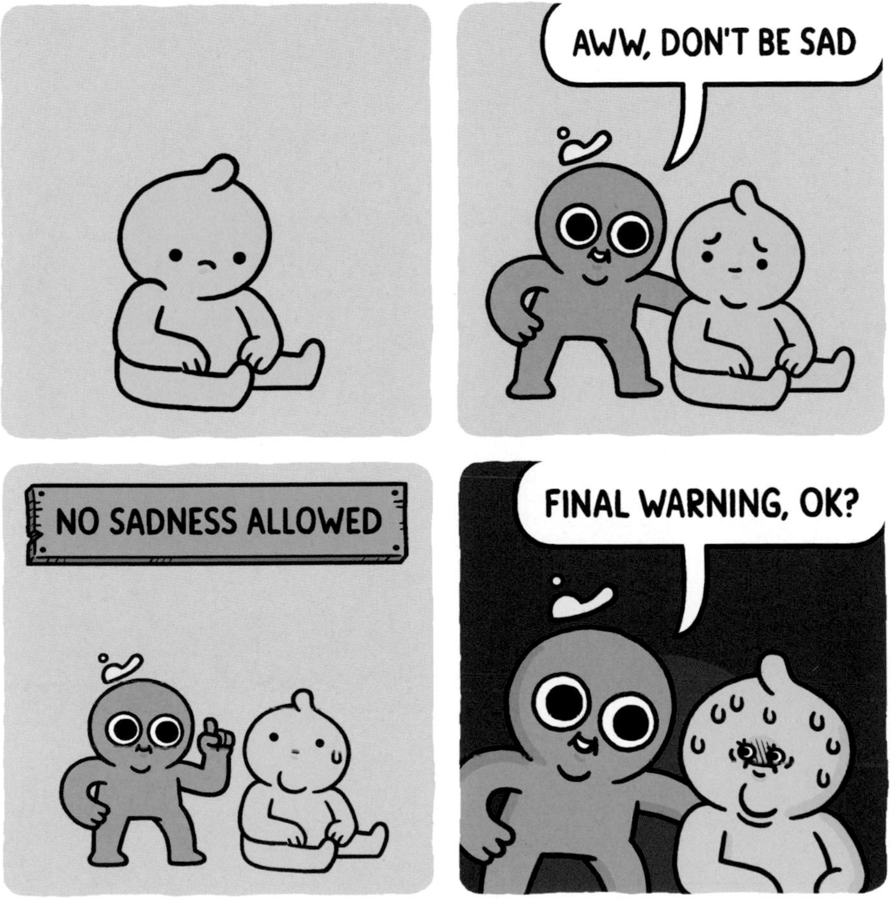
AWW, DON'T BE SAD
NO SADNESS ALLOWED
FINAL WARNING, OK?

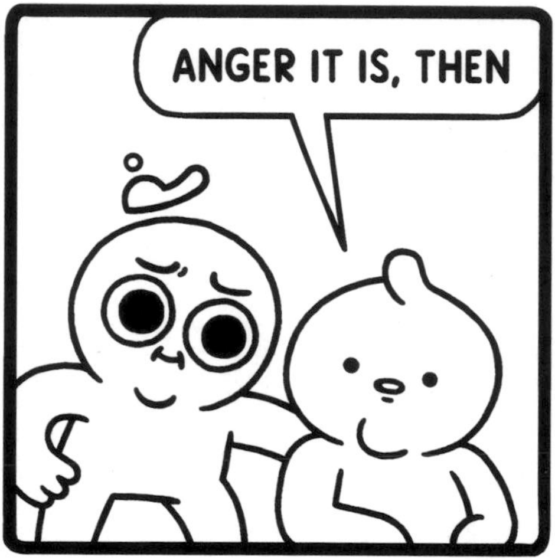
ANGER IT IS, THEN

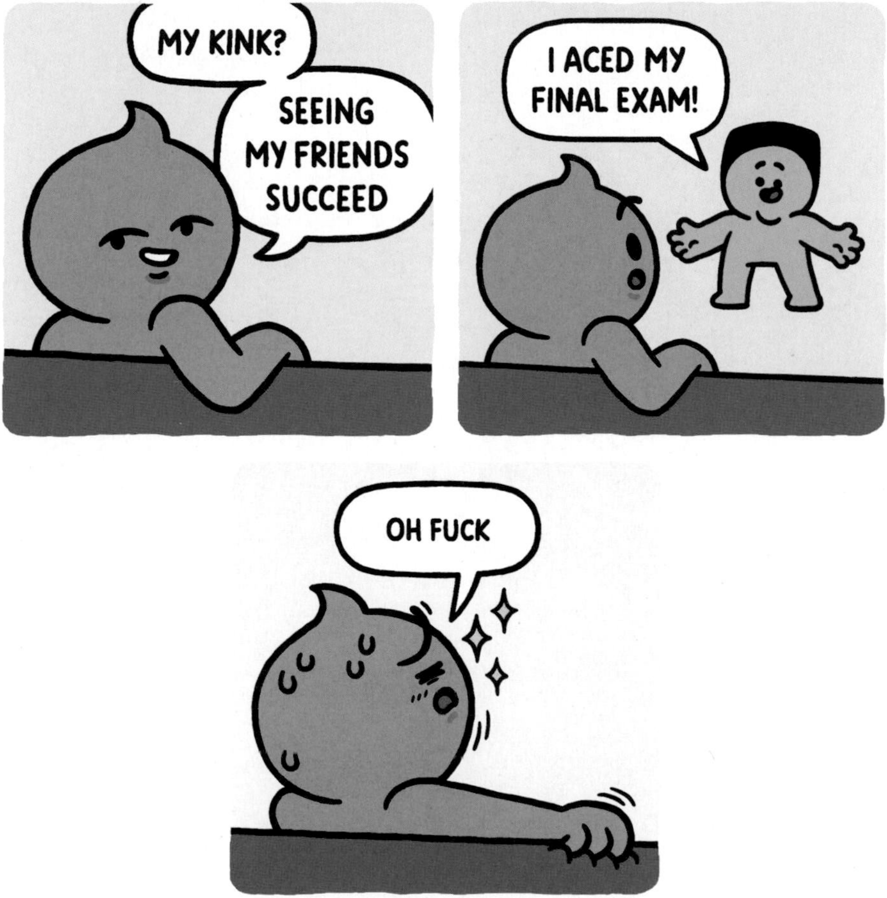
MY KINK?
SEEING MY FRIENDS SUCCEED
I ACED MY FINAL EXAM!
OH FUCK

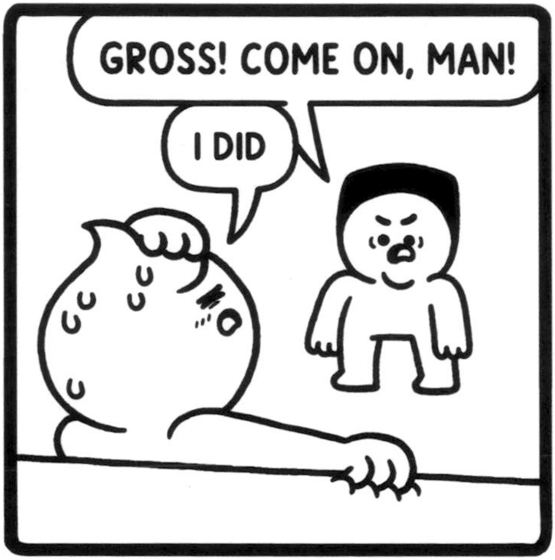
GROSS! COME ON, MAN!
I DID

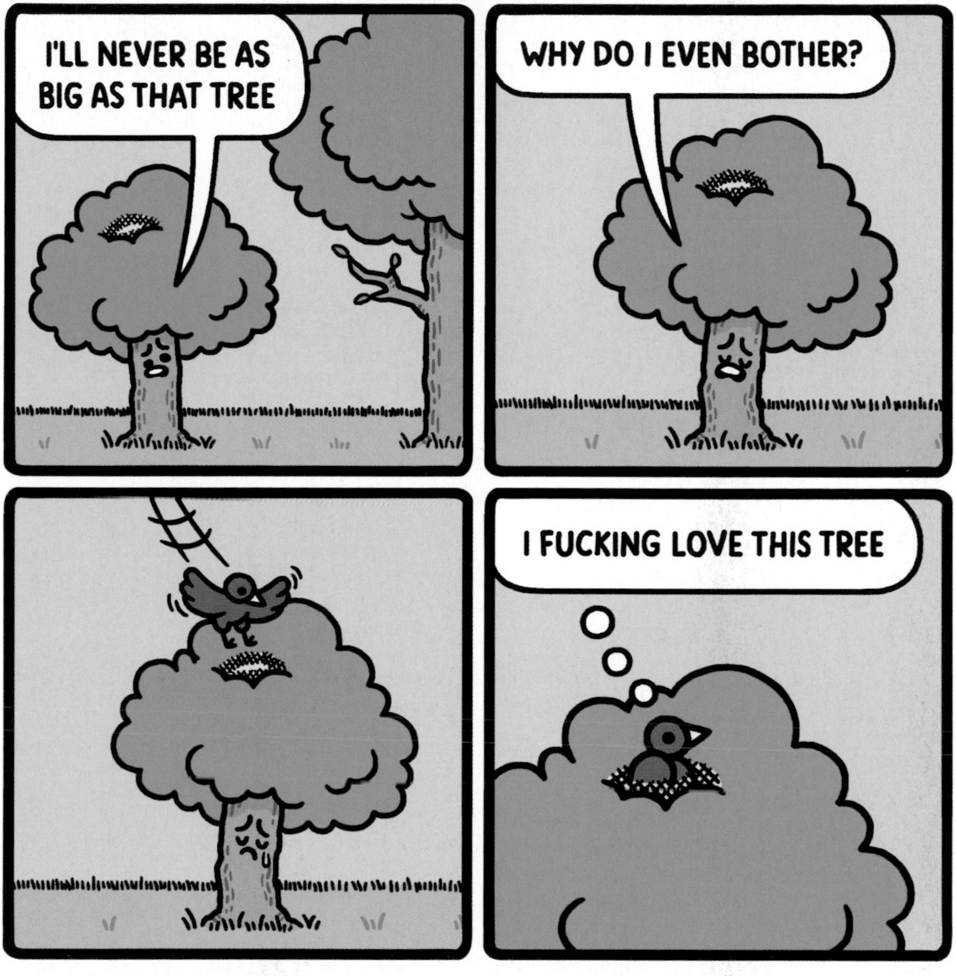
I'LL NEVER BE AS BIG AS THAT TREE
WHY DO I EVEN BOTHER?
I FUCKING LOVE THIS TREE

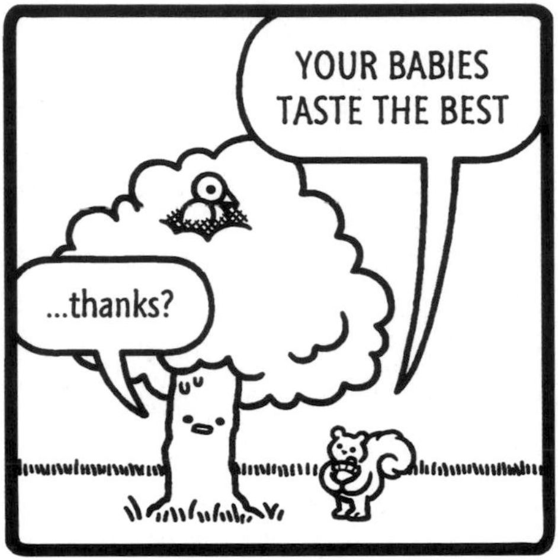
YOUR BABIES TASTE THE BEST
...thanks?

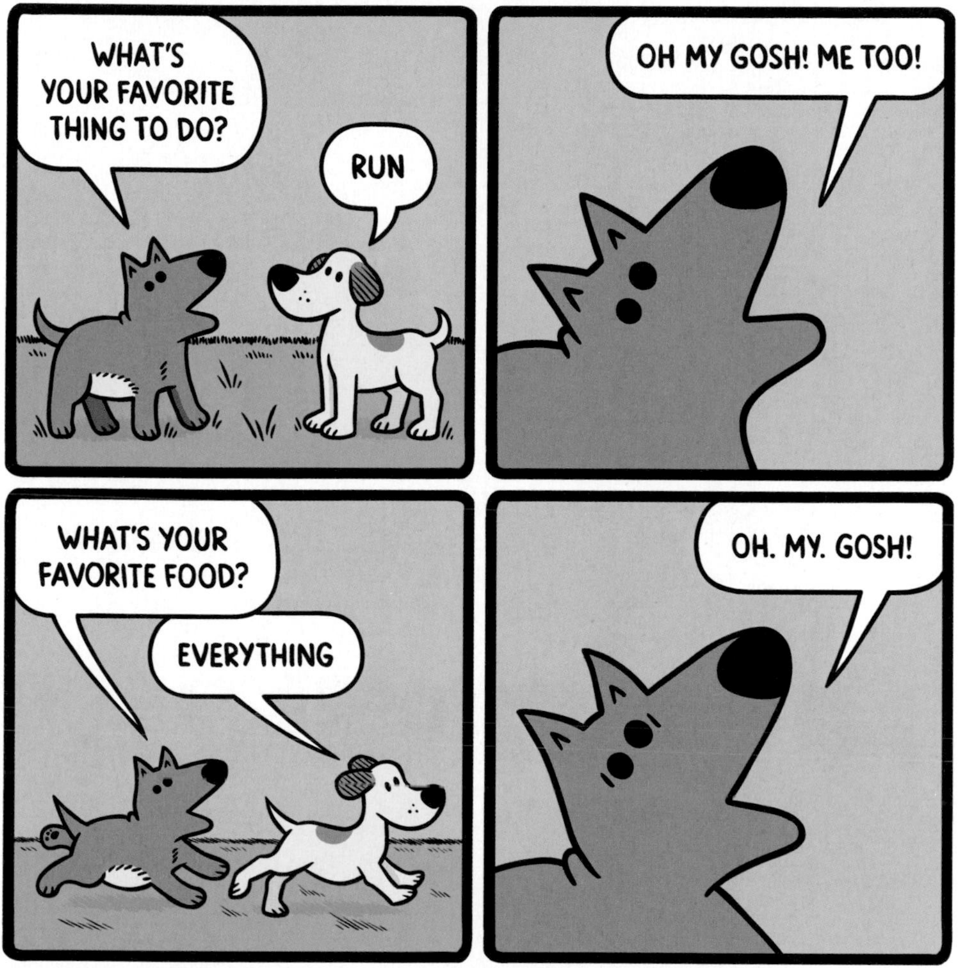
WHAT'S YOUR FAVORITE THING TO DO?
RUN
OH MY GOSH! ME TOO!
WHAT'S YOUR FAVORITE FOOD?
EVERYTHING
OH. MY. GOSH!

DO YOU LIKE TO BARK?
IT'S MY FAVORITE THING

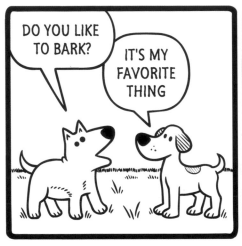

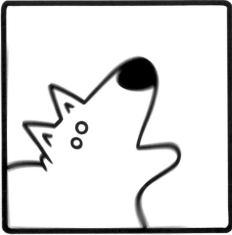

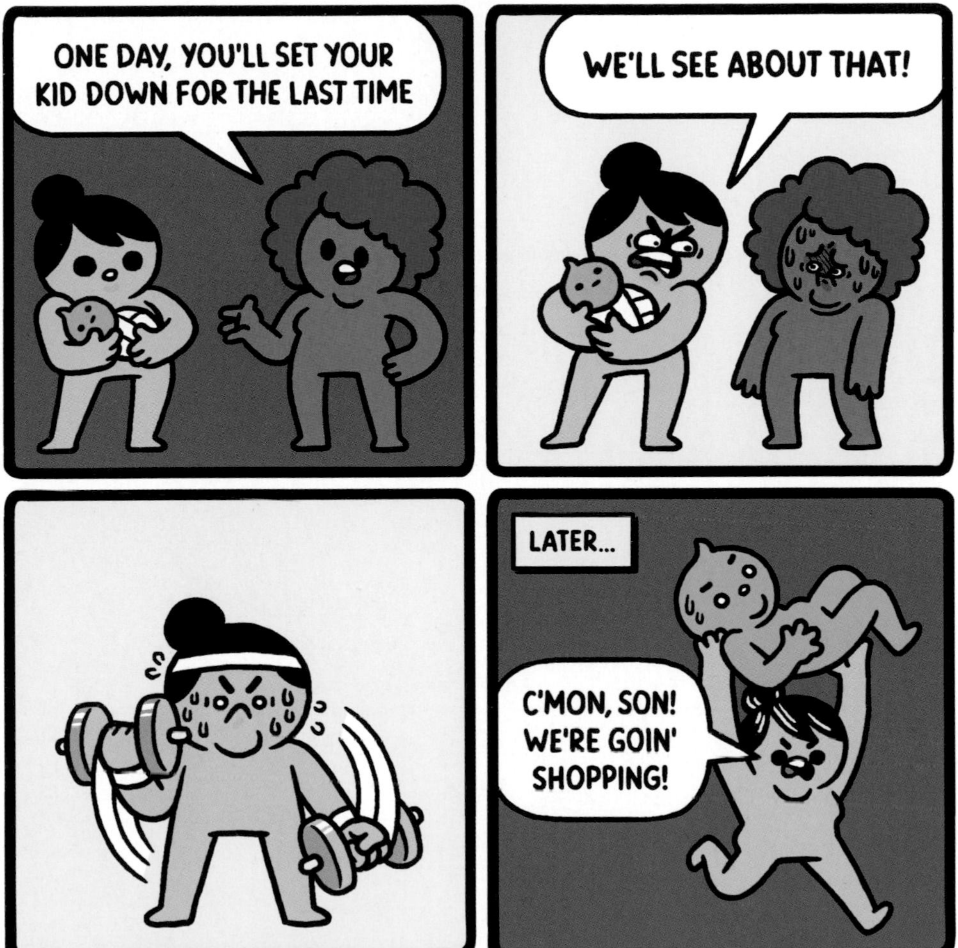
ONE DAY, YOU'LL SET YOUR KID DOWN FOR THE LAST TIME
WE'LL SEE ABOUT THAT!
LATER...
C'MON, SON! WE'RE GOIN' SHOPPING!

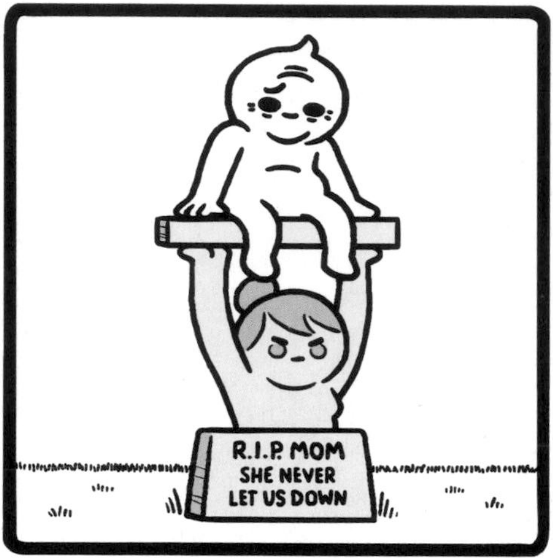
R.I.P. MOM
SHE NEVER
LET US DOWN

BUG CLASS REUNION

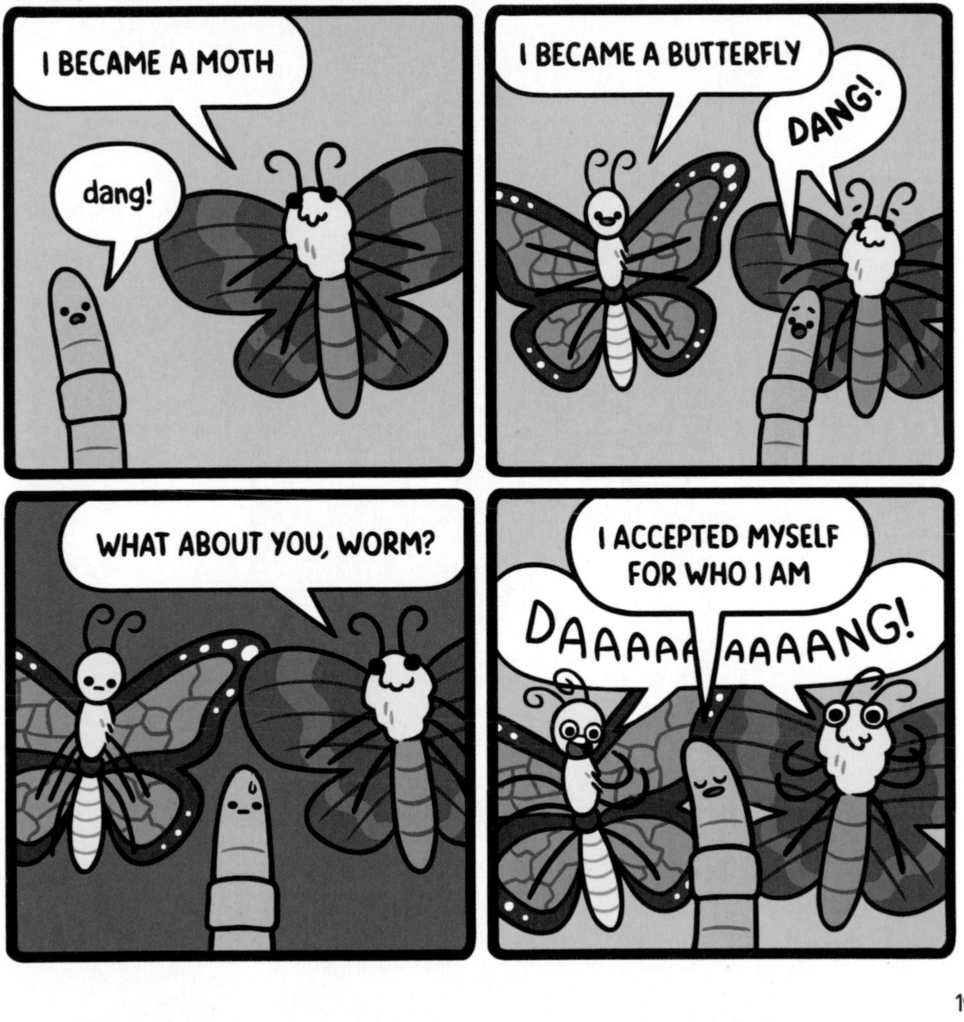
I BECAME A MOTH
dang!
I BECAME A BUTTERFLY
DANG!
WHAT ABOUT YOU, WORM?
I ACCEPTED MYSELF FOR WHO I AM
DAAAAA AAAANG!

I ALSO ATE A DEAD BODY

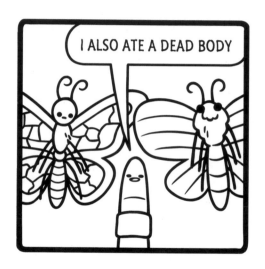

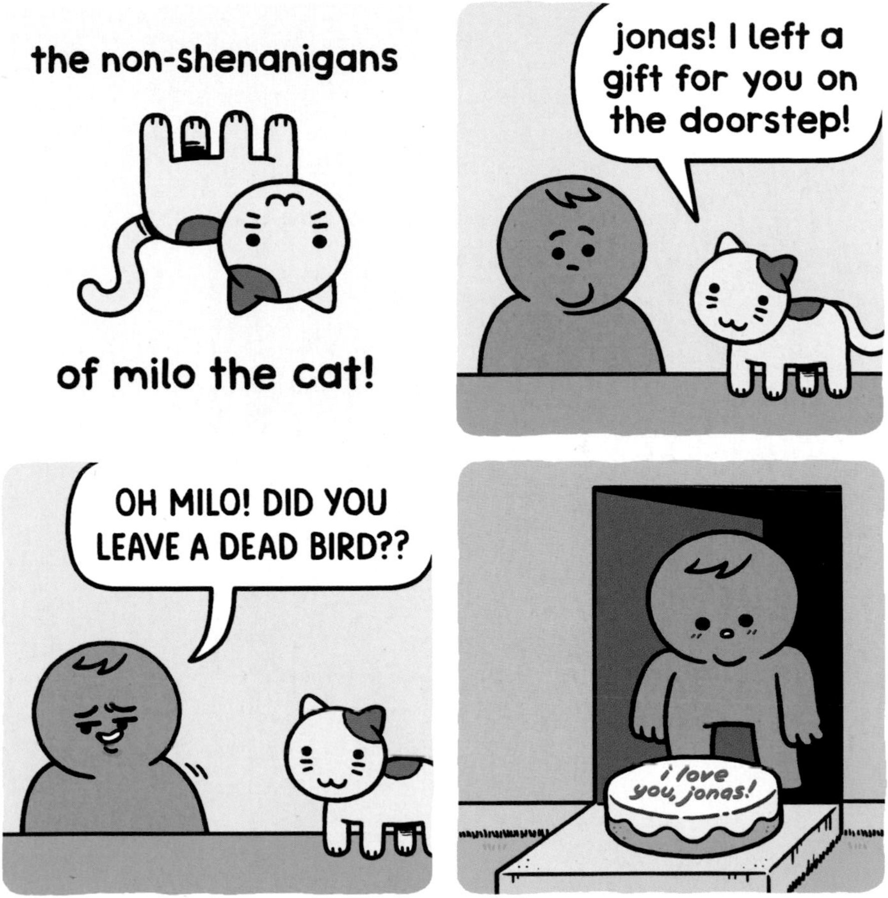
the non-shenanigans
of milo the cat!
jonas! I left a gift for you on the doorstep!
OH MILO! DID YOU LEAVE A DEAD BIRD??
i love you, jonas!

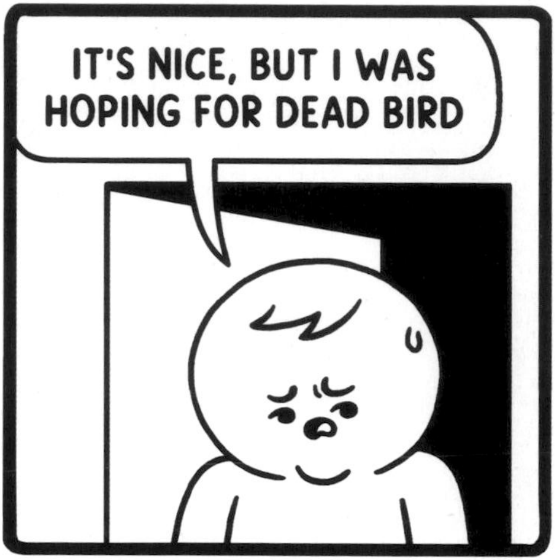
IT'S NICE, BUT I WAS HOPING FOR DEAD BIRD

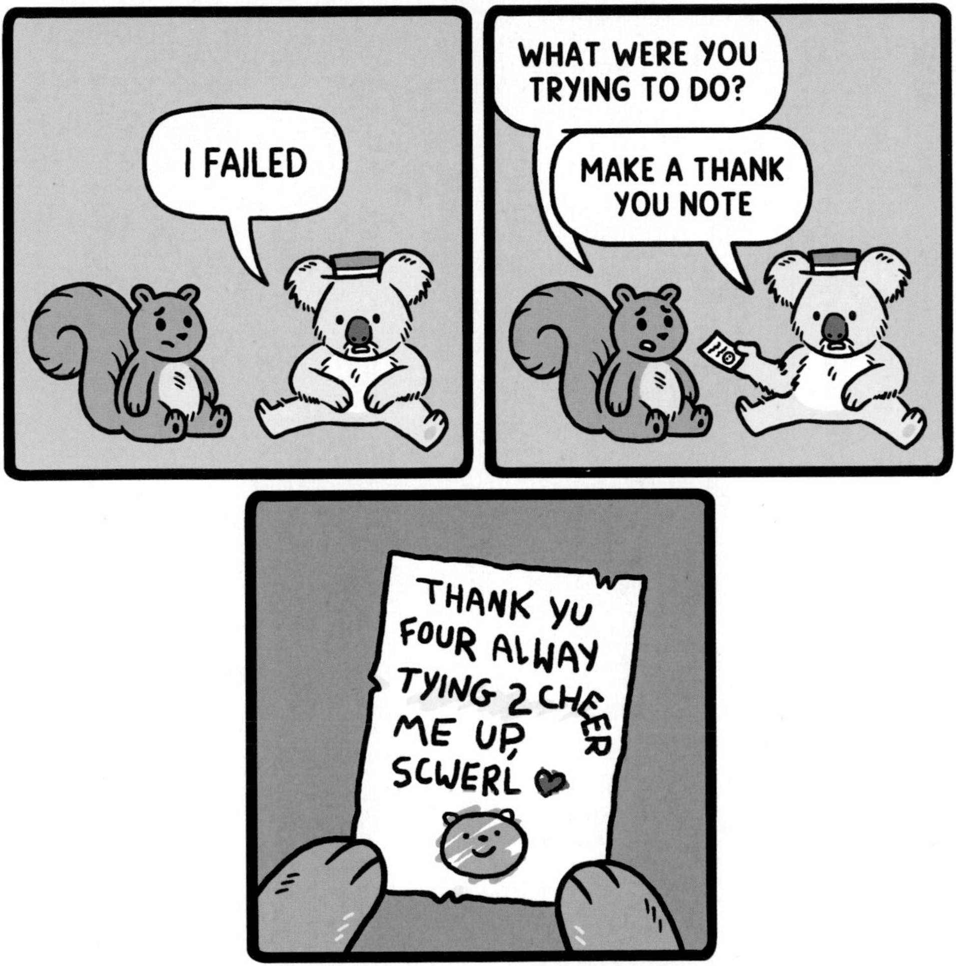
I FAILED
WHAT WERE YOU TRYING TO DO?
MAKE A THANK YOU NOTE
THANK YU FOUR ALWAY TYING 2 CHEER ME UP, SCWERL

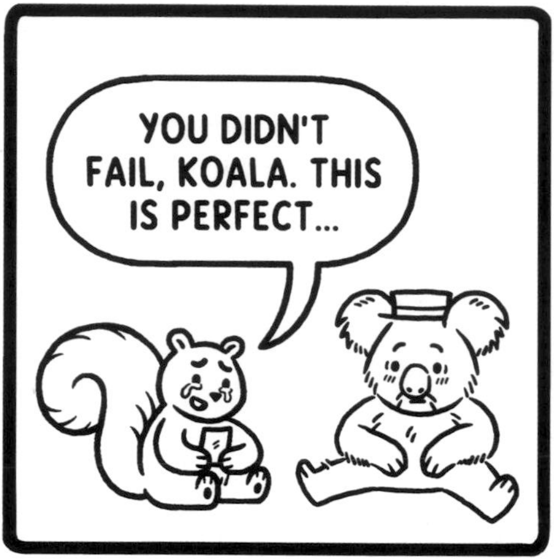
YOU DIDN'T FAIL, KOALA. THIS IS PERFECT...

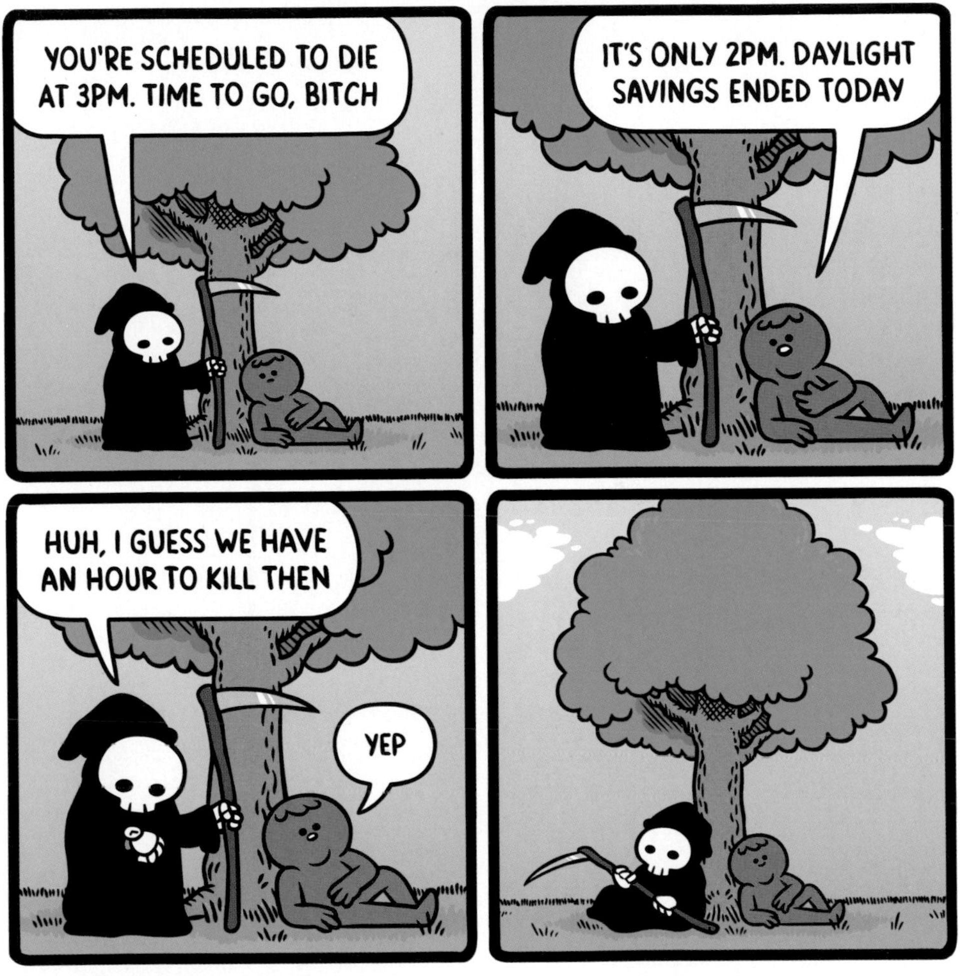
YOU'RE SCHEDULED TO DIE AT 3PM. TIME TO GO, BITCH
IT'S ONLY 2PM. DAYLIGHT SAVINGS ENDED TODAY
HUH, I GUESS WE HAVE AN HOUR TO KILL THEN
YEP

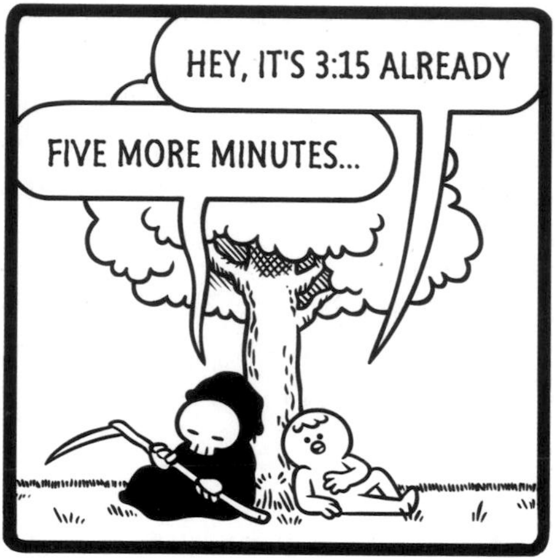
HEY, IT'S 3:15 ALREADY
FIVE MORE MINUTES...

BOOK EXCLUSIVE COMICS

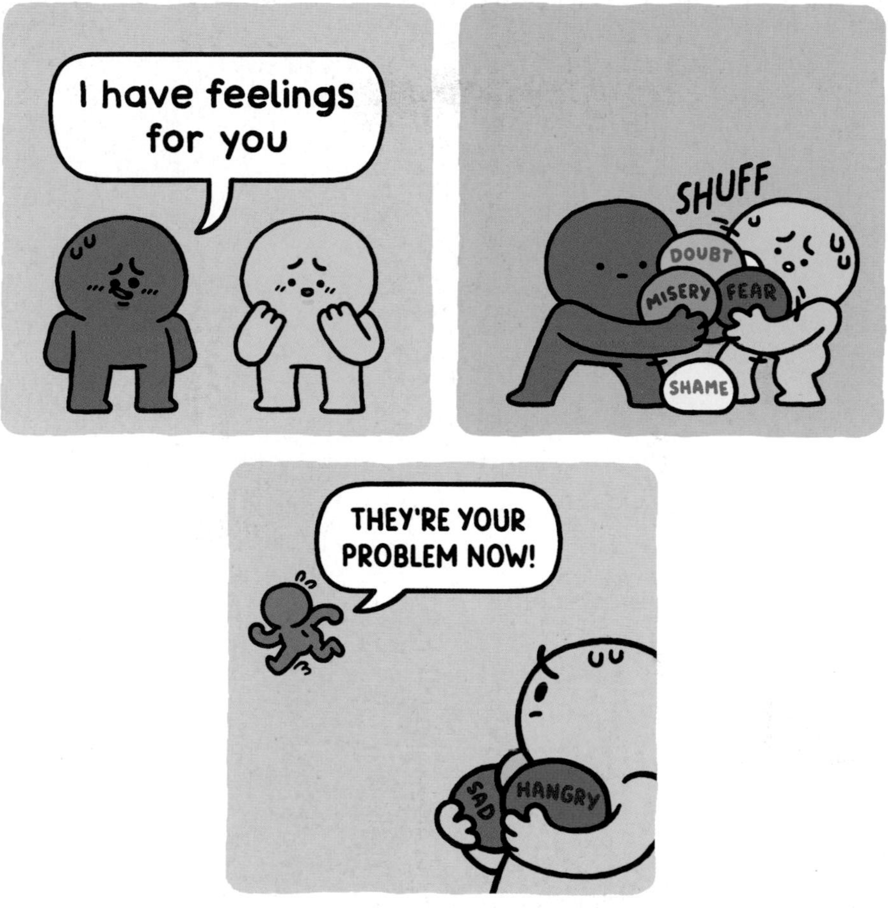
I have feelings for you
SHUFF
DOUBT
MISERY
FEAR
SHAME
THEY'RE YOUR PROBLEM NOW!
SAD
HANGRY

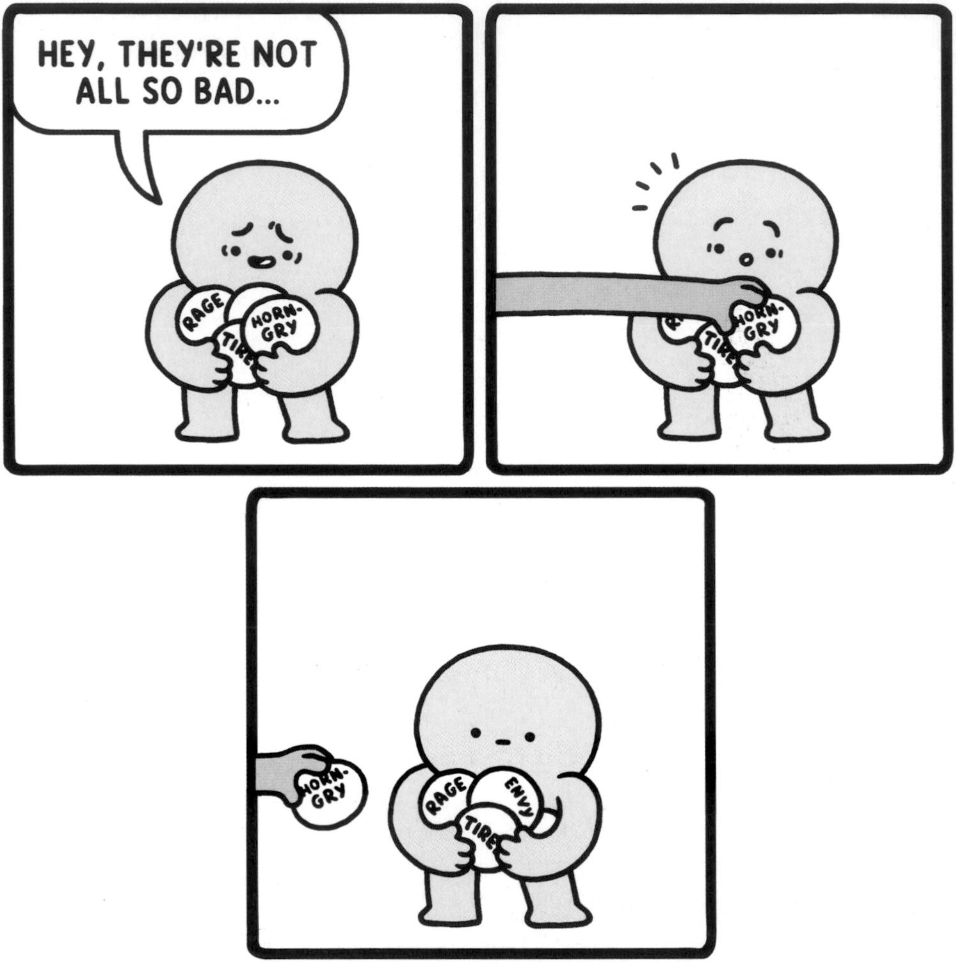
HEY, THEY'RE NOT ALL SO BAD...
RAGE
TIRE
HORN-GRY
TIRE
HORN-GRY
HORN-GRY
RAGE
ENVY
TIRE

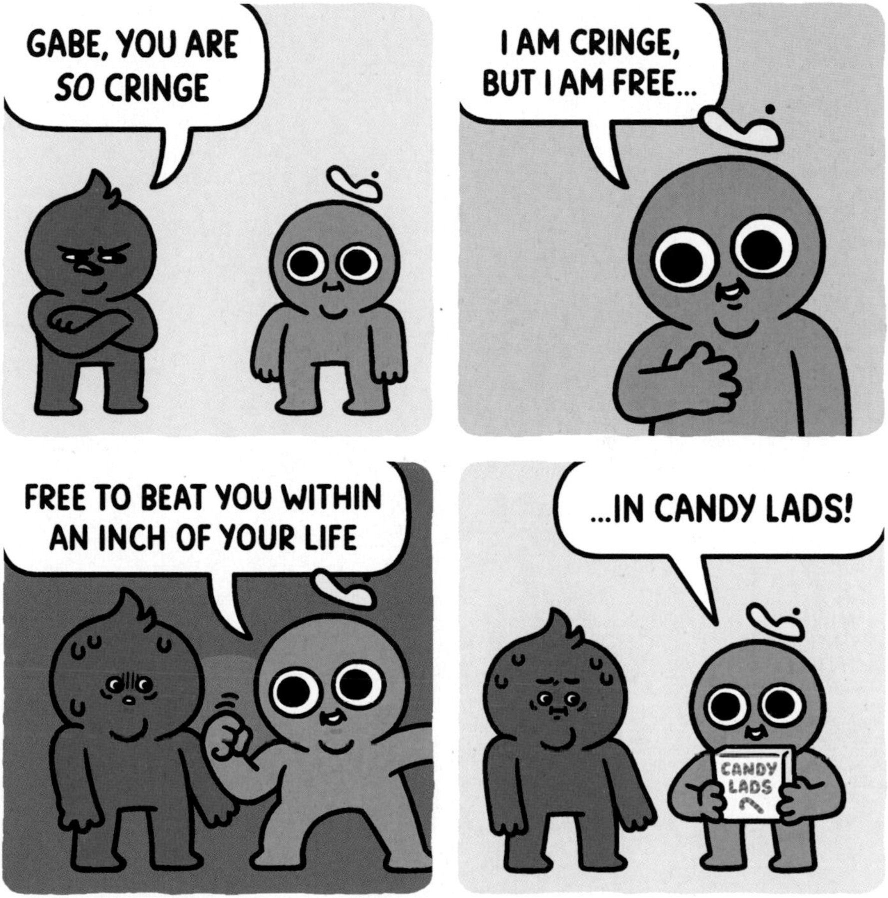
GABE, YOU ARE *SO* CRINGE
I AM CRINGE, BUT I AM FREE...
FREE TO BEAT YOU WITHIN AN INCH OF YOUR LIFE
...IN CANDY LADS!
CANDY LADS

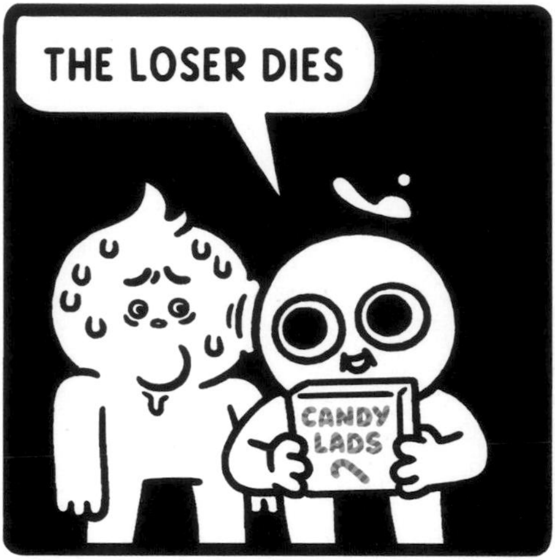
THE LOSER DIES
CANDY LADS

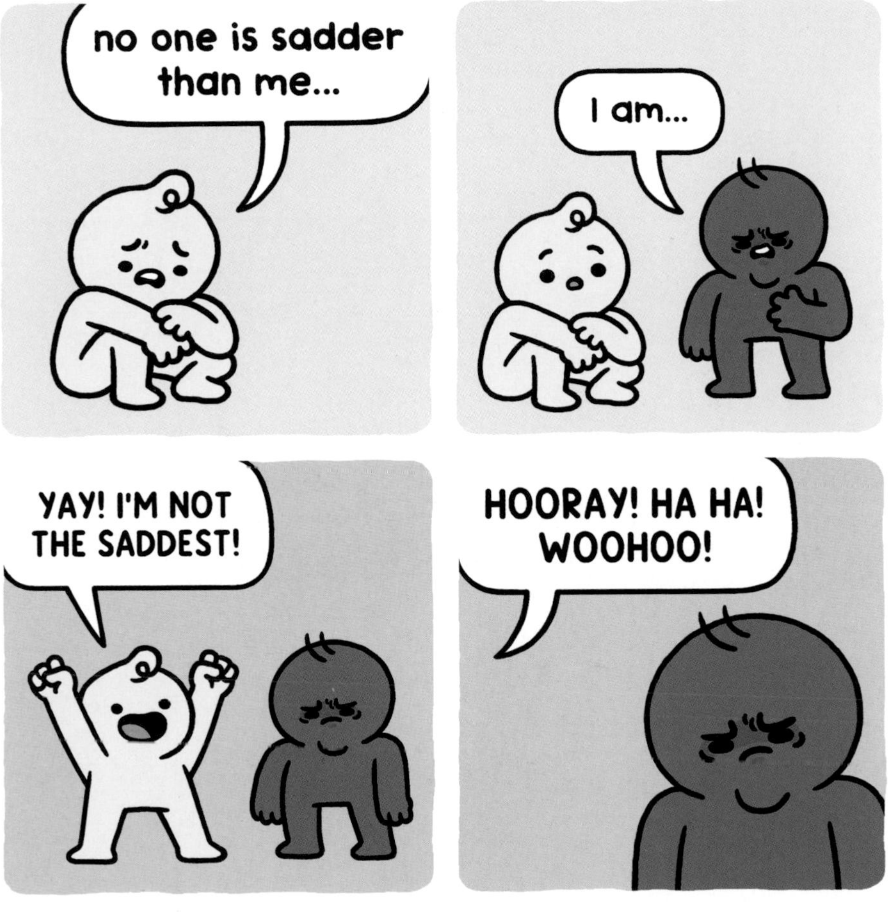
no one is sadder than me...
I am...
YAY! I'M NOT THE SADDEST!
HOORAY! HA HA! WOOHOO!

NO... I AM THE SADDEST...
YIPPEE!!

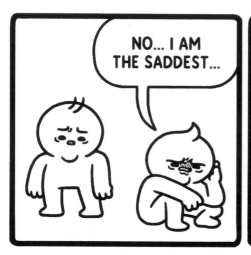

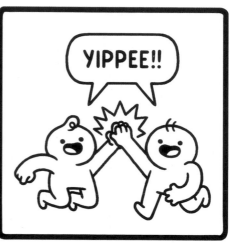

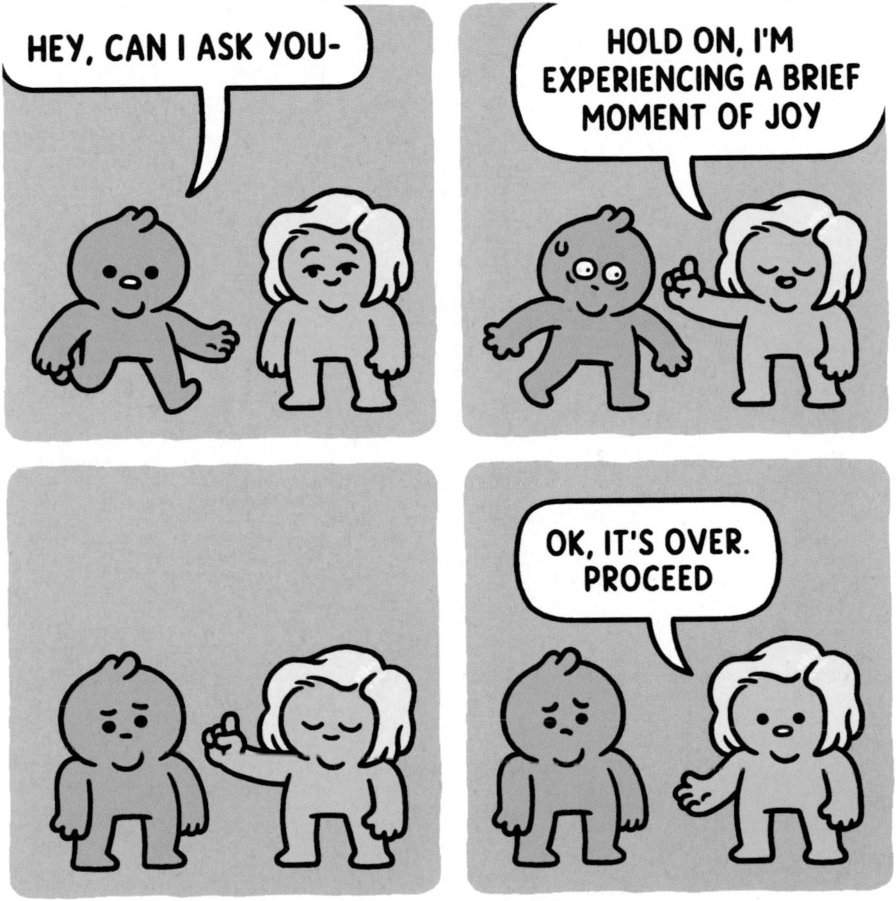
HEY, CAN I ASK YOU-
HOLD ON, I'M EXPERIENCING A BRIEF MOMENT OF JOY
OK, IT'S OVER. PROCEED

LATER...
OH, THE JOY IS COMING BACK!
AND IT'S GONE AGAIN

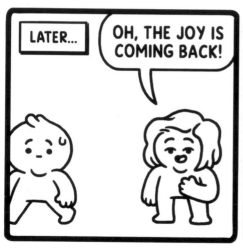

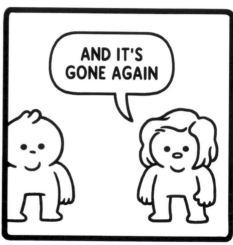

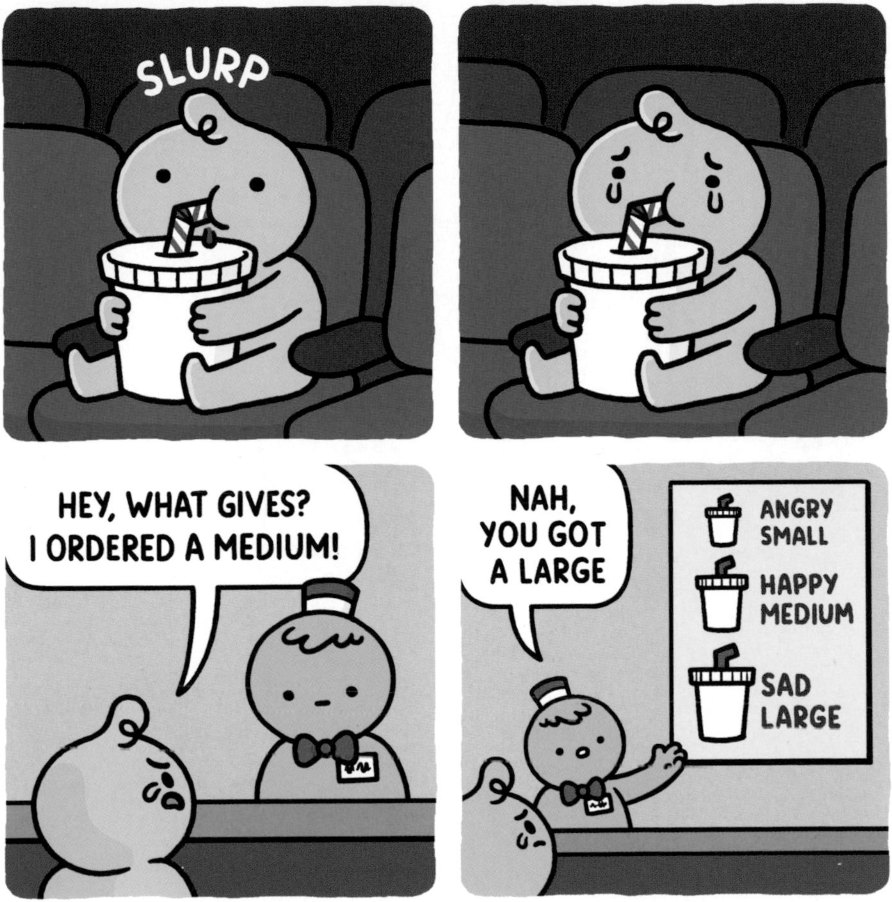
SLURP
HEY, WHAT GIVES? I ORDERED A MEDIUM!
NAH, YOU GOT A LARGE
ANGRY SMALL
HAPPY MEDIUM
SAD LARGE

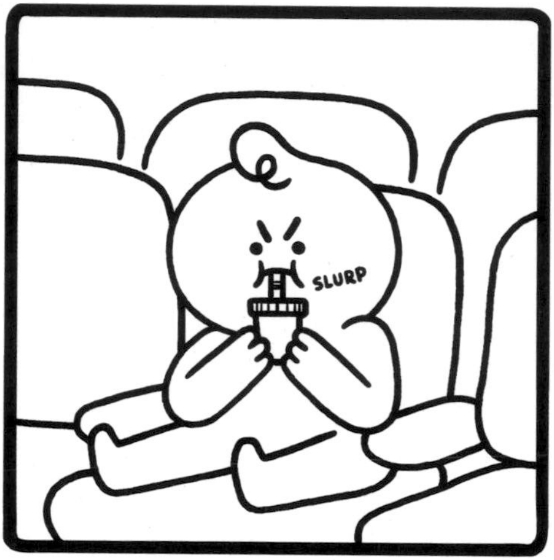
SLURP

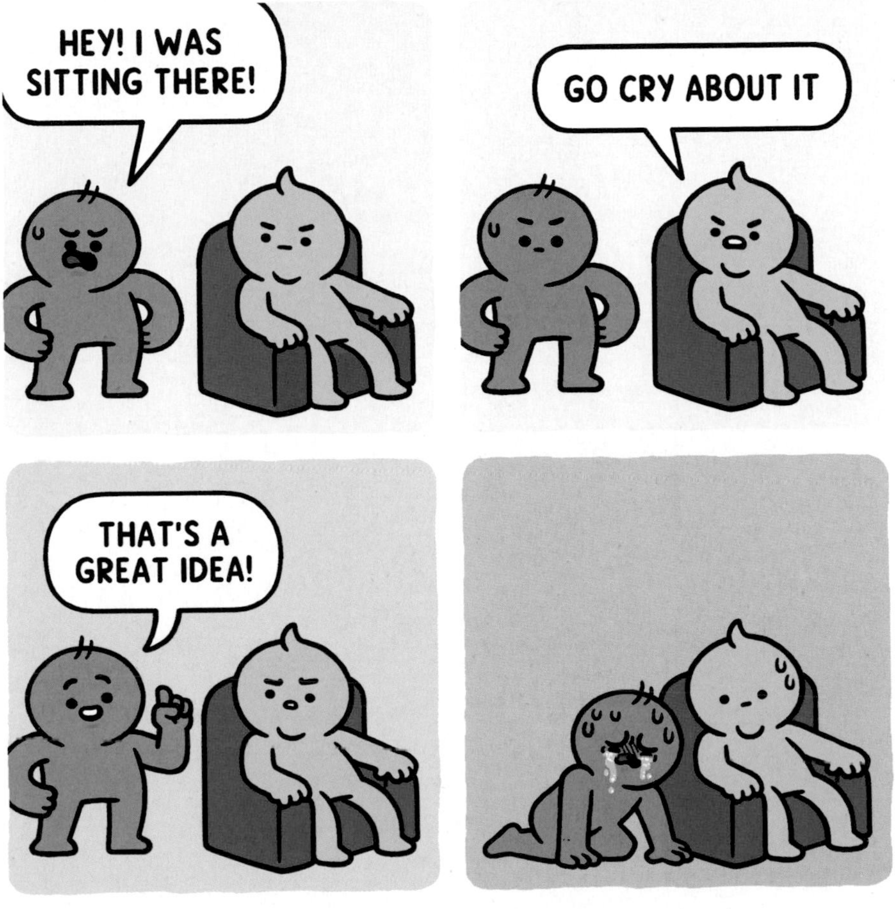
HEY! I WAS SITTING THERE!
GO CRY ABOUT IT
THAT'S A GREAT IDEA!

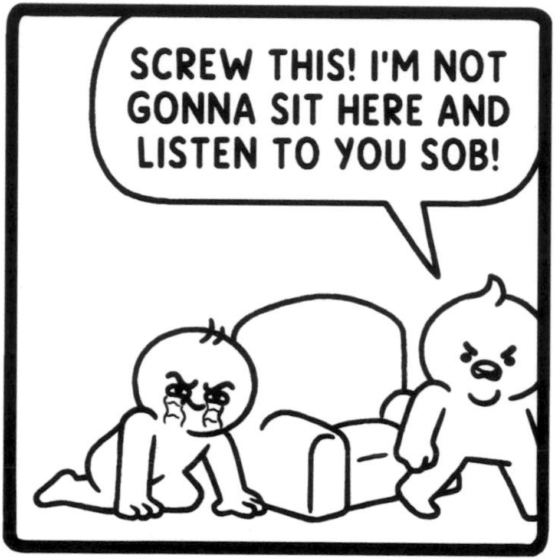
SCREW THIS! I'M NOT GONNA SIT HERE AND LISTEN TO YOU SOB!

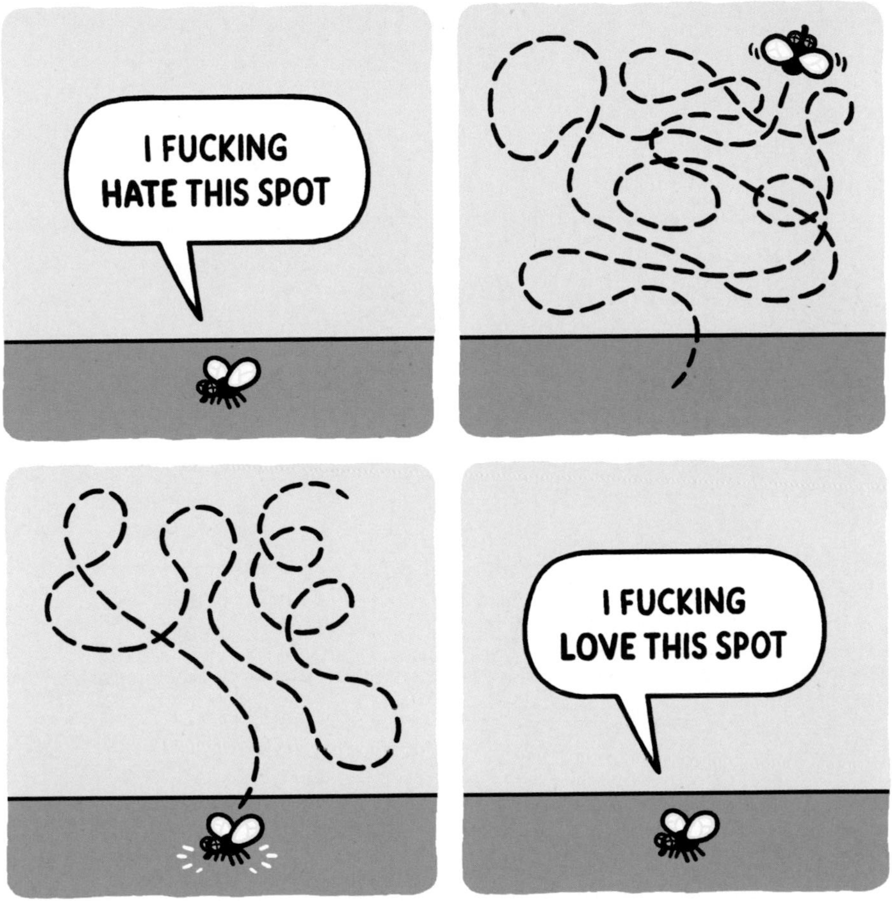
I FUCKING HATE THIS SPOT
I FUCKING LOVE THIS SPOT

THIS WAS MY DAD'S FAVORITE SPOT
THAT'S SWEET
HE FUCKING HATED IT

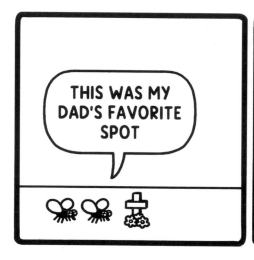

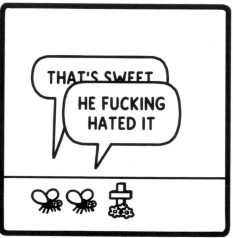

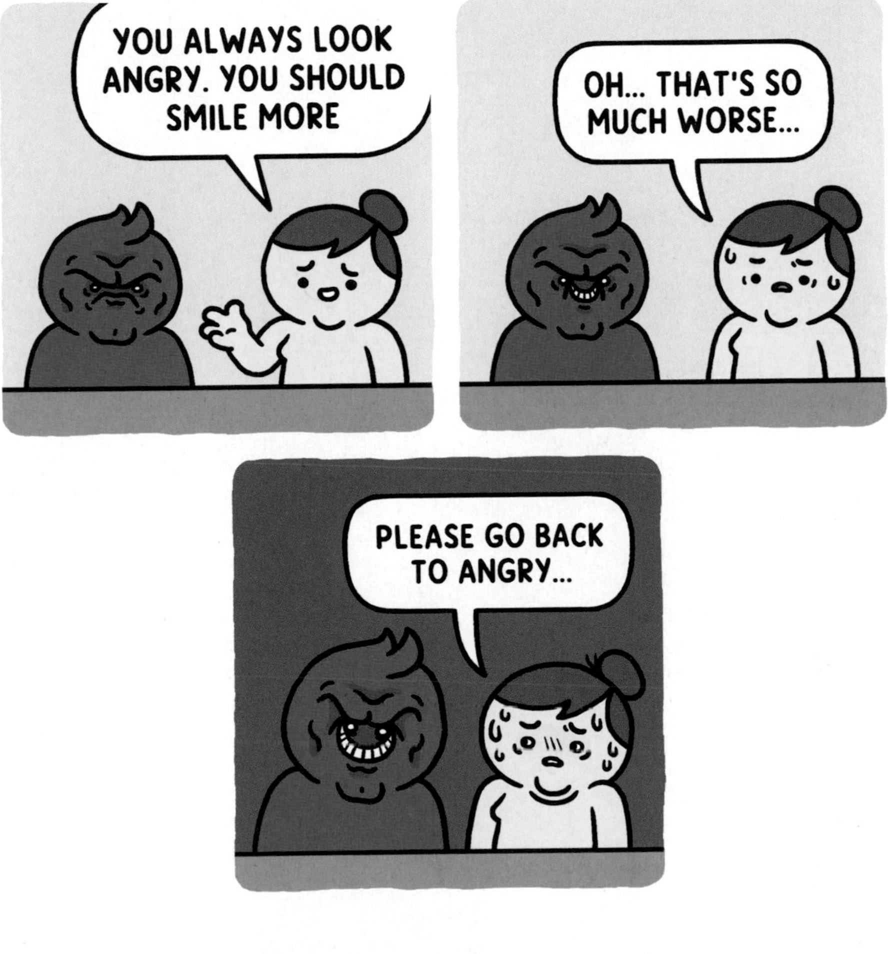
YOU ALWAYS LOOK ANGRY. YOU SHOULD SMILE MORE
OH... THAT'S SO MUCH WORSE...
PLEASE GO BACK TO ANGRY...

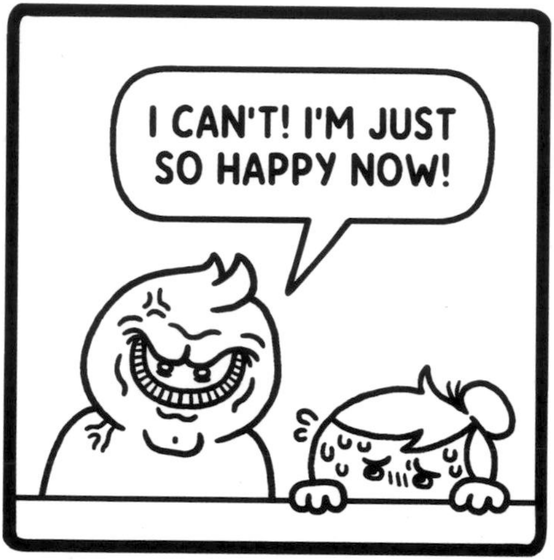
I CAN'T! I'M JUST SO HAPPY NOW!

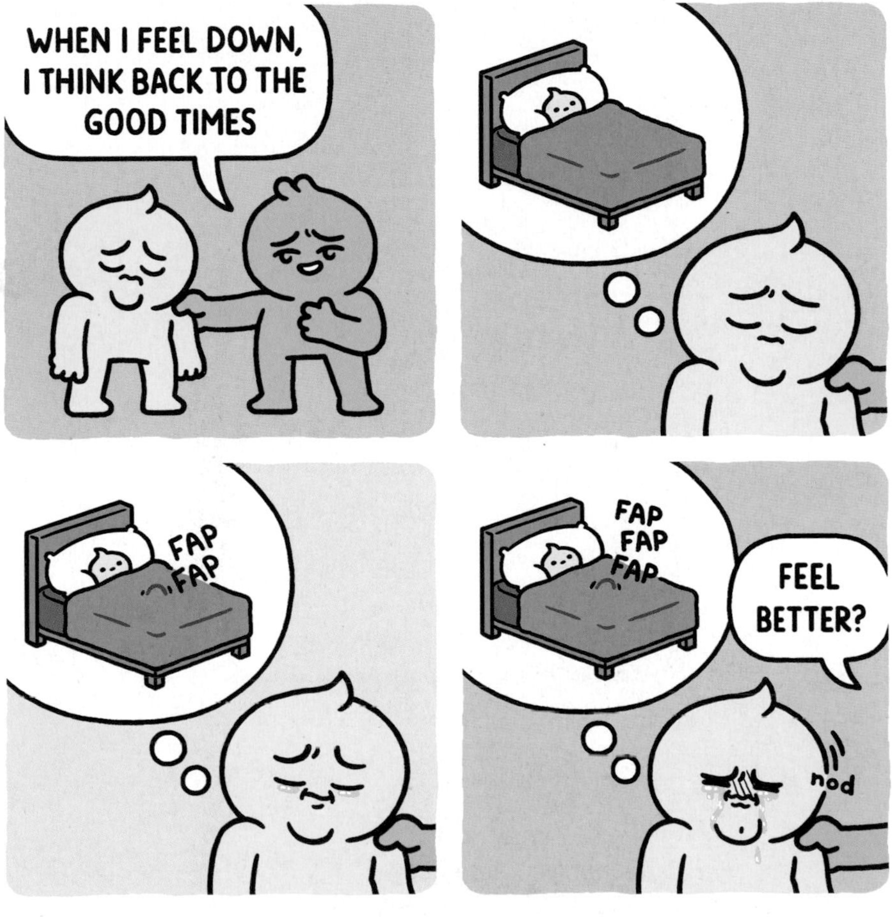
WHEN I FEEL DOWN, I THINK BACK TO THE GOOD TIMES
FAP FAP
FAP FAP FAP
FEEL BETTER?
nod

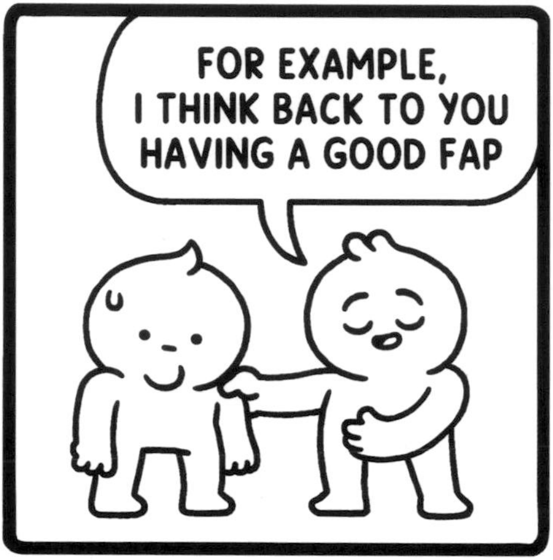
FOR EXAMPLE,
I THINK BACK TO YOU
HAVING A GOOD FAP

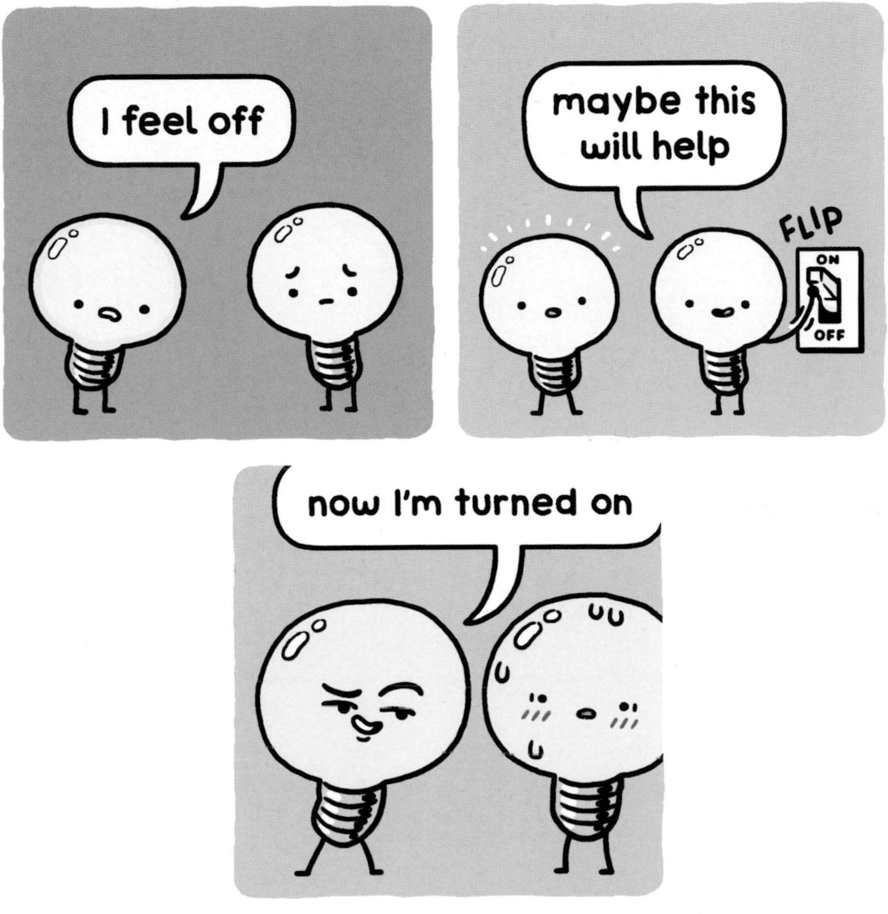
I feel off
maybe this will help
FLIP
ON
OFF
now I'm turned on

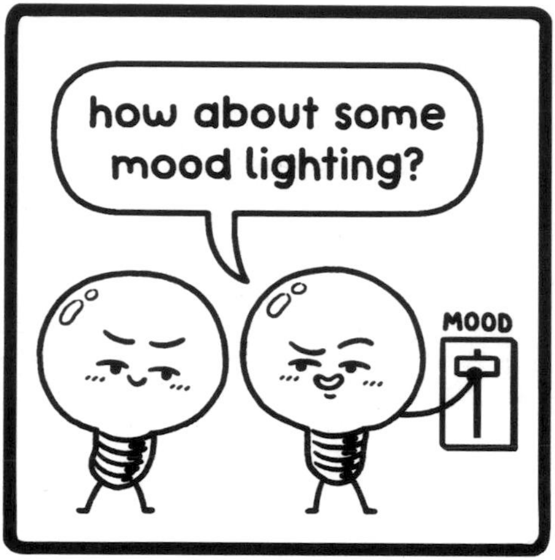
how about some mood lighting?
MOOD

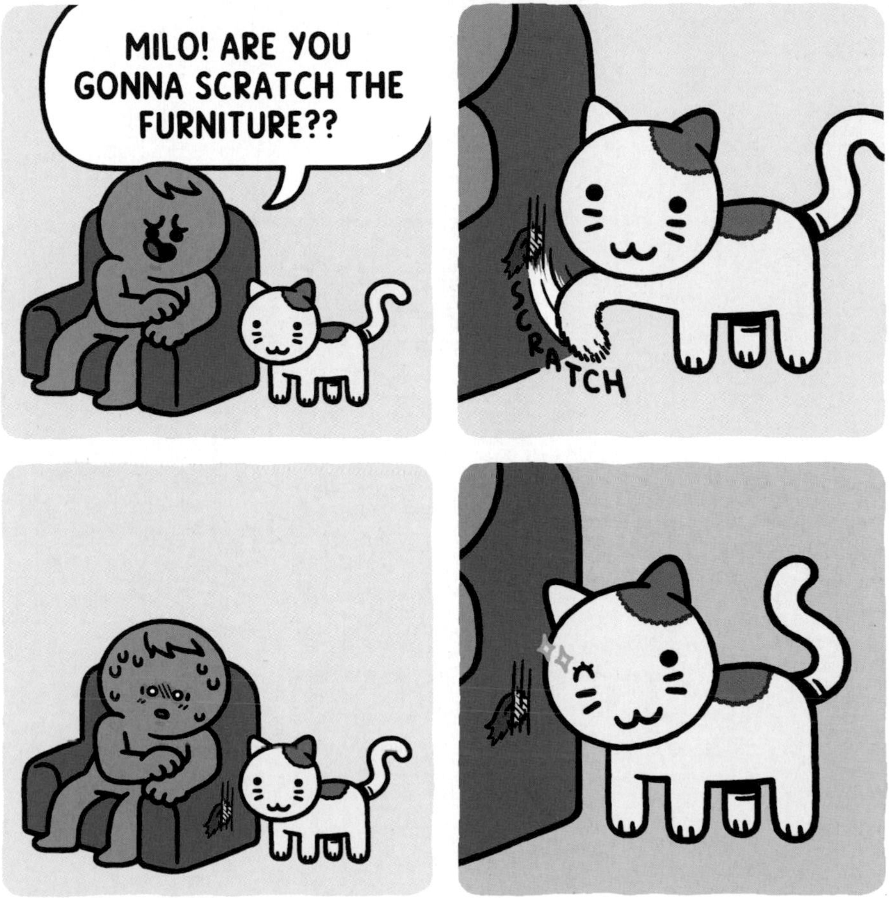
MILO! ARE YOU GONNA SCRATCH THE FURNITURE??
SCRATCH

milo, actually

the *best* cat in the world!

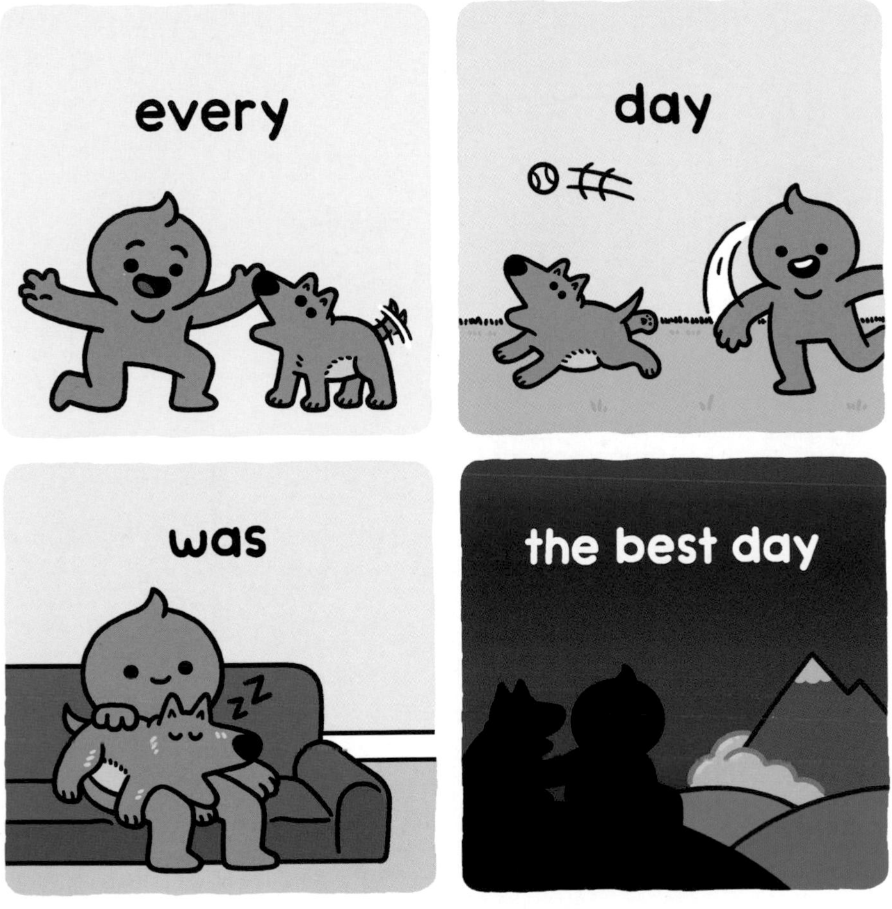
every
day
was
the best day

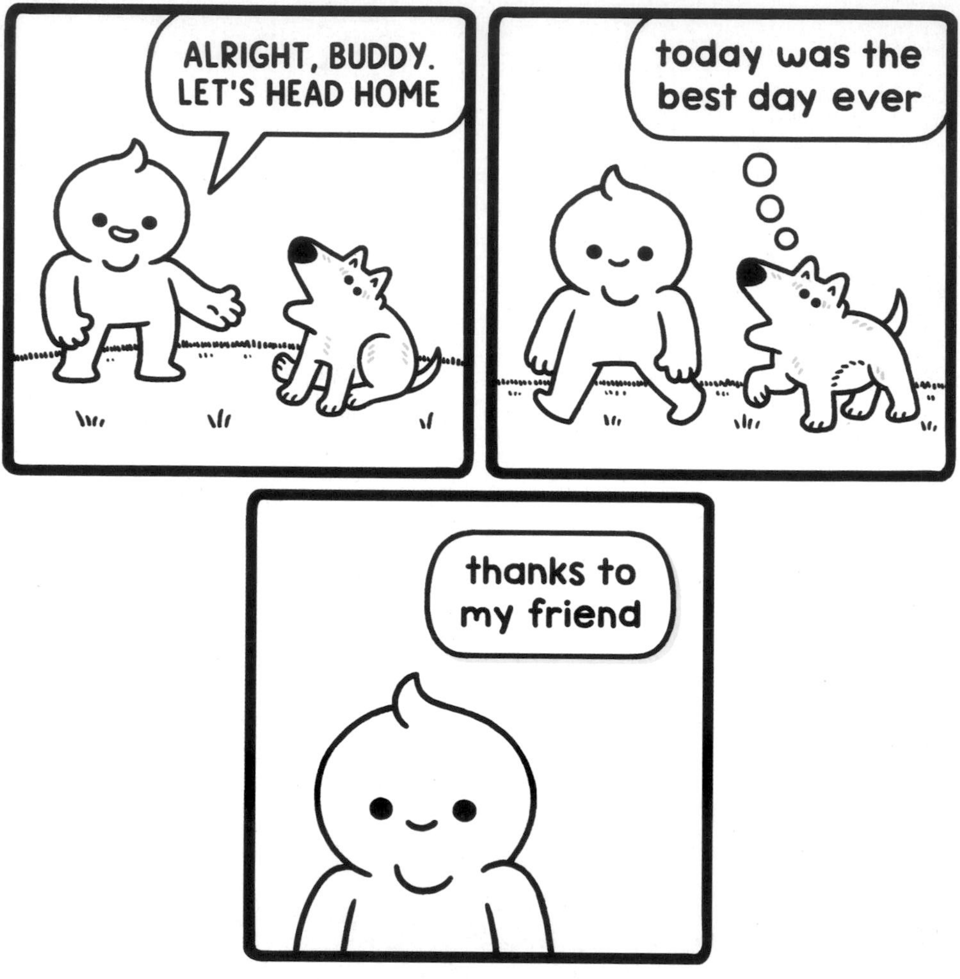
ALRIGHT, BUDDY.
LET'S HEAD HOME
today was the
best day ever
thanks to
my friend

AFTERWORD

The release of FEELINGS has truly been an emotional journey for me. Mr. Lovenstein has always been a place to channel my feelings. Consequently, there's a lot of crying in my comics. I don't mind crying. It purges all the gunk churning in the pit of my soul. The act of crying is also oddly funny to me. Perhaps it's because we're not used to seeing people cry so brazenly. Usually, we're so afraid of crying that we'll go out of our way to avoid it. We don't even like being near people crying for fear of catching it like a cold. It's exaggerated and silly in my comics, but there's a lot of pathos between the lines. My characters cry for us. They cry when we're afraid to. Therefore, much like FAILURE, I chose to celebrate that which we fear.

It's not all one big downer, though. There's plenty of joy to be found in this collection. More than I expected to find, to be honest. Regardless of if I'm happy or sad, it's soothing to draw something positive. I knew that if I could cheer someone up, that would cheer me up as well. Ironically, the nicest comics make me tear up the most.

And that's where I intended to end this afterword. A little navel gazing on creating this collection and my thoughts on feelings, but it turns out I hadn't fully reckoned with FEELINGS. I pour my emotions into Mr. Lovenstein, that's true, but I rarely let it get too personal. I'm always expressing myself from a safe distance through layers of abstraction. That was the case until very recently. Just as I was about to send this book off to the presses, things changed.

Caleb Guenther, one of my closest and dearest friends, unexpectedly passed away. We were born on the same day. December 17, 1989. We always joked that it was destiny that we would find each other. Since grade school, we forged a creative partnership that lasted a lifetime. We did a lot of amazing things together, and it was largely thanks to his brilliance. He designed the website and home for Mr. Lovenstein, and it's safe to say I wouldn't be doing what I do now without him. This loss has been heartbreaking. I've cried more than any character in this book. At the same time, it's been bittersweet thinking back on all the wonderful memories. In the end, I've come through this experience with a deeper appreciation of what it means to *feel*. To feel anything is to feel alive, and to feel alive is the most powerful feeling of them all.

For the first time, I turned to Mr. Lovenstein as a vessel to share something raw and personal. I knew I had to do it for Caleb. It was the least I could do for him. So, I leave you with one last comic. A tribute to my friend. A tribute to all friends. A tribute to love. A tribute to grief. A tribute to joy. A tribute to pain. A tribute to life.

A tribute to feelings.

- J.L. Westover
May 2024

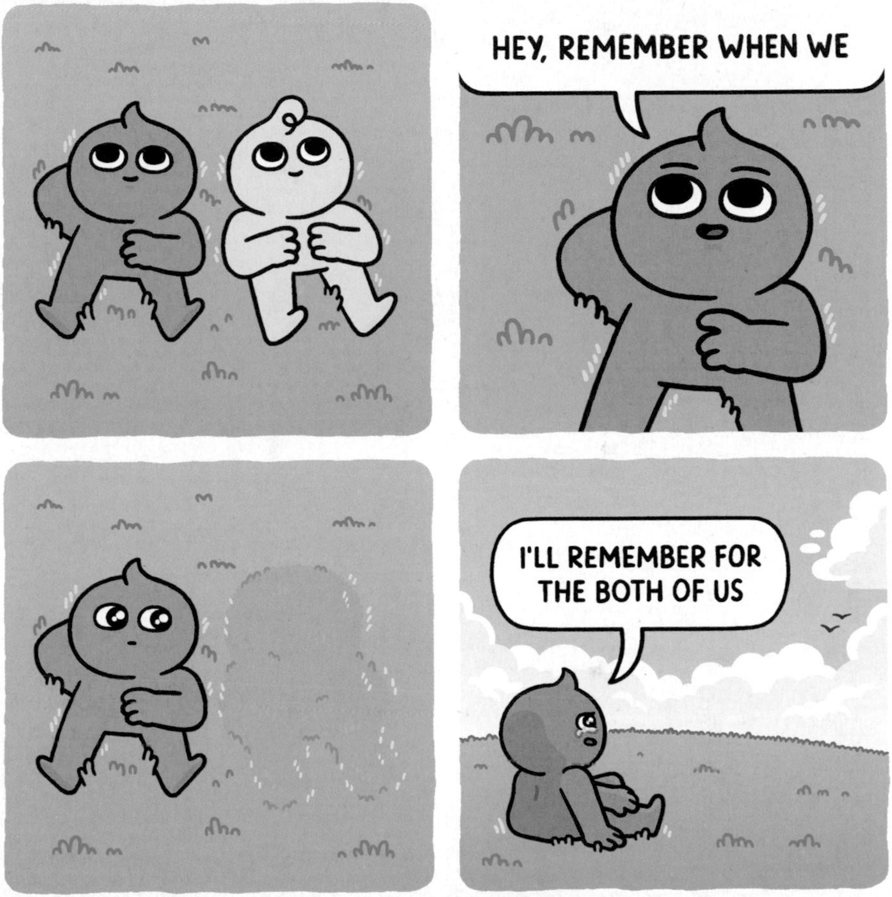
HEY, REMEMBER WHEN WE
I'LL REMEMBER FOR THE BOTH OF US

IN MEMORY OF CALEB GUENTHER • 1989 – 2024

Celebrate Failure!

"Sometimes I think of a great comic idea but then I realize
Justin has already made it. Thanks a lot, Justin."

-Chris McCoy *(Safely Endangered)*

AVAILABLE NOW
Everywhere Books Are Sold!

ABOUT THE AUTHOR

J. L. Westover is the creator of the world's sweatiest comic, *Mr. Lovenstein*. *Mr. Lovenstein* was launched out of his humble college dorm room, much like Facebook. It has gone on to unravel the fabric of society, much like Facebook. J. L. views writing *Mr. Lovenstein* as a form of therapy for him because actual therapy would be too expensive. The creation process allows him to get in touch with all of his feelings such as sadness, unhappiness, melancholy, and ennui. What he loves most about making comics is putting smiles on thousands of faces, and blank stares on millions more. He currently resides in North Carolina with his wife and ever-growing army of salukis.

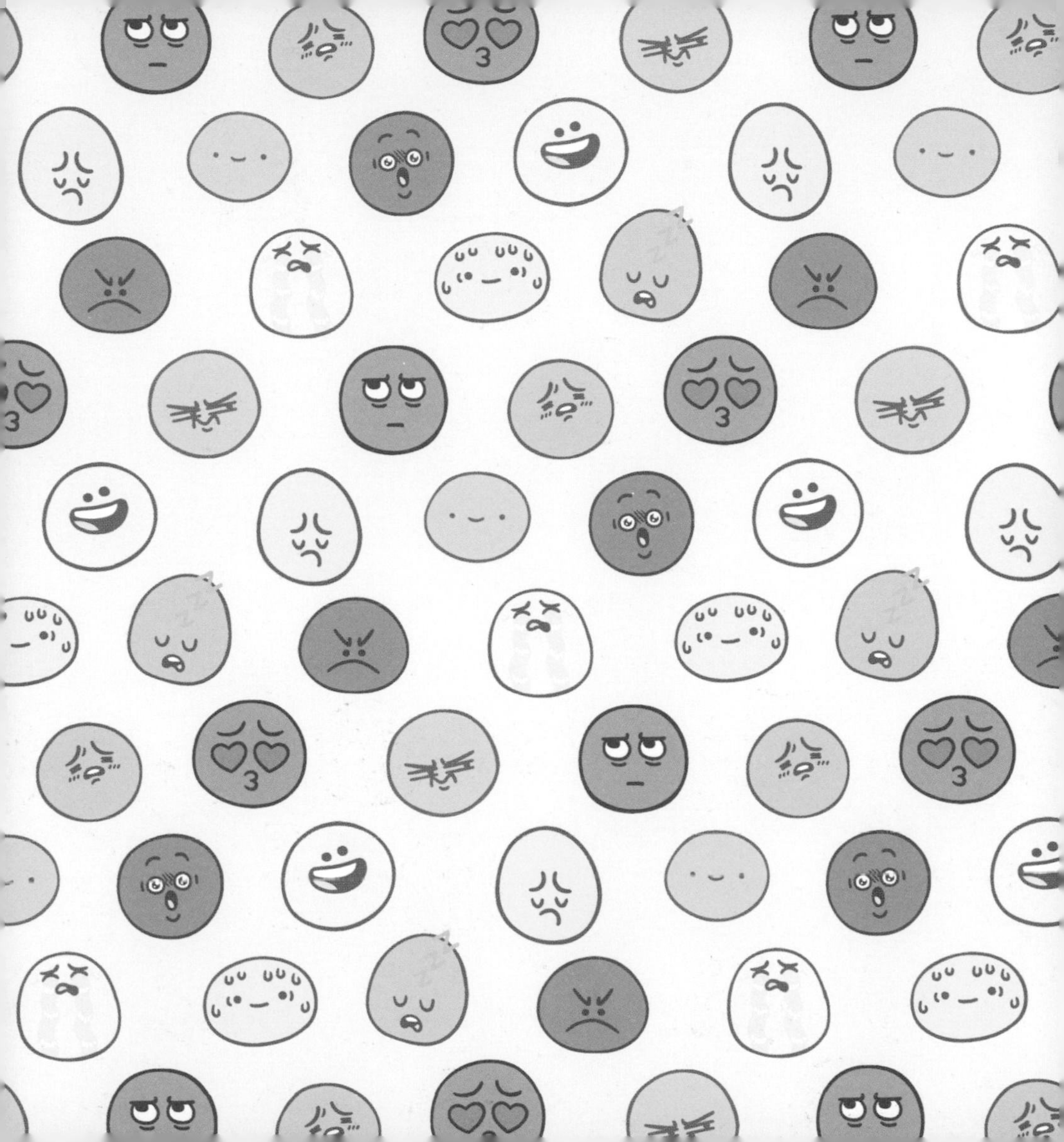

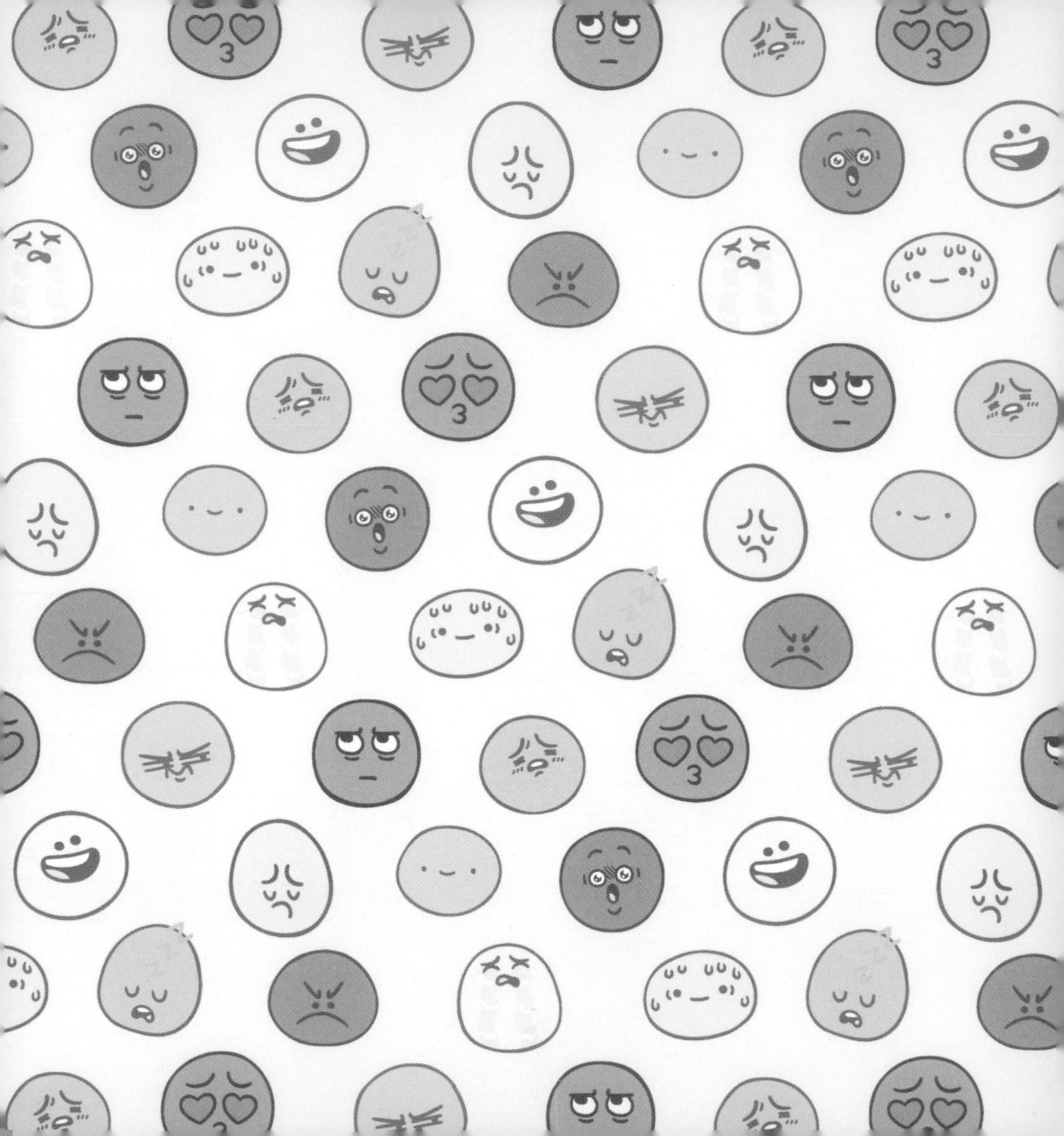